hush, hush

hush, hush

BECCA FITZPATRICK

SIMON & SCHUSTER BFYR

NEW YORK LONDON TORONTO SYDNEY NEW DELHI

An imprint of Simon & Schuster Children's Publishing Division
1230 Avenue of the Americas, New York, New York 10020
This book is a work of fiction. Any references to historical events, real people, or real locales are used fictitiously. Other names, characters, places, and incidents are products of the author's imagination, and any resemblance to actual events or locales or persons, living or dead, is entirely coincidental.
Copyright © 2009 by Becca Fitzpatrick
All rights reserved, including the right of reproduction in whole or in part in any form.
SIMON & SCHUSTER BFYR is a trademark of Simon & Schuster, Inc.
For information about special discounts for bulk purchases, please contact Simon & Schuster Special Sales at 1-866-506-1949 or business@simonandschuster.com.
The Simon & Schuster Speakers Bureau can bring authors to your live event.
For more information or to book an event, contact the Simon & Schuster Speakers Bureau at 1-866-248-3049 or visit our website at www.simonspeakers.com.
Also available in a SIMON & SCHUSTER BFYR hardcover edition
Book design by Lucy Ruth Cummins
The text for this book is set in Seria, Lunix, and Aviano.
Manufactured in the United States of America
This SIMON & SCHUSTER BFYR paperback edition May 2012
2 4 6 8 10 9 7 5 3 1
The Library of Congress has cataloged the hardcover edition as follows:
Fitzpatrick, Becca.
Hush, hush / Becca Fitzpatrick. — 1st ed.
p. cm.
Summary: High school sophomore Nora has always been very cautious in her relationships, but when Patch, who has a dark side she can sense, enrolls at her school, she is mysteriously and strongly drawn to him, despite warnings from her best friend, the school counselor, and her own instincts.
ISBN 978-1-4169-8941-7 (hc)
[1.Supernatural—Fiction. 2. Angels—Fiction. 3. Dating (Social customs)—Fiction. 4. Best friends—Fiction. 5. Friendship—Fiction. 6. High schools—Fiction. 7. Schools—Fiction.] I. Title.
PZ7.F5777Hus 2010
[Fic]—dc22
2009012936
ISBN 978-1-4169-8942-4 (pbk)
ISBN 978-1-4424-6513-8 (special edition pbk)
ISBN 978-1-4169-9820-4 (eBook)

For Heather, Christian, and Michael.
Our childhood was nothing if not imaginative.
And to Justin. Thanks for not choosing
the Japanese cooking class—love you.

. . . GOD SPARED NOT THE ANGELS THAT SINNED,
BUT CAST THEM DOWN TO HELL,
AND DELIVERED THEM INTO CHAINS OF DARKNESS,
TO BE RESERVED UNTO JUDGMENT . . .

—2 PETER 2:4

PROLOGUE

LOIRE VALLEY, FRANCE
NOVEMBER 1565

CHAUNCEY WAS WITH A FARMER'S DAUGHTER ON the grassy banks of the Loire River when the storm rolled in, and having let his gelding wander in the meadow, was left to his own two feet to carry him back to the château. He tore a silver buckle off his shoe, placed it in the girl's palm, and watched her scurry away, mud slinging on her skirts. Then he tugged on his boots and started for home.

Rain sheeted down on the darkening countryside surrounding

the Château de Langeais. Chauncey stepped easily over the sunken graves and humus of the cemetery; even in the thickest fog he could find his way home from here and not fear getting lost. There was no fog tonight, but the darkness and onslaught of rain were deceiving enough.

There was movement along the fringe of Chauncey's vision, and he snapped his head to the left. At first glance what appeared to be a large angel topping a nearby monument rose to full height. Neither stone nor marble, the boy had arms and legs. His torso was naked, his feet were bare, and peasant trousers hung low on his waist. He hopped down from the monument, the ends of his black hair dripping rain. It slid down his face, which was dark as a Spaniard's.

Chauncey's hand crept to the hilt of his sword. "Who goes there?"

The boy's mouth hinted at a smile.

"Do not play games with the Duc de Langeais," Chauncey warned. "I asked for your name. Give it."

"Duc?" The boy leaned against a twisted willow tree. "Or bastard?"

Chauncey unsheathed his sword. "Take it back! My father was the Duc de Langeais. I'm the Duc de Langeais now," he added clumsily, and cursed himself for it.

The boy gave a lazy shake of his head. "Your father wasn't the old duc."

Chauncey seethed at the outrageous insult. "And your father?"

he demanded, extending the sword. He didn't yet know all his vassals, but he was learning. He would brand the family name of this boy to memory. "I'll ask once more," he said in a low voice, wiping a hand down his face to clear away the rain. "Who are you?"

The boy walked up and pushed the blade aside. He suddenly looked older than Chauncey had presumed, maybe even a year or two older than Chauncey. "One of the Devil's brood," he answered.

Chauncey felt a clench of fear in his stomach. "You're a raving lunatic," he said through his teeth. "Get out of my way."

The ground beneath Chauncey tilted. Bursts of gold and red popped behind his eyes. Hunched with his fingernails grinding into his thighs, he looked up at the boy, blinking and gasping, trying to make sense of what was happening. His mind reeled like it was no longer his to command.

The boy crouched to level their eyes. "Listen carefully. I need something from you. I won't leave until I have it. Do you understand?"

Gritting his teeth, Chauncey shook his head to express his disbelief—his defiance. He tried to spit at the boy, but it trickled down his chin, his tongue refusing to obey him.

The boy clasped his hands around Chauncey's; their heat scorched him and he cried out.

"I need your oath of fealty," the boy said. "Bend on one knee and swear it."

Chauncey commanded his throat to laugh harshly, but his

throat constricted and he choked on the sound. His right knee buckled as if kicked from behind, though no one was there, and he stumbled forward into the mud. He bent sideways and retched.

"Swear it," the boy repeated.

Heat flushed Chauncey's neck; it took all his energy to curl his hands into two weak fists. He laughed at himself, but there was no humor. He had no idea how, but the boy was inflicting the nausea and weakness inside him. It would not lift until he took the oath. He would say what he had to, but he swore in his heart he would destroy the boy for this humiliation.

"Lord, I become your man," Chauncey said venomously.

The boy raised Chauncey to his feet. "Meet me here at the start of the Hebrew month of Cheshvan. During the two weeks between new and full moons, I'll need your service."

"A . . . fortnight?" Chauncey's whole frame trembled under the weight of his rage. "I am the Duc de Langeais!"

"You are a Nephil," the boy said on a sliver of a smile.

Chauncey had a profane retort on the tip of his tongue, but he swallowed it. His next words were spoken with icy venom. "What did you say?"

"You belong to the biblical race of Nephilim. Your real father was an angel who fell from heaven. You're half mortal." The boy's dark eyes lifted, meeting Chauncey's. "Half fallen angel."

Chauncey's tutor's voice drifted up from the recesses of his mind, reading passages from the Bible, telling of a deviant race created when angels cast from heaven mated with mortal women. A fearsome and powerful race. A chill that wasn't entirely revulsion crept through Chauncey. "Who are you?"

The boy turned, walking away, and although Chauncey wanted to go after him, he couldn't command his legs to hold his weight. Kneeling there, blinking up through the rain, he saw two thick scars on the back of the boy's naked torso. They narrowed to form an upside-down V.

"Are you—fallen?" he called out. "Your wings have been stripped, haven't they?"

The boy—angel—whoever he was did not turn back. Chauncey did not need the confirmation.

"This service I'm to provide," he shouted. "I demand to know what it is!"

The air resonated with the boy's low laughter.

CHAPTER

COLDWATER, MAINE
PRESENT DAY

WALKED INTO BIOLOGY AND MY JAW FELL OPEN. Mysteriously adhered to the chalkboard was a Barbie doll, with Ken at her side. They'd been forced to link arms and were naked except for artificial leaves placed in a few choice locations. Scribbled above their heads in thick pink chalk was the invitation:

WELCOME TO HUMAN REPRODUCTION (SEX)

At my side Vee Sky said, "This is exactly why the school outlaws camera phones. Pictures of this in the eZine would be all the evidence I'd need to get the board of education to ax biology. And then we'd have this hour to do something productive—like receive one-on-one tutoring from cute upperclass guys."

"Why, Vee," I said, "I could've sworn you've been looking forward to this unit all semester."

Vee lowered her lashes and smiled wickedly. "This class isn't going to teach me anything I don't already know."

"Vee? As in virgin?"

"Not so loud." She winked just as the bell rang, sending us both to our seats, which were side by side at our shared table.

Coach McConaughy grabbed the whistle swinging from a chain around his neck and blew it. "Seats, team!" Coach considered teaching tenth-grade biology a side assignment to his job as varsity basketball coach, and we all knew it.

"It may not have occurred to you kids that sex is more than a fifteen-minute trip to the backseat of a car. It's science. And what is science?"

"Boring," some kid in the back of the room called out.

"The only class I'm failing," said another.

Coach's eyes tracked down the front row, stopping at me. "Nora?"

"The study of something," I said.

He walked over and jabbed his index finger on the table in front of me. "What else?"

"Knowledge gained through experimentation and observation." Lovely. I sounded like I was auditioning for the audiobook of our text.

BECCA FITZPATRICK

"In your own words."

I touched the tip of my tongue to my upper lip and tried for a synonym. "Science is an investigation." It sounded like a question.

"Science is an investigation," Coach said, sanding his hands together. "Science requires us to transform into spies."

Put that way, science almost sounded fun. But I'd been in Coach's class long enough not to get my hopes up.

"Good sleuthing takes practice," he continued.

"So does sex," came another back-of-the-room comment. We all bit back laughter while Coach pointed a warning finger at the offender.

"That won't be part of tonight's homework." Coach turned his attention back to me. "Nora, you've been sitting beside Vee since the beginning of the year." I nodded but had a bad feeling about where this was going. "Both of you are on the school eZine together." Again I nodded. "I bet you know quite a bit about each other."

Vee kicked my leg under our table. I knew what she was thinking. That he had no idea how much we knew about each other. And I don't just mean the secrets we entomb in our diaries. Vee is my un-twin. She's green-eyed, minky blond, and a few pounds over curvy. I'm a smoky-eyed brunette with volumes of curly hair that holds its own against even the best flatiron. And I'm all legs, like a bar stool. But there is an invisible thread that ties us together; both of us swear that tie began long before birth. Both of us swear it will continue to hold for the rest of our lives.

Coach looked out at the class. "In fact, I'll bet each of you knows the person sitting beside you well enough. You picked the seats you did for a reason, right? Familiarity. Too bad the best sleuths avoid familiarity. It dulls the investigative instinct. Which is why, today, we're creating a new seating chart."

I opened my mouth to protest, but Vee beat me to it. "What the crap? It's April. As in, it's almost the end of the year. You can't pull this kind of stuff now."

Coach hinted at a smile. "I can pull this stuff clear up to the last day of the semester. And if you fail my class, you'll be right back here next year, where I'll be pulling this kind of stuff all over again."

Vee scowled at him. She is famous for that scowl. It's a look that does everything but audibly hiss. Apparently immune to it, Coach brought his whistle to his lips, and we got the idea.

"Every partner sitting on the left-hand side of the table—that's your left—move up one seat. Those in the front row—yes, including you, Vee—move to the back."

Vee shoved her notebook inside her backpack and ripped the zipper shut. I bit my lip and waved a small farewell. Then I turned slightly, checking out the room behind me. I knew the names of all my classmates . . . except one. The transfer. Coach never called on him, and he seemed to prefer it that way. He sat slouched one table back, cool black eyes holding a steady gaze forward. Just like always. I didn't for one moment believe he just sat there, day after day, staring into space. He was thinking *something*, but instinct told me I probably didn't want to know what.

He set his bio text down on the table and slid into Vee's old chair.

I smiled. "Hi. I'm Nora."

His black eyes sliced into me, and the corners of his mouth tilted up. My heart fumbled a beat and in that pause, a feeling of gloomy darkness seemed to slide like a shadow over me. It vanished in an instant, but I was still staring at him. His smile wasn't friendly. It was a smile that spelled trouble. With a promise.

I focused on the chalkboard. Barbie and Ken stared back with strangely cheerful smiles.

Coach said, "Human reproduction can be a sticky subject—"

"Ewww!" groaned a chorus of students.

"It requires mature handling. And like all science, the best approach is to learn by sleuthing. For the rest of class, practice this technique by finding out as much as you can about your new partner. Tomorrow, bring a write-up of your discoveries, and believe me, I'm going to check for authenticity. This is biology, not English, so don't even think about fictionalizing your answers. I want to see real interaction and teamwork." There was an implied *Or else.*

I sat perfectly still. The ball was in his court—I'd smiled, and look how well that turned out. I wrinkled my nose, trying to figure out what he smelled like. Not cigarettes. Something richer, fouler.

Cigars.

I found the clock on the wall and tapped my pencil in time to the second hand. I planted my elbow on the table and propped my chin on my fist. I blew out a sigh.

Great. At this rate I would fail.

I had my eyes pinned forward, but I heard the soft glide of his pen. He was writing, and I wanted to know what. Ten minutes of sitting together didn't qualify him to make any assumptions about me. Flitting a look sideways, I saw that his paper was several lines deep and growing.

"What are you writing?" I asked.

"And she speaks English," he said while scrawling it down, each stroke of his hand both smooth and lazy at once.

I leaned as close to him as I dared, trying to read what else he'd written, but he folded the paper in half, concealing the list.

"What did you write?" I demanded.

He reached for my unused paper, sliding it across the table toward him. He crumpled it into a ball. Before I could protest, he tossed it at the trash can beside Coach's desk. The shot dropped in.

I stared at the trash can a moment, locked between disbelief and anger. Then I flipped open my notebook to a clean page. "What is your name?" I asked, pencil poised to write.

I glanced up in time to catch another dark grin. This one seemed to dare me to pry anything out of him.

"Your name?" I repeated, hoping it was my imagination that my voice faltered.

"Call me Patch. I mean it. Call me."

He winked when he said it, and I was pretty sure he was making fun of me.

"What do you do in your leisure time?" I asked.

"I don't have free time."

"I'm assuming this assignment is graded, so do me a favor?"

He leaned back in his seat, folding his arms behind his head. "What kind of favor?"

I was pretty sure it was an innuendo, and I grappled for a way to change the subject.

"Free time," he repeated thoughtfully. "I take pictures."

I printed Photography on my paper.

"I wasn't finished," he said. "I've got quite a collection going of an eZine columnist who believes there's truth in eating organic, who writes poetry in secret, and who shudders at the thought of having to choose between Stanford, Yale, and . . . what's that big one with the H?"

I stared at him a moment, shaken by how dead on he was. I didn't get the feeling it was a lucky guess. He knew. And I wanted to know how—right now.

"But you won't end up going to any of them."

"I won't?" I asked without thinking.

He hooked his fingers under the seat of my chair, dragging me closer to him. Not sure if I should scoot away and show fear, or do nothing and feign boredom, I chose the latter.

He said, "Even though you'd thrive at all three schools, you scorn them for being a cliché of achievement. Passing judgment is your third biggest weakness."

"And my second?" I said with quiet rage. Who was this guy? Was this some kind of disturbing joke?

"You don't know how to trust. I take that back. You trust—just all the wrong people."

"And my first?" I demanded.

"You keep life on a short leash."

"What's that supposed to mean?"

"You're scared of what you can't control."

The hair at the nape of my neck stood on end, and the temperature in the room seemed to chill. Ordinarily I would have gone straight to Coach's desk and requested a new seating chart. But I refused to let Patch think he could intimidate or scare me. I felt an irrational need to defend myself and decided right then and there I wouldn't back down until he did.

"Do you sleep naked?" he asked.

My mouth threatened to drop, but I held it in check. "You're hardly the person I'd tell."

"Ever been to a shrink?"

"No," I lied. The truth was, I was in counseling with the school psychologist, Dr. Hendrickson. It wasn't by choice, and it wasn't something I liked to talk about.

"Done anything illegal?"

"No." Occasionally breaking the speed limit wouldn't count. Not with him. "Why don't you ask me something normal? Like . . . my favorite kind of music?"

"I'm not going to ask what I can guess."

"You do not know the type of music I listen to."

"Baroque. With you, it's all about order, control. I bet you play . . . the cello?" He said it like he'd pulled the guess out of thin air.

"Wrong." Another lie, but this one sent a chill rippling along my skin. Who was he really? If he knew I played the cello, what else did he know?

"What's that?" Patch tapped his pen against the inside of my wrist. Instinctively I pulled away.

"A birthmark."

"Looks like a scar. Are you suicidal, Nora?" His eyes connected with mine, and I could feel him laughing. "Parents married or divorced?"

"I live with my mom."

"Where's dad?"

"My dad passed away last year."

"How did he die?"

I flinched. "He was—murdered. This is kind of personal territory, if you don't mind."

There was a count of silence and the edge in Patch's eyes seemed to soften a touch. "That must be hard." He sounded like he meant it.

The bell rang and Patch was on his feet, making his way toward the door.

"Wait," I called out. He didn't turn. "Excuse me!" He was through the door. "Patch! I didn't get anything on you."

He turned back and walked toward me. Taking my hand, he scribbled something on it before I thought to pull away.

I looked down at the seven numbers in red ink on my palm and made a fist around them. I wanted to tell him no way was his phone ringing tonight. I wanted to tell him it was his fault for taking all the time questioning me. I wanted a lot of things, but I just stood there looking like I didn't know how to open my mouth.

At last I said, "I'm busy tonight."

"So am I." He grinned and was gone.

I stood nailed to the spot, digesting what had just happened. Did he eat up all the time questioning me on purpose? So I'd *fail*? Did he think one flashy grin would redeem him? Yes, I thought. Yes, *he did*.

"I won't call!" I called after him. "Not—ever!"

"Have you finished your column for tomorrow's deadline?" It was Vee. She came up beside me, jotting notes on the notepad she carried everywhere. "I'm thinking of writing mine on the injustice of seating charts. I got paired with a girl who said she just finished lice treatment this morning."

"My new partner," I said, pointing into the hallway at the back of Patch. He had an annoyingly confident walk, the kind you find paired with faded T-shirts and a cowboy hat. Patch wore neither. He was a dark-Levi's-dark-henley-dark-boots kind of guy.

"The senior transfer? Guess he didn't study hard enough the first time around. Or the second." She gave me a knowing look. "Third time's a charm."

"He gives me the creeps. He knew my music. Without any hints whatsoever, he said, 'Baroque.'" I did a poor job of mimicking his low voice.

"Lucky guess?"

"He knew . . . other things."

"Like what?"

I let go of a sigh. He knew more than I wanted to comfortably contemplate. "Like how to get under my skin," I said at last. "I'm going to tell Coach he has to switch us back."

"Go for it. I could use a hook for my next eZine article. 'Tenth Grader Fights Back.' Better yet, 'Seating Chart Takes Slap in the Face.' Mmm. I like it."

At the end of the day, I was the one who took a slap in the face. Coach shot down my plea to rethink the seating chart. It appeared I was stuck with Patch.

For now.

CHAPTER

2

MY MOM AND I LIVE IN A DRAFTY EIGHTEENTH-
century farmhouse on the outskirts of Coldwater.
It's the only house on Hawthorne Lane, and the
nearest neighbors are almost a mile away. I sometimes wonder if
the original builder realized that out of all the plots of land available, he chose to construct the house in the eye of a mysterious
atmospheric inversion that seems to suck all the fog off Maine's
coast and transplant it into our yard. The house was at this moment

veiled by gloom that resembled escaped and wandering spirits.

I spent the evening planted on a stool in the kitchen in the company of algebra homework and Dorothea, our housekeeper. My mom works for the Hugo Renaldi Auction Company, coordinating estate and antique auctions all along the East Coast. This week she was in upstate New York. Her job required a lot of travel, and she paid Dorothea to cook and clean, but I was pretty sure the fine print on Dorothea's job description included keeping a watchful, parental eye on me.

"How was school?" Dorothea asked with a slight German accent. She stood at the sink, scrubbing overbaked lasagna off a casserole dish.

"I have a new biology partner."

"This is a good thing, or a bad thing?"

"Vee was my old partner."

"Humph." More vigorous scrubbing, and the flesh on Dorothea's upper arm jiggled. "A bad thing, then."

I sighed in agreement.

"Tell me about the new partner. This girl, what is she like?"

"He's tall, dark, and annoying." And eerily closed off. Patch's eyes were black orbs. Taking in everything and giving away nothing. Not that I wanted to know more about Patch. Since I hadn't liked what I'd seen on the surface, I doubted I'd like what was lurking deep inside.

Only, this wasn't exactly true. I'd liked a lot of what I'd seen.

Long, lean muscles down his arms, broad but relaxed shoulders, and a smile that was part playful, part seductive. I was in an uneasy alliance with myself, trying to ignore what had started to feel irresistible.

At nine o'clock Dorothea finished for the evening and locked up on her way out. I flashed the porch lights twice to say good-bye; they must have penetrated the fog, because she answered with a honk. I was alone.

I took inventory of the feelings playing out inside me. I wasn't hungry. I wasn't tired. I wasn't even all that lonely. But I *was* a little bit restless about my biology assignment. I'd told Patch I wouldn't call, and six hours ago I'd meant it. All I could think now was that I didn't want to fail. Biology was my toughest subject. My grade tottered problematically between A and B. In my mind, that was the difference between a full and half scholarship in my future.

I went to the kitchen and picked up the phone. I looked at what was left of the seven numbers still tattooed on my hand. Secretly I hoped Patch didn't answer my call. If he was unavailable or uncooperative on assignments, it was evidence I could use against him to convince Coach to undo the seating chart. Feeling hopeful, I keyed in his number.

Patch answered on the third ring. "What's up?"

In a matter-of-fact tone I said, "I'm calling to see if we can meet tonight. I know you said you're busy, but—"

"Nora." Patch said my name like it was the punch line to a joke. "Thought you weren't going to call. Ever."

I hated that I was eating my words. I hated Patch for rubbing it in. I hated Coach and his deranged assignments. I opened my mouth, hoping something smart would come out. "Well? Can we meet or not?"

"As it turns out, I can't."

"Can't, or won't?"

"I'm in the middle of a pool game." I heard the smile in his voice. "An important pool game."

From the background noise I heard on his end, I believed he was telling the truth—about the pool game. Whether it was more important than my assignment was up for debate.

"Where are you?" I asked.

"Bo's Arcade. It's not your kind of hangout."

"Then let's do the interview over the phone. I've got a list of questions right—"

He hung up on me.

I stared at the phone in disbelief, then ripped a clean sheet of paper from my notebook. I scribbled Jerk on the first line. On the line beneath it I added, Smokes cigars. Will die of lung cancer. Hopefully soon. Excellent physical shape.

I immediately scribbled over the last observation until it was illegible.

The microwave clock blinked to 9:05. As I saw it, I had two

hush, hush

choices. Either I fabricated my interview with Patch, or I drove to Bo's Arcade. The first option might have been tempting, if I could just block out Coach's voice warning that he'd check all answers for authenticity. I didn't know enough about Patch to bluff my way through a whole interview. And the second option? Not even remotely tempting.

I delayed making a decision long enough to call my mom. Part of our agreement for her working and traveling so much was that I act responsibly and not be the kind of daughter who required constant supervision. I liked my freedom, and I didn't want to do anything to give my mom a reason to take a pay cut and get a local job to keep an eye on me.

On the fourth ring her voice mail picked up.

"It's me," I said. "Just checking in. I've got some biology homework to finish up, then I'm going to bed. Call me at lunch tomorrow, if you want. Love you."

After I hung up, I found a quarter in the kitchen drawer. Best to leave complicated decisions to fate.

"Heads I go," I told George Washington's profile, "tails I stay." I flipped the quarter in the air, flattened it to the back of my palm, and dared a peek. My heart squeezed out an extra beat, and I told myself I wasn't sure what it meant.

"It's out of my hands now," I said.

Determined to get this over with as quickly as possible, I grabbed a map off the fridge, snagged my keys, and backed my

Fiat Spider down the driveway. The car had probably been cute in 1979, but I wasn't wild about the chocolate brown paint, the rust spreading unchecked across the back fender, or the cracked white leather seats.

Bo's Arcade turned out to be farther away than I would have liked, nestled close to the coast, a thirty-minute drive. With the map flattened to the steering wheel, I pulled the Fiat into a parking lot behind a large cinder-block building with an electric sign flashing BO'S ARCADE, MAD BLACK PAINTBALL & OZZ'S POOL HALL. Graffiti splashed the walls, and cigarette butts dotted the foundation. Clearly Bo's would be filled with future Ivy Leaguers and model citizens. I tried to keep my thoughts lofty and nonchalant, but my stomach felt a little uneasy. Double-checking that I'd locked all the doors, I headed inside.

I stood in line, waiting to get past the ropes. As the group ahead of me paid, I squeezed past, walking toward the maze of blaring sirens and blinking lights.

"Think you deserve a free ride?" hollered a smoke-roughened voice.

I swung around and blinked at the heavily tattooed cashier. I said, "I'm not here to play. I'm looking for someone."

He grunted. "You want past me, you pay." He put his palms on the counter, where a price chart had been duct-taped, showing I owed fifteen dollars. Cash only.

I didn't have cash. And if I had, I wouldn't have wasted it to

hush, hush

spend a few minutes interrogating Patch about his personal life. I felt a flush of anger at the seating chart and at having to be here in the first place. I only needed to find Patch, then we could hold the interview outside. I was not going to drive all this way and leave empty-handed.

"If I'm not back in two minutes, I'll pay the fifteen dollars," I said. Before I could exercise better judgment or muster up a tad more patience, I did something completely out of character and ducked under the ropes. I didn't stop there. I hurried through the arcade, keeping my eyes open for Patch. I told myself I couldn't believe I was doing this, but I was like a rolling snowball, gaining speed and momentum. At this point I just wanted to find Patch and get out.

The cashier followed after me, shouting, "Hey!"

Certain Patch was not on the main level, I jogged downstairs, following signs to Ozz's Pool Hall. At the bottom of the stairs, dim track lighting illuminated several poker tables, all in use. Cigar smoke almost as thick as the fog enveloping my house clouded the low ceiling. Nestled between the poker tables and the bar was a row of pool tables. Patch was stretched across the one farthest from me, attempting a difficult bank shot.

"Patch!" I called out.

Just as I spoke, he shot his pool stick, driving it into the tabletop. His head whipped up. He stared at me with a mixture of surprise and curiosity.

The cashier clomped down the steps behind me, vising my shoulder with his hand. "Upstairs. Now."

Patch's mouth moved into another barely-there smile. Hard to say if it was mocking or friendly. "She's with me."

This seemed to hold some sway with the cashier, who loosened his grip. Before he could change his mind, I shook off his hand and weaved through the tables toward Patch. I took the first several steps in stride, but found my confidence slipping the closer I got to him.

I was immediately aware of something different about him. I couldn't quite put my finger on it, but I could feel it like electricity. More animosity?

More confidence.

More freedom to be himself. And those black eyes were getting to me. They were like magnets clinging to my every move. I swallowed discreetly and tried to ignore the queasy tap dance in my stomach. I couldn't quite put my finger on it, but something about Patch wasn't right. Something about him wasn't normal. Something wasn't . . . safe.

"Sorry about the hang-up," Patch said, coming beside me. "The reception's not great down here."

Yeah, right.

With a tilt of his head, Patch motioned the others to leave. There was an uneasy silence before anybody moved. The first guy to leave bumped into my shoulder as he walked past. I took a step back to balance myself and looked up just in time to receive cold eyes from the other two players as they departed.

Great. It wasn't my fault Patch was my partner.

"Eight ball?" I asked him, raising my eyebrows and trying to sound completely sure of myself, of my surroundings. Maybe he was right and Bo's wasn't my kind of place. That didn't mean I was going to bolt for the doors. "How high are the stakes?"

His smile widened. This time I was pretty sure he was mocking me. "We don't play for money."

I set my handbag on the edge of the table. "Too bad. I was going to bet everything I have against you." I held up my assignment, two lines already filled. "A few quick questions and I'm out of here."

"Jerk?" Patch read out loud, leaning on his pool stick. "Lung cancer? Is that supposed to be prophetic?"

I fanned the assignment through the air. "I'm assuming you contribute to the atmosphere. How many cigars a night? One? Two?"

"I don't smoke." He sounded sincere, but I didn't buy it.

"Mm-hmm," I said, setting the paper down between the eight ball and the solid purple. I accidentally nudged the solid purple while writing *Definitely cigars* on line three.

"You're messing up the game," Patch said, still smiling.

I caught his eye and couldn't help but match his smile—briefly. "Hopefully not in your favor. Biggest dream?" I was proud of this one because I knew it would stump him. It required forethought.

"Kiss you."

"That's not funny," I said, holding his eyes, grateful I didn't stutter.

"No, but it made you blush."

I boosted myself onto the side of the table, trying to look impassive. I crossed my legs, using my knee as a writing board. "Do you work?"

"I bus tables at the Borderline. Best Mexican in town."

"Religion?"

He didn't seem surprised by the question, but he didn't seem overjoyed by it either. "I thought you said a few quick questions. You're already at number four."

"Religion?" I asked more firmly.

Patch dragged a hand thoughtfully along the line of his jaw. "Not religion . . . cult."

"You belong to a cult?" I realized too late that while I sounded surprised, I shouldn't have.

"As it turns out, I'm in need of a healthy female sacrifice. I'd planned on luring her into trusting me first, but if you're ready now . . ."

Any smile left on my face slid away. "You're not impressing me."

"I haven't started trying yet."

I edged off the table and stood up to him. He was a full head taller. "Vee told me you're a senior. How many times have you failed tenth-grade biology? Once? Twice?"

"Vee isn't my spokesperson."

"Are you denying failing?"

"I'm telling you I didn't go to school last year." His eyes taunted me. It only made me more determined.

"You were truant?"

Patch laid his pool stick across the tabletop and crooked a finger for me to come closer. I didn't. "A secret?" he said in confidential tones. "I've never gone to school before. Another secret? It's not as dull as I expected."

He was lying. Everyone went to school. There were laws. He was lying to get a rise out of me.

"You think I'm lying," he said around a smile.

"You've never been to school, ever? If that's true—and you're right, I don't think it is—what made you decide to come this year?"

"You."

The impulse to feel scared pounded through me, but I told myself that was exactly what Patch wanted. Standing my ground, I tried to act annoyed instead. Still, it took me a moment to find my voice. "That's not a real answer."

He must have taken a step closer, because suddenly our bodies were separated by nothing more than a shallow margin of air. "Your eyes, Nora. Those cold, pale gray eyes are surprisingly irresistible." He tipped his head sideways, as if to study me from a new angle. "And that killer curvy mouth."

Startled not so much by his comment, but that part of me responded positively to it, I stepped back. "That's it. I'm out of here."

But as soon as the words were out of my mouth, I knew they weren't true. I felt the urge to say something more. Picking through the thoughts tangled in my head, I tried to find what it was I felt I had to say. Why was he so derisive, and why did he act like I'd done something to deserve it?

"You seem to know a lot about me," I said, making the understatement of the year. "More than you should. You seem to know exactly what to say to make me uncomfortable."

"You make it easy."

A spark of anger fired through me. "You admit you're doing this on purpose?"

"This?"

"This—provoking me."

"Say 'provoking' again. Your mouth looks provocative when you do."

"We're done. Finish your pool game." I grabbed his pool stick off the table and pushed it at him. He didn't take it.

"I don't like sitting beside you," I said. "I don't like being your partner. I don't like your condescending smile." My jaw twitched—something that typically happened only when I lied. I wondered if I was lying now. If I was, I wanted to kick myself. "I don't like you," I said as convincingly as I could, and thrust the stick against his chest.

"I'm glad Coach put us together," he said. I detected the slightest irony on the word "Coach," but I couldn't figure out any hidden meaning. This time he took the pool stick.

"I'm working to change that," I countered.

Patch thought this was so funny, his teeth showed through his smile. He reached for me, and before I could move away, he untangled something from my hair.

"Piece of paper," he explained, flicking it to the ground. As he reached out, I noticed a marking on the inside of his wrist. At first I assumed it was a tattoo, but a second look revealed a ruddy brown, slightly raised birthmark. It was the shape of a splattered paint drop.

"That's an unfortunate place for a birthmark," I said, more than a little unnerved that it was so similarly positioned to my own scar.

Patch casually but noticeably slid his sleeve down over his wrist. "You'd prefer it someplace more private?"

"I wouldn't prefer it anywhere." I wasn't sure how this sounded and tried again. "I wouldn't care if you didn't have it at all." I tried a third time. "I don't care about your birthmark, period."

"Any more questions?" he asked. "Comments?"

"No."

"Then I'll see you in bio."

I thought about telling him he'd never see me again. But I wasn't going to eat my words twice in one day.

Later that night a *crack!* pulled me out of sleep. With my face mashed into my pillow, I held still, all my senses on high alert. My mom was out of town at least once a month for work, so I was used to sleeping alone, and it had been months since I'd imagined the sound of footsteps creeping down the hall toward my bedroom. The truth was, I never felt completely alone. Right after my dad was shot to death in Portland while buying my mom's birthday gift, a strange presence entered my life. Like someone was orbiting my world, watching from a distance. At first the phantom presence had creeped me out, but when nothing had came of it, my anxiety lost its edge. I started wondering if there was a cosmic purpose for the way I was feeling. Maybe my dad's spirit was close by. The thought was usually comforting, but tonight was different. The presence felt like ice on the skin.

Turning my head a fraction, I saw a shadowy form stretching across my floor. I flipped around to face the window, the gauzy shaft of moonlight the only light in the room capable of casting a shadow. But nothing was there. I squeezed my pillow against me and told myself it was a cloud passing over the moon. Or a piece of trash blowing in the wind. Still, I spent the next several minutes waiting for my pulse to calm down.

By the time I found the courage to get out of bed, the yard below my window was silent and still. The only noise came from tree branches scraping against the house, and my own heart thrumming under my skin.

CHAPTER

COACH MCCONAUGHY STOOD AT THE CHALKBOARD
droning on and on about something, but my mind was
far from the complexities of science.

I was busy formulating reasons why Patch and I should no
longer be partners, making a list of them on the back of an old
quiz. As soon as class was over, I would present my argument to
Coach. *Uncooperative on assignments,* I wrote. *Shows little interest
in teamwork.*

But it was the things not listed that bothered me most. I found the location of Patch's birthmark eerie, and I was spooked by the incident at my window last night. I didn't outright suspect Patch of spying on me, but I couldn't ignore the coincidence that I was almost positive I'd seen someone looking in my window just hours after I'd met him.

At the thought of Patch spying on me, I reached inside the front compartment of my backpack and shook two iron pills from a bottle, swallowing them whole. They caught in my throat a moment, then found their way down.

Out of the corner of my eye, I caught Patch's raised eyebrows.

I considered explaining that I was anemic and had to take iron a few times a day, especially when I was under stress, but I thought better. The anemia wasn't life threatening . . . as long as I took regular doses of iron. I wasn't paranoid to the point that I thought Patch meant me harm, but somehow, my medical condition was a vulnerability that felt better kept secret.

"Nora?"

Coach stood at the front of the room, his hand outstretched in a gesture that showed he was waiting for one thing—my answer. A slow burn made its way up my cheeks.

"Could you repeat the question?" I asked.

The class snickered.

Coach said, with slight irritation, "What qualities are you attracted to in a potential mate?"

hush, hush

"Potential mate?"

"Come on now, we haven't got all afternoon."

I could hear Vee laughing behind me.

My throat seemed to constrict. "You want me to list characteristics of a . . . ?"

"Potential mate, yes, that would be helpful."

Without meaning to, I looked sideways at Patch. He was eased back in his seat, one notch above a slouch, studying me with satisfaction. He flashed his pirate smile and mouthed, *We're waiting*.

I stacked my hands on the table, hoping I looked more composed than I felt. "I've never thought about it before."

"Well, think fast."

"Could you call on someone else first?"

Coach gestured impatiently to my left. "You're up, Patch."

Unlike me, Patch spoke with confidence. He had himself positioned so his body was angled slightly toward mine, our knees mere inches apart.

"Intelligent. Attractive. Vulnerable."

Coach was busy listing the adjectives on the board. "Vulnerable?" he asked. "How so?"

Vee spoke up. "Does this have anything to do with the unit we're studying? Because I can't find anything about desired characteristics of a mate anywhere in our text."

Coach stopped writing long enough to look over his shoulder. "Every animal on the planet attracts mates with the goal of

BECCA FITZPATRICK

reproduction. Frogs swell their bodies. Male gorillas beat their chests. Have you ever watched a male lobster rise up on the tips of his legs and snap his claws, demanding female attention? Attraction is the first element of all animal reproduction, humans included. Why don't you give us your list, Miss Sky?"

Vee held up five fingers. "Gorgeous, wealthy, indulgent, fiercely protective, and just a little bit dangerous." A finger went down with each description.

Patch laughed under his breath. "The problem with human attraction is not knowing if it will be returned."

"Excellent point," Coach said.

"Humans are vulnerable," Patch continued, "because they're capable of being hurt." At this, Patch's knee knocked against mine. I scooted away, not daring to let myself wonder what he meant by the gesture.

Coach nodded. "The complexity of human attraction—and reproduction—is one of the features that set us apart from other species."

I thought I heard Patch snort at this, but it was a very soft sound, and I couldn't be sure.

Coach continued, "Since the dawn of time, women have been attracted to mates with strong survival skills—like intelligence and physical prowess—because men with these qualities are more likely to bring home dinner at the end of the day." He stuck his thumbs in the air and grinned. "Dinner equals survival, team."

hush, hush

No one laughed.

"Likewise," he continued, "men are attracted to beauty because it indicates health and youth—no point mating with a sickly woman who won't be around to raise the children." Coach pushed his glasses up the bridge of his nose and chuckled.

"That is so sexist," Vee protested. "Tell me something that relates to a woman in the twenty-first century."

"If you approach reproduction with an eye to science, Miss Sky, you'll see that children are the key to the survival of our species. And the more children you have, the greater your contribution to the gene pool."

I practically heard Vee's eyes rolling. "I think we're finally getting close to today's topic. Sex."

"Almost," said Coach, holding up a finger. "Before sex comes attraction, but after attraction comes body language. You have to communicate 'I'm interested' to a potential mate, only not in so many words."

Coach pointed beside me. "All right, Patch. Let's say you're at a party. The room is full of girls of all different shapes and sizes. You see blonds, brunettes, redheads, a few girls with black hair. Some are talkative, while others appear shy. You've found one girl who fits your profile—attractive, intelligent, and vulnerable. How do you let her know you're interested?"

"Single her out. Talk to her."

"Good. Now for the big question—how do you know if she's game or if she wants you to move on?"

BECCA FITZPATRICK

"I study her," Patch said. "I figure out what she's thinking and feeling. She's not going to come right out and tell me, which is why I have to pay attention. Does she turn her body toward mine? Does she hold my eyes, then look away? Does she bite her lip and play with her hair, the way Nora is doing right now?"

Laughter rose in the room. I dropped my hands to my lap.

"She's game," said Patch, bumping my leg again. Of all things, I blushed.

"Very good! Very good!" Coach said, his voice charged, smiling broadly at our attentiveness.

"The blood vessels in Nora's face are widening and her skin is warming," Patch said. "She knows she's being evaluated. She likes the attention, but she's not sure how to handle it."

"I am not blushing."

"She's nervous," Patch said. "She's stroking her arm to draw attention away from her face and down to her figure, or maybe her skin. Both are strong selling points."

I nearly choked. He's joking, I told myself. No, he's insane. I had no experience dealing with lunatics, and it showed. I felt like I spent most of our time together staring at Patch, mouth agape. If I had any illusions about keeping up with him, I was going to have to figure out a new approach.

I placed my hands flat against the table, held my chin high, and tried to look as if I still possessed some dignity. "This is ridiculous."

hush, hush

Stretching his arm out to his side with exaggerated slyness, Patch hung it on the back of my chair. I had the strange feeling that this was a threat aimed entirely at me, and that he was unaware and uncaring of how the class received it. They laughed, but he didn't seem to hear it, holding my eyes so singly with his own that I almost believed he'd carved a small, private world for us that no one else could reach.

Vulnerable, he mouthed.

I locked my ankles around the legs of my chair and jerked forward, feeling the weight of his arm drop off the back of the seat. I was *not* vulnerable.

"And there you have it!" Coach said. "Biology in motion."

"Can we please talk about sex now?" asked Vee.

"Tomorrow. Read chapter seven and be ready for a discussion first thing."

The bell rang, and Patch scraped his chair back. "That was fun. Let's do it again sometime." Before I could come up with something more pithy than *No, thanks,* he edged behind me and disappeared out the door.

"I'm starting a petition to have Coach fired," Vee said, coming to my table. "What was up with class today? It was watered-down porn. He practically had you and Patch on top of your lab table, horizontal, minus your clothes, doing the Big Deed—"

I nailed her with a look that said, *Does it look like I want a replay?*

"Yeesh," Vee said, stepping back.

"I need to talk to Coach. I'll meet you at your locker in ten minutes."

"Sure thing."

I made my way up to Coach's desk, where he sat hunched over a book of basketball plays. At first glance all the Xs and Os made it look like he'd been playing tic-tac-toe.

"Hi, Nora," he said without looking up. "What can I do for you?"

"I'm here to tell you the new seating chart and lesson plan is making me uncomfortable."

Coach kicked back in his chair and folded his hands behind his head. "I like the seating chart. Almost as much as I like this new man-to-man play I'm working on for Saturday's game."

I set a copy of the school code of conduct and student rights down on top of it. "By law, no student should feel threatened on school property."

"You feel threatened?"

"I feel uncomfortable. And I'd like to propose a solution." When Coach didn't cut me off, I drew a confident breath. "I will tutor any student from any of your biology classes—if you will seat me beside Vee again."

"Patch could use a tutor."

I resisted gritting my teeth. "That defeats the point."

"Did you see him today? He was involved in the discussion. I haven't heard him say one word all year, but I put him next to you and—bingo. His grade in here is going to improve."

"And Vee's is going to drop."

"That happens when you can't look sideways to get the right answer," he said dryly.

"Vee's problem is lack of dedication. I'll tutor her."

"No can do." Glancing at his watch, he said, "I'm late for a meeting. Are we done here?"

I squeezed my brain for one more argument, but it appeared I was fresh out of inspiration.

"Let's give the seating chart a few more weeks. Oh, and I was serious about tutoring Patch. I'll count you in." Coach didn't wait for my answer; he whistled the tune to Jeopardy and ducked out the door.

By seven o'clock the sky had glowered into an inky blue, and I zipped up my coat for warmth. Vee and I were on our way from the movie theater to the parking lot, having just watched *The Sacrifice*. It was my job to review movies for the eZine, and since I'd already seen every other movie showing at the theater, we'd resigned ourselves to the latest urban chiller.

"That," Vee said, "was the freakiest movie I have ever seen. As a rule, we are no longer allowed to see anything suggestive of horror."

Fine by me. Take into consideration that someone had been

lurking outside my bedroom window last night and compound it with watching a fully developed stalker movie tonight, and I was starting to feel a little bit paranoid.

"Can you imagine?" Vee said. "Living your whole life never having a clue that the only reason you're being kept alive is to be used as a sacrifice?"

We both shuddered.

"And what was up with that altar?" she continued, annoyingly unaware that I would have rather talked about the life cycle of fungi than about the movie. "Why did the bad guy light the stone on fire before tying her down? When I heard her flesh sizzle—"

"Okay!" I practically shouted. "Where to next?"

"And can I just say if a guy ever kisses me like that, I will start dry heaving. Repulsive doesn't begin to describe what was going on with his mouth. That was makeup, right? I mean, nobody actually has a mouth like that in real life—"

"My review is due by midnight," I said, cutting across her.

"Oh. Right. To the library, then?" Vee unlocked the doors to her 1995 purple Dodge Neon. "You're being awfully touchy, you know."

I slid into the passenger seat. "Blame the movie." Blame the Peeping Tom at my window last night.

"I'm not talking about just tonight. I've noticed," she said with a mischievous curve of her mouth, "that you've been unusually crabby for a good half hour at the end of bio the past two days."

"Also easy. Blame Patch."

Vee's eyes flicked to the rearview mirror. She adjusted it for a better look at her teeth. She licked them, giving a practiced smile. "I have to admit, his dark side calls to me."

I had no desire to admit it, but Vee wasn't alone. I felt drawn to Patch in a way I'd never felt drawn to anyone. There was a dark magnetism between us. Around him, I felt lured to the edge of danger. At any moment, it felt like he could push me over the edge.

"Hearing you say that makes me want to—" I paused, trying to think of exactly what our attraction to Patch did make me want to do. Something unpleasant.

"Tell me you don't think he's good-looking," Vee said, "and I promise I'll never bring up his name again."

I reached to turn on the radio. Of all things, there had to be something better to do than ruin our evening by inviting Patch, albeit abstractly, into it. Sitting beside him for one hour every day, five days a week, was plenty more than I could take. I wasn't giving him my evenings, too.

"Well?" Vee pressed.

"He could be good-looking. But I'd be the last to know. I'm a tainted juror on this one, sorry."

"What's that supposed to mean?"

"It means I can't get beyond his personality. No amount of beauty could make up for it."

"Not beauty. He's . . . hard-edged. Sexy."

I rolled my eyes.

Vee honked and tapped her brake as a car pulled in front of her. "What? You disagree, or rough-and-roguish isn't your type?"

"I don't have a type," I said. "I'm not that narrow."

Vee laughed. "You, babe, are more than narrow—you're confined. Cramped. Your spectrum is about as wide as one of Coach's microorganisms. There are very few, if any, boys at school you would fall for."

"That's not true." I said the words automatically. It wasn't until I'd spoken them that I wondered how accurate they were. I had never been seriously interested in anyone. How weird was I? "It isn't about the boys, it's about . . . love. I haven't found it."

"It isn't about love," Vee said. "It's about fun."

I lifted my eyebrows, doubtful. "Kissing a guy I don't know—I don't care about—is fun?"

"Haven't you been paying attention in bio? It's about a lot more than kissing."

"Oh," I said in an enlightened voice. "The gene pool is warped enough without me contributing to it."

"Want to know who I think would be really good?"

"Good?"

"Good," she repeated with an indecent smile.

"Not particularly."

"Your partner."

"Don't call him that," I said. "'Partner' has a positive connotation."

Vee squeezed into a parking space near the library doors and killed the engine. "Have you ever fantasized about kissing him? Have you ever stolen a peek sideways and imagined flinging yourself at Patch and crushing your mouth to his?"

I stared at her with a look I hoped spoke appalled shock. "Have you?"

Vee grinned.

I tried to imagine what Patch would do if presented with this information. As little as I knew about him, I sensed his aversion to Vee as if it were concrete enough to touch.

"He's not good enough for you," I said.

She moaned. "Careful, you'll only make me want him more."

Inside the library we took a table on the main level, near adult fiction. I opened my laptop and typed: *The Sacrifice, two and a half stars.* Two and a half was probably on the low side. But I had a lot on my mind and wasn't feeling particularly equitable.

Vee opened a bag of dried apple chips. "Want some?"

"I'm good, thanks."

She peered into the bag. "If you're not going to eat them, I'll have to. And I really don't want to."

Vee was on the color-wheel fruit diet. Three red fruits a day, two blue, a handful of green . . .

She held up an apple chip, examining it front to back.

"What color?" I asked.

"Make-me-gag-Granny-Smith-green. I think."

Just then Marcie Millar, the only sophomore to make varsity cheerleading in the history of Coldwater High, took a seat on the edge of our table. Her strawberry blond hair was combed into low pigtails, and like always, her skin was concealed under half a bottle of foundation. I was fairly certain I'd guessed the right amount, since there wasn't a trace of her freckles in sight. I hadn't seen any of Marcie's freckles since seventh grade, the same year she discovered Mary Kay. There was three-quarters of an inch between the hem of her skirt and the start of her underwear . . . if she was even wearing any.

"Hi, Supersize," Marcie said to Vee.

"Hi, Freakshow," Vee said back.

"My mom is looking for models this weekend. The pay is nine dollars an hour. I thought you'd be interested."

Marcie's mom manages the local JCPenney, and on weekends she has Marcie and the rest of the cheerleaders model bikinis in the store's street-facing display windows.

"She's having a really hard time finding plus-size lingerie models," said Marcie.

"You've got food stuck in your teeth," Vee told Marcie. "In the crack between your two front teeth. Looks like chocolate Ex-Lax . . ."

Marcie licked her teeth and slid off the table. As she sashayed off, Vee stuck her finger in her mouth and made gagging gestures at Marcie's back.

"She's lucky we're at the library," Vee told me. "She's lucky we didn't cross paths in a dark alley. Last chance—any chips?"

"Pass."

Vee wandered off to discard the chips. A few minutes later she returned with a romance novel. She took the seat next to me and, displaying the novel's cover, said, "Someday this is going to be us. Ravished by half-dressed cowboys. I wonder what it's like to kiss a pair of sunbaked, mud-crusted lips?"

"Dirty," I murmured, typing away.

"Speaking of dirty." There was an unexpected rise in her voice. "There's our guy."

I stopped typing long enough to peer over my laptop, and my heart skipped a beat. Patch stood across the room in the checkout line. As if he sensed me watching, he turned. Our eyes locked for one, two, three counts. I broke away first, but not before receiving a slow grin.

My heartbeat turned erratic, and I told myself to pull it together. I was not going down this path. Not with Patch. Not unless I was out of my mind.

"Let's go," I told Vee. Shutting my laptop, I zipped it inside its carrying case. I pushed my books inside my backpack, dropping a few on the floor as I did.

Vee said, "I'm trying to read the title he's holding . . . hang on . . . How to Be a Stalker."

"He is not checking out a book with that title." But I wasn't sure.

"It's either that or How to Radiate Sexy Without Trying."

"Shh!" I hissed.

"Calm down, he can't hear. He's talking to the librarian. He's checking out."

Confirming this with a quick glance over, I realized that if we left now, we'd probably meet him at the exit doors. And then I would be expected to say something to him. I ordered myself back into my chair and searched diligently through my pockets for nothing whatsoever while he finished checking out.

"Do you think it's creepy he's here at the same time we are?" Vee asked.

"Do you?"

"I think he's following you."

"I think it's a coincidence." This wasn't entirely true. If I had to make a list of the top ten places I would expect to find Patch on any given night, the public library wouldn't make it. The library wouldn't make the top hundred places. So what was he doing here?

The question was particularly disturbing after what had happened last night. I hadn't mentioned it to Vee because I was hoping it would shrink and shrivel in my memory until it ceased to have happened. Period.

"Patch!" Vee stage-whispered. "Are you stalking Nora?"

I clamped my hand over her mouth. "Stop it. I mean it." I put on a severe face.

"I bet he is following you," said Vee, prying my hand away.

"I bet he has a history of it too. I bet he has restraining orders. We should sneak into the front office. It would all be in his student file."

"We are not sneaking into the front office."

"I could create a diversion. I'm good at diversions. No one would see you go in. We could be like spies."

"We are not spies."

"Do you know his last name?" Vee asked.

"No."

"Do you know anything about him?"

"No. And I'd like to keep it that way."

"Oh, come on. You love a good mystery, and it doesn't get better than this."

"The best mysteries involve a dead body. We don't have a dead body."

Vee squealed. "Not yet!"

Shaking two iron pills from the bottle in my backpack, I swallowed them together.

Vee bounced the Neon into her driveway just after nine thirty. She killed the engine and dangled the keys in front of me.

"You're not going to drive me home?" I asked. A waste of breath, since I knew her answer.

"There's fog."

"Patchy fog."

Vee grinned. "Oh, boy. He is so on your mind. Not that I blame you. Personally, I'm hoping I dream about him tonight."

Ugh.

"And the fog always gets worse near your house," Vee continued. "It freaks me out after dark."

I grabbed the keys. "Thanks a lot."

"Don't blame me. Tell your mom to move closer. Tell her there's this new club called civilization and you guys should join."

"I suppose you expect me to pick you up before school tomorrow?"

"Seven thirty would be nice. Breakfast is on me."

"It better be good."

"Be nice to my baby." She patted the Neon's dash. "But not too nice. Can't have her thinking there's better out there."

On the drive home I allowed my thoughts a brief trip to Patch. Vee was right—something about him was incredibly alluring. And incredibly creepy. The more I thought about it, the more I was convinced something about him was . . . off. The fact that he liked to antagonize me wasn't exactly a news flash, but there was a difference between getting under my skin in class and possibly going as far as following me to the library to accomplish it. Not many people would go to that much trouble . . . unless they had a very good reason.

Halfway home a pattering rain flushed out the wispy clouds of fog hovering above the road. Dividing my attention between the road and the controls on the steering wheel, I tried to locate the windshield wipers.

The streetlights flickered overhead, and I wondered if a heavier storm was blowing in. This close to the ocean the weather changed constantly, and a rainstorm could quickly escalate into a flash flood. I fed the Neon more gas.

The outside lights flickered again. A cold feeling prickled up the back of my neck, and the hairs on my arms tingled. My sixth sense graduated to high alert. I asked myself if I thought I was being followed. There were no headlights in the rearview mirror. No cars ahead, either. I was all alone. It wasn't a very comforting thought. I pushed the car to forty-five.

I found the wipers, but even at top speed they couldn't keep up with the hammering rain. The stoplight ahead turned yellow. I rolled to a stop, checked to see that traffic was clear, then pulled into the intersection.

I heard the impact before I registered the dark silhouette skidding across the hood of the car.

I screamed and stomped on the brake. The silhouette thumped into the windshield with a splintering crack.

On impulse, I jerked the steering wheel a hard right. The back end of the Neon fishtailed, sending me spinning across the intersection. The silhouette rolled and disappeared over the edge of the hood.

I was holding my breath, squeezing the steering wheel between white-knuckled hands. I lifted my feet off the pedals. The car bucked and stalled out.

He was crouched a few feet away, watching me. He didn't look at all . . . injured.

He was dressed in total black and blended with the night, making it hard to tell what he looked like. At first I couldn't distinguish any facial features, and then I realized he was wearing a ski mask.

He rose to his feet, closing the distance between us. He flattened his palms to the driver's-side window. Our eyes connected through the holes in the mask. A lethal smile seemed to rise in his.

He gave another pound, the glass vibrating between us.

I started the car. I tried to synchronize shoving it into first gear, pushing on the gas pedal, and releasing the clutch. The engine revved, but the car bucked again and died.

I turned the engine over once more, but was distracted by an off-key metallic groan. I watched with horror as the door began to bow. He was tearing it off.

I rammed the car into first. My shoes slipped over the pedals. The engine roared, the RPM needle on the dash spiking into the red zone.

His fist came through the window in an explosion of glass. His hand fumbled over my shoulder, clamping around my arm. I gave a hoarse cry, stomped the gas pedal, and released the clutch. The Neon screeched into motion. He hung on, gripping my arm, running beside the car several feet before dropping away.

I sped forward with the force of adrenaline. I checked the rearview mirror to make sure he wasn't chasing me, then shoved the mirror to face away. I had to press my lips together to keep from sobbing.

CHAPTER

FLYING DOWN HAWTHORNE, I DROVE PAST MY
house, circled back, cut over to Beech, and headed back
toward the center of Coldwater. I speed-dialed Vee.
"Something happened—I—he—it—out of nowhere—the Neon—"

"You're breaking up. What?"

I wiped my nose with the back of my hand. I was trembling
down to my toes. "He came out of nowhere."

"Who?"

"He—" I tried to net my thoughts and funnel them into words. "He jumped in front of the car!"

"Oh, man. Oh-man-oh-man-oh-man. You hit a deer? Are you okay? What about Bambi?" She half wailed, half groaned. "The Neon?"

I opened my mouth, but Vee cut me off.

"Forget it. I've got insurance. Just tell me there aren't deer parts all over my baby. . . . No deer parts, right?"

Whatever answer I was about to give faded into the background. My mind was two steps ahead. A deer. Maybe I could pass the whole thing off as hitting a deer. I wanted to confide in Vee, but I didn't want to sound crazy, either. How was I going to explain watching the guy I hit rise to his feet and begin tearing off the car door? I stretched my collar down past my shoulder. No red marks where he'd gripped me that I could see . . .

I came to myself with a start. Was I actually considering denying it had happened? I knew what I'd seen. It was not my imagination.

"Holy freak show," Vee said. "You're not answering. The deer is lodged in my headlights, isn't he? You're driving around with him stuck to the front of the car like a snowplow."

"Can I sleep at your place?" I wanted to get off the streets. Out of the dark. With a sudden intake of air, I realized to get to Vee's, I'd have to drive back through the intersection where I'd hit him.

"I'm down in my room," said Vee. "Let yourself in. See you in a few."

With my hands tight on the steering wheel, I pushed the Neon through the rain, praying the light at Hawthorne would be green in my favor. It was, and I floored it through the intersection, keeping my eyes straight ahead, but at the same time, stealing glimpses into the shadows along the side of the road. There was no sign of the guy in the ski mask.

Ten minutes later I parked the Neon in Vee's driveway. The damage to the door was extensive, and I had to put my foot to it and kick my way out. Then I jogged to the front door, bolted myself inside, and hurried down the basement stairs.

Vee was sitting cross-legged on her bed, notebook propped between her knees, earbuds plugged in, iPod turned up all the way. "Do I want to see the damage tonight, or should I wait until I've had at least seven hours of sleep?" she called over the music.

"Maybe option number two."

Vee snapped the notebook shut and tugged out the earbuds. "Let's get it over with."

When we got outside, I stared at the Neon for a long moment. It wasn't a warm night, but the weather wasn't the cause of the goose bumps rippling over my arms. No smashed driver's-side window. No bend in the door.

"Something's not right," I said. But Vee wasn't listening. She was busy inspecting every square inch of the Neon.

I stepped forward and poked the driver's-side window. Solid

glass. I closed my eyes. When I reopened them, the window was still intact.

I walked around the back of the car. I'd completed almost a full circle when I came up short.

A fine crack bisected the windshield.

Vee saw it at the same time. "Are you sure it wasn't a squirrel?"

My mind flashed back to the lethal eyes behind the ski mask. They were so black I couldn't distinguish the pupils from the irises. Black like . . . Patch's.

"Look at me, I'm crying tears of joy," Vee said, sprawling herself across the Neon's hood in a hug. "A teeny-tiny crack. That's it!"

I manufactured a smile, but my stomach soured. Five minutes ago, the window was smashed out and the door was bowed. Looking at the car now, it seemed impossible. No, it seemed crazy. But I *saw* his fist punch through the glass, and I *felt* his fingernails bite into my shoulder.

Hadn't I?

The harder I tried to recall the crash, the more I couldn't. Little blips of missing information cut across my memory. The details were fading. Was he tall? Short? Thin? Bulky? Had he said anything?

I couldn't remember. That was the most frightening part.

Vee and I left her house at seven fifteen the following morning and drove to Enzo's Bistro to grab a breakfast of steamed milk. With my hands wrapped around my china cup, I tried to warm away the deep chill inside me. I'd showered, pulled on a camisole and cardigan borrowed from Vee's closet, and swept on some makeup, but I hardly remembered doing it.

"Don't look now," Vee said, "but Mr. Green Sweater keeps looking this way, estimating your long legs through your jeans. . . . Oh! He just saluted me. I am not kidding. A little two-finger military salute. How adorable."

I wasn't listening. Last night's accident had replayed itself in my head all night, chasing away any chance of sleep. My thoughts were in tangles, my eyes were dry and heavy, and I couldn't concentrate.

"Mr. Green Sweater looks normal, but his wingman looks hardcore bad boy," said Vee. "Emits a certain don't-mess-with-me signal. Tell me he doesn't look like Dracula's spawn. Tell me I'm imagining things."

Lifting my eyes just high enough to get a look at him without appearing that I was, I took in his fine-boned, handsome face. Blond hair hung at his shoulders. Eyes the color of chrome. Unshaven. Impeccably dressed in a tailored jacket over his green sweater and dark designer jeans. I said, "You're imagining things."

"Did you miss the deep-set eyes? The widow's peak? The tall, lanky build? He might even be tall enough for me."

Vee is closing in on six feet tall, but she has a thing for heels. High heels. She also has a thing about not dating shorter guys.

"Okay, what's wrong?" Vee asked. "You've gone all incommunicado. This isn't about the crack in my windshield, is it? So what if you hit an animal? It could happen to anyone. Granted, the chances would be a lot slimmer if your mom relocated out of the wilderness."

I was going to tell Vee the truth about what happened. Soon. I just needed a little time to sort out the details. The problem was, I didn't see how I could. The only details left were spotty, at best. It was as if an eraser had scrubbed my memory blank. Thinking back, I remembered the heavy rain cascading down the Neon's windows, causing everything outside to blur. Had I in fact hit a deer?

"Mmm, check it out," said Vee. "Mr. Green Sweater is getting out of his seat. Now that's a body that hits the gym regularly. He is definitely making his way toward us, his eyes pursuing the real estate, your real estate, that is."

A half beat later we were greeted with a low, pleasant "Hello."

Vee and I looked up at the same time. Mr. Green Sweater stood just back from our table, his thumbs hooked in the pockets of his jeans. He was blue-eyed, with stylishly shaggy blond hair swept across his forehead.

"Hello yourself," Vee said. "I'm Vee. This is Nora Grey."

I frowned at Vee. I did not appreciate her tagging on my last name, feeling that it violated an unspoken contract between girls, let alone best friends, upon meeting unknown boys. I gave a half-hearted wave and brought my cup to my lips, immediately scalding my tongue.

He dragged a chair over from the next table and sat backward

BECCA FITZPATRICK

on it, his arms resting where his back should have been. Holding a hand out to me, he said, "I'm Elliot Saunders." Feeling way too formal, I shook it. "And this is Jules," he added, jerking his chin toward his friend, whom Vee had grossly underestimated by calling "tall."

Jules lowered all of himself into a seat beside Vee, dwarfing the chair.

She said to him, "I think you might be the tallest guy I've ever seen. Seriously, how tall are you?"

"Six foot ten," Jules muttered, slumping in his seat and crossing his arms.

Elliot cleared his throat. "Can I get you ladies something to eat?"

"I'm fine," I said, raising my cup. "I already ordered."

Vee kicked me under the table. "She'll have a vanilla-cream-filled doughnut. Make it two."

"So much for the diet, huh?" I asked Vee.

"Huh yourself. The vanilla bean is a fruit. A brown fruit."

"It's a legume."

"You sure about that?"

I wasn't.

Jules closed his eyes and pinched the bridge of his nose. Apparently he was as thrilled to be sitting with us as I was to have them here.

As Elliot walked to the front counter, I let my eyes trail after him. He was definitely in high school, but I hadn't seen him at

CHS before. I would remember. He had a charming, outgoing personality that didn't fade into the background. If I wasn't feeling so shaken, I might have actually taken an interest. In friendship, maybe more.

"Do you live around here?" Vee asked Jules.

"Mmm."

"Go to school?"

"Kinghorn Prep." There was a tinge of superiority in the way he said it.

"Never heard of it."

"Private school. Portland. We start at nine." He lifted his sleeve and glanced at his watch.

Vee dipped a finger in the froth of her milk and licked it off. "Is it expensive?"

Jules looked at her directly for the first time. His eyes stretched, showing a little white around the edges.

"Are you rich? I bet you are," she said.

Jules eyed Vee like she'd just killed a fly on his forehead. He scraped his chair back several inches, distancing himself from us.

Elliot returned with a box of a half-dozen doughnuts.

"Two vanilla creams for the ladies," he said, pushing the box toward me, "and four glazed for me. Guess I'd better fill up now, since I don't know what the cafeteria is like at Coldwater High."

Vee nearly spewed her milk. "You go to CHS?"

"As of today. I just transferred from Kinghorn Prep."

"Nora and I go to CHS," Vee said. "I hope you appreciate your good fortune. Anything you need to know—including who you should invite to Spring Fling—just ask. Nora and I don't have dates . . . yet."

I decided it was time to part ways. Jules was obviously bored and irritated, and being in his company wasn't helping my already restless mood. I made a big presentation of looking at the clock on my cell phone and said, "We better get to school, Vee. We have a bio test to study for. Elliot and Jules, it was nice meeting you."

"Our bio test isn't until Friday," said Vee.

On the inside, I cringed. On the outside, I smiled through my teeth. "Right. I meant to say I have an English test. The works of . . . Geoffrey Chaucer." Everyone knew I was lying.

In a remote way my rudeness bothered me, especially since Elliot hadn't done anything to deserve it. But I didn't want to sit here any longer. I wanted to keep moving forward, distancing myself from last night. Maybe the diminishing memory wasn't such a bad thing after all. The sooner I forgot the accident, the sooner my life would resume its normal pace.

"I hope you have a really great first day, and maybe we'll see you at lunch," I told Elliot. Then I dragged Vee up by her elbow and steered her out the door.

The school day was almost over, only biology left, and after a quick stop by my locker to exchange books, I headed to class. Vee and I arrived before Patch; she slid into his empty seat and dug through her backpack, pulling out a box of Hot Tamales.

"One red fruit coming right up," she said, offering me the box.

"Let me guess . . . cinnamon is a fruit?" I pushed the box away.

"You didn't eat lunch, either," Vee said, frowning.

"I'm not hungry."

"Liar. You're always hungry. Is this about Patch? You're not worried he's really stalking you, are you? Because last night, that whole thing at the library, I was joking."

I massaged small circles into my temples. The dull ache that had taken up residence behind my eyes flared at the mention of Patch. "Patch is the least of my worries," I said. It wasn't exactly true.

"My seat, if you don't mind."

Vee and I looked up simultaneously at the sound of Patch's voice.

He sounded pleasant enough, but he kept his eyes trained on Vee as she rose and slung her backpack over her shoulder. It appeared she couldn't move fast enough; he swept his arm toward the aisle, inviting her out of his way.

"Looking good as always," he said to me, taking his chair. He leaned back in it, stretching his legs out in front of him. I'd known all along he was tall, but I'd never put a measurement to it. Looking at the length of his legs now, I guessed him to top out at six feet. Maybe even six-one.

"Thank you," I answered without thinking. Immediately I wanted to take it back. Thank you? Of all the things I could have said, "thank you" was the worst. I didn't want Patch thinking I liked his compliments. Because I didn't . . . for the most part. It didn't take much perception to realize he was trouble, and I had enough trouble in my life already. No need to invite more. Maybe if I ignored him, he'd eventually give up initiating conversation. And then we could sit side by side in silent harmony, like every other partnership in the room.

"You smell good too," said Patch.

"It's called a shower." I was staring straight ahead. When he didn't answer, I turned sideways. "Soap. Shampoo. Hot water."

"Naked. I know the drill."

I opened my mouth to change the subject when the bell cut me off.

"Put your textbooks away," Coach said from behind his desk. "I'm handing out a practice quiz to get you warmed up for this Friday's real one." He stopped in front of me, licking his finger as he tried to separate the quizzes. "I want fifteen minutes of silence while you answer the questions. Then we'll discuss chapter seven. Good luck."

I worked through the first several questions, answering them with a rhythmic outpouring of memorized facts. If nothing else, the quiz stole my concentration, pushing last night's accident and the voice at the back of my mind questioning my sanity to the sidelines. Pausing to shake a cramp out of my writing hand, I felt Patch lean toward me.

"You look tired. Rough night?" he whispered.

"I saw you at the library." I was careful to keep my pencil gliding over my quiz, seemingly hard at work.

"The highlight of my night."

"Were you following me?"

He tipped his head back and laughed softly.

I tried a new angle. "What were you doing there?"

"Getting a book."

I felt Coach's eyes on me and dedicated myself to my quiz. After answering several more questions, I stole a glimpse to my left. I was surprised to find Patch already watching me. He grinned.

My heart did an unexpected flip, startled by his bizarrely attractive smile. To my horror, I was so taken aback, I dropped my pencil. It bounced on the tabletop a few times before rolling over the edge. Patch bent to pick it up. He held it out in the palm of his hand, and I had to focus not to touch his skin as I took it back.

"After the library," I whispered, "where did you go?"

"Why?"

"Did you follow me?" I demanded in an undertone.

"You look a little on edge, Nora. What happened?" His eyebrows lifted in concern. It was all for show, because there was a taunting spark at the center of his black eyes.

"Are you following me?"

"Why would I want to follow you?"

"Answer the question."

"Nora." The warning in Coach's voice pulled me back to my quiz, but I couldn't help speculating about what Patch's answer might have been, and it had me wanting to slide far away from him. Across the room. Across the universe.

Coach chirped his whistle. "Time's up. Pass your quizzes forward. Be expecting similar questions this Friday. Now"—he sanded his hands together, and the dry sound of it made me shiver—"for today's lesson. Miss Sky, want to take a stab at our topic?"

"S-e-x," Vee announced.

Precisely after she did, I tuned out. Was Patch following me? Was he the face behind the ski mask—if there even was a face behind a mask? What did he want? I hugged my elbows, suddenly feeling very cold. I wanted my life to go back to the way it was before Patch barged into my life.

At the end of class, I stopped Patch from leaving. "Can we talk?"

He was already standing, so he took a seat on the edge of the table. "What's up?"

"I know you don't want to sit next to me any more than I want to sit next to you. I think Coach might consider changing our seats if you talk to him. If you explain the situation—"

"The situation?"

"We're not—compatible."

He rubbed a hand over his jaw, a calculating gesture I'd grown accustomed to in only a few short days of knowing him. "We're not?"

"I'm not announcing groundbreaking news here."

"When Coach asked for my list of desired characteristics in a mate, I gave him you."

"Take that back."

"Intelligent. Attractive. Vulnerable. You disagree?"

He was doing this for the sole purpose of antagonizing me, and that only flustered me more. "Will you ask Coach to change our seats or not?"

"Pass. You've grown on me."

What was I supposed to say to that? He was obviously aiming to get a reaction out of me. Which wasn't difficult, seeing as how I could never tell when he was joking, and when he was sincere.

I tried to inject a measure of self-composure into my voice. "I think you'd be much better seated with someone else. And I think you know it." I smiled, tense but polite.

"I think I could end up next to Vee." His smile appeared just as polite. "I'm not going to press my luck."

Vee appeared beside our table, glancing between me and Patch. "Interrupting something?"

"No," I said, yanking my backpack shut. "I was asking Patch about tonight's reading. I couldn't remember which pages Coach assigned."

Vee said, "The assignment's on the board, same as always. As if you haven't already read it."

Patch laughed, seemingly sharing a private joke with himself.

Not for the first time, I wished I knew what he was thinking. Because sometimes I was positive these private jokes had everything to do with me. "Anything else, Nora?" he said.

"No," I said. "See you tomorrow."

"Looking forward to it." He winked. Actually winked.

After Patch was out of earshot, Vee gripped my arm. "Good news. Cipriano. That's his last name. I saw it on Coach's class roster."

"And that's something to smile about because . . . ?"

"Everybody knows students are required to register prescription drugs with the nurse's office." She tugged at the front pocket of my backpack, where I kept my iron pills. "Likewise, everybody knows the nurse's office is conveniently located inside the front office, where, as it happens, student files are also kept."

Eyes aglow, Vee locked her arm in mine and pulled me toward the door. "Time to do some real sleuthing."

CHAPTER 5

"CAN I HELP YOU?"

I forced myself to smile at the front office secretary, hoping I didn't look as dishonest as I felt. "I have a prescription I take daily at school, and my friend—"

My voice caught on the word, and I wondered if after today I would ever feel like calling Vee my friend again.

"—my friend informed me that I'm supposed to register it with the nurse. Do you know if that's correct?" I couldn't believe I was standing here, intending to do something illegal. As of late, I was exhibiting a lot of uncharacteristic behavior. First I'd followed Patch to a disreputable arcade late at night. Now I was on the verge of snooping in his student file. What was the matter with me? No—what was the matter with Patch, that when it came to him, I couldn't seem to stop exercising bad judgment?

"Oh, yes," the secretary said solemnly. "All drugs need to be registered. Nurse's office is back through there, third door on the left, across from student records." She gestured into the hallway behind her. "If the nurse isn't there, you can take a seat on the cot inside her office. She should be back any minute."

I fabricated another smile. I'd really hoped it wouldn't be this easy.

Heading down the hall, I stopped several times to check over my shoulder. Nobody came up behind me. The phone out in the front office was ringing, but it sounded a world apart from the dim corridor where I stood. I was all alone, free to do as I pleased.

I came to a stop at the third door on the left. I sucked in a breath and knocked, but it was obvious from the darkened window that the room was empty. I pushed on the door. It moved with reluctance, creaking open on a compact room with scuffed white tiles. I stood in the entrance a moment, almost wishing the nurse would appear so I'd have no choice but to register my iron pills and leave. A quick glance across the hall revealed a door with a window marked STUDENT RECORDS. It too was dark.

I focused my attention on a nagging thought at the back of my mind. Patch claimed that he hadn't gone to school last year. I was pretty sure he was lying, but if he wasn't, would he even have a student record? He'd have a home address at the very least, I reasoned. And an immunization card, and last semester's grades. Still. Possible suspension seemed like a large price to pay for a peek at Patch's immunization card.

I leaned one shoulder against the wall and checked my watch. Vee had told me to wait for her signal. She said it would be obvious.

Great.

The phone in the front office rang again, and the secretary picked up.

Chewing my lip, I stole a second glimpse at the door labeled STUDENT RECORDS. There was a good chance it was locked. Student files were probably considered high security. It didn't matter what kind of diversion Vee created; if the door was locked, I wasn't getting in.

I shifted my backpack to the opposite shoulder. Another minute ticked down. I told myself maybe I should leave. . . .

On the other hand, what if Vee was right and he was stalking me? As his bio partner, regular contact with him could place me in danger. I had a responsibility to protect myself . . . didn't I?

If the door was unlocked and the files were alphabetized, I would have no trouble locating Patch's quickly. Add another few seconds to skim his file for red flags, and I could probably be in and out of the room in under a minute. Which was so brief it might not feel like I'd entered at all.

Things had grown unusually quiet out in the front office. Suddenly Vee rounded the corner. She edged down the wall toward me, walking in a crouch, dragging her hands along the wall, stealing surreptitious glances over her shoulder. It was the kind of walk spies adopted in old movies.

"Everything is under control," she whispered.

"What happened to the secretary?"

"She had to leave the office for a minute."

"Had to? You didn't incapacitate her, did you?"

"Not this time."

Thank goodness for small mercies.

"I called in a bomb threat from the pay phone outside," Vee said. "The secretary dialed the police, then ran off to find the principal."

"Vee!"

She tapped her wrist. "Clock's ticking. We don't want to be in here when the cops arrive."

Tell me about it.

Vee and I sized up the door to student records.

"Move over," Vee said, giving me her hip.

She drew her sleeve down over her fist and drilled it into the window. Nothing happened.

"That was just for practice," she said. She drew back for another punch and I grabbed her arm.

"It might be unlocked." I turned the knob and the door swung open.

"That wasn't near as much fun," said Vee.

A matter of opinion.

"You go in," Vee instructed. "I'm going to keep surveillance. If all goes well, we'll rendezvous in an hour. Meet me at the Mexican restaurant on the corner of Drake and Beech." She crouch-walked back down the hall.

I was left standing half in, half out of the narrow room lined wall-to-wall with filing cabinets. Before my conscience talked me out of it, I stepped inside and shut the door behind me, pressing my back against it.

With a deep breath I slouched off my backpack and hurried forward, dragging my finger along the faces of the cabinets. I found the drawer marked CAR–CUV. With one tug the drawer rattled open. The tabs on the files were labeled by hand, and I wondered if Coldwater High was the last school in the country not computerized.

My eyes brushed over the name "Cipriano."

I wrenched the file from the crammed drawer. I held it in my hands a moment, trying to convince myself there was nothing too wrong with what I was about to do. So what if there was private information inside? As Patch's biology partner, I had a right to know these things.

Outside, voices filled the hall.

I fumbled the file open and immediately flinched. It didn't make any sense.

The voices advanced.

I shoved the file randomly inside the drawer and gave it a push, sending it rattling back into the cabinet. As I turned, I froze. On the other side of the window, the principal stopped midstride, his gaze latching onto me.

Whatever he'd been saying to the group, which probably consisted of every major player on the school's faculty, trailed off. "Excuse me a moment," I heard him say. The group continued hustling forward. He did not.

He opened the door. "This area is off-limits to students."

I tried on a helpless face. "I'm so sorry. I'm trying to find the nurse's office. The secretary said third door on the right, but I think I miscounted. . . . " I threw my hands up. "I'm lost."

Before he could respond, I tugged at the zipper on my backpack. "I'm supposed to register these. Iron pills," I explained. "I'm anemic."

He studied me for a moment, his brow creasing. I thought I could see him weighing his options: stick around and deal with me, or deal with a bomb threat. He jerked his chin out the door. "I need you to exit the building immediately."

He propped the door wide and I ducked out under his arm, my smile collapsing.

An hour later I slid into a corner booth at the Mexican restaurant on the corner of Drake and Beech. A ceramic cactus and a stuffed coyote were mounted on the wall above me. A man wearing a sombrero wider than he was tall sauntered over. Strumming chords on his guitar, he serenaded me while the hostess laid menus on the table. I frowned at the insignia on the front cover. The Borderline. I hadn't eaten here before, yet something about the name sounded vaguely familiar.

Vee came up behind me and flopped into the opposite seat. Our waiter was on her heels.

"Four chimis, extra sour cream, a side of nachos, and a side of black beans," Vee told him without consulting the menu.

"One red burrito," I said.

"Separate bills?" he asked.

"I'm not paying for her," Vee and I said at the same time.

After our waiter left, I said, "Four chimis. I'm looking forward to hearing the fruit connection."

"Don't even start. I'm starving. Haven't eaten since lunch." She paused. "If you don't count the Hot Tamales, which I don't."

Vee is voluptuous, Scandinavian fair, and in an unorthodox way, incredibly sexy. There have been days when our friendship was the only thing standing in the way of my jealousy. Next to Vee, the only thing I have going for me are my legs. And maybe my metabolism. But definitely not my hair.

"He'd better bring chips soon," said Vee. "I'll break out in hives if I don't eat something salty within the next forty-five seconds. And anyway, the first three letters in the word diet should tell you what I want it to do."

"They make salsa with tomatoes," I pointed out. "That's a red. And avocados are a fruit. I think."

Her face brightened. "And we'll order virgin strawberry daiquiris."

Vee was right. This diet was easy.

"Be right back," she said, sliding out of the booth. "That time of the month. After that, I want to get the scoop."

While waiting for her, I found myself concentrating on the busboy some tables away. He was hard at work scrubbing a rag over the top of a table. There was something strangely familiar about the way he moved, about the way his shirt fell over the arch of his well-defined back. Almost as if he suspected he was being watched, he straightened and turned, his eyes fixing on mine at the exact same moment I figured out what was so familiar about this particular busboy.

Patch.

I couldn't believe it. I thought about slapping my forehead when I remembered he'd told me he worked at the Borderline.

Wiping his hands on his apron, he walked over, apparently enjoying my discomfort as I looked around for some way to escape, finding I had nowhere to go but deeper into the booth.

"Well, well," he said. "Five days a week isn't enough of me? Had to give me an evening, too?"

"I apologize for the unfortunate coincidence."

He slid into Vee's seat. When he laid his arms down, they were so long, they crossed into my half of the table. He reached for my glass, twirling it in his hands.

"All the seats here are taken," I said. When he didn't answer, I grabbed my glass back and took a sip of water, accidentally swallowing an ice cube. It burned the whole way down. "Shouldn't you be working instead of fraternizing with customers?" I choked.

He smiled. "What are you doing Sunday night?"

I snorted. By accident. "Are you asking me out?"

"You're getting cocky. I like that, Angel."

"I don't care what you like. I'm not going out with you. Not on a date. Not alone." I wanted to kick myself for experiencing a hot thrill upon speculating what a night alone with Patch might entail. Most likely, he hadn't even meant it. Most likely, he was baiting me for reasons known only to him. "Hang on, did you just call me Angel?" I asked.

"If I did?"

"I don't like it."

He grinned. "It stays. Angel."

He leaned across the table, raised his hand to my face, and brushed his thumb along one corner of my mouth. I pulled away, too late.

He rubbed lip gloss between his thumb and forefinger. "You'd look better without it."

I tried to remember what we'd been talking about, but not nearly as hard as I tried to appear unmoved by his touch. I tossed my hair back over my shoulder, picking up the tail of our previous conversation. "Anyway, I'm not allowed to go out on school nights."

"Too bad. There's a party on the coast. I thought we could go." He actually sounded sincere.

I could not figure him out. At all. The earlier hot thrill still lingered in my blood, and I took a long pull on my straw, trying to cool my feelings with a shot of ice water. Time alone with Patch would be intriguing, and dangerous. I wasn't sure how exactly, but I was trusting my instincts on this one.

I affected a yawn. "Well, like I said, it's a school night." In hopes of convincing myself more than him, I added, "If this party is something you'd be interested in, I can almost guarantee I won't be."

There, I thought. Case closed.

And then, without any warning whatsoever, I said, "Why are you asking me anyway?"

Up until this very moment, I'd been telling myself I didn't care what Patch thought of me. But right now, I knew it was a lie. Even though it would probably come back to haunt me, I was curious enough about Patch to go almost anywhere with him.

"I want to get you alone," Patch said. Just like that, my defenses shot back up.

"Listen, Patch, I don't want to be rude, but—"

"Sure you do."

hush, hush   77

"Well, you started it!" Lovely. Very mature. "I can't go to the party. End of story."

"Because you can't go out on a school night, or because you're scared of being alone with me?"

"Both." The confession just slipped out.

"Are you scared of all guys . . . or just me?"

I rolled my eyes as if to say I *am not answering such an inane question.*

"I make you uneasy?" His mouth held a neutral line, but I detected a speculative smile trapped behind it.

Yes, actually, he had that effect on me. He also had the tendency to wipe all logical thought from my mind.

"I'm sorry," I said. "What were we talking about?"

"You."

"Me?"

"Your personal life."

I laughed, unsure what other response to give. "If this is about me . . . and the opposite sex . . . Vee already gave me this speech. I don't need to hear it twice."

"And what did wise old Vee say?"

I was playing with my hands, and slid them out of sight. "I can't imagine why you're so interested."

He softly shook his head. "Interested? We're talking about you. I'm fascinated." He smiled, and it was a fantastic smile. The effect was a ratcheted pulse—my ratcheted pulse.

"I think you should get back to work," I said.

"For what it's worth, I like the idea that there's not a guy at school who matches up to your expectations."

"I forgot you're the authority on my so-called expectations," I scoffed.

He studied me in a way that had me feeling transparent. "You're not cagey, Nora. Not shy, either. You just need a very good reason to go out of your way to get to know someone."

"I don't want to talk about me anymore."

"You think you've got everyone all figured out."

"Not true," I said. "For example, well, for instance, I don't know much about . . . you."

"You aren't ready to know me."

There was nothing light about the way he said it. In fact, his expression was razor sharp.

"I looked in your student file."

My words hung in the air a moment before Patch's eyes aligned with mine. "I'm pretty sure that's illegal," he said calmly

"Your file was empty. Nothing. Not even an immunization record."

He didn't even pretend to look surprised. He eased back in his seat, eyes gleaming obsidian "And you're telling me this because you're afraid I might cause an outbreak? Measles or mumps?"

"I'm telling you this because I want you to know that I know something about you isn't right. You haven't fooled everybody. I'm going to find out what you're up to. I'm going to expose you."

"Looking forward to it."

I flushed, catching the innuendo too late. Over the top of Patch's head, I could see Vee weaving her way through the tables.

I said, "Vee's coming. You have to go."

He stayed put, eyeing me, considering.

"Why are you looking at me like that?" I challenged.

He tipped forward, preparing to stand. "Because you're nothing like what I expected."

"Neither are you," I countered. "You're worse."

CHAPTER 6

THE FOLLOWING MORNING I WAS SURPRISED TO SEE Elliot walk into first-hour PE just as the tardy bell sounded. He was dressed in knee-length basketball shorts and a white Nike sweatshirt. His high-tops looked new and expensive. After handing a slip of paper to Miss Sully, he caught my eye. He gave a low wave and joined me in the bleachers.

"I was wondering when we'd bump into each other again," he said. "The front office realized I haven't had PE for the past two years. It's not required in private school. They're debating how they're going to fit four years' worth of PE into the next two. So here I am. I've got PE first and fourth hours."

"I never heard why you transferred here," I said.

"I lost my scholarship and my parents couldn't afford the tuition."

Miss Sully blew her whistle.

"I take it the whistle means something," Elliot said to me.

"Ten laps around the gym, no cutting corners." I pushed up from the bleachers. "Are you an athlete?"

Elliot jumped up, dancing on the balls of his feet. He threw a few hooks and jabs into the air. He finished with an uppercut that stopped just short of my chin. Grinning, he said, "An athlete? To the core."

"Then you're going to love Miss Sully's idea of fun."

Elliot and I jogged the ten laps together, then headed outdoors, where the air was laced with a ghostly fog. It seemed to clog my lungs, choking me. The sky leaked a few raindrops, trying hard to push a storm down on the city of Coldwater. I eyed the building doors but knew it was to no avail; Miss Sully was hard-core.

"I need two captains for softball," she hollered. "Come on, look alive. Let's see some hands in the air! Better volunteer, or I'll pick teams, and I don't always play fair."

Elliot raised his hand.

"All right," Miss Sully said to him. "Up here, by home plate. And how about . . . Marcie Millar as captain of the red team."

Marcie's eyes swept over Elliot. "Bring it on."

"Elliot, go ahead and take first pick," Miss Sully said.

Steepling his fingers at his chin, Elliot examined the class, seemingly sizing up our batting and fielding skills just by the look of us. "Nora," he said.

Marcie tipped her neck back and laughed. "Thanks," she told Elliot, flashing him a toxic smile that, for reasons beyond me, mesmerized the opposite sex.

"For what?" said Elliot.

"For handing us the game." Marcie pointed a finger at me. "There's a hundred reasons why I'm a cheerleader and Nora's not. Coordination tops the list."

I narrowed my eyes at Marcie, then made my way over beside Elliot and tugged a blue jersey over my head.

"Nora and I are friends," Elliot told Marcie calmly, almost coolly. It was an overstatement, but I wasn't about to correct him. Marcie looked like she'd had a bucket of ice water flung at her, and I was enjoying it.

"That's because you haven't met anyone better. Like me." Marcie twisted her hair around her finger. "Marcie Millar. You'll hear all about me soon enough." Either her eye twitched, or she winked at him.

Elliot gave no response whatsoever, and my approval rating of him shot up a few notches. A lesser guy would have dropped to his knees and begged Marcie for any attention she saw fit to toss.

"Do we want to stand out here all morning waiting for the rain to come, or get down to business?" Miss Sully asked.

After divvying up teams, Elliot led ours to the dugout and determined the batting order. Handing me a bat, he pushed a helmet on my head. "You're up first, Grey. All we need is a base hit."

Taking a practice swing, and almost nailing him with it, I said, "But I was in the mood for a home run."

"We'll take one of those, too." He directed me toward home plate. "Step into the pitch and swing all the way through."

I balanced the bat on my shoulder, thinking maybe I should have paid more attention during the World Series. Okay, maybe I should have *watched* the World Series. My helmet slipped low on my eyes, and I pushed it up, trying to size up the infield, which was lost under ghoulish wisps of mist.

Marcie Millar took her place on the pitcher's mound. She held the ball out in front of her, and I noticed her middle finger was raised at me. She flashed another toxic smile and lobbed the softball at me.

I got a piece of it, sending it flying into the dirt on the wrong side of the foul line.

"That's a strike!" Miss Sully called from her position between first and second bases.

Elliot hollered from the dugout, "That had a lot of spin on it— send her a clean one!" It took me a moment to realize he was talking to Marcie and not me.

BECCA FITZPATRICK

Again the ball left Marcie's hand, arching through the dismal sky. I swung, a pure miss.

"Strike two," Anthony Amowitz said through the catcher's mask.

I gave him a hard look.

Stepping away from the plate, I took a few more practice swings. I almost missed Elliot coming up behind me. He reached his arms around me and positioned his hands on the bat, flush with mine.

"Let me show you," he said in my ear. "Like this. Feel that? Relax. Now pivot your hips—it's all in the hips."

I could feel my face heat up with the eyes of the entire class on us. "I think I've got it, thanks."

"Get a room!" Marcie called to us. The infield laughed.

"If you'd throw her a decent pitch," Elliot called back, "she'd hit the ball."

"My pitch is on."

"Her swing is on." Elliot dropped his voice, speaking to me alone. "You lose eye contact the minute she lets go of the ball. Her pitches aren't clean, so you're going to have to work to get them."

"We're holding up the game here, people!" Miss Sully called out.

Just then, something in the parking lot beyond the dugout drew my attention. I thought I'd heard my name called. I turned, but even as I did, I knew my name hadn't been said out loud. It had been spoken quietly to my mind.

Nora.

Patch wore a faded blue baseball cap and had his fingers hooked in the chain-link fence, leaning against it. No coat, despite the weather. Just head-to-toe black. His eyes were opaque and inaccessible as he watched me, but I suspected there was a lot going on behind them.

Another string of words crept into my mind.

Batting lessons? Nice . . . touch.

I drew a steadying breath and told myself I'd imagined the words. Because the alternative was considering that Patch held the power to channel thoughts into my mind. Which couldn't be. It just couldn't. Unless I was delusional. That scared me more than the idea that he'd breached normal communication methods and could, at will, speak to me without ever opening his mouth.

"Grey! Head in the game!"

I blinked, jerking to life just in time to see the ball rolling through the air toward me. I started to swing, then heard another trickle of words.

Not . . . yet.

I held back, waiting for the ball to come to me. As it descended, I stepped toward the front of the plate. I swung with everything I had.

A huge crack sounded, and the bat vibrated in my hands. The ball drove at Marcie, who fell flat on her backside. Squeezing between shortstop and second base, the ball bounced in the outfield grass.

"Run!" my team shouted from the dugout. "Run, Nora!"

I ran.

"Drop the bat!" they screamed.

I flung it aside.

"Stay on first base!"

I didn't.

Stepping on a corner of first base, I rounded it, sprinting toward second. Left field had the ball now, in position to throw me out. I put my head down, pumped my arms, and tried to remember how the pros on ESPN slid into base. Feetfirst? Headfirst? Stop, drop, and roll?

The ball sailed toward the second baseman, spinning white somewhere in my peripheral vision. An excited chanting of the word "Slide!" came from the dugout, but I still hadn't made up my mind which was hitting the dirt first—my shoes in my hands.

The second baseman snagged the ball out of the air. I dove headfirst, arms outstretched. The glove came out of nowhere, swooping down on me. It collided with my face, smelling strongly of leather. My body crumpled on the dirt, leaving me with a mouthful of grit and sand dissolving under my tongue.

"She's out!" cried Miss Sully.

I tumbled sideways, surveying myself for injuries. My thighs burned a strange mix of hot and cold, and when I raised my sweats, to say it looked like two cats had been set free on my thighs would be an understatement. Limping to the dugout, I collapsed on the bench.

"Cute," Elliot said.

"The stunt I pulled or my torn-up leg?" Tucking my knee against my chest, I gently brushed as much of the dirt away as I could.

Elliot bent sideways and blew on my knee. Several of the larger bits of dirt fell to the ground.

A moment of awkward silence followed.

"Can you walk?" he asked.

Standing, I demonstrated that while my leg was a mess of scratches and dirt, I still had the use of it.

"I can take you the nurse's office if you want. Get you bandaged," he said.

"Really, I'm fine." I glanced at the fence where I'd last seen Patch. He was no longer there.

"Was that your boyfriend standing by the fence?" Elliot asked.

I was surprised that Elliot had noticed Patch. He'd had his back to him. "No," I said. "Just a friend. Actually, not even that. He's my bio partner."

"You're blushing."

"Probably windburn."

Patch's voice still echoed in my head. My heart pumped faster, but if anything, my blood ran colder. Had he talked directly to my thoughts? Was there some inexplicable link between us that allowed it to happen? Or was I losing my mind?

Elliot didn't look fully convinced. "You sure nothing's going on between the two of you? I don't want to chase after an unavailable girl."

"Nothing." Nothing I was going to allow, anyway.

Wait. What did Elliot say?

"Sorry?" I said.

He smiled. "Delphic Seaport reopens Saturday night, and Jules and I are thinking about driving out. Weather's not supposed to be too bad. Maybe you and Vee want to come?"

I took a moment to think over his offer. I was pretty sure that if I turned Elliot down, Vee would kill me. Besides, going out with Elliot seemed like a good way to escape my uncomfortable attraction to Patch.

"Sounds like a plan," I said.

CHAPTER

IT WAS SATURDAY NIGHT, AND DOROTHEA AND I WERE IN the kitchen. She had just popped a casserole into the oven and was sizing up a list of tasks my mom had hanging from a magnet on the fridge.

"Your mother called. She won't arrive home until late Sunday night," Dorothea said as she scrubbed Ajax into our kitchen sink with a vigor that made my own elbow ache. "She left a message on the machine. She wants you to give her a call. You've been calling every night before bed?"

I sat on a stool, eating a buttered bagel. I'd just taken a huge bite, and now Dorothea was looking at me like she wanted an answer. "Mm-hmm," I said, nodding.

"A letter from school came today." She flicked her chin at the stack of mail on the counter. "Maybe you know why?"

I gave my best innocent shrug and said, "No clue." But I had a pretty good idea what this was about. Twelve months ago I'd opened the front door to find the police on the doorstep. *We have some bad news,* they said. My dad's funeral was a week later. Every Monday afternoon since then, I'd shown up at my scheduled time slot with Dr. Hendrickson, school psychologist. I'd missed the last two sessions, and if I didn't make amends this week, I was going to get in trouble. Most likely the letter was a warning.

"You have plans tonight? You and Vee have something up your sleeves? Maybe a movie here at the house?"

"Maybe. Honestly, Dorth, I can clean the sink later. Come sit and . . . have the other half of my bagel."

Dorothea's gray bun was coming undone as she scrubbed. "I am going to a conference tomorrow," she said. "In Portland. Dr. Melissa Sanchez will speak. She says you think your way to a sexier you. Hormones are powerful drugs. Unless we tell them what we want, they backfire. They work against us." Dorothea turned, pointing the Ajax can at me for emphasis. "Now I wake in the morning and take red lipstick to my mirror. 'I am sexy,' I write. 'Men want me. Sixty-five is the new twenty-five.'"

"Do you think it's working?" I asked, trying very hard not to smile.

"It's working," Dorothea said soberly.

I licked butter off my fingers, stalling for a suitable response. "So you're going to spend the weekend reinventing your sexy side."

"Every woman needs to reinvent her sexy side—I like that. My daughter got implants. She said she did it for herself, but what woman gets boobs for herself? They are a burden. She got the boobs for a man. I hope you do not do stupid things for a boy, Nora." She shook her finger at me.

"Trust me, Dorth, there are no boys in my life." Okay, maybe there were two lurking on the fringe, circling from afar, but since I didn't know either very well, and one outright frightened me, it felt safer to close my eyes and pretend they weren't there.

"This is a good thing, and a bad thing," Dorothea said scoldingly. "You find the wrong boy, you ask for trouble. You find the right boy, you find love." Her voice softened reminiscently. "When I was a little girl in Germany, I had to choose between two boys. One was a very wicked boy. The other was my Henry. We are happily married for forty-one years."

It was time to change the subject. "How's, um, your godson . . . Lionel?"

Her eyes stretched. "You have a thing for little Lionel?"

"Noooo."

"I can work something out—"

"No, Dorothea, really. Thank you, but—I'm really concentrating on my grades right now. I want to get into a top-tier college."

"If in the future—"

"I'll let you know."

I finished my bagel to the sounds of Dorothea's monotone chatter, interjecting a few nods or "uh-huh's" whenever she stopped talking long enough to wait for my response. I was preoccupied debating whether or not I really wanted to meet Elliot tonight. At first, meeting up had seemed like a great idea. But the more I thought about it, the more doubt crept in. I'd only known Elliot a couple of days, for one. And I wasn't sure how my mom would feel about the arrangement, for another. It was getting late, and Delphic was at least a half-hour drive. More to the point, on weekends Delphic had a reputation for being wild.

The phone rang, and Vee's number showed on the caller ID.

"Are we doing anything tonight?" she wanted to know.

I opened my mouth, weighing my answer carefully. Once I told Vee about Elliot's offer, there was no turning back.

Vee shrieked. "Oh, man! Oh-man-oh-man oh-man. I just spilled nail polish on the sofa. Hang on, I'm going to get some paper towels. Is nail polish water-soluble?" A moment later she returned. "I think I ruined the sofa. We have to go out tonight. I don't want to be here when my latest work of accidental art is discovered."

Dorothea had moved down the hall to the powder room. I had no desire to spend the whole night listening to her grunt over the bathroom fixtures as she cleaned, so I made my decision. "How about Delphic Seaport? Elliot and Jules are going. They want to meet up."

"You buried the lead! Vital information here, Nora. I'll pick you up in fifteen." I was left listening to the dial tone.

I went upstairs and pulled on a snug white cashmere sweater, dark jeans, and navy blue driving moccasins. I shaped the hair framing my face around my finger, the way I'd learned to manage my natural curls, and . . . voilà! Half-decent spirals. I stepped back from the mirror for a twice-over and called myself a cross between carefree and *almost* sexy.

Fifteen minutes later to the dot, Vee bounced the Neon up the driveway and beeped the horn staccato-style. It took me ten minutes to make the drive between our houses, but I usually paid attention to the speed limit. Vee understood the word speed, but limit wasn't part of her vocabulary.

"I'm going to Delphic Seaport with Vee," I called to Dorothea. "If my mom calls, would you mind relaying the message?"

Dorothea waddled out of the powder room. "All the way to Delphic? This late?"

"Have fun at your conference!" I said, escaping out the door before she could protest or get my mom on the phone.

Vee's blond hair was pulled up in a high ponytail, big fat curls spilling down. Gold hoops dangled from her ears. Cherry red lipstick. Black, lengthening mascara.

"How do you do it?" I asked. "You had five minutes to get ready."

"Always prepared." Vee shot me a grin. "I'm a Boy Scout's dream."

She gave me a critical once-over.

"What?" I said.

"We're meeting up with boys tonight."

"Last I checked, yes."

"Boys like girls who look like . . . girls."

I arched my eyebrows. "And what do I look like?"

"Like you stepped out of the shower and decided that alone was enough to pass as presentable. Don't get me wrong. The clothes are good, the hair is okay, but the rest . . . Here." She reached inside her purse. "Being the friend that I am, I'll loan you my lipstick. And my mascara, but only if you swear you don't have a contagious eye disease."

"I do not have an eye disease!"

"Just covering my bases."

"I'll pass."

Vee's mouth dropped, half-playful, half-serious. "You'll feel naked without it!"

"Sounds like just the kind of look you'd go for," I said.

In all honesty, I had mixed feelings about going makeup free.

Not because I did feel a little bit naked, but because Patch had put the no-makeup suggestion in my mind. In an effort to make myself feel better, I told myself my dignity wasn't at stake. Neither was my pride. I'd been given a suggestion, and I was open-minded enough to try it. What I didn't want to acknowledge was I'd specifically chosen a night I knew I wouldn't see Patch to test it out.

A half hour later Vee drove under the gates to Delphic Seaport. We were forced to park at the farthest end of the lot, due to heavy opening-weekend traffic. Nestled right on the coast, Delphic is not known for its mild weather. A low wind had picked up, sweeping popcorn bags and candy wrappers around our ankles as Vee and I walked toward the ticket counter. The trees had long since lost their leaves, and the branches loomed over us like disjointed fingers. Delphic Seaport boomed all summer long with an amusement park, masquerades, fortune-telling booths, gypsy musicians, and a freak show. I could never be sure if the human deformities were real or an illusion.

"One adult, please," I told the woman at the ticket counter. She took my money and slid a wristband under the window. Then she smiled, exposing white plastic vampire teeth, smudged red with lipstick.

"Have a good time," she said in a breathless voice. "And don't forget to try our newly remodeled ride." She tapped her side of the glass, pointing to a stack of park maps and a flier.

I grabbed one of each on my way through the revolving gates.
The flier read:

DELPHIC AMUSEMENT PARK'S

NEWEST SENSATION!

THE ARCHANGEL

REMODELED AND RENOVATED!

FALL FROM GRACE ON THIS

ONE-HUNDRED-FOOT VERTICAL DROP.

Vee read the flier over my shoulder. Her nails threatened to
puncture the skin on my arm. "We have to do it!" she squealed.

"Last," I promised, hoping if we did all the other rides first,
she'd forget about this one. I hadn't been afraid of heights for
years, probably because I had conveniently avoided them. I wasn't
sure I was ready just yet to find out if time had faded my fear of
them.

After we hit the Ferris wheel, the bumper cars, the Magic Carpet
ride, and a few of the game booths, Vee and I decided it was time to
look for Elliot and Jules.

"Hmm," said Vee, looking both ways down the path looping the
park. We shared a thoughtful silence.

"The arcade," I said at last.

"Good call."

We had just walked through the doors to the arcade when I saw him. Not Elliot. Not Jules.

Patch.

He glanced up from his video game. The same baseball cap he'd worn when I saw him during PE shielded most of his face, but I was certain I saw a flicker of a smile. At first glance it appeared friendly, but then I remembered how he'd entered my thoughts, and I went cold to the bone.

If I was lucky, Vee hadn't seen him. I edged her forward through the crowd, letting Patch fall out of sight. The last thing I needed was for her to suggest we go over and strike up a conversation.

"There they are!" Vee said, waving her arm over her head. "Jules! Elliot! Over here!"

"Good evening, ladies," Elliot said, making his way through the crowd. Jules moved in his wake, looking about as enthusiastic as three-day-old meat loaf. "Can I buy you both a Coke?"

"Sounds good," said Vee. She was looking right at Jules. "I'll take a Diet."

Jules muttered an excuse about needing to use the restroom and slipped back into the crowd.

Five minutes later Elliot returned with Cokes. After splitting them between us, he rubbed his hands together and surveyed the floor. "Where should we start?"

"What about Jules?" Vee asked.

"He'll find us."

"Air hockey," I said immediately. Air hockey was on the other side of the arcade. The farther away from Patch, the better. I told myself it was a coincidence he was here, but my instincts disagreed.

"Ooh, look!" Vee interjected. "Foosball!" She was already zigzagging her way toward an open table. "Jules and me against the two of you. Losers buy pizza."

"Fair enough," said Elliot.

Foosball would have been fine, had the table not been a short distance from where Patch stood playing his game. I told myself to ignore him. If I kept my back to him, I'd hardly notice he was there. Maybe Vee wouldn't notice him either.

"Hey, Nora, isn't that Patch?" Vee said.

"Hmm?" I said innocently.

She pointed. "Over there. That's him, isn't it?"

"I doubt it. Are Elliot and I the white team, then?"

"Patch is Nora's bio partner," Vee explained to Elliot. She winked slyly at me but made a face of innocence the moment Elliot gave her his attention. I shook my head subtly but firmly at her, transmitting a silent message—stop.

"He keeps looking this way," Vee said in a lowered voice. She leaned across the foosball table, attempting to make her conversation with me appear private, but she whispered loud enough that Elliot had no choice but to overhear. "He's bound to wonder what you're doing here with—" She bobbed her head at Elliot.

I shut my eyes and envisioned banging my head against the wall.

"Patch has made it very clear he'd like to be more than biology partners with Nora," Vee continued. "Not that anyone can blame him."

"That so?" said Elliot, eyeing me with a look that said he wasn't surprised. He'd suspected it all along. I noticed he took a step closer.

Vee shot me a triumphant smile. *Thank me later*, it said.

"It's not like that," I corrected. "It's—"

"Twice as bad," Vee said. "Nora suspects he's stalking her. The police are on the brink of becoming involved."

"Should we play?" I said loudly. I dropped the foosball in the center of the table. Nobody noticed.

"Do you want me to talk to him?" Elliot asked me. "I'll explain we're not looking for trouble. I'll tell him you're here with me, and if he's got a problem, he can discuss it with me."

This was not the direction I wanted the conversation to go. At all. "What happened to Jules?" I said. "He's been gone for a while."

"Yeah, maybe he fell in the toilet," said Vee.

"Let me talk to Patch," Elliot said.

While I appreciated the concern, I did not like the idea of Elliot going head-to-head with Patch. Patch was an X factor: intangible, scary, and unknown. Who knew what he was capable of? Elliot was far too nice to be sent up against Patch.

"He doesn't scare me," Elliot said, as if to disprove my thoughts.

Obviously this was something Elliot and I disagreed on.

"Bad idea," I said.

"Great idea," Vee said. "Otherwise, Patch might get . . . violent. Remember last time?"

Last time?! I mouthed at her.

I had no idea why Vee was doing this, other than that she had a penchant for making everything as dramatic as possible. Her idea of drama was my idea of morbid humiliation.

"No offense, but this guy sounds like a creep," said Elliot. "Give me two minutes with him." He started to walk over.

"No!" I said, yanking on his sleeve to stop him. "He, uh, might get violent again. Let me handle this." I narrowed a look at Vee.

"You sure?" Elliot said. "I'm more than happy to do it."

"I think it's best coming from me."

I wiped my palms on my jeans, and after taking a mostly steady breath, I started closing the distance between me and Patch, which was only the width of a few game consoles. I had no idea what I was going to say when I reached him. Hopefully just a brief hello. Then I could go back and reassure Elliot and Vee that everything was under control.

Patch was dressed in the usual: black shirt, black jeans, and a thin silver necklace that flashed against his dark complexion. His sleeves were pushed up his forearms, and I could see his muscles working as he punched buttons. He was tall and lean and hard, and I wouldn't have been surprised if under his clothes he bore several scars, souvenirs from street fights and other reckless behavior. Not that I wanted a look under his clothes.

When I got to Patch's console, I tapped a hand against the side of it to get his attention. In the calmest voice I could manage, I said, "Pac-Man? Or is it Donkey Kong?" In truth, it looked a little more violent and military.

A slow grin spread over his face. "Baseball. Think maybe you could stand behind me and give me a few pointers?"

Firebombs erupted on the screen, and screaming bodies sailed through the air. Obviously not baseball.

"What's his name?" Patch asked, directing an almost imperceptible nod at the foosball table.

"Elliot. Listen, I have to keep this short. They're waiting."

"Have I seen him before?"

"He's new. Just transferred."

"First week at school and he's already made friends. Lucky guy." He slid me a look. "Could have a dark and dangerous side we know nothing about."

"Seems to be my specialty."

I waited for him to catch my meaning, but he only said, "Up for a game?" He tilted his head toward the back of the arcade. Through the crowd I could just make out pool tables.

"Nora!" Vee called out. "Get over here. Elliot is cramming defeat down my throat!"

"Can't," I told Patch.

"If I win," he said, as if he had no intention of being refused, "you'll tell Elliot something came up. You'll tell him you're no longer free tonight."

I couldn't help it; he was way too arrogant. I said, "And if *I* win?"

His eyes skimmed me, head to toe. "I don't think we have to worry."

Before I could stop myself, I punched his arm.

"Careful," he said in a low voice. "They might think we're flirting."

I felt like kicking myself, because that's exactly what we were doing. But it wasn't my fault—it was Patch's. In close contact with him, I experienced a confusing polarity of desires. Part of me wanted to run away from him screaming, Fire! A more reckless part was tempted to see how close I could get without . . . combusting.

"One game of pool," he tempted.

"I'm here with someone else."

"Head toward the pool tables. I'll take care of it."

I crossed my arms, hoping to look stern and a little exasperated, but at the same time, I had to bite my lip to keep from showing a slightly more positive reaction. "What are you going to do? Fight Elliot?"

"If it comes to that."

I was almost sure he was joking. Almost.

"A pool table just opened up. Go claim it." I . . . *dare* . . . *you*.

I stiffened. "How did you do that?"

When he didn't immediately deny it, I felt a squeeze of panic. It was real. He knew exactly what he was doing. The palms of my hands touched with sweat.

"How did you do that?" I repeated.

He gave me a sly smile. "Do what?"

"Don't," I warned. "Don't pretend you're not doing it."

He leaned a shoulder against the console and gazed down at me. "Tell me what I'm supposed to be doing."

"My . . . thoughts."

"What about them?"

"Cut it out, Patch."

He glanced around theatrically. "You don't mean—talking to your mind? You know how crazy that sounds, right?"

Swallowing, I said in the calmest voice I could manage, "You scare me, and I'm not sure you're good for me."

"I could change your mind."

"Noooora!" Vee called over the din of voices and electronic beeps.

"Meet me at the Archangel," Patch said.

I took a step back. "No," I said on impulse.

Patch came around behind me, and a chill shimmied up my spine. "I'll be waiting," he said into my ear. Then he slipped out of the arcade.

CHAPTER

I WALKED BACK TO THE FOOSBALL TABLE IN A COLD DAZE. Elliot was bent over it, his face showing competitive concentration. Vee was shrieking and laughing. Jules was still missing.

Vee looked up from the game. "Well? What happened? What'd he say to you?"

"Nothing. I told him not to bother us. He left." My voice sounded flat.

"He didn't look mad when he left," Elliot said. "Whatever you said, it must have worked."

"Too bad," Vee said. "I was hoping for some excitement."

"Are we ready to play?" Elliot asked. "I'm getting hungry for some hard-won pizza."

"Yeah, if Jules would ever come back," said Vee. "I'm starting to think maybe he doesn't like us. He keeps disappearing. I'm starting to think it's a nonverbal cue."

"You kidding me? He loves you guys," Elliot said with too much enthusiasm. "He's just slow to warm up to strangers. I'll go find him. Don't go anywhere."

As soon as Vee and I were alone, I said, "You know I'm going to kill you, right?"

Vee raised her palms and took a step back. "I was doing you a favor. Elliot is wild about you. After you left, I told him you have, like, ten guys calling you every night. You should have seen his face. Barely contained jealousy."

I groaned.

"It's the law of supply and demand," Vee said. "Who would've thought economics would come in useful?"

I looked to the arcade doors. "I need something."

"You need Elliot."

"No, I need sugar. Lots of it. I need cotton candy." What I needed was an eraser big enough to scrub away all evidence of Patch from my life. Particularly the mind-speaking. I shuddered. How was he doing it? And why me? Unless . . . I'd imagined it. Just like I'd imagined hitting someone with the Neon.

"I could use a little sugar myself," Vee said. "I saw a vendor near the park entrance on our way in. I'll stay here so Jules and Elliot don't think we ran off, and you can get the cotton candy."

Outside, I backtracked to the entrance, but when I found the vendor selling cotton candy, I was distracted by a sight farther down the walkway. The Archangel rose up above the treetops. A snake of cars zipped over the lighted tracks and dove out of view. I wondered why Patch wanted to meet. I felt a jab in my stomach and probably should have taken it for an answer, but despite my best intentions, I found myself continuing down the walkway toward the Archangel.

I stayed with the flow of foot traffic, keeping my eyes on the distant track of the Archangel looping through the sky. The wind had changed from chilly to icy, but that wasn't the reason I felt increasingly ill at ease. The feeling was back. That cold, heart-stopping feeling that someone was watching me.

I stole a look to both sides. Nothing abnormal in my peripheral vision. I spun a full 180 degrees. A little ways back, standing in a small courtyard of trees, a hooded figure turned and disappeared into the darkness.

With my heart beating faster, I bypassed a large group of pedestrians, putting distance between me and the clearing. Several strides farther on, I glanced back again. Nobody stood out as following me.

hush, hush

When I faced forward again, I ran smack into someone. "Sorry!" I blurted, trying to regain my balance.

Patch grinned down at me. "I'm hard to resist."

I blinked up at him. "Leave me alone." I tried to sidestep him, but he caught me by the elbow.

"What's wrong? You look ready to throw up."

"You have that effect on me," I snapped.

He laughed. I felt like kicking his shins.

"You could use a drink." He still had me by the elbow, and he tugged me toward a lemonade cart.

I dug in my heels. "You want to help? Stay away from me."

He brushed a curl off my face. "Love the hair. Love when it's out of control. It's like seeing a side of you that needs to come out more often."

I smoothed my hair furiously. As soon as I realized I looked like I was trying to make myself more presentable for him, I said, "I have to go. Vee is waiting." A frazzled pause. "I guess I'll see you in class on Monday."

"Ride the Archangel with me."

I craned my neck, staring up at it. High-pitched screams echoed down as the cars thundered over the tracks.

"Two people to a seat." His smile changed to a slow, daring grin.

"No." No *way*.

"If you keep running from me, you're never going to figure out what's really going on."

BECCA FITZPATRICK

That comment right there should have sent me running. But it didn't. It was almost as if Patch knew exactly what to say to pique my curiosity. Exactly what to say, at exactly the right moment.

"What is going on?" I asked.

"Only one way to find out."

"I can't. I'm afraid of heights. Besides, Vee's waiting." Only, suddenly the thought of going up that high in the air didn't scare me. Not anymore. In an absurd way, knowing I'd be with Patch made me feel safe.

"If you ride the whole way through without screaming, I'll tell Coach to switch our seats."

"I already tried. He won't budge."

"I could be more convincing than you."

I took his comment as a personal insult. "I don't scream," I said. "Not for carnival rides." Not for you.

In step with Patch, I made my way to the back of the line leading up to the Archangel. A rush of screams lifted, then faded, far above in the night sky.

"I haven't seen you at Delphic before," Patch said.

"You're here a lot?" I made a mental note not to take any more weekend trips to Delphic.

"I have a history with the place."

We edged up the line as the cars emptied and a new set of thrill seekers boarded the ride.

"Let me guess," I said. "You played hooky here instead of going to school last year."

hush, hush

I was being sarcastic, but Patch said, "Answering that would mean shedding light on my past. And I'd like to keep it in the dark."

"Why? What's wrong with your past?"

"I don't think now is a good time to talk about it. My past might frighten you."

Too late, I thought.

He stepped closer and our arms met, a brushed connection that caused the hairs on my arm to rise. "The things I have to confess aren't the kind of things you tell your flippant bio partner," he said.

The frigid wind wrapped around me, and when I breathed in, it filled me with ice. But it didn't compare to the chill Patch's words sent through me.

Patch jerked his chin up the ramp. "Looks like we're up."

I pushed through the revolving gate. By the time we made it to the boarding platform, the only empty cars were at the very front and the very back of the roller coaster. Patch headed toward the former.

The roller coaster's construction didn't inspire my confidence, remodeled or not. It looked more than a century old and was made of wood that had spent a lot of time exposed to Maine's harsh elements. The artwork painted on the sides was even less inspiring.

The car Patch chose had a grouping of four paintings. The first

depicted a mob of horned demons ripping the wings off a screaming male angel. The next painting showed the wingless angel
perched on a headstone, watching children play from a distance. In
the third painting, the wingless angel stood close to the children,
crooking a finger at one little green-eyed girl. In the final painting, the wingless angel drifted through the girl's body like a ghost.
The girl's eyes were black, her smile was gone, and she'd sprouted
horns like the demons from the first painting. A slivered moon
hung above the paintings.

I averted my eyes and assured myself it was the frigid air making my legs tremble. I slid into the car beside Patch.

"Your past wouldn't frighten me," I said, buckling my seat belt
across my lap. "I'm guessing I'd be more appalled than anything."

"Appalled," he repeated. The tone of his voice led me to believe
he'd accepted the accusation. Strange, since Patch never degraded
himself.

The cars rolled backward, then lurched forward. Not in a
smooth way, we headed away from the platform, climbing steadily
uphill. The smell of sweat, rust, and saltwater blowing in from
the sea filled the air. Patch sat close enough to smell. I caught the
slightest trace of rich mint soap.

"You look pale," he said, leaning in to be heard above the clicking tracks.

I felt pale, but did not admit it.

At the crest of the hill there was a moment's hesitation. I could see for miles, noting where the dark countryside blended with the sparkle of the suburbs and gradually became the grid of Portland's lights. The wind held its breath, allowing the damp air to settle on my skin.

Without meaning to, I stole a look at Patch. I found a measure of consolation in having him at my side. Then he flashed a grin.

"Scared, Angel?"

I clenched the metal bar drilled into the front of the car as I felt my weight tip forward. A shaky laugh slipped out of me.

Our car flew demonically fast, my hair flapping out behind me. Swerving to the left, then to the right, we clattered over the tracks. Inside, I felt my organs float and fall in response to the ride. I looked down, trying to concentrate on something not moving.

It was then that I noticed my seat belt had come undone.

I tried to shout at Patch, but my voice was swallowed up in the rush of air. I felt my stomach go hollow, and I let go of the metal bar with one hand, trying to secure the seat belt around my waist with the other. The car lunged to the left. I slammed shoulders with Patch, pressing against him so hard it hurt. The car soared up, and I felt it lift from the tracks, not fully riveted to them.

We were plunging. The flashing lights along the tracks blinded me; I couldn't see which way the track turned at the end of the dive.

It was too late. The car swerved to the right. I felt a jolt of panic, and then it happened. My left shoulder slammed against the car door. It flung open, and I was ripped out of the car while the roller coaster sped off without me. I rolled onto the tracks and grappled for something to anchor myself. My hands found nothing, and I tumbled over the edge, plunging straight down through the black air. The ground rushed up at me, and I opened my mouth to scream.

The next thing I knew, the ride screeched to a stop at the unloading platform.

My arms hurt from how tightly Patch held me. "Now that's what I call a scream," he said, grinning at me.

In a daze, I watched him place a hand over his ear as if my scream still echoed there. Not at all certain what had just happened, I stared at the place on his arm where my nails had left semicircles tattooed on his skin. Then my eyes moved to my seat belt. It was secured around my waist.

"My seat belt . . . ," I began. "I thought—"

"Thought what?" Patch asked, sounding genuinely interested.

"I thought . . . I flew out of the car. I literally thought . . . I was going to die."

"I think that's the point."

At my sides, my arms trembled. My knees wobbled slightly under the weight of my body.

"Guess we're stuck as partners," said Patch. I suspected a small degree of victory in his voice. I was too stunned to argue.

"The Archangel," I murmured, looking back over my shoulder at the ride, which had started its next ascent.

husH, husH

"It means high-ranking angel." There was a definite smugness to his voice. "The higher up, the harder the fall."

I started to open my mouth, meaning to say again how I was sure I'd left the car for a moment and forces beyond my ability to explain had put me safely back behind my seat belt. Instead I said, "I think I'm more of a guardian angel girl."

Patch smirked again. Guiding me down the walk, he said, "I'll take you back to the arcade."

CHAPTER

I CUT THROUGH THE CROWD INSIDE THE ARCADE, PASSING the concession counter and restrooms. When the foosball tables came into view, Vee wasn't at any of them. Neither were Elliot or Jules.

"Looks like they left," Patch said. His eyes might have held a sliver of amusement. Then again, with Patch, it could just as easily have been something entirely different. "Looks like you need a ride."

"Vee wouldn't leave me," I said, standing on my tiptoes to see over the top of the crowd. "They're probably playing table tennis."

I edged sideways through the crowd while Patch followed behind, tipping back a can of soda he'd bought on our way in. He'd offered to buy me one, but in my current state, I wasn't sure I could hold it down.

There was no trace of Vee or Elliot at table tennis.

"Maybe they're at the pinball machines," Patch suggested. He was definitely making fun of me.

I felt myself go a little red in the face. Where was Vee?

Patch held out his soda. "Sure you don't want a drink?"

I looked from the can to Patch. Just because my blood warmed at the thought of putting my mouth where his had been didn't mean I had to tell him.

I dug through my purse and pulled out my cell. The screen on my phone was black and refused to turn on. I didn't understand how the battery could be dead when I'd charged it right before I left. I pushed the on button again and again, but nothing happened.

Patch said, "My offer's still on the table."

I thought I'd be safer hitching a ride from a stranger. I was still shaken over what had happened on the Archangel, and no matter how many times I tried to flush it out, the image of falling repeated through my head. I was falling . . . and then the ride was over. Just like that. It was the most terrifying thing I'd ever been through. Almost as terrifying, I was the only one who'd seemed to notice. Not even Patch, who'd been right beside me.

I smacked my palm to my forehead. "Her car. She's probably waiting for me in the parking lot."

Thirty minutes later I'd canvassed the entire lot. The Neon was gone. I couldn't believe Vee had left without me. Maybe there'd been an emergency. I had no way of knowing, since I couldn't check the messages on my cell. I tried to hold my emotions in check, but if she had left me, I had an ample amount of anger simmering under the surface, ready to spill out.

"Out of options yet?" asked Patch.

I bit my lip, pondering my other options. I had no other options. Unfortunately, I wasn't sure I was ready to take Patch up on his offer. On an ordinary day he exuded danger. Tonight there was a potent mix of danger, threat, and mystery all thrown together.

Finally I blew out a sigh and prayed I wasn't about to make a mistake.

"You'll take me straight home," I said. It sounded more like a question than an order.

"If that's what you want."

I was about to ask Patch if he'd noticed anything strange on the Archangel, when I stopped myself. I was too scared to ask. What if I hadn't fallen? What if I'd imagined the whole thing? What if I was seeing things that weren't really happening? First the guy in the ski mask. Now this. I was pretty sure Patch's mind-speaking was real, but everything else? Not so sure.

Patch walked a few parking spaces over. A shiny black

motorcycle rested on its kickstand. He swung on and tipped his head at the seat behind him. "Hop on."

"Wow. Nice bike," I said. Which was a lie. It looked like a glossy black death trap. I had never been on a motorcycle in my life, ever. I wasn't sure I wanted to change that tonight.

"I like the feel of the wind on my face," I continued, hoping my bravado masked my terror of moving at speeds upward of sixty-five miles an hour with nothing standing between me and the road.

There was one helmet—black with a tinted visor—and he held it out for me.

Taking it, I swung my leg over the bike and realized how insecure I felt with nothing but a narrow strip of seat beneath me. I slid the helmet over my curls and strapped it under my chin.

"Is it hard to drive?" I asked. What I really meant was, Is it safe?

"No," Patch said, answering both my spoken and unspoken questions. He laughed softly. "You're tense. Relax."

When he pulled out of the parking space, the explosion of movement startled me; I'd been holding on to his shirt with just enough of the fabric between my fingers to keep my balance. Now I wrapped my arms around him in a backward bear hug.

Patch accelerated onto the highway, and my thighs squeezed around him. I hoped I was the only one who noticed.

When we reached my house, Patch eased the bike up the fog-drenched driveway, killed the engine, and swung off. I removed my helmet, balancing it carefully on the seat in front of me, and

BECCA FITZPATRICK

opened my mouth to say something along the lines of *Thanks for the ride, I'll see you on Monday.*

The words dissolved as Patch crossed the driveway and headed up the porch steps.

I couldn't begin to speculate what he was doing. Walking me to the door? Highly improbable. Then . . . what?

I climbed the porch after him and found him at the door. I watched, divided between confusion and escalating concern, as he drew a set of familiar keys from his pocket and inserted my house key into the bolt.

I lowered my handbag down my shoulder and unzipped the compartment where I stored my keys. They weren't inside.

"Give me back my keys," I said, disconcerted at not knowing how my keys had come into his possession.

"You dropped them in the arcade when you were hunting for your cell," he said.

"I don't care where I dropped them. Give them back."

Patch held up his hands, claiming innocence, and backed away from the door. He leaned one shoulder against the bricks and watched me step up to the lock. I attempted to turn the key. It wouldn't budge.

"You jammed it," I said, rattling the key. I dropped back a step. "Go ahead. Try it. It's stuck."

With a sharp click, he turned the key. Hand poised on the handle, he arched his eyebrows as if to say *May I?*

I swallowed, burying a surge of mutual fascination and dis-quiet. "Go ahead. You're not going to walk in on anyone. I'm home alone."

"The whole night?"

Immediately, I realized it might not have been the smartest thing to say. "Dorothea will be coming soon." That was a lie. Dorothea was long gone. It was close to midnight.

"Dorothea?"

"Our housekeeper. She's old—but strong. Very strong." I tried to squeeze past him. Unsuccessfully.

"Sounds frightening," he said, retrieving the key from the lock. He held it out for me.

"She can clean a toilet inside and out in under a minute. More like terrifying." Taking the key, I edged around him. I fully intended to shut the door between us, but as I turned about, Patch filled the doorway, his arms braced on either side of the frame.

"You're not going to invite me in?" he asked.

I blinked. Invite him in? To my house? With no one else home?

Patch said, "It's late." His eyes followed mine closely, reflecting a wayward glint. "You must be hungry."

"No. Yes. I mean, yes, but—"

Suddenly he was inside.

I took three steps back; he nudged the door closed with his foot. "You like Mexican?" he asked.

"I—" I'd like to know what you're doing inside my house!

"Tacos?"

"Tacos?" I echoed.

This seemed to amuse him. "Tomatoes, lettuce, cheese."

"I know what a taco is!"

Before I could stop him, he strode past me into the house. At the end of the hall, he steered left. To the kitchen.

He went to the sink and ran the tap while scrubbing soap halfway up his arms. Apparently having made himself at home, he went to the pantry first, then browsed the fridge, bringing out items here and there—salsa, cheese, lettuce, a tomato. Then he dug through the drawers and found a knife.

I suspect I was halfway to panicking at the image of Patch holding a knife when something else caught my eye. I took two steps forward and squinted at my reflection in one of the skillets hanging from the pot rack. My hair! It looked like a giant tumbleweed had rolled on top of my head. I clapped a hand to my mouth.

Patch smiled. "You come by your red hair naturally?"

I stared at him. "I don't have red hair."

"I hate to break it to you, but it's red. I could light it on fire and it wouldn't turn any redder."

"It's brown." So maybe I had the teeniest, tiniest, most infinitesimal amount of auburn in my hair. I was still a brunette. "It's the lighting," I said.

hush, hush

"Yeah, maybe it's the lightbulbs." His smile brought up both sides of his mouth, and a dimple surfaced.

"I'll be right back," I said, hurrying out of the kitchen.

I went upstairs and coaxed my hair into a ponytail. With that out of the way, I pulled my thoughts together. I wasn't entirely comfortable with the idea of Patch roaming freely through my house—armed with a knife. And my mom would kill me if she found out I'd invited Patch inside when Dorothea wasn't here.

"Can I take a rain check?" I asked upon finding him still hard at work in the kitchen two minutes later. I placed a hand on my stomach, signaling that it was bothering me. "Queasy," I said. "I think it was the ride home."

He paused in his chopping and looked up. "I'm almost finished."

I noticed he'd exchanged knives for a bigger—and sharper—blade.

As if he had a window to my thoughts, he held up the knife, examining it. The blade gleamed in the light. My stomach clenched.

"Put the knife down," I instructed quietly.

Patch looked from me to the knife and back again. After a minute he laid it down in front of him. "I'm not going to hurt you, Nora."

"That's . . . reassuring," I managed to say, but my throat was tight and dry.

He spun the knife, handle pointing toward me. "Come here. I'll teach you how to make tacos."

I didn't move. There was a glint to his eye that made me think I should be frightened of him . . . and I was. But that fright was equal part allure. There was something extremely unsettling about being near him. In his presence, I didn't trust myself.

"How about a . . . deal?" His face was bent down, shadowed, and he looked up at me through his lashes. The effect was an impression of trustworthiness. "Help me make tacos, and I'll answer a few of your questions."

"My questions?"

"I think you know what I mean."

I knew exactly what he meant. He was giving me a glimpse into his private world. A world where he could speak to my mind. Again he knew exactly what to say, at exactly the right moment.

Without a word, I moved beside him. He slid the cutting board in front of me.

"First," he said, coming behind me and placing his hands on the counter, just outside of mine, "choose your tomato." He dipped his head so his mouth was at my ear. His breath was warm, tickling my skin. "Good. Now pick up the knife."

"Does the chef always stand this close?" I asked, not sure if I liked or feared the flutter his closeness caused inside me.

"When he's revealing culinary secrets, yes. Hold the knife like you mean it."

"I am."

"Good." Stepping back, he gave me a thorough twice-over,

seemingly scrutinizing any imperfections—his eyes shifted up and down, here and there. For one unnerving moment, I thought I saw a secret smile of approval. "Cooking isn't taught," Patch said. "It's inherent. Either you've got it or you don't. Like chemistry. You think you're ready for chemistry?"

I pressed the knife down through the tomato; it split in two, each half rocking gently on the cutting board. "You tell me. Am I ready for chemistry?"

Patch made a deep sound I couldn't decipher and grinned.

After dinner Patch carried our plates to the sink. "I'll wash, you dry." Hunting through the drawers to the side of the sink, he found a dish towel and slung it playfully at me.

"I'm ready to ask you those questions," I said. "Starting with that night at the library. Did you follow me . . ."

I trailed off. Patch leaned lazily against the counter. Dark hair flipped out from under his ball cap. A smile tugged at his mouth. My thoughts dissolved and just like that, a new thought broke the surface of my mind.

I wanted to kiss him. Right now.

Patch arched his eyebrows. "What?"

"Uh—nothing. Nothing at all. You wash, I'll dry."

It didn't take long to finish the dishes, and when we had, we found ourselves cramped in the space near the sink. Patch moved to take the dish towel from me, and our bodies touched. Neither of us moved, holding to the fragile link that welded us together.

I stepped back first.

"Scared?" he murmured.

"No."

"Liar."

My pulse edged up a degree. "I'm not scared of you."

"No?"

I spoke without thinking. "Maybe it's just that I'm scared of—" I cursed myself for even beginning the sentence. What was I supposed to say now? I was not about to admit to Patch that everything about him frightened me. It would be giving him permission to provoke me further. "Maybe it's just that I'm scared of . . . of—"

"Liking me?"

Relieved that I didn't have to finish my own sentence, I automatically answered, "Yes." I realized too late what I'd confessed. "I mean, no! Definitely no. That is not what I was trying to say!"

Patch laughed softly.

"The truth is, part of me is definitely not comfortable around you," I said.

"But?"

I gripped the counter behind me for support. "But at the same time I feel a scary attraction to you."

Patch grinned.

"You are way too cocky," I said, using my hand to push him back a step.

He trapped my hand against his chest and yanked my sleeve down past my wrist, covering my hand with it. Just as quickly, he did the same thing with the other sleeve. He held my shirt by the cuffs, my hands captured. My mouth opened in protest.

Reeling me closer, he didn't stop until I was directly in front of him. Suddenly he lifted me onto the counter. My face was level with his. He fixed me with a dark, inviting smile. And that's when I realized this moment had been dancing around the edge of my fantasies for several days now.

"Take off your hat," I said, the words tumbling out before I could stop them.

He slid it around, the brim facing backward.

I scooted to the edge of the counter, my legs dangling one on either side of him. Something inside of me was telling me to stop—but I swept that voice to the far back of my mind.

He spread his hands on the counter, just outside my hips. Tilting his head to one side, he moved closer. His scent, which was all damp dark earth, overwhelmed me.

I inhaled two sharp breaths. No. This wasn't right. Not this, not with Patch. He was frightening. In a good way, yes. But also in a bad way. A very bad way.

"You should go," I breathed. "You should definitely go."

"Go here?" His mouth was on my shoulder. "Or here?" It moved up my neck.

My brain couldn't process one logical thought. Patch's mouth was roaming north, up over my jaw, gently sucking at my skin. . . .

"My legs are falling asleep," I blurted. It wasn't a total lie. I was experiencing tingling sensations all through my body, legs included.

"I could solve that." Patch's hands closed on my hips.

Suddenly my cell phone rang. I jumped at the sound of it and fumbled it out of my pocket.

"Hi, sweetheart," my mom said cheerfully.

"Can I call you back?"

"Sure. What's going on?"

I shut the phone. "You need to leave," I told Patch. "Right now."

He'd slid his baseball cap back around. His mouth was the only feature I could see beneath it, and it curved in a mischievous smile. "You're not wearing makeup."

"I must have forgotten it."

"Sweet dreams tonight."

"Sure. No problem." What had he said?

"About that party tomorrow night . . ."

"I'll think about it," I managed to say.

Patch tucked a piece of paper inside my pocket, his touch sending hot sensations down my legs. "Here's the address. I'll be looking for you. Come alone."

A moment later I heard the front door close behind him. A fiery blush worked its way up my face. Too close, I thought. There was nothing wrong with fire . . . as long as you didn't stand too close. Something to keep in mind.

I leaned back against the cabinets, taking short, shallow breaths.

CHAPTER 10

I WAS YANKED AWAKE BY THE SOUND OF MY PHONE RINGING. Caught with one foot still in a dream, I tugged my pillow over my head and tried to block out the noise. But the phone rang. And rang.

The call went to voice mail. Five seconds later, the ringing started up again.

I reached an arm over the side of the bed, groped around until I found my jeans, and wiggled my cell out of the pocket.

"Yes?" I said with a wide yawn, leaving my eyes shut.

Someone was breathing angrily on the other end. "What happened to you? What happened to bringing back cotton candy? And while you're at it, how about telling me where you are so I can come strangle you—barehanded!"

I knocked the heel of my hand against my forehead a few times.

"I thought you'd been kidnapped!" Vee went on. "I thought you'd been abducted! I thought you were *murdered!*"

I tried to find the clock in the dark. I bumped a picture frame on the nightstand, and all the frames behind it played dominoes.

"I was sort of delayed," I said. "By the time I made it back to the arcade, you were gone."

"'Delayed'? What kind of excuse is 'delayed'?"

The red numbers on the clock swam into focus. It was just after two in the morning.

"I drove around the parking lot for an hour," Vee said. "Elliot walked the park flashing the only photo I had of you on my cell phone. I tried your cell a zillion times. Hang on. Are you at home? How did you get home?"

I rubbed the corners of my eyes. "Patch."

"*Stalker Patch?*"

"Well, I didn't have much of a choice, did I?" I said tersely. "You left without me."

"You sound worked up. Really worked up. No, that's not it. You sound agitated . . . flustered . . . *aroused*." I could feel her eyes widen. "He kissed you, didn't he?"

No answer.

"He did! I knew it! I've seen the way he looks at you. I knew this was coming. I saw it from a mile away."

I didn't want to think about it.

"What was it like?" Vee pressed. "A peach kiss? A plum kiss? Or maybe an al-fal-fa kiss?"

"What?"

"Was it a peck, did mouths part, or was there tongue? Never mind. You don't have to answer that. Patch isn't the kind of guy to deal with preliminaries. There was tongue involved. Guaranteed."

I covered my face with my hands, hiding behind them. Patch probably thought I didn't have any self-control. I'd fallen apart in his arms. I'd melted like butter. Right before I told him he should go, I was pretty sure I'd made a sound that was a cross between a sigh of sheer bliss and a moan of ecstasy.

That would explain his arrogant grin.

"Can we talk about this later?" I asked, pinching the bridge of my nose.

"No way."

I sighed. "I'm dead tired."

"I can't believe you're thinking about keeping me in suspense."

"I'm hoping you'll forget about it."

"Fat chance."

hush, hush

I tried to envision the muscles along my neck relaxing, forestalling the headache I felt creeping on. "Are we still on for shopping?"

"I'll pick you up at four."

"I thought we weren't meeting until five."

"Circumstances have changed. I'll be there even earlier if I can get out of family time. My mom's having a nervous breakdown. She blames my bad grades on her parenting skills. Apparently spending time together is the solution. Wish me luck."

I snapped my phone shut and slid deep into my bed. I pictured Patch's unprincipled grin and his glittering black eyes. After thrashing around in bed for several minutes, I gave up trying to get comfortable. The truth was, as long as Patch was on my mind, comfort was out of the question.

When I was little, Dorothea's godson Lionel shattered one of the kitchen glasses. He swept up all the shards of glass except one, and he dared me to lick it. I imagined falling for Patch was a little like licking that shard. I knew it was stupid. I knew I'd get cut. After all these years one thing hadn't changed: I was still lured by danger.

Suddenly I sat up straight in bed and reached for my cell. I switched on the lamp.

The battery showed fully charged.

My spine tingled ominously. My cell was supposed to be dead. So how had my mom and Vee gotten through?

BECCA FITZPATRICK

Rain battered the colorful awnings of the shops along the pier and spilled to the sidewalk below. The antique gas lamps that were staggered down both sides of the street glowed to life. With our umbrellas bumping together, Vee and I hustled down the sidewalk and under the pink-and-white-striped awning of Victoria's Secret. We shook out our umbrellas in unison and propped them just outside the entrance.

A boom of thunder sent us flying through the doors.

I stamped rain from my shoes and shuddered off the cold. Several oil diffusers burned on a display at the center of the store, surrounding us with an exotic, lusty smell.

A woman in black slacks and a stretchy black tee stepped forward. She had a measuring tape snaked around her neck, and she started to reach for it. "Would you girls like a free measuring—"

"Put the damn measuring tape away," Vee ordered. "I already know my size. I don't need reminding."

I gave the woman a smile that was part apology as I trailed after Vee, who was heading toward the clearance bins at the back.

"A D cup is nothing to be ashamed of," I told Vee. I picked up a blue satin bra and hunted for the price tag.

"Who said anything about being ashamed?" Vee said. "I'm not ashamed. Why would I be ashamed? The only other sixteen-year-olds with boobs as big as mine are suffused with silicone—and everyone knows it. Why would I have reason to be ashamed?" She rummaged through a bin. "Think they have any bras in here that can get my babies to lie flat?"

"They're called sports bras, and they have a nasty side effect called the uniboob," I said, my eyes picking out a lacy black bra from the pile.

I shouldn't have been looking at lingerie. It naturally made me think about sexy things. Like kissing. Like Patch.

I closed my eyes and replayed our night together. The touch of Patch's hand on my thigh, his lips tasting my neck . . .

Vee caught me off guard with a pair of turquoise leopard print undies slung at my chest. "These would look nice on you," she said. "All you need is a booty like mine to fill them."

What had I been thinking? I'd come this close to kissing Patch. The same Patch who just might be invading my mind. The same Patch who saved me from plunging to my death on the Archangel— because that's what I was sure had happened, although I had zero logical explanations. I wondered if he had somehow suspended time and caught me during the fall. If he was capable of talking to my thoughts, maybe, just maybe, he was capable of other things.

Or maybe, I thought with a chill, I could no longer trust my mind.

I still had the scrap of paper Patch had tucked inside my pocket, but there was no way I was going to the party tonight. I secretly enjoyed the attraction between us, but the mystery and eeriness outweighed it. From now on, I was going to flush Patch out of my

BECCA FITZPATRICK

system—and this time, I meant it. It would be like a cleansing diet. The problem was, the only diet I'd ever been on backfired. Once I tried to go an entire month without chocolate. Not one bite. At the end of two weeks, I broke down and binged on more chocolate than I would have eaten in three months.

I hoped my chocolate-free diet didn't foreshadow what would happen if I tried to avoid Patch.

"What are you doing?" I asked, my attention drawn to Vee.

"What does it look like I'm doing? I'm peeling the clearance price stickers off these clearance bras and sticking them on the not-on-sale bras. That way I can get sexy bras at trashy bra prices."

"You can't do that. She'll scan the bar codes when you checkout. She'll know what you're up to."

"Bar codes? They don't scan bar codes." She didn't sound too sure.

"They do. I swear. Cross my heart." I figured lying was better than watching Vee get hauled off to jail.

"Well, it seemed like a good idea. . . ."

"You have to get these," I told Vee, tossing a scrap of silk at her, hoping to distract her.

She held up the panties. Tiny red crabs embroidered the fabric. "That is the most disgusting thing I've ever seen. I like that black bra you're holding, on the other hand. I think you should get it. You go pay and I'll keep looking."

I paid. Then, thinking it would be easier to forget about Patch

hush, hush

if I was looking at something more benign, I wandered over to the wall of lotions. I was sniffing a bottle of Dream Angels when I felt a familiar presence nearby. It was like someone had dropped a scoop of ice cream down the back of my shirt. It was the same shivery jolt I experienced whenever Patch approached.

Vee and I were still the only two customers in the shop, but on the other side of the plate-glass window, I saw a hooded figure step back under a shadowed awning across the street. Freshly unsettled, I stood immobile for a whole minute before I pulled myself together and went to find Vee.

"Time to go," I told her.

She was flipping through a rack of nightgowns. "Wow. Look at this—flannel pajamas, fifty percent off. I need a pair of flannel pj's."

I kept one eye glued to the window. "I think I'm being followed."

Vee's head jerked up. "Patch?"

"No. Look across the street."

Vee squinted. "I don't see anyone."

Neither did I anymore. A car had driven past, interrupting my line of vision. "I think they went inside the shop."

"How do you know they're following you?"

"A bad feeling."

"Did they look like anyone we know? For example . . . a cross between Pippi Longstocking and the Wicked Witch of the West would obviously give us Marcie Millar."

BECCA FITZPATRICK

"It wasn't Marcie," I said, eyes still trained across the street. "When I left the arcade last night to buy cotton candy, I saw someone watching me. I think the same person is here now."

"Are you serious? Why are you just telling me this now? Who is it?"

I didn't know. And that scared me more than anything.

I directed my voice at the saleslady. "Is there a back door to the shop?"

She looked up from tidying a drawer. "Employees only."

"Is the person male or female?" Vee wanted to know.

"I can't tell."

"Well, why do you think they're following you? What do they want?"

"To scare me." It seemed reasonable enough.

"Why would they want to scare you?"

Again, I didn't know.

"We need a diversion," I told Vee.

"Exactly what I was thinking," she said. "And we know I'm really good at diversions. Give me your jean jacket."

I stared at her. "No way. We know nothing about this person. I'm not letting you go out there dressed like me. What if they're armed?"

"Sometimes your imagination scares me," Vee said.

I had to admit, the idea that they were armed and out to kill was a little far-fetched. But with all the creepy things happening lately,

I didn't blame myself for feeling on edge and assuming the worst.

"I'll go out first," said Vee. "If they follow me, you follow them. I'll head up the hill toward the cemetery, and then we'll bookend them and get some answers."

A minute later Vee left the store wearing my jean jacket. She picked up my red umbrella, holding it low on her head. Other than the fact that she was a few inches too tall, and a few pounds too voluptuous, she passed as me. From where I crouched behind the rack of nightgowns, I watched the hooded figure step out of the store across the street and follow after Vee. I crept closer to the window. Though the figure's baggy sweatshirt and jeans were meant to look androgynous, the walk was feminine. Definitely feminine.

Vee and the girl turned the corner and disappeared, and I jogged to the door. Outside, the rain had turned into a downpour.

Grabbing Vee's umbrella, I picked up my pace, keeping under the awnings, steering clear of the pelting rain. I could feel the bottoms of my jeans dampening. I wished I'd worn boots.

Behind me the pier extended out to the cement-gray ocean. In front of me, the strip of shops ended at the base of a steep, grassy hill. At the top of the hill, I could just make out the high cast-iron fence of the local cemetery.

I unlocked the Neon, cranked the defroster to high, and set the windshield wipers to full power. I drove out of the lot and turned left, accelerating up the winding hill. The trees of the cemetery loomed ahead, their branches deceptively coming to life through

BECCA FITZPATRICK

the mad chop of the wipers. The white marble headstones seemed to stab up from the darkness. The gray headstones dissolved into the atmosphere.

Out of nowhere, a red object hurtled into the windshield. It smacked the glass directly in my line of vision, then flew up and over the car. I stomped on the brakes and the Neon skidded to a stop on the shoulder of the road.

I opened the door and got out. I jogged to the back of the car, searching for what had hit me.

There was a moment of confusion as my mind processed what I was seeing. My red umbrella was tangled in the weeds. It was broken; one side was collapsed in the exact way I might expect if it had been hurled with force against another, harder object.

Through the onslaught of rain I heard a choked sob.

"Vee?" I said. I jogged across the road, shielding my eyes from the rain as I swept my gaze over the landscape. A body lay crumpled just ahead. I started running.

"Vee!" I dropped to my knees beside her. She was on her side, her legs drawn up to her chest. She groaned.

"What happened? Are you okay? Can you move?" I threw my head back, blinking rain. Think! I told myself. My cell phone. Back in the car. I had to call 911.

"I'm going to get help," I told Vee.

She moaned and clutched my hand.

I lowered myself down on her, holding her tightly. Tears burned

hush, hush

behind my eyes. "What happened? Was it the person who followed you? Did they do this to you? What did they do?"

Vee murmured something unintelligible that might have been "handbag." Sure enough, her handbag was missing.

"You're going to be all right." I worked to hold my voice steady. I had a dark feeling stirring inside me, and I was trying to keep it at bay. I was certain the same person who'd watched me at Delphic and followed me shopping today was responsible, but I blamed myself for putting Vee in harm's way. I ran back to the Neon and punched 911 into my cell.

Trying to keep the hysteria out of my voice, I said, "I need an ambulance. My friend was attacked and robbed."

CHAPTER

11

MONDAY PASSED IN A DAZE. I WENT FROM CLASS TO
class waiting for the final bell of the day. I'd called
the hospital before school and was told that Vee
was heading into the OR. Her left arm had been broken during
the attack, and since the bone wasn't aligned, she needed surgery.
I wanted to see her but couldn't until later in the afternoon, when
the anesthesia wore off and hospital staff moved her to her own
room. It was especially important that I hear her version of the

attack before she either forgot the details or embellished them. Anything she remembered might fill a hole in the picture and help me figure out who had done this.

As the hours stretched toward afternoon, my focus shifted from Vee to the girl outside Victoria's Secret. Who was she? What did she want? Maybe it was a disturbing coincidence that Vee had been attacked minutes after I'd watched the girl follow after her, but my instincts disagreed. I wished I had a better picture of what she looked like. The bulky hoodie and jeans, compounded with the rain, had done a good job of disguising her. For all I knew it could've been Marcie Millar. But deep inside it didn't feel like the right match.

I swung by my locker to pick up my biology textbook, then headed to my last class. I walked in to find Patch's chair empty. Typically, he arrived at the last possible moment, tying with the tardy bell, but the bell rang and Coach took his place at the chalkboard and started lecturing on equilibrium.

I pondered Patch's empty chair. A tiny voice at the back of my head speculated that his absence might be connected to Vee's attack. It was a little strange that he was missing on the morning after. And I couldn't forget the icy chill I'd felt moments before looking outside Victoria's Secret and realizing I was being watched. Every other time I'd felt that way, it was because Patch was near.

The voice of reason quickly extinguished Patch's involvement. He could have caught a cold. Or he could have run out of gas on the drive to school and was stranded miles away. Or maybe there was a high-bets pool game going on at Bo's Arcade and he figured it was more profitable than an afternoon spent learning the intricacies of the human body.

At the end of class, Coach stopped me on my way out the door.

"Hang on a minute, Nora."

I turned back and hiked my backpack up my shoulder. "Yes?"

He extended a folded piece of paper. "Miss Greene stopped by before class and asked me to give this to you," he said.

I accepted the note. "Miss Greene?" I didn't have any teachers by that name.

"The new school psychologist. She just replaced Dr. Hendrickson."

I unfolded the note and read the message scrawled inside.

Dear Nora,
I'll be taking over Dr. Hendrickson's role as your school psychologist. I noticed you missed your last two appointments with Dr. H. Please come in right away so we can get acquainted. I've mailed a letter to your mother to make her aware of the change.
All best,
Miss Greene

"Thanks," I told Coach, folding the note until it was small enough to tuck inside my pocket.

Out in the hall I merged with the flow of the crowd. No avoiding it now—I had to go. I steered my way through the halls until I could see the closed door to Dr. Hendrickson's office. Sure enough, there was a new name plaque on the door. The polished brass gleamed against the drab oak door: MISS D. GREENE, SCHOOL PSYCHOLOGIST.

I knocked on the door, and a moment later it opened from within. Miss Greene had flawless pale skin, sea blue eyes, a lush mouth, and fine, straight blond hair that tumbled past her elbows. It was parted at the crown of her oval-shaped face. A pair of turquoise cat's-eye glasses sat at the tip of her nose, and she was dressed formally in a gray herringbone pencil skirt and a pink silk blouse. Her figure was willowy but feminine. She couldn't have been more than five years older than me.

"You must be Nora Grey. You look just like the picture in your file," she said, giving my hand a firm pump. Her voice was abrupt, but not rude. Businesslike.

Stepping back, she signaled me to enter the office.

"Can I get you juice, water?" she asked.

"What happened to Dr. Hendrickson?"

"He took early retirement. I've had my eye on this job for a while, so I jumped on the opening. I went to Florida State, but I grew up in Portland, and my parents still live there. It's nice to be close to family again."

I surveyed the small office. It had changed drastically since I'd

·

last been in a few weeks ago. The wall-to-wall bookshelves were now filled with academic but generic-looking hardcovers, all bound in neutral colors with gold lettering. Dr. Hendrickson had used the shelves to display family pictures, but there were no snapshots of Miss Greene's private life. The same fern hung by the window, but under Dr. Hendrickson's care, it had been far more brown than green. A few days with Miss Greene and already it looked pert and alive. There was a pink paisley chair opposite the desk, and several moving boxes stacked in the far corner.

"Friday was my first day," she explained, seeing my eyes fall on the moving boxes. "I'm still unpacking. Have a seat."

I lowered my backpack down my arm and sat on the paisley chair. Nothing in the small room gave me any clues as to Miss Greene's personality. She had a stack of file folders on her desk—not neat, but not messy, either—and a white mug of what looked like tea. There wasn't a trace of perfume or air freshener. Her computer monitor was black.

Miss Greene crouched in front of a file cabinet behind her desk, tugged out a clean manila folder, and printed my name on the tab in black Magic Marker. She placed it on her desk next to my old file, which bore a few of Dr. Hendrickson's coffee-mug stains.

"I spent the whole weekend going through Dr. Hendrickson's files," she said. "Just between the two of us, his handwriting gives me a migraine, so I'm copying over all the files. I was amazed to find he didn't use a computer to type his notes. Who still uses longhand in this day and age?"

She settled back into her swivel chair, crossed her legs, and smiled politely at me. "Well. Why don't you tell me a little bit about the history of your meetings with Dr. Hendrickson? I could barely decipher his notes. It appeared the two of you were discussing how you feel about your mom's new job."

"It's not all that new. She's been working for a year."

"She used to be a stay-at-home mom, correct? And after your dad's passing, she took on a full-time job." She squinted at a sheet of paper in my file. "She works for an auction company, correct? It looks like she coordinates estate auctions all down the coast." She peeked at me over her glasses. "That must require a lot of time away from home."

"We wanted to stay in our farmhouse," I said, my tone touching on the defensive. "We couldn't afford the mortgage if she took a local job." I hadn't exactly loved my sessions with Dr. Hendrickson, but I found myself resenting him for retiring and abandoning me to Miss Greene. I was starting to get a feel for her, and she seemed attentive to detail. I sensed her itching to dig into every dark corner of my life.

"Yes, but you must be very lonely all by yourself at the farmhouse."

"We have a housekeeper who stays with me every afternoon until nine or ten at night."

"But a housekeeper isn't the same thing as a mother."

I eyed the door. I didn't even try to be discreet.

"Do you have a best friend? A boyfriend? Someone you can talk to when your housekeeper doesn't quite . . . fit the bill?" She dunked a tea bag in the mug, then raised it for a sip.

"I have a best friend." I'd made up my mind to say as little as possible. The less I said, the shorter the appointment. The shorter the appointment, the sooner I could visit Vee.

Her eyebrows peaked. "Boyfriend?"

"No."

"You're an attractive girl. I imagine there must be some interest from the opposite sex."

"Here's the thing," I said as patiently as possible. "I really appreciate that you're trying to help me, but I had this exact conversation with Dr. Hendrickson a year ago when my dad died. Rehashing it with you isn't helping. It's like going back in time and reliving it all over again. Yes, it was tragic and horrible, and I'm still dealing with it every day, but what I really need is to move on."

The clock on the wall ticked between us.

"Well," Miss Greene said at last, plastering on a smile. "It's very helpful to know your viewpoint, Nora. Which is what I was trying to understand all along. I'll make a note of your feelings in your file. Anything else you want to talk about?"

"Nope." I smiled to confirm that, really, I was doing fine.

She leafed through a few more pages of my file. I had no idea what observations Dr. Hendrickson had immortalized there, and I didn't want to wait around long enough to find out.

I lifted my backpack off the floor and scooted to the edge of the chair. "I don't mean to cut things short, but I need to be somewhere at four."

"Oh?"

I had no desire to go into Vee's attack with Miss Greene. "Library research," I lied.

"For which class?"

I said the first answer that popped to mind. "Biology."

"Speaking of classes, how are yours going? Any concerns in that department?"

"No."

She flipped a few more pages in my file. "Excellent grades," she observed. "It says here you're tutoring your biology partner, Patch Cipriano." She looked up, apparently wanting my confirmation.

I was surprised my tutoring assignment was important enough to make it into the school psychologist's file. "So far we haven't been able to meet. Conflicting schedules." I gave a *What can you do?* shrug.

She tapped my file on her desk, tidying all the loose sheets of paper into one clean stack, then inserted it into the new file she'd hand-labeled. "To give you fair warning, I'm going to talk with Mr. McConaughy and see about setting some parameters for your tutoring sessions. I'd like all meetings to be held here at school, under the direct supervision of a teacher or other faculty member. I don't want you tutoring Patch off school property. I especially don't want the two of you meeting alone."

A chill tiptoed along my skin. "Why? What's going on?"

"I can't discuss it."

The only reason I could think why she didn't want me alone with Patch was that he was dangerous. *My past might frighten you,* he'd said on the loading platform of the Archangel.

"Thanks for your time. I won't keep you any longer," Miss Greene said. She strode to the door, propping it open with her slender hip. She gave a parting smile, but it looked perfunctory.

After leaving Miss Greene's office, I called the hospital. Vee's surgery was over, but she was still in the recovery room and couldn't have visitors until seven p.m. I consulted the clock on my phone. Three hours. I found the Fiat in the student parking lot and dropped inside, hoping an afternoon spent doing homework at the library would keep my mind off the long wait.

I stayed at the library through the afternoon, and before I realized it, the clock on the wall had passed quietly into evening. My stomach rumbled against the quiet of the library, and my thoughts went to the vending machine just inside the entrance.

The last of my homework could wait until later, but there was still one project that required the help of library resources. I had a vintage IBM computer at home with dial-up Internet service, and I typically tried to save myself a lot of unnecessary shouting and hair pulling by using the library's computer lab. I had a theater review of *Othello* due on the eZine editor's desk by nine p.m., and I made a deal with myself, promising I'd go hunt down food as soon as I finished it.

Packing up my belongings, I walked to the elevators. Inside the cage I pushed the button to close the doors, but didn't immediately request a floor. I pulled out my cell and called the hospital again.

"Hi," I told the answering nurse. "My friend is recovering from surgery, and when I checked in earlier this afternoon, I was told she'd be out tonight. Her name is Vee Sky."

There was a pause and the clicking of computer keys. "Looks like they'll be bringing her to a private room within the hour."

"What time do visiting hours end?"

"Eight."

"Thank you." I disconnected and pressed the third-floor button, sending me up.

On the third floor I followed signs to collections, hoping that if I read several theater reviews in the local newspaper, it would spark my muse.

"Excuse me," I said to the librarian behind the collections desk. "I'm trying to find copies of the *Portland Press Herald* from the past year. Particularly the theater guide."

"We don't keep anything that current in collections," she said, "but if you look online, I believe the *Portland Press Herald* keeps archives on their website. Head straight down the hallway behind you and you'll see the media lab on your left."

Inside the lab I signed onto a computer. I was about to dive into my assignment when an idea struck me. I couldn't believe I hadn't thought of it earlier. After confirming no one was watching over my shoulder, I Googled "Patch Cipriano." Maybe I'd find an article that would shed light on his past. Or maybe he kept a blog.

I frowned at the search results. Nothing. No Facebook, no MySpace, no blog. It was like he didn't exist.

"What's your story, Patch?" I murmured. "Who are you—really?"

Half an hour later, I'd read several reviews and my eyes were glazing over. I spread my online search to all newspapers in Maine. A link to Kinghorn Prep's school paper popped up. A few seconds passed before I placed the familiar name. Elliot had transferred from Kinghorn Prep. On a whim, I decided to check it out. If the school was as elite as Elliot claimed, it probably had a respectable paper.

I clicked on the link, scrolled over the archives page, and randomly chose March 21 of earlier this year. A moment later I had a headline.

STUDENT QUESTIONED IN KINGHORN PREP MURDER

I scooted my chair closer, lured by the idea of reading something more exciting than theater reviews.

A sixteen-year-old Kinghorn Preparatory student who police were questioning in what has
been dubbed "The Kinghorn Hanging" has been
released without charge. After eighteen-year-old
Kjirsten Halverson's body was found hanging from
a tree on the wooded campus of Kinghorn Prep,
police questioned sophomore Elliot Saunders,
who was seen with the victim on the night of her
death.

My mind was slow to process the information. Elliot was questioned as part of a murder investigation?

Halverson worked as a waitress at Blind Joe's.
Police confirm that Halverson and Saunders were
seen walking the campus together late Saturday
night. Halverson's body was discovered Sunday
morning, and Saunders was released Monday
afternoon after a suicide note was discovered in
Halverson's apartment.

"Find anything interesting?"

I jumped at the sound of Elliot's voice behind me. I whirled
around to find him leaning against the doorjamb. His eyes were
narrowed ever so slightly, his mouth set in a line. Something

BECCA FITZPATRICK

cold flushed through me, like a blush, only opposite.

I wheeled my chair slightly to the right, trying to position myself in front of the computer's monitor. "I'm—I'm just finishing up homework. How about you? What are you doing? I didn't hear you come in. How long have you been standing there?" My pitch was all over the place.

Elliot pushed away from the doorjamb and walked inside the lab. I groped blindly behind me for the monitor's on/off button.

I said, "I'm attempting to jump-start my inspiration on a theater review I'm supposed to have to my editor by later tonight." I was still speaking much too fast. Where was the button?

Elliot peered around me. "Theater reviews?"

My fingers brushed a button, and I heard the monitor drain to black. "I'm sorry, what did you say you're doing here?"

"I was walking by when I saw you. Something wrong? You seem . . . jumpy."

"Uh—low blood sugar." I swept my papers and books into a pile and shoehorned them inside my backpack. "I haven't eaten since lunch."

Elliot hooked a nearby chair and wheeled it next to mine. He sat backward on it and leaned close, invading my personal space. "Maybe I can help with the review."

I leaned away. "Wow, that's really nice of you, but I'm going to call it quits for now. I need to grab something to eat. It's a good time to break."

"Let me buy you dinner," he said. "Isn't there a diner just around the corner?"

"Thanks, but my mom will be expecting me. She's been out of town all week and gets back tonight." I stood and tried to step around him. He held his cell phone out, and it caught me in the navel.

"Call her."

I lowered my gaze to the phone and scrambled for an excuse. "I'm not allowed to go out on school nights."

"It's called lying, Nora. Tell her homework is taking longer than you expected. Tell her you need another hour at the library. She's not going to know the difference."

Elliot's voice had taken on an edge I'd never heard before. His blue eyes snapped with a newfound coldness, his mouth looked thinner.

"My mom doesn't like me going out with guys she hasn't met," I said.

Elliot smiled, but there was no warmth. "We both know you're not too concerned with your mom's rules, since Saturday night you were with me at Delphic."

I had my backpack slung over one shoulder, and I was clutching the strap. I didn't say anything. I brushed past Elliot and walked out of the lab in a hurry, realizing that if he turned the monitor on, he'd see the article. But there wasn't anything I could do now.

Halfway to the collections desk, I dared a glance over my shoulder. The plate-glass walls showed that the lab was empty. Elliot was nowhere to be seen. I retraced my steps to the computer, keeping my eyes on guard in case he reappeared. I turned on the monitor; the murder investigation article was still up. Sending a copy to the nearest printer, I tucked it inside my binder, logged off, and hurried out.

CHAPTER

12

MY CELL PHONE BUZZED IN MY POCKET, AND after confirming I wasn't being evil-eyed by a librarian, I answered. "Mom?"

"Good news," she said. "The auction wrapped up early. I got on the road an hour ahead of schedule and should be home soon. Where are you?"

"Hi! I wasn't expecting you until later. I'm just leaving the library. How was upstate New York?"

"Upstate New York was . . . long." She laughed, but she sounded drained. "I can't wait to see you."

I looked around for a clock. I wanted to stop by the hospital and see Vee before heading home.

"Here's the deal," I told my mom. "I need to visit Vee. I might be a few minutes late. I'll hurry—I promise."

"Of course." I detected the tiniest disappointment. "Any updates? I got your message this morning about her surgery."

"Surgery is over. They're taking her to a private room any minute now."

"Nora." I heard the swell of emotion in her voice. "I'm so glad it wasn't you. I couldn't live with myself if anything happened to you. Especially since your dad—" She broke off. "I'm just glad we're both safe. Say hi to Vee for me. See you soon. Hugs and kisses."

"Love you, Mom."

Coldwater's Regional Medical Center is a three-story redbrick structure with a covered walkway leading up to the main entrance. I passed through the revolving glass doors and stopped at the main desk to inquire about Vee. I was told she'd been moved to a room half an hour ago, and that visiting hours ended in fifteen minutes. I located the elevators and punched the button to send me up a floor.

At room 207 I pushed on the door. "Vee?" I coaxed a bouquet of balloons inside behind me, crossed the small foyer, and found Vee reclining in bed, her left arm in a cast and slung across her body.

hush, hush

"Hi!" I said when I saw she was awake.

Vee expelled a luxurious sigh. "I love drugs. Really. They're amazing. Even better than an Enzo cappuccino. Hey, that rhymed. Enzo cappuccino. It's a sign. I'm destined to be a poet. Want to hear another poem? I'm good at impromptu."

"Uh—"

A nurse swished in and tinkered around with Vee's IV. "Feeling okay?" she asked Vee.

"Forget being a poet," Vee said. "I'm destined for stand-up comedy. Knock, knock."

"What?" I said.

The nurse rolled her eyes. "Who's there?"

"Crab," said Vee.

"Crab who?"

"Crab your towel, we're going to the beach!"

"Maybe a little less painkillers," I told the nurse.

"Too late. I just gave her another dose. Wait until you see her in ten minutes." She swished back out the door.

"So?" I asked Vee. "What's the verdict?"

"The verdict? My doctor is a lard-arse. Closely resembles an Oompa-Loompa. Don't give me your severe look. Last time he came in, he broke into the Funky Chicken. And he's forever eating chocolate. Mostly chocolate animals. You know the solid chocolate bunnies they're selling for Easter? That's what the Oompa-Loompa ate for dinner. Had a chocolate duck at lunch with a side of yellow Peeps."

"I meant the verdict . . ." I pointed at the medical paraphernalia adorning her.

"Oh. One busted arm, a concussion, and assorted cuts, scrapes, and bruises. Fortunately for my quick reflexes, I jumped out of the way before any major damage was done. When it comes to reflexes, I'm like a cat. I'm Catwoman. I'm invulnerable. The only reason he got a piece of me is because of the rain. Cats don't like water. It impairs us. It's our kryptonite."

"I'm so sorry," I told Vee sincerely. "I should be the one in the hospital bed."

"And get all the drugs? Uh-uh. No way."

"Have the police found any leads?" I asked.

"Nada, zilch, zero."

"No eyewitnesses?"

"We were at a cemetery in the middle of a rainstorm," Vee pointed out. "Most normal people were indoors."

She was right. Most normal people had been indoors. Of course, Vee and I had been out . . . along with the mysterious girl who followed Vee out of Victoria's Secret.

"How did it happen?" I asked.

"I was walking to the cemetery like we planned, when all of a sudden I heard footsteps closing in behind me," Vee explained. "That's when I looked back, and everything came together really fast. There was the flash of a gun, and him lunging for me. Like I told the cops, my brain wasn't exactly transmitting, 'Get a visual

ID.' It was more like, 'Holy freak show, I'm about to go splat!' He growled, whacked me three or four times with the gun, grabbed my handbag, and ran."

I was more confused than ever. "Wait. It was a guy? You saw his face?"

"Of course it was a guy. He had dark eyes . . . charcoal eyes. But that's all I saw. He was wearing a ski mask."

At the mention of the ski mask, my heart skittered through several beats. It was the same guy who'd jumped in front of the Neon, I was sure of it. I hadn't imagined him—Vee was proof. I remembered the way all evidence of the crash had disappeared. Maybe I hadn't imagined that part either. This guy, whoever he was, was real. And he was out there. But if I hadn't imagined the damage to the Neon, what really happened that night? Was my vision, or my memory, somehow . . . being altered?

After a moment, a slew of secondary questions raced to mind. What did he want this time? Was he connected to the girl outside Victoria's Secret? Had he known I'd be shopping at the pier? Wearing a ski mask constituted advance planning, so he must have known beforehand where I'd be. And he didn't want me to recognize his face.

"Who did you tell we were going shopping?" I asked Vee suddenly.

She rammed a pillow behind her neck, trying to get comfortable. "My mom."

"That's it? Nobody else?"

"I might have brought it up to Elliot."

My blood seemed to suddenly stop flowing. "You told Elliot?"

"What's the big deal?"

"There's something I need to tell you," I said soberly. "Remember the night I drove the Neon home and hit a deer?"

"Yeah?" she said, frowning.

"It wasn't a deer. It was a guy. A guy in a ski mask."

"Shut up," she whispered. "You're telling me my attack wasn't random? You're telling me this guy wants something from me? No, wait. He wants something from you. I was wearing your jacket. He thought I was you."

My whole body felt leaden.

After a count of silence, she said, "Are you sure you didn't tell Patch about shopping? Because on further reflection, I'm thinking the guy had Patch's build. Tallish. Leanish. Strongish. Sexyish, aside from the attacking part."

"Patch's eyes aren't charcoal, they're black," I pointed out, but I was uncomfortably aware that I had told Patch we were going shopping at the pier.

Vee raised an indecisive shoulder. "Maybe his eyes were black. I can't remember. It happened really fast. I can be specific about the gun," she said helpfully. "It was aimed at me. Like, right at me."

I pushed a few puzzle pieces around my mind. If Patch had attacked Vee, he must have seen her leave the store wearing my jacket and thought it was me. When he figured out he was following the wrong girl, he hit Vee with the gun out of anger and vanished. The only problem was, I couldn't imagine Patch brutalizing Vee. It felt off. Besides, he was supposedly at a party on the coast all night.

"Did your attacker look at all like Elliot?" I asked.

I watched Vee absorb the question. Whatever drug she'd been given, it seemed to slow her thought process, and I could practically hear each gear in her brain grind into action.

"He was about twenty pounds too light and four inches too tall to be Elliot."

"This is all my fault," I said. "I never should have let you leave the store wearing my jacket."

"I know you don't want to hear this," said Vee, looking like she was fighting a drug-induced yawn. "But the more I think on it, the more similarities I see between Patch and my attacker. Same build. Same long-legged stride. Too bad his school file was empty. We need an address. We need to canvass his neighborhood. We need to find a gullible little granny neighbor who could be coaxed into mounting a webcam in her window and aiming it at his house. Because something about Patch just isn't right."

"You honestly think Patch could have done this to you?" I asked, still unconvinced.

Vee chewed at her lip. "I think he's hiding something. Something big."

BECCA FITZPATRICK

I wasn't going to argue that.

Vee sank deeper in her bed. "My body's tingling. I feel good all over."

"We don't have an address," I said, "but we do know where he works."

"Are you thinking what I'm thinking?" Vee asked, eyes brightening briefly through the haze of chemical sedation.

"Based on past experience, I hope not."

"The truth is, we need to brush up on our sleuthing skills," said Vee. "Use them or lose them, that's what Coach said. We need to find out more about Patch's past. Hey, I bet if we document, Coach will even give us extra credit."

Highly doubtful, given that if Vee was involved, the sleuthing would likely take an illegal turn. Not to mention, this particular sleuthing job had nothing to do with biology. Even remotely.

The slight smile Vee had dragged out of me faded. Fun as it was to be lighthearted about the situation, I was frightened. The guy in the ski mask was out there, planning his next attack. It kind of made sense that Patch might know what was going on. The guy in the ski mask jumped in front of the Neon the day after Patch became my biology partner. Maybe it wasn't a coincidence.

Just then the nurse popped her head inside the door. "It's eight o'clock," she told me, tapping her watch. "Visiting hours are over."

"I'll be right out," I said.

As soon as her footsteps faded down the hall, I shut the door to Vee's room. I wanted privacy before I told her about the murder investigation surrounding Elliot. However, when I got back to Vee's bed, it was apparent that her medication had kicked in.

"Here it comes," she said with an expression of pure bliss. "Drug rush . . . any moment now . . . the surge of warmth . . . bye-bye, Mr. Pain . . ."

"Vee—"

"Knock, knock."

"This is really important—"

"Knock, knock."

"It's about Elliot—"

"Knock, knoooock," she said in a singsong voice.

I sighed. "Who's there?"

"Boo."

"Boo who?"

"Boo-hoo, somebody's crying, and it's not me!" She broke into hysterical laughter.

Realizing it was pointless to push the issue, I said, "Call me tomorrow after you're discharged." I unzipped my backpack. "Before I forget, I brought your homework. Where do you want me to put it?"

She pointed at the trash can. "Right there will be fine."

I pulled the Fiat into the garage and pocketed the keys. The sky lacked stars on the drive home, and sure enough, a light rain started to fall. I tugged on the garage door, lowering it to the ground and locking it. I let myself into the kitchen. A light was on somewhere upstairs, and a moment later my mom came running down the stairs and threw her arms around me.

My mom has dark wavy hair and green eyes. She's an inch shorter than I am, but we share the same bone structure. She always smells like Love by Ralph Lauren.

"I'm so glad you're safe," she said, squeezing me tight.

Safe-ish, I thought.

CHAPTER

13

THE FOLLOWING NIGHT AT SEVEN, THE BORDERLINE'S
parking lot was packed. After nearly an hour of begging,
Vee and I had convinced her parents that we needed to
celebrate her first night out of the hospital over chiles rellenos
and virgin strawberry daiquiris. At least, that's what we were
claiming. But we had an ulterior motive.

I tucked the Neon into a tight parking space and turned off the
engine.

"Ew," said Vee when I passed the keys back and my fingers brushed hers. "Think you could sweat a little more?"

"I'm nervous."

"Gee, I had no clue."

I inadvertently looked at the door.

"I know what you're thinking," Vee said, tightening her lips. "And the answer is no. No as in no *way*."

"You don't know what I'm thinking," I said.

Vee vised my arm. "The heck I don't."

"I wasn't going to run," I said. "Not me."

"Liar."

Tuesday was Patch's night off, and Vee had put it into my head that it would be the perfect time to interrogate his coworkers. I envisioned myself sashaying up to the bar, giving the bartender a coy Marcie Millar look, then segueing to the topic of Patch. I needed his home address. I needed any prior arrests. I needed to know if he had a connection to the guy in the ski mask, no matter how tenuous. And I needed to figure out why the guy in the ski mask and the mysterious girl were in my life.

I peeked inside my handbag, double-checking to make sure the list of interrogation questions I'd prepared were still with me. One side of the list dealt with questions about Patch's personal life. The flip side had flirting prompts. Just in case.

"Whoa, whoa, whoa," Vee said. "What is *that*?"

"Nothing," I said, folding the list.

Vee tried to grab the list, but I was faster and had it crammed deep in my handbag before she could get to it.

"Rule number one," Vee said. "There is no such thing as notes in flirting."

"There's an exception to every rule."

"And you're not it!" She grabbed two plastic 7-Eleven sacks from the backseat and swiveled out of the car. As soon as I stepped out, she used her good arm to hurl the sacks over the top of the Neon at me.

"What's this?" I asked, catching the sacks. The handles were tied and I couldn't see inside, but the unmistakable shaft of a stiletto heel threatened to poke through the plastic.

"Size eight and a half," Vee said. "Sharkskin. It's easier to play the part when you look the part."

"I can't walk in high heels."

"Good thing they're not high, then."

"They look high," I said, eying the protruding stiletto.

"Almost five inches. They left 'high' behind at four."

Lovely. If I didn't break my neck, I just might get to humiliate myself while seducing secrets out of Patch's coworkers.

"Here's the deal," said Vee as we strode down the sidewalk to the front doors. "I sort of invited a couple of people. The more the merrier, right?"

"Who?" I asked, feeling the dark stirrings of foreboding in the pit of my stomach.

"Jules and Elliot."

BECCA FITZPATRICK

Before I had time to tell Vee exactly how bad I thought this idea was, she said, "Moment of truth: I've sort of been seeing Jules. On the sly."

"What?"

"You should see his house. Bruce Wayne can't compete. His parents are either South American drug lords or come from serious old money. Since I haven't met them yet, I can't say which."

I was at a loss for words. My mouth opened and shut, but nothing came out. "When did this happen?" I finally managed to ask.

"Pretty much right after that fateful morning at Enzo's."

"Fateful? Vee, you have no idea—"

"I hope they got here first and reserved a table," Vee said, stretching her neck while eying the crowd accumulating around the doors. "I don't want to wait. I am seriously two thin minutes away from death by starvation."

I grabbed Vee by her good elbow, pulling her aside. "There's something I need to tell you—"

"I know, I know," she said. "You think there's a slim chance Elliot attacked me Sunday night. Well, I think you've got Elliot confused with Patch. And after you do some sleuthing tonight, the facts will back me up. Believe me, I want to know who attacked me just as much as you. Probably even more. It's personal now. And while we're handing each other advice, here's mine. Stay away from Patch. Just to be safe."

"I'm glad you've thought this through," I said tersely, "but here's the thing. I found an article—"

The doors to the Borderline opened. A fresh wave of heat, carrying the smell of limes and cilantro, swirled out at us, along with the sound of a mariachi band playing through the speakers.

"Welcome to the Borderline," a hostess greeted us. "Just the two of you tonight?"

Elliot was standing behind her inside the dimmed foyer. We saw each other at the same moment. His mouth smiled but his eyes did not.

"Ladies," he said, sanding his hands together as he walked over. "Looking magnificent, as always."

My skin prickled.

"Where's your partner in crime?" Vee asked, glancing around the foyer. Paper lanterns hung from the ceiling, and a mural of a Mexican pueblo spanned two walls. The waiting benches were filled to capacity. There was no sign of Jules.

"Bad news," said Elliot. "The man is sick. You're going to have to settle for me."

"Sick?" Vee demanded. "How sick? What kind of excuse is sick?"

"Sick as in it's coming out both ends."

Vee scrunched her nose. "Too much information."

I was still having a difficult time grasping the idea that something was going on between Vee and Jules. Jules came across sullen, brooding, and completely disinterested in Vee's company or anyone else's. Not one part of me felt comfortable with the idea of Vee spending time alone with Jules. Not necessarily because of how unpleasant he was or how little I knew about him, but because of the one thing I did know: He was close friends with Elliot.

The hostess plucked three menus out of a slotted cubbyhole and led us to a booth so close to the kitchen I could feel the fire of the ovens coming through the walls. To our left was the salsa bar. To our right glass doors moist with condensation led out to a patio. My poplin blouse was already clinging to my back. My sweat might have had more to do with the news about Vee and Jules than with the heat, however.

"Is this good?" the hostess asked, gesturing at the booth.

"It's great," Elliot said, shrugging out of his bomber jacket. "I love this place. If the room doesn't make you sweat, the food will."

The hostess's smile lit up. "You've been here before. Can I start you with chips and our newest jalapeño salsa? It's our hottest yet."

"I like things hot," said Elliot.

I was pretty sure he was being slimy. I'd been way too generous in thinking he wasn't as low as Marcie. I'd been way too generous about his character, period. Especially now that I knew he had a murder investigation hiding along with who knew how many other skeletons in his closet.

The hostess swept him an appraising once-over. "I'll be right back with chips and salsa. Your waitress will be here shortly to take your orders."

Vee plopped into the booth first. I slid in beside her, and Elliot took the seat across from me. Our eyes connected, and there was a fleck of something dark in his. Very likely resentment. Maybe even hostility. I wondered if he knew I'd seen the article.

"Purple is your color, Nora," he said, nodding at my scarf as I loosened it from my neck and tied it around the handle of my handbag. "Brightens your eyes."

Vee nudged my foot. She actually thought he meant it as a compliment.

"So," I said to Elliot with an artificial smile, "why don't you tell us about Kinghorn Prep?"

"Yeah," Vee chimed in. "Are there secret societies there? Like in the movies?"

"What's to tell?" Elliot said. "Great school. End of story." He picked up his menu and scanned it. "Anyone interested in an appetizer? My treat."

"If it's so great, why did you transfer?" I met his eyes and held them. Ever so slightly, I arched my eyebrows, challenging.

A muscle in Elliot's jaw jumped just before he cracked a smile. "The girls. I heard they were a lot finer around these parts. The rumor proved true." He winked at me, and an ice-cold feeling shot from my head to my toes.

"Why didn't Jules transfer too?" asked Vee. "We could have

been the fabulous four, only with a lot more punch. The phenomenal four."

"Jules's parents are obsessed with his education. Intense doesn't begin to cover it. I swear on my life, he's going all the way to the top. The guy can't be stopped. I mean, I confess, I do okay in school. Better than most. But nobody tops Jules. He's an academic god."

The dreamy look returned to Vee's eyes. "I've never met his parents," she said. "Both times I've gone over, they're either out of town or working."

"They work a lot," Elliot agreed, returning his eyes to the menu, making it hard for me to read anything in them.

"Where do they work?" I asked.

Elliot took a long drink of his water. It seemed to me like he was buying time while he devised an answer. "Diamonds. They spend a lot of time in Africa and Australia."

"I didn't know Australia was big in the diamond business," I said.

"Yeah, neither did I," said Vee.

In fact, I was pretty sure Australia had no diamonds. Period.

"Why are they living in Maine?" I asked. "Why not Africa?"

Elliot studied his menu more intensely. "What are you both having? I'm thinking the steak fajitas look good."

"If Jules's parents are in the diamond business, I bet they know a lot about choosing the perfect engagement ring," Vee said. "I've always wanted an emerald-cut solitaire."

I kicked Vee under the table. She jabbed me with her fork.

"Oww!" I said.

Our waitress paused at the end of the table long enough to ask, "Anything to drink?"

Elliot looked over the top of his menu, first at me, then at Vee.

"Diet Coke," Vee said.

"Water with lime wedges, please," I said.

The waitress returned amazingly quickly with our drinks. Her return was my cue to leave the table and initiate step one of the Plan, and Vee reminded me with a second under-the-table prod from her fork.

"Vee," I said through my teeth, "would you like to accompany me to the ladies' room?" I suddenly didn't want to go through with the Plan. I didn't want to leave Vee alone with Elliot. What I did want was to drag her out, tell her about the murder investigation, then find some way to make both Elliot and Jules disappear from our lives.

"Why don't you go alone?" said Vee. "I think that would be a better plan." She jerked her head at the bar and mouthed Go, while making discreet shooing motions below the table.

"I was planning on going alone, but I'd really like you to join me."

"What is it with girls?" Elliot said, splitting a smile between us. "I swear, I've never known a girl who could go to the bathroom alone." He leaned forward and grinned conspiratorially. "Let me in on the secret. Seriously. I'll pay you five bucks each." He reached for his back pocket. "Ten, if I can come along and see what the big deal is."

Vee flashed a grin. "Pervert. Don't forget these," she told me, stuffing the 7-Eleven sacks into my arms.

Elliot's eyebrows lifted.

"Trash," Vee explained to him with a touch of snark. "Our garbage can is full. My mom asked if I could throw these away since I was going out."

Elliot didn't look like he believed her, and Vee didn't look like she cared. I got up, my arms loaded with costume gear, and swallowed my burning frustration.

Weaving through the tables, I took the hall leading back to the restrooms. The hall was painted terra-cotta and was decorated with maracas, straw hats, and wooden dolls. It was hotter back here, and I wiped my forehead. The Plan now was to get this over with as quickly as possible. As soon as I was back at the table, I'd formulate an excuse about needing to leave, and haul Vee out. With or without her consent.

After peeking below the three stalls in the ladies' room and confirming I was alone, I locked the main door and dumped the contents of the 7-Eleven sacks onto the counter. One platinum blond wig, one purple push-up bra, one black tube top, one sequined miniskirt, hot pink fishnet tights, and one pair of size eight and a half sharkskin stiletto heels.

hush, hush

I stuffed the bra, the tube top and the tights back inside the sacks. After sloughing off my jeans, I pulled on the miniskirt. I tucked my hair under the wig and applied the lipstick. I topped it off with a generous coat of high-shine lip gloss.

"You can do this," I told my reflection, snapping the cap back on the gloss and blotting my lips together. "You can pull a Marcie Millar. Seduce men for secrets. How hard can it be?"

I kicked off my driving mocs, stuffed them into a sack along with my jeans, then pushed the sack under the counter, out of sight. "Besides," I continued, "there's nothing wrong with sacrificing a little pride for the sake of intelligence. If you want to approach this with a morbid outlook, you could even say if you don't get answers, you could wind up dead. Because like it or not, someone out there means you harm."

I dangled the sharkskin heels in my line of vision. They weren't the ugliest things I'd ever seen. In fact, they could be considered sexy. *Jaws* meets Coldwater, Maine. I strapped myself into them and practiced walking across the bathroom several times.

Two minutes later I eased myself on top of a bar stool at the bar.

The bartender eyed me. "Sixteen?" he guessed. "Seventeen?"

He looked about ten years older than me and had receding brown hair that he wore shaved close. A silver hoop hung from his right earlobe. White T-shirt and Levi's. Not bad looking . . . not great, either.

BECCA FITZPATRICK

"I'm not an underage drinker," I called loudly above the music and surrounding conversation. "I'm waiting for a friend. I've got a great view of the doors here." I retrieved the list of questions from my handbag and covertly positioned the paper under a glass salt shaker.

"What's that?" the bartender asked, wiping his hands on a towel and nodding at the list.

I slid the list farther under the salt shaker. "Nothing," I said, all innocence.

He raised an eyebrow.

I decided to be loose with the truth. "It's a . . . shopping list. I have to pick up some groceries for my mom on the way home." *What happened to flirting? I asked myself. What happened to Marcie Millar?*

He gave me a scrutinizing look that I decided wasn't all negative. "After working this job for five years, I'm pretty good at spotting liars."

"I'm not a liar," I said. "Maybe I was lying a moment ago, but it was just one lie. One little lie doesn't make a liar."

"You look like a reporter," he said.

"I work for my high school's eZine." I wanted to shake myself. Reporters didn't instill trust in people. People were generally suspicious of reporters. "But I'm not working tonight," I amended quickly. "Strictly pleasure tonight. No business. No underlying agendas. None whatsoever."

After a count of silence I decided the best move was to plow ahead. I cleared my throat and said, "Is the Borderline a popular place of employment for high school students?"

"We get a lot of those, yeah. Hostesses and busboys and the like."

"Really?" I said, feigning surprise. "Maybe I know some of them. Try me."

The bartender angled his eyes toward the ceiling and scratched the stubble on his chin. His blank stare wasn't inspiring my confidence. Not to mention that I didn't have a lot of time. Elliot could be slipping lethal drugs into Vee's Diet Coke.

"How about Patch Cipriano?" I asked. "Does he work here?"

"Patch? Yeah. He works here. A couple nights, and weekends."

"Was he working Sunday night?" I tried not to sound too curious. But I needed to know if it was possible for Patch to have been at the pier. He said he had a party on the coast, but maybe his plans had changed. If someone verified that he was at work Sunday evening, I could rule out his involvement in the attack on Vee.

"Sunday?" More scratching. "The nights blur together. Try the hostesses. One of them will remember. They all giggle and go a little screwy when he's around." He smiled as if I might somehow sympathize with them.

I said, "You wouldn't happen to have access to his job application?" Including his home address.

"That would be a no."

"Just out of curiosity," I said, "do you know if it's possible to get hired here if you have a felony on your record?"

"A felony?" He gave a bark of laughter. "You kidding me?"

"Okay, maybe not a felony, but how about a misdemeanor?"

He spread his palms on the counter and leaned close. "No." His tone had shifted from humoring to insulted.

"That's good. That's really good to know." I repositioned myself on the bar stool, and felt the skin on my thighs peel away from the vinyl. I was sweating. If rule number one of flirting was no lists, I was fairly certain rule number two was no sweating.

I consulted my list.

"Do you know if Patch has ever had any restraining orders? Does he have a history of stalking?" I suspected the bartender was getting a bad vibe from me, and I decided to throw all my questions out in a last-ditch effort before he sent me away from the bar—or worse, had me evicted from the restaurant for harassment and suspicious behavior. "Does he have a girlfriend?" I blurted.

"Go ask him," he said.

I blinked. "He's not working tonight."

At the bartender's grin, my stomach seemed to unravel.

"He's not working tonight . . . is he?" I asked, my voice inching up an octave. "He's supposed to have Tuesdays off!"

"Usually, yeah. But he's covering for Benji. Benji went to the hospital. Ruptured appendix."

"You mean Patch is here? Right now?" I glanced over my shoulder, brushing the wig to cover my profile while I scanned the dining area for him.

"He walked back to the kitchen a couple minutes ago."

I was already disengaging myself from the bar stool. "I think I left my car running. But it was great talking to you!" I hurried as quickly as I could to the restrooms.

Inside the ladies' room I locked the door behind me, drew a few breaths with my back pressed to the door, then went to the sink and splashed cold water on my face. Patch was going to find out I'd spied on him. My memorable performance guaranteed that. On the surface, this was a bad thing because it was, well, humiliating. But when I thought about it, I had to face the fact that Patch was very secretive. Secretive people didn't like their lives pried into. How would he react when he learned I was holding him under a magnifying glass?

And now I wondered why I'd come here at all, since deep inside, I didn't believe Patch was the guy behind the ski mask. Maybe he had dark, disturbing secrets, but running around in a ski mask wasn't one of them.

I turned off the tap, and when I looked up, Patch's face was reflected in the mirror. I shrieked and swung around.

He wasn't smiling, and he didn't look particularly amused.

"What are you doing here?" I gasped.

"I work here."

"I mean here. Can't you read? The sign on the door—"

"I'm starting to think you're following me. Every time I turn around, there you are."

"I wanted to take Vee out," I explained. "She's been in the hospital." I sounded defensive. I was certain that only made me look more guilty. "I never dreamed I'd run into you. It's supposed to be your night off. And what are you talking about? Every time I turn around, there you are."

Patch's eyes were sharp, intimidating, extracting. They calculated my every word, my every movement.

"Want to explain the tacky hair?" he said.

I yanked off the wig and tossed it on the counter. "Want to explain where you've been? You missed the last two days of school."

I was almost certain Patch wouldn't reveal his whereabouts, but he said, "Playing paintball. What were you doing at the bar?"

"Talking with the bartender. Is that a crime?" Balancing one hand against the counter, I raised my foot to unbuckle a sharkskin heel. I bent over slightly, and as I did, the interrogation list fluttered out of my neckline and onto the floor.

I went down on my knees for it, but Patch was faster. He held it over his head while I jumped for it.

"Give it back!" I said.

"'Does Patch have a restraining order against him?'" he read. "'Is Patch a felon?'"

"Give—me—that!" I hissed furiously.

Patch gave a soft laugh, and I knew he'd seen the next question. "'Does Patch have a girlfriend?'"

Patch put the paper in his back pocket. I was sorely tempted to go after it, despite its location.

He leaned back against the counter and leveled our eyes. "If you're going to dig around for information, I'd prefer that you ask me."

"Those questions"—I waved where he'd hidden them—"were a joke. Vee wrote them," I added in a flash of inspiration. "It's all her fault."

"I know your handwriting, Nora."

"Well, okay, fine," I began, hunting for a smart reply, but I took too long and lost my chance.

"No restraining orders," he said. "No felonies."

I tilted my chin up. "Girlfriend?" I told myself I didn't care how he answered. Either way was fine with me.

"That's none of your business."

"You tried to kiss me," I reminded him. "You made it my business."

The ghost of a pirate smile lurked at his mouth. I got the impression he was recalling every last detail of that near kiss, including my sigh-slash-moan.

"Ex-girlfriend," he said after a moment.

My stomach dropped as a sudden thought popped into my mind. What if the girl from Delphic and Victoria's Secret was

Patch's ex? What if she saw me talking to Patch at the arcade and—mistakenly—assumed there was a lot more to our relationship? If she was still attracted to Patch, it made sense that she might be jealous enough to follow me around. A few puzzle pieces seemed to fall into place. . . .

And then Patch said, "But she's not around."

"What do you mean she's not around?"

"She's gone. She's never coming back."

"You mean . . . she's dead?" I asked.

Patch didn't deny it.

My stomach suddenly felt heavy and twisted. I hadn't expected this. Patch had a girlfriend, and now she was dead.

The door to the ladies' room rattled as someone tried to enter. I'd forgotten I'd locked it. Which made me wonder how Patch got in. Either he had a key, or there was another explanation. An explanation I probably didn't want to think about, such as gliding under the door like air. Like smoke.

"I need to get back to work," Patch said. He gave me a once-over that lingered a bit below the hips. "Killer skirt. Deadly legs."

Before I'd formed a single coherent thought, he was through the door.

The older woman waiting for admittance looked at me, then over her shoulder at Patch, who was vanishing down the hall. "Honey," she told me, "he looks slippery as soap."

"Good description," I mumbled.

She fluffed her short, corkscrew gray hair. "A girl could lather up in soap like that."

After I changed back into my clothes, I returned to the booth and slid in beside Vee. Elliot checked his watch and lifted his eyebrows at me.

"Sorry I was gone so long," I said. "Did I miss anything?"

"Nope," said Vee. "Same old, same old." She bumped my knee, and the question was implied. Well?

Before I could return the bump, Elliot said, "You missed the waitress. I ordered you a red burrito." A creepy smile tugged at the corners of his mouth.

I saw my chance.

"Actually, I'm not sure I'm up to eating." I managed a nauseated face that wasn't altogether contrived. "I think I caught what Jules has."

"Oh, man," Vee said. "Are you okay?"

I shook my head.

"I'll hunt down our waitress and get her to box the food," Vee suggested, digging in her purse for keys.

"What about me?" said Elliot, sounding only half joking.

"Rain check?" Vee said.

Bingo, I thought.

CHAPTER
14

GOT BACK TO THE FARMHOUSE SHORTLY BEFORE EIGHT.
I turned my key in the lock, grabbed the doorknob, and shoved
my hip against the door. I'd called my mom a few hours before
dinner; she was at the office, tying up a few loose ends, not sure
when she'd be home, and I expected to find the house quiet, dark,
and cold.

On the third shove, the door gave way, and I hurled my handbag into the darkness, then wrestled with the key still jammed

in the lock. Ever since the night Patch came over, the lock had developed a greedy disposition. I wondered if Dorothea had noticed it earlier in the day.

"Give—me—the—dumb—key," I said, jiggling it free.

The grandfather clock in the hall ticked on the hour, and eight loud dongs reverberated through the silence. I was walking into the living room to start a fire in the wood-burning stove when there was the rustle of fabric and a low creak from across the room.

I screamed.

"Nora!" my mom said, throwing off a blanket and scrambling into a sitting position on the sofa. "What in the world's the matter?"

I had one hand splayed across my heart and the other flattened against the wall, supporting me. "You scared me!"

"I fell asleep. If I'd heard you come in, I would have said something." She pushed her hair off her face and blinked owlishly. "What time is it?"

I collapsed into the nearest armchair and tried to recover my normal heart rate. My imagination had conjured up a pair of ruthless eyes behind a ski mask. Now that I was positive he wasn't a figment of my imagination, I had an overwhelming desire to tell my mom everything, from the way he'd jumped on the Neon to his role as Vee's attacker. He was stalking me, and he was violent. We'd get new locks on the doors. And it seemed logical that the police would get involved. I'd feel much safer at night with an officer parked on the curb.

"I was going to wait to bring this up," my mom said, interrupting my thought process, "but I'm not sure the perfect moment is ever going to present itself."

I frowned. "What's going on?"

She gave a long, troubled sigh. "I'm thinking about putting the farmhouse up for sale."

"What? Why?"

"We've been struggling for a year, and I'm not pulling in as much as I'd hoped. I've considered taking a second job, but honestly, I'm not sure there are enough hours in the day." She laughed without any trace of humor. "Dorothea's wages are modest, but it's extra money we don't have. The only other thing I can think of is moving into a smaller house. Or an apartment."

"But this is our house." All my memories were here. The memory of my dad was here. I couldn't believe she didn't feel the same way. I would do whatever it took to stay.

"I'll give it three more months," she said. "But I don't want to get your hopes up."

Right then I knew I couldn't tell my mom about the guy in the ski mask. She'd quit work tomorrow. She'd get a local job, and there'd be absolutely no choice but to sell the farmhouse.

"Let's talk about something brighter," Mom said, pushing her mouth into a smile. "How was dinner?"

"Fine," I said morosely.

"And Vee? How's she recovering?"

"She can go back to school tomorrow."

Mom smiled wryly. "It's a good thing she broke her left arm. Otherwise she wouldn't be able to take notes in class, and I can only imagine how disappointing that would have been for her."

"Ha, ha," I said. "I'm going to make hot chocolate." I stood and pointed over my shoulder into the kitchen. "Want some?"

"That actually sounds perfect. I'll start the fire."

After a quick trip to the kitchen to round up mugs, sugar, and the cocoa canister, I came back to find that Mom had a kettle of water on the wood-burning stove. I perched myself on the arm of the sofa and handed her a mug.

"How did you know you were in love with Dad?" I asked, striving to sound casual. There was always the chance that discussing Dad would bring on a tearfest, something I hoped to avoid.

Mom settled into the sofa and propped her feet up on the coffee table. "I didn't. Not until we'd been married about a year."

It wasn't the answered I'd expected. "Then . . . why did you marry him?"

"Because I thought I was in love. And when you think you're in love, you're willing to stick it out and make it work until it is love."

"Were you scared?"

"To marry him?" She laughed. "That was the exciting part. Shopping for a gown, reserving the chapel, wearing my diamond solitaire."

I pictured Patch's mischievous smile. "Were you ever scared of Dad?"

"Whenever the New England Patriots lost."

Whenever the Patriots lost, my dad went to the garage and revved up his chainsaw. Two autumns ago he hauled the chainsaw to the woods behind our property, felled ten trees, and diced them into firewood. We still have more than half the pile to burn through.

Mom patted the sofa beside her, and I curled up against her, resting my head on her shoulder. "I miss him," I said.

"Me too."

"I'm afraid I'll forget what he looked like. Not in pictures, but hanging around on a Saturday morning in sweats, making scrambled eggs."

Mom laced her fingers through mine. "You've always been so much like him, right from the start."

"Really?" I sat up. "In what way?"

"He was a good student, very clever. He wasn't flashy or outspoken, but people respected him."

"Was Dad ever . . . mysterious?"

Mom seemed to turn this over in her mind. "Mysterious people have a lot of secrets. Your father was very open."

"Was he ever rebellious?"

She gave a short, startled laugh. "Did you see him that way? Harrison Grey, the world's most ethical accountant . . . rebellious?"

She gave a theatrical gasp. "Heaven forbid! He did wear his hair long for a while. It was wavy and blond—like a surfer's. Of course, his horn-rimmed glasses killed the look. So . . . do I dare ask what got us on this subject?"

I had no idea how to explain my conflicting feelings for Patch to my mom. I had no idea how to explain Patch, period. My mom was probably expecting a description that included his parents' names, his GPA, the varsity sports he played, and which colleges he planned on applying to. I didn't want to alarm her by saying I was willing to bet my piggy bank that Patch had a rap sheet. "There's this guy," I said, unable to hold back a smile at the thought of Patch. "We've been hanging out lately. Mostly school stuff."

"Ooh, a boy," she said mysteriously. "Well? Is he in the Chess Club? Student Council? The tennis team?"

"He likes pool," I offered optimistically.

"A swimmer! Is he as cute as Michael Phelps? Of course, I always leaned toward Ryan Lochte when it came to appearances."

I thought about correcting my mom. On second thought, it was probably best not to clarify. Pool, swimming . . . close enough, right?

The phone rang and Mom stretched across the sofa to answer it. Ten seconds into the call she flopped back against the sofa and slapped a hand to her forehead. "No, it's not a problem. I'll run over, pick it up, and bring it by first thing tomorrow morning."

"Hugo?" I asked after she hung up. Hugo was my mom's boss,

and to say he called *all the time* was putting it mildly. Once, he'd called her into work on a Sunday because he couldn't figure out how to operate the copy machine.

"He left some unfinished paperwork in the office and needs me to run over. I have to make copies, but I shouldn't be gone more than an hour. Have you finished your homework?"

"Not yet."

"Then I'll tell myself we couldn't have spent time together even if I was here." She sighed and rose to her feet. "See you in an hour?"

"Tell Hugo he should pay you more."

She laughed. "A lot more."

As soon as I had the house to myself, I cleared the breakfast dishes off the kitchen table and made room for my textbooks. English, world history, biology. Arming myself with a brand-new number two pencil, I flipped open the top book and went to work.

Fifteen minutes later my mind rebelled, refusing to digest another paragraph on European feudal systems. I wondered what Patch was doing after he got off work. Homework? Hard to believe. Eating pizza and watching basketball on TV? Maybe, but it didn't feel right. Placing bets and playing pool at Bo's Arcade? It seemed like a good guess.

I had the unexplainable desire to drive to Bo's and defend my earlier behavior, but the thought was quickly put into perspective by the simple fact that I didn't have time. My mom would be home in less time than it took to make the half-hour drive there. Not to mention, Patch wasn't the kind of guy I could just go hunt down. In the past, our meetings had operated on his schedule, not mine. Always.

I climbed the stairs to change into something comfy. I pushed on my bedroom door and took three steps inside before stopping short. My dresser drawers were yanked out, clothes strewn across the floor. The bed was ripped apart. The closet doors were open, hanging askew by their hinges. Books and picture frames littered the floor.

I saw the reflection of movement in the window across the room and swung around. He stood against the wall behind me, dressed head to toe in black and wearing the ski mask. My brain was in a swirling fog, just beginning to transmit run! to my legs, when he lunged for the window, threw it open, and ducked lithely out.

I took the stairs down three at a time. I flung myself around the banister, flew down the hall to the kitchen, and dialed 911.

Fifteen minutes later a patrol car bumped into the driveway. Shaking, I unbolted the door and let the two officers in. The first officer to step inside was short and thick-waisted with salt-and-pepper hair. The other was tall and lean with hair almost as dark as Patch's, but cropped above his ears. In a strange way, he vaguely resembled Patch. Mediterranean complexion, symmetrical face, eyes with an edge.

They introduced themselves; the dark-haired officer was Detective Basso. His partner was Detective Holstijic.

"Are you Nora Grey?" Detective Holstijic asked.

I nodded.

"Your parents home?"

"My mom left a few minutes before I called 911."

"So you're home alone?"

Another nod.

"Why don't you tell us what happened?" he asked, crossing his arms and planting his feet wide, while Detective Basso walked a few paces inside the house and took a look around.

"I came home at eight and did some homework," I said. "When I went up to my bedroom, I saw him. Everything was a mess. He tore my room apart."

"Did you recognize him?"

"He was wearing a ski mask. And the lights were off."

"Any distinguishing marks? Tattoos?"

"No."

"Height? Weight?"

I delved reluctantly into my short-term memory. I didn't want to relive the moment, but it was important that I recall any clues. "Average weight, but a little on the tall side. About the same size as Detective Basso."

"Did he say anything?"

I shook my head.

Detective Basso reappeared and said, "All clear," to his partner. Then he climbed to the second floor. The floorboards creaked overhead as he moved down the hall, opening and shutting doors.

Detective Holstijic cracked the front door and squatted to examine the deadbolt. "Was the door unlocked or damaged when you came home?"

"No. I used my key to get in. My mom was asleep in the living room."

Detective Basso appeared at the top of the stairs.

"Can you show us what's damaged?" he asked me.

Detective Holstijic and I climbed the stairs together, and I led the way down the hall to where Detective Basso stood just inside my bedroom door with his hands on his hips, surveying my room.

I held perfectly still, a tingle of fear creeping through me. My bed was made. My pajamas were in a heap on my pillow, just the way I'd left them this morning. My dresser drawers were shut, picture frames arranged neatly on top. The trunk at the foot of the bed was closed. The floors were clean. The window drapes hung in long, smooth panels, one on either side of the closed window.

"You said you saw the intruder," said Detective Basso. He was staring down at me with hard eyes that didn't miss a thing. Eyes that were expert at filtering lies.

I stepped inside the room, but it lacked the familiar touch of comfort and safety. There was an underlying note of violation and menace. I pointed across the room at the window, trying to hold

BECCA FITZPATRICK

my hand steady. "When I walked in, he jumped out the window."

Detective Basso glanced out the window. "Long way to the ground," he observed. He attempted to open the window. "Did you lock it after he left?"

"No. I ran downstairs and called 911."

"Somebody locked it." Detective Basso was still eyeing me with razor eyes, his mouth pressed in a tight line.

"Not sure anybody'd be able to get away after a jump like that," Detective Holstijic said, joining his partner at the window. "They'd be lucky to get off with a broken leg."

"Maybe he didn't jump, maybe he climbed down the tree," I said.

Detective Basso whipped his head around. "Well? Which is it? Did he climb or jump? He could have pushed past you and gone out the front door. That would be the logical option. That's what I'd have done. I'm going to ask once more. Think real careful. Did you really see someone in your room tonight?"

He didn't believe me. He thought I'd invented it. For a moment I was tempted to think similarly. What was wrong with me? Why was my reality convoluted? Why did the truth never match up? For the sake of my sanity, I told myself it wasn't me. It was him. The guy in the ski mask. He was doing this. I didn't know how, but he was to blame.

Detective Holstijic broke the tense silence by saying, "When will your parents be home?"

"I live with my mom. She had to make a quick trip to the office."

"We need to ask you both a few questions," he continued. He pointed for me to take a seat on my bed, but I shook my head numbly. "Have you recently broken up with a boyfriend?"

"No."

"How about drugs? Have you had a problem, now or in the past?"

"No."

"You mentioned that you live with your mom. How about Dad? Where's he?"

"This was a mistake," I said. "I'm sorry. I shouldn't have called."

The two officers exchanged looks. Detective Holstijic shut his eyes and massaged the inner corners. Detective Basso looked like he'd wasted enough time and was ready to blow it off.

"We've got things to do," he said. "Are you going to be all right here alone until your mom gets back?"

I hardly heard him; I couldn't pull my eyes off the window. How was he doing it? Fifteen minutes. He had *fifteen* minutes to find a way back inside and put the room in order before the police arrived. And with me downstairs the whole time. At the realization that we'd been alone in the house together, I shuddered.

Detective Holstijic extended his business card. "Could you have your mom call us when she gets in?"

"We'll see ourselves out," Detective Basso said. He was already halfway down the hall.

YOU THINK ELLIOT *MURDERED* SOMEONE?"

"Shh!" I hissed at Vee, glancing across the rows of lab tables to make sure no one had overheard.

"No offense, babe, but this is starting to get ridiculous. First he attacked me. Now he's a killer. I'm sorry, but Elliot? A murderer? He's, like, the nicest guy I've ever met. When was the last time he forgot to hold open a door for you? Oh, yeah, that's right . . . *never*."

Vee and I were in biology, and Vee was lying faceup on a table.

We were running a lab on blood pressure, and Vee was supposed to be resting silently for five minutes. Normally I would have worked with Patch, but Coach had given us a free day, which meant we were free to choose our own partners. Vee and I were at the back of the room; Patch was working with a jock named Thomas Rookery at the front of the room.

"He was questioned as a suspect in a murder investigation," I whispered, feeling Coach's eyes gravitate toward us. I scribbled a few notes on my lab sheet. *Subject is calm and relaxed. Subject has refrained from speaking for three and a half minutes.* "The police obviously thought he had motive and means."

"Are you sure it's the same Elliot?"

"How many Elliot Saunderses do you think there were at Kinghorn in February?"

Vee strummed her fingers on her stomach. "It just seems really, really hard to believe. And anyway, so what if he was questioned? The important thing is, he was released. They didn't find him guilty."

"Because police found a suicide note written by Halverson."

"Who's Halverson again?"

"Kjirsten Halverson," I said impatiently. "The girl who supposedly hanged herself."

"Maybe she did hang herself. I mean, what if one day she said, 'Hey, life sucks,' and strung herself to a tree? It has happened."

"You don't find it a little too coincidental that her apartment showed evidence of a break-in when they discovered the suicide note?"

"She lived in Portland. Break-ins happen."

"I think someone placed the note. Someone who wanted Elliot off the hook."

"Who would want Elliot off the hook?" Vee asked.

I gave her my best *duh* look.

Vee propped herself up with her good elbow. "So you're saying Elliot hauled Kjirsten up a tree, tied a rope around her neck, pushed her off the limb, then did a breaking-and-entering job on her apartment and planted evidence pointing to a suicide."

"Why not?"

Vee returned the *duh* look. "Because the cops already analyzed everything. If they're ruling it a suicide, so am I."

"How about this," I said. "Just weeks after Elliot was released from questioning, he transferred schools. Why would someone leave Kinghorn Prep to come to CHS?"

"You've got a point there."

"I think he's trying to escape his past. I think it became too uncomfortable attending school on the same campus where he killed Kjirsten. He has a guilty conscience." I tapped my pencil against my lip. "I need to drive out to Kinghorn and ask questions. She just died two months ago; everyone will still be buzzing about it."

"I don't know, Nora. I'm getting bad vibes about initiating a spy operation at Kinghorn. I mean, are you going to ask about Elliot specifically? What if he finds out? What's he going to think?"

I looked down at her. "He only has something to worry about if he's guilty."

"And then he'll kill you to silence you." Vee grinned like the Cheshire cat. I didn't. "I want to find out who attacked me just as much as you do," she continued on a more serious note, "but I swear on my life it wasn't Elliot. I've replayed the memory, like, a hundred times. It's not a match. Not even close. Trust me."

"Okay, maybe Elliot didn't attack you," I said, trying to appease Vee but not about to clear Elliot's name. "He still has a lot going against him. He was involved in a murder investigation, for one. And he's almost too nice, for two. It's creepy. And he's friends with Jules, for three."

Vee frowned. "Jules? What's wrong with Jules?"

"Don't you think it's odd that every time we're with them, Jules bails?"

"What's that supposed to mean?"

"The night we went to Delphic, Jules left almost immediately to use the bathroom. Did he ever come back? After I left to buy cotton candy, did Elliot find him?"

"No, but I chalked it up to internal plumbing issues."

"Then, last night, he mysteriously called in sick." I scrubbed my pencil's eraser down the length of my nose, thinking. "He seems to get sick a lot."

"I think you're overanalyzing this. Maybe . . . maybe he has IBS."

BECCA FITZPATRICK

"IBS?"

"Irritable bowel syndrome."

I discarded Vee's suggestion in favor of mentally stretching for an idea that floated just out of reach. Kinghorn Prep was easily an hour away by car. If the school was as academically rigorous as Elliot claimed, how did Jules continually have time to make the drive to Coldwater to visit? I saw him nearly every morning on my way to school at Enzo's Bistro with Elliot. Plus, he gave Elliot a ride home after school. It was almost like Elliot had Jules in the palm of his hand.

But that wasn't all of it. I scrubbed the eraser more furiously against my nose. What was I missing?

"Why would Elliot kill Kjirsten?" I wondered out loud. "Maybe she saw him do something illegal, and he killed her to silence her."

Vee let go of a sigh. "This is starting to drift into the land of This Makes Absolutely No Sense."

"There's something else. Something we're not seeing."

Vee looked at me like my logic was vacationing in outer space. "Personally, I think you're seeing too much. This feels a lot like a witch hunt."

And then all of a sudden I knew what I was missing. It had been nagging me all day, calling to me from the back of my mind, but I'd been too overwhelmed with everything else to pay attention. Detective Basso had asked me if anything was missing. It just now hit me that something was. I'd set the article about Elliot on top of my dresser last night. But this morning—I consulted my memory to be sure—it was gone. Definitely gone.

"Omigosh," I said. "Elliot broke into my house last night. It was him! He stole the article." Since the article was in plain sight, it was obvious Elliot had torn apart my room to terrorize me—possibly as punishment for finding the article in the first place.

"Whoa, what?" Vee said.

"What's wrong?" asked Coach, coming to a stop beside me.

"Yeah, what's wrong?" Vee chimed in. She pointed and laughed at me from behind Coach's back.

"Um—the subject doesn't appear to have a pulse," I said, giving Vee's wrist a hard pinch.

While Coach probed for Vee's pulse, she made swooning motions and fanned herself. Coach flicked his eyes to mine, looking at me over the top of his glasses. "Right here, Nora. Beating loud and strong. Are you sure the subject refrained from activity, including talking, for the full five minutes? This pulse isn't as slow as I would have expected."

"The subject struggled with the no-talking step," Vee interjected. "And the subject has a hard time relaxing on a rock-hard biology table. The subject would like to propose switching places so Nora can be the new subject." Vee used her right hand to grab me and pull herself upright.

"Don't make me regret allowing you to choose your own partners," Coach told us.

"Don't make me regret coming to school today," said Vee sweetly.

Coach shot her a warning look, then picked up my lab sheet, eyes skimming the all-but-blank page.

"The subject equates biology labs with overdosing on prescription-strength sedatives," Vee said.

Coach chirped his whistle, and all eyes in the class swung our way.

"Patch?" he said. "Mind taking over here? We seem to have run into a partner problem."

"I was so kidding," Vee said quickly. "Here—I'll do the lab."

"You should have thought of that fifteen minutes ago," Coach said.

"Please forgive me?" she asked, batting her eyelashes angelically.

Coach tucked her notebook under her good arm. "No."

Sorry! Vee mouthed over her shoulder at me as she walked reluctantly to the front of the room.

A moment later Patch took a seat on the table beside me. He clasped his hands loosely between his knees and kept a steady gaze on me.

"What?" I said, feeling unnerved by the weight of his stare.

He smiled. "I was remembering the shark shoes. Last night."

I got the usual Patch-induced flutter in my stomach, and like usual, I couldn't distinguish if it was a good thing or a bad thing.

"How was your night?" I asked, my voice carefully neutral as

hush, hush

I attempted to break the ice. My spying adventures still hung uncomfortably between us.

"Interesting. Yours?"

"Not so much."

"Homework was brutal, huh?"

He was making fun of me. "I didn't do homework."

He had the smile of a fox. "Who did you do?"

I was speechless a moment. I stood there with my mouth slightly open. "Was that an innuendo?"

"Just curious what my competition is."

"Grow up."

His smile stretched. "Loosen up."

"I'm already walking on thin ice with Coach, so do me a favor and let's concentrate on the lab. I'm not in the mood to play test subject, so if you don't mind . . ." I looked pointedly at the table.

"Can't," he said. "I don't have a heart."

I told myself he wasn't being literal.

I lowered myself down on the table and stacked my hands on my stomach. "Tell me when five minutes are up." I shut my eyes, preferring not to watch Patch's black eyes examine me.

A few minutes later I opened one eye a slit.

"Time's up," said Patch.

I held one upturned wrist out so he could take my pulse.

Patch took my hand, and a jolt of heat shot up my arm and ended with a squeeze in my stomach.

"The subject's pulse increased on contact," he said.

"Don't write that." It was supposed to sound indignant. If anything, it sounded like I was repressing a smile.

"Coach wants us to be thorough."

"What do you want?" I asked him.

Patch's eyes connected with mine. On the inside, he was grinning. I could tell.

"Except, you know, *that*," I said.

After school I swung by Miss Greene's office for our scheduled appointment. At the end of the school day, Dr. Hendrickson had always kept his door wide open, a nonverbal invitation for students to stop by. Every time I passed down this stretch of hallway now, Miss Greene had the door closed. All the way. The Do not disturb was implicit.

"Nora," she said, opening the door after my knock, "please come in. Have a seat."

Her office was fully unpacked and decorated today. She'd brought in several more plants, and a panel of framed botanical prints hung in a row on the wall above her desk.

Miss Greene said, "I've been thinking a lot about what you said last week. I came to the obvious conclusion that our relationship needs to be built on trust and respect. We won't discuss your dad again, unless you specify."

"Okay," I said warily. What were we going to talk about?

hush, hush

"I heard some rather disappointing news," she said. Her smile faded and she leaned forward, resting her elbows on the desk. She was holding a pen, and she rolled it between her palms. "I don't mean to pry into your private life, Nora, but I thought I made myself perfectly clear concerning your involvement with Patch."

I wasn't quite sure where she was going with this. "I haven't tutored him." And, really, was it any of her business?

"Saturday night Patch gave you a ride home from Delphic Seaport. And you invited him inside your house."

I fought to hold in a choke of protest. "How do you know about that?"

"Part of my job as your school psychologist is to give you guidance," Miss Greene said. "Please promise me you'll be very, very careful around Patch." She looked at me like she was actually waiting for my oath of promise.

"It's kind of complicated," I said. "My ride left me stranded at Delphic. I didn't have a choice. It's not like I seek out opportunities to spend time with Patch." Well, except for last night at the Borderline. In my defense, I honestly hadn't expected to see Patch. He was supposed to have the night off.

"I'm very glad to hear it," Miss Greene answered, but she didn't sound fully convinced of my innocence. "With that out of the way, is there anything else you'd like to talk about today? Anything weighing on your mind?"

I wasn't about to tell her that Elliot broke into my house. I didn't trust Miss Greene. I couldn't put my finger on it, but something about her bothered me. And I didn't like the way she kept hinting that Patch was dangerous but wouldn't tell me why. It was almost like she had an agenda.

I hoisted my backpack off the ground and opened the door. "No," I said.

CHAPTER 16

Vee was leaning against my locker, doodling on her cast with a purple marker.

"Hi," she said when there was nothing of the hallway left between us. "Where've you been? I checked the eZine lab and the library."

"I had a meeting with Miss Greene, the new school psych." I said it very matter-of-factly, but on the inside, I had a hollow, trembly feeling. I couldn't stop thinking about Elliot breaking into my house. What was stopping him from doing it again? Or from doing something worse?

"What happened?" Vee asked.

I spun my locker combination and traded out books. "Do you know how much a good alarm system costs?"

"No offense, babe, but nobody's going to steal your car."

I pinned Vee with a black look. "For my house. I want to make sure Elliot can't get inside again."

Vee glanced around and cleared her throat.

"What?" I said.

Vee did a hands-up. "Nothing. Nothing at all. If you're still bent on nailing this to Elliot . . . that's your prerogative. It's a crazy prerogative, but hey, it's yours."

I shoved my locker door closed, and the rattle echoed down the hall. I bit back an accusatory response that she of all people should believe me and instead said, "I'm on my way to the library, and I'm sort of in a hurry." We exited the building and crossed the grounds to the parking lot, and I came up short. I looked around for the Fiat, but that's when I remembered my mom had dropped me off on her way to work this morning. And with Vee's arm broken, she wasn't driving.

"Crap," Vee said, reading my thoughts, "we're carless."

Shielding my eyes from the sun, I squinted down the street. "Guess this means we'll have to walk."

"Not we. You. I'd come with, but once a week is my library limit."

hush, hush

"You haven't been to the library this week," I pointed out.

"Yeah, but I might have to go tomorrow."

"Tomorrow's Thursday. In all your life, have you ever studied on a Thursday?"

Vee tapped a fingernail to her lip and adopted a thoughtful expression. "Have I ever studied on a Wednesday?"

"Not that I recall."

"There you have it. I can't go. It would be anti-tradition."

Thirty minutes later, I hiked up the steps leading to the library's main doors. Once inside, I put homework on the back burner and went directly to the media lab, where I combed the Internet trying to find more information on the "Kinghorn Hanging." I didn't find much. Originally there had been a lot of hype, but after the suicide note was discovered and Elliot was released, the news moved on.

It was time to take a trip to Portland. I wasn't going to learn much more sifting through archived news articles, but maybe I'd have better luck doing legwork there.

I logged off and called my mom.

"Do I need to be home by nine tonight?"

"Yes, why?"

"I was thinking of taking a bus out to Portland."

She gave me one of her *You must think I'm crazy* laughs.

"I need to interview some students at Kinghorn Prep," I said. "It's for a project I've been researching." It wasn't a lie. Not really. Of course, it would have been much easier to justify if I weren't burdened by the guilt of keeping the break-in and ensuing police visit from her. I'd thought about telling her, but every time I opened my mouth to say the words, they slipped away. We were struggling to survive. We needed my mom's income. If I told her about Elliot, she'd quit immediately.

"You can't go to the city alone. It's a school night and it will be dark soon. Besides, by the time you get there, the students will have left."

I heaved a sigh. "Okay, I'll be home soon."

"I know I promised you a ride, but I'm stuck at my office." I heard her shuffling papers in the background, and I imagined she had the phone cradled under her chin and the phone cord wrapped around her body several times. "Is it too much to ask you to walk?"

The weather was just this side of cool, I had my jean jacket, and I had two legs. I could walk. The plan sounded a lot more reasonable in my head, because the thought of walking home left my insides hollow. But aside from spending the night in the library, I didn't see any other choice.

I was almost through the library doors when I heard my name called. Turning around, I found Marcie Millar closing the distance between us.

"I heard about Vee," she said. "It's really sad. I mean, who would attack her? Unless, you know, they couldn't help it. Maybe it was self-defense. I heard it was dark and raining. It would be easy to mistake Vee for a moose. Or a bear, or a buffalo. Really, any hulking animal would do."

"Gosh, it was nice talking to you, but I've got a lot of things I'd rather be doing. Like sticking my hand in the garbage disposal." I continued toward the exit.

"I hope she stayed clear of those hospital meals," Marcie said, keeping at my heels. "I hear they're high in fat. She can't stand to gain a lot of weight."

I spun around. "That's it. One more word, and I'll . . ." We both knew it was an empty threat.

Marcie simpered. "You'll what?"

"Skank," I said.

"Geek."

"Slut."

"Freak."

"Anorexic pig."

"Wow," said Marcie, staggering back melodramatically with a hand pressed to her heart. "Am I supposed to act offended? Try this on for size. Old news. At least I know how to exercise a little self-control."

The security guard standing at the doors cleared his throat. "All right, break it up. Take this outside or I'm going to cart the both of you inside my office and start calling parents."

"Talk to her," Marcie said, pointing a finger at me. "I'm the one who's trying to be nice. She verbally attacked me. I was just offering my condolences to her friend."

"I said outside."

"You look good in uniform," Marcie told him, flashing her trademark toxic smile.

He jerked his head at the doors. "Get out of here." But it didn't sound half so gruff.

Marcie sashayed up to the doors. "Mind getting the door for me? I'm short on hands." She was holding one book. A paperback.

The guard pushed on the handicapped button, and the doors automatically glided open.

"Why, thank you," Marcie said, blowing him a kiss.

I didn't follow her. I wasn't sure what would happen if I did, but I was filled with enough negative emotion that I just might do something I'd regret. Name-calling and fighting were beneath me. Unless I was dealing with Marcie Millar.

I turned around and headed back into the library. At the elevators, I stepped into the metal cage and punched the button for the basement level. I could've waited around a few minutes for Marcie to leave, but I knew another way out and decided to take it. Five years ago the city had approved moving the public library into a historic building smack in the center of Old Town Coldwater. The red brick dated back to the 1850s, and the building was complete with a romantic cupola and a widow's walk to watch for vessels coming in from sea. Unfortunately, the building didn't include a parking lot, so an underground tunnel had been dug to connect the library to the underground parking garage of the courthouse

hush, hush

across the street. The garage now served both buildings.

The elevator clanked to a stop and I stepped off. The tunnel was lit with fluorescent lights that flickered pale purple. It took me a moment to force my feet to walk. I was struck by the sudden thought of my dad the night he was killed. I wondered if he'd been on a street as remote and dark as the tunnel ahead.

Pull it together, I told myself. It was a random act of violence. You've spent the last year paranoid about every dark alley, dark room, dark closet. You can't live the rest of your life terrified of having a gun pulled on you.

Determined to prove my fear was all in my head, I headed down the tunnel, hearing the soft tap of my shoes on concrete. Shifting my backpack to my left shoulder, I calculated how long it would take to walk home, and whether or not I was up for taking a short-cut across the railroad tracks now that it was dusk. I hoped that if I kept my thoughts upbeat and busy, I wouldn't have time to concentrate on my growing sense of alarm.

The tunnel ended, and a dark form stood straight ahead.

I stopped midstride, and my heart dropped a few beats. Patch was wearing a black T-shirt, loose jeans, steel-toed boots. His eyes looked like they didn't play by the rules. His smile was a little too cunning for comfort.

"What are you doing here?" I asked, pushing a handful of hair off my face and glancing past him to the car exit leading above ground. I knew it was straight ahead, but several of the overhead fluorescent lights were out of service, making it difficult to see clearly. If rape, murder, or any other miscreant activities were on Patch's mind, he'd cornered me in the perfect place.

As Patch moved toward me, I backed up. I came up short against a car and saw my chance. I scrambled around it, positioning myself opposite Patch, with the car between us.

Patch looked at me over the top of the car. His eyebrows lifted.

"I have questions," I said. "A lot of them."

"About?"

"About everything."

His mouth twitched, and I was pretty sure he was fighting a smile. "And if my answers don't make the cut, you're going to make a break for it?" He gave a nod in the direction of the garage's exit.

That was the plan. More or less. Give or take a few glaring holes, like the fact that Patch was a lot faster than me.

"Let's hear those questions," he said.

"How did you know I'd be at the library tonight?"

"Seemed like a good guess."

I didn't for one moment believe Patch was here on a hunch. There was a side to him that was almost predatory. If the armed forces knew about him, they'd do everything in their power to recruit him.

Patch lunged to his left. I countered his move, scurrying toward the rear of the car. When Patch came up short, I did too. He was at the nose of the car, and I was at the tail.

"Where were you Sunday afternoon?" I asked. "Did you follow

me when I went shopping with Vee?" Patch may not have been the guy in the ski mask, but that didn't mean he hadn't been involved in the chain of recent disturbing events. He was keeping something from me. He'd been keeping something from me since the day we met. Was it a coincidence that the last normal day in my life had been right before that fateful day? I didn't think so.

"No. How did that go, by the way? Buy anything?"

"Maybe," I said, thrown off guard.

"Like?"

I thought back. Vee and I had only made it as far as Victoria's Secret. I'd spent thirty dollars on the lacy black bra, but I wasn't about to go there. Instead I related my evening, starting with sensing I was being followed, and ending with finding Vee on the side of the road, the victim of a brutal mugging.

"Well?" I demanded when I finished. "Do you have anything to say?"

"No."

"You have no idea what happened to Vee?"

"Again, no."

"I don't believe you."

"That's because you have trust issues." He splayed both hands on the car, leaning across the hood. "We've been over this."

I felt my temper spark. Patch had flipped the conversation again. Instead of shining on him, the spotlight was directed back on me. I especially didn't like being reminded that he knew all sorts of things about me. Private things. Like my trust issues.

Patch lunged clockwise. I ran away from him, halting when he did. While we were at a standstill again, his eyes locked on mine, almost as if he was trying to glean my next move from them.

"What happened on the Archangel? Did you save me?" I asked.

"If I'd saved you, we wouldn't be standing here having this conversation."

"You mean if you *hadn't* saved me we wouldn't be here. I'd be dead."

"That's not what I said."

I had no idea what he meant. "Why wouldn't we be standing here?"

"You'd still be here." He paused. "I probably wouldn't."

Before I could figure out what he was talking about, he darted for me again, this time attacking from the right. Momentarily confused, I gave up some of the distance between us. Instead of stopping, Patch skirted around the car. I made a break for it, running down the straightaway of the garage.

I made it three cars before he caught hold of my arm. He spun me around and backed me against a cement beam.

"So much for that plan," he said.

I glared at him. There was a lot of panic behind it, though. He flashed a grin brimming with dark intent, confirming that I had every reason to sweat freely.

"What's going on?" I said, working hard to sound hostile. "How come I swear I can hear your voice in my head? And why did you say you came to school for me?"

"I was tired of admiring your legs from a distance."

"I want the truth." I swallowed hard. "I deserve full disclosure."

"Full disclosure," he repeated with a sly grin. "Does this have anything to do with the promise you made to expose me? What exactly are we talking about here?"

I couldn't remember what we were talking about. All I knew was that Patch's gaze felt especially hot. I had to break eye contact, so I trained my eyes on my hands. They were glistening with sweat, and I slid them behind my back.

"I have to go," I said. "I have homework."

"What happened in there?" He tilted his chin back at the elevators.

"Nothing."

Before I could stop him, he had my palm pressed to his, forming a steeple with our hands. He slid his fingers between mine, locking me to him. "Your knuckles are white," he said, brushing his mouth across them. "And you came out looking worked up."

"Let go. And I'm not worked up. Not really. If you'll excuse me, I have homework—"

"Nora." Patch spoke my name softly, yet with every intention of getting what he wanted.

"I had a fight with Marcie Millar." I had no idea where the confession came from. The last thing I wanted was to give Patch another window inside me. "Okay?" I said, pushing a note of exasperation into my voice. "Satisfied? Will you please let go now?"

"Marcie Millar?"

I tried to unlace my fingers, but Patch had a different idea.

"You don't know Marcie?" I said cynically. "Hard to believe, considering you attend Coldwater High, for one. And you have a Y chromosome, for two."

"Tell me about the fight," he said.

"She called Vee fat."

"And?"

"I called her an anorexic pig."

Patch looked like he was trying not to crack a grin. "That's it? No punches? No biting, clawing, or hair pulling?"

I narrowed a look at him.

"Are we going to have to teach you to fight, Angel?"

"I can fight." I tipped my chin up in spite of the lie.

This time he didn't bother restraining the grin.

"In fact, I've had boxing lessons." Kickboxing. At the gym. Once.

Patch held out his hand as a target. "Give me a shot. Hard as you can."

"I'm—not a fan of senseless violence."

"We're all alone down here." Patch's boots were flush with the toes of my shoes. "A guy like me could take advantage of a girl like you. Better show me what you've got."

I inched backward, and Patch's black motorcycle came into view. "Let me give you a ride," he offered.

"I'll walk."

"It's late, and dark."

He had a point. Whether or not I liked it.

But inwardly, I was caught in a fierce game of tug-of-war. I'd been idiotic to walk home in the first place, and now I was stuck between two bad decisions: ride with Patch, or risk the chance there was someone worse out there.

"I'm starting to think the only reason you keep offering me a ride is because you know how *not* fond I am of this thing." I blew out a jittery sigh, scrunched the helmet on, then swung on behind him. It wasn't entirely my fault that I was snuggled up close to him. The seat wasn't exactly spacious.

Patch made a low sound of amusement. "I can think of a couple other reasons."

He sped down the straightaway of the garage, gunning it toward the exit. A red-and-white-striped traffic arm and an automatic ticket machine barred the exit. I was just wondering if Patch would slow long enough to feed money into the machine, when he brought the bike to a smooth stop, jolting me even closer into him. He fed the machine, then floored the bike up onto the street above.

Patch edged his bike up my driveway, and I held on to him to keep my balance while I climbed off. I handed back the helmet.

"Thanks for the ride," I said.

"What are you doing Saturday night?"

A moment's pause. "I have a date with the usual."

This appeared to spark his interest. "The usual?"

"Homework."

"Cancel."

I was feeling a lot more relaxed. Patch was warm and solid, and he smelled fantastic. Like mint and rich, dark earth. Nobody had jumped out at us on the ride home, and all the windows on the lower level of the farmhouse glowed with light. For the first time all day I felt safe.

Except that Patch had cornered me in a dark tunnel and was possibly stalking me. Maybe not so safe.

"I don't go out with strangers," I said.

"Good thing I do. I'll pick you up at five."

CHAPTER

17

THERE WAS COLD RAIN ALL SATURDAY, AND I SAT NEAR the window watching it pepper down on the growing puddles in the lawn. I had a dog-eared copy of *Hamlet* in my lap, a pen tucked behind my ear, and an empty mug of hot chocolate at my feet. The sheet of reading comprehension questions on the side table was just as white as it had been when Mrs. Lemon passed it out two days ago. Always a bad thing.

My mom had left for yoga class almost thirty minutes ago, and while I'd practiced a few different ways of breaking the news of my date with Patch to her, in the end I'd let her walk out the door without vocalizing any of them. I told myself it was no big deal, I was sixteen and could decide when and why I left the house, but the truth was, I should have told her I was going out. Perfect. Now I was going to be carting around my guilt all night.

When the grandfather clock in the hall chimed to announce 4:30, I gladly tossed aside the book and jogged upstairs to my bedroom. I'd burned through most of the day with homework and chores, and that had kept my mind off tonight's date. But now that I was down to the final minutes, nervous anticipation overruled all. Whether or not I wanted to think about it, Patch and I had unfinished business. Our last kiss got cut short. Sooner or later, the kiss would need resolving. I had no doubt I wanted resolution, I just wasn't sure I was ready for it tonight. On top of all this, it didn't help that Vee's warning kept popping up like a red flag at the back of my mind. *Stay away from Patch.*

I positioned myself in front of the bureau mirror and took inventory. Makeup was minimal, reserved to a sweep of mascara. Too much tumbleweed hair, but what else was new? Lips could use some gloss. I licked my bottom lip, giving it a wet shine. That got me thinking more about my almost-kiss with Patch, and I got an involuntary rush of heat. If an almost-kiss could do that, I wondered what a full-on kiss could do. My reflection smiled.

"No big deal," I told myself while trying on earrings. The first pair was big, loopy, and turquoise . . . and tried too hard. I put them aside and tried again with topaz teardrops. Better. I wondered what Patch had in mind. Dinner? A movie? "It's a lot like a biology study date," I told my reflection nonchalantly. "Only . . . without the biology and studying."

I tugged on matchstick jeans and ballet flats. I wrapped a Hally-blue silk scarf around my waist, up over my torso, then tied the ends behind my neck to fashion a halter-style blouse. I fluffed my hair, and there was a knock at the door.

"Coming!" I hollered down the stairs.

I did one final check in the hall mirror, then opened the front door and found two men in dark trench coats standing on the porch.

"Nora Grey," said Detective Basso, holding up his police badge. "We meet again."

It took a moment to find my voice. "What are you doing here?"

He tipped his head sideways. "You remember my partner, Detective Holstijic. Mind if we step inside and ask you a few questions?" It didn't sound like he was asking permission. In fact, it sounded just this side of a threat.

"What's wrong?" I asked, dividing a glance between them.

"Is your mom home?" Detective Basso asked.

"She's at yoga. Why? What's going on?"

They wiped their feet and stepped inside.

"Can you tell us what happened between you and Marcie Millar at the library Wednesday evening?" Detective Holstijic asked, plunking down on the sofa. Detective Basso remained standing, scrutinizing the family pictures arranged on the mantel.

His words took a moment to register. The library. Wednesday evening. Marcie Millar.

"Is Marcie okay?" I asked. It was no secret I didn't hold a warm, affectionate place in my heart for Marcie. But that didn't mean I wanted her in trouble, or worse, in danger. I especially didn't want her in trouble if it appeared to involve me.

Detective Basso put his hands on his hips. "What makes you think she's not okay?"

"I didn't do anything to Marcie."

"What were the two of you arguing about?" Detective Holstijic asked. "Library security told us things were getting heated."

"It wasn't like that."

"What was it like?"

"We called each other a few names," I said, hoping we could leave it at that.

"What kind of names?"

"Stupid names," I said in retrospect.

"I'm going to need to hear those names, Nora."

"I called her an anorexic pig." My cheeks stung and my voice was humiliated. If the situation hadn't been so serious, I might have wished I'd invented something a lot more cruel and demeaning. Not to mention something that made a little more sense.

The detectives exchanged a look.

"Did you threaten her?" asked Detective Holstijic.

"No."

"Where did you go after the library?"

"Home."

"Did you follow Marcie?"

"No. Like I said, I came home. Are you going to tell me what happened to Marcie?"

"Can anyone vouch for that?" Detective Basso asked.

"My biology partner. He saw me at the library and offered me a ride."

I had a shoulder propped against one side of the French doors leading into the room, and Detective Basso walked over and took up a post on the opposite side, across from me. "Let's hear about this biology partner."

"What kind of question is that?"

He spread his hands. "It's a pretty basic question. But if you want me to get more specific, I can. When I was in high school, I only offered rides to girls I was interested in. Let's carry that a step further. What's your relationship with your bio partner . . . outside the classroom?"

"You're joking, right?"

One side of Detective Basso's mouth hitched up. "That's what I thought. Did you have your boyfriend beat up Marcie Millar?"

"Marcie was beat up?"

He pushed up from the doorway and positioned himself directly in front of me, sharp eyes boring into me. "Did you want to show her what happens when girls like her don't keep their mouths shut? Did you think she deserved to get a little roughed up? I knew girls like Marcie when I went to school. They ask for it, don't they? Was Marcie asking for it, Nora? Someone beat her up pretty bad Wednesday night, and I think you know more than you're saying."

I was working hard to suppress my thoughts, afraid they might somehow show on my face. Maybe it was a coincidence that on the same night I complained to Patch about Marcie, she took a beating. Then again, maybe it wasn't.

"We're going to need to talk to your boyfriend," Detective Holstijic said.

"He's not my boyfriend. He's my biology partner."

"Is he on his way here now?"

I knew I should be up-front. But on further reflection, I could not accept that Patch would hurt Marcie. Marcie wasn't the nicest person, and she'd acquired more than a handful of enemies. A few of those enemies might be capable of brutality, but Patch wasn't one of them. Senseless beating wasn't his style. "No," I said.

Detective Basso gave a stiff smile. "All dressed up for a Saturday night in?"

"Something like that," I said in the coldest tone I dared.

Detective Holstijic pulled a small notepad out of his coat pocket, flipped it open, and clicked his pen. "We're going to need his name and number."

Ten minutes after the detectives left, a black Jeep Commander rolled to the curb. Patch jogged through the rain to the porch, wearing dark jeans, boots, and a thermal gray T-shirt.

"New car?" I asked after I opened the door.

He gave me a mysterious smile. "I won it a couple nights ago off a game of pool."

"Someone bet their car?"

"He wasn't happy about it. I'm trying to stay clear of dark alleys for the next little while."

"Did you hear about Marcie Millar?" I threw it out there, hoping the question would take him by surprise.

"No. What's up?" His answer came easily, and I decided it probably meant he was telling the truth. Unfortunately, when it came to telling lies, Patch didn't strike me as an amateur.

"Someone beat her up."

"A shame."

"Any idea who might have done it?"

If Patch heard the concern in my voice, he didn't show it. He leaned back against the porch railing and rubbed a hand thoughtfully across his jaw. "Nope."

I asked myself if I thought he was hiding something. But reading lies wasn't a strong point of mine. I didn't have a lot of experience. Typically I hung around people I trusted . . . typically.

Patch parked the Jeep behind Bo's Arcade. When we got to the front of the line, the cashier laid eyes first on Patch, then on me. Back and forth they went, trying to make a connection.

"What's up?" Patch said, and put three tens on the counter.

The cashier trained his watchful stare on me. He'd noticed that I couldn't stop staring at the moldy-green tattoos covering every available inch of skin on his forearms. He moved a wad of gum? tobacco? to the other side of his bottom lip and said, "You looking at something?"

"I like your tat—," I began. He bared pointed dog teeth.

"I don't think he likes me," I whispered to Patch when we were a safe distance away.

"Bo doesn't like anybody."

"That's Bo of Bo's Arcade?"

"That's Bo Junior of Bo's Arcade. Bo Senior died a few years ago."

"How?" I asked.

"Bar brawl. Downstairs."

I felt an overwhelming desire to run back to the Jeep and peel out of the lot.

"Are we safe?" I asked.

Patch slanted a look sideways. "Angel."

"Just asking."

Downstairs, the pool hall looked exactly like it had the first night I'd come. Cinder-block walls painted black. Red felt pool tables at the center of the room. Poker tables scattered around the fringe. Low track lighting curving across the ceiling. The congested smell of cigar smoke clogging the air.

Patch chose the table farthest from the stairs. He retrieved two

7UPs from the bar and popped their caps on the edge of the counter.

"I've never played pool before," I confessed.

"Choose a cue." He motioned to the rack of pool sticks mounted on the wall. I lifted one down and carried it back to the pool table.

Patch wiped a hand down his mouth to erase a smile.

"What?" I said.

"Can't hit a home run in pool."

I nodded. "No home runs. Got it."

His smiled stretched. "You're holding your cue like a bat."

I looked down at my hands. He was right. I *was* holding it like a bat. "It feels comfortable this way."

He moved behind me, put his hands on my hips, and positioned me in front of the table. He slid his arms around me and took hold of the pool stick.

"Like this," he said, repositioning my right hand up several inches. "And . . . this," he went on, taking my left hand and forming a circle with my thumb and index finger. Then he planted my left hand on the pool table, like a tripod. He pushed the tip of the pool stick through the circle and over the knuckle of my middle finger. "Bend at the waist."

I leaned into the pool table, with Patch's breath warming my neck. He pulled back on the pool stick, and it glided through the circle.

"Which ball do you want to hit?" he asked, referring to the

triangle of balls arranged at the far end of the table. "The yellow one in front's a good choice."

"Red's my favorite color."

"Red it is."

Patch drew the stick back and forth through the circle, aiming at the cue ball, practicing my stroke.

I squinted at the cue ball, then at the triangle of balls farther down the table. "You're a tiny bit off," I said.

I felt him smile. "How much you want to bet?"

"Five dollars."

I felt him give a soft shake of his head. "Your jacket."

"You want my jacket?"

"I want it off."

My arm jerked forward, and the pool stick shot through my fingers, ramming the cue ball. In turn, the cue ball shot forward, impacted with the solid red, and shattered the triangle, balls ricocheting in all directions.

"Okay," I said, shucking off my jean jacket, "maybe I'm a little bit impressed."

Patch examined my silk-scarf-slash-halter. His eyes were as black as a midnight ocean, his expression contemplative. "Nice," he said. Then he moved around the table, scrutinizing the layout of balls.

"Five dollars says you can't sink the blue striped one," I said, selecting it purposely; it was shielded from the white cue ball by a mass of colorful balls.

"I don't want your money," Patch said. Our eyes locked, and the tiniest dimple surfaced in his cheek.

My internal temperature rose another degree.

"What do you want?" I asked.

Patch lowered his pool stick to the table, took one practice stroke, and drilled the cue ball. The momentum of the cue ball transferred to the solid green, then to the eight ball, and punched the striped blue into a pocket.

I gave a nervous laugh and tried to cover it up by cracking my knuckles, a bad habit I never succumbed to. "Okay, maybe I'm more than a little impressed."

Patch was still bent over the table, and he looked up at me. The look warmed my skin.

"We never agreed on a bet," I said, resisting the urge to shift my weight. The pool stick felt a little slick in my hands, and I discreetly wiped a hand on my thigh.

As if I wasn't already sweating enough, Patch said, "You owe me. Someday I'll come to collect."

I laughed, but it wasn't quite on pitch. "You wish."

Footsteps barreled down the stairs across the room. A tall, stringy guy with a hawk nose and shaggy blue-black hair appeared at the bottom. He looked at Patch first, then shifted his gaze to me. A slow grin appeared, and he strode over and tipped back my 7UP, which I'd left on the rim of the pool table.

"Excuse me, I believe that's—," I began.

"You didn't tell me she was so soft on the eyes," he said to Patch, wiping his mouth with the back of his hand. He spoke with a heavy Irish accent.

"I didn't tell her how hard you are on them either," Patch returned, his mouth at the relaxed stage just before a grin.

The guy backed up against the pool table beside me and stuck his hand out sideways. "The name's Rixon, love," he told me.

I reluctantly slid my hand into his. "Nora."

"Am I interrupting something here?" Rixon said, dividing an inquiring look between me and Patch.

"No," I said at the same time Patch said, "Yes."

Suddenly Rixon lunged playfully at Patch, and the two dropped to the floor, rolling and throwing punches. There was the sound of husky laughter, fists laying into flesh, and fabric tearing, and Patch's bare back came into view. Two thick gashes ran the length of it. They started near his kidneys and ended at his shoulder blades, widening to form an upside-down V. The gashes were so grotesque I almost gasped in horror.

"Aye, get off me!" Rixon bellowed.

Patch swung off him, and as he got to his feet, his torn shirt fluttered open. He sloughed it off and tossed it into the trash can in the corner. "Give me your shirt," he told Rixon.

Rixon directed a wicked wink at me. "What do you think, Nora? Should we give him a shirt?"

Patch made a playful lunge forward, and Rixon's hands flew up to his shoulders.

"Easy now," he said, backing up. He peeled off his sweatshirt and tossed it at Patch, revealing a fitted white tee underneath.

As Patch rolled the sweatshirt down over abs hard enough to put a flutter in my stomach, Rixon turned to me. "He told you how he got his nickname, didn't he?"

"Sorry?"

"Before our good friend Patch here got mixed up in pool, the lad favored Irish bare-knuckle boxing. Wasn't very good at it." Rixon wagged his head. "Truth be told, he was downright pathetic. I spent most nights patching him up, and soon after, everyone started calling him Patch. Told him to give up boxing, but he wouldn't listen."

Patch caught my eye and passed me a gold-medal bar-fight grin. The grin alone was scary enough, but under the rough exterior, it held a note of desire. More than a note, actually. A whole symphony of desire.

Patch tipped his head at the stairs and held his hand out to me. "Let's get out of here," he said.

"Where are we going?" I asked, my stomach tumbling to my knees.

"You'll see."

As we ascended the stairs, Rixon called out to me, "Good luck with that one, love!"

CHAPTER

18

ON THE DRIVE BACK, PATCH TOOK THE TOPSHAM EXIT
and parked alongside the historic Topsham paper
mill sitting on the bank of the Androscoggin River.
At one point, the mill had been used to turn tree pulp into paper.
Now a big sign across the side of the building read SEA DOG BREWING
CO. The river was wide and choppy, with mature trees shooting up
on both sides.

It was still raining hard, and night had settled down around us. I had to beat my mom home. I hadn't told her I was going out because . . . well, the honest truth was, Patch wasn't the kind of guy mothers smiled on. He was the kind of guy they changed the house locks for.

"Can we get takeout?" I asked.

Patch opened the driver's-side door. "Any requests?"

"A turkey sandwich. But no pickles. Oh, and no mayonnaise."

I could tell I'd earned one of his smiles that never quite made it to the surface. I seemed to earn a lot of those. This time, I couldn't figure out what I'd said.

"I'll see what I can do," he said, sliding out.

Patch left the keys in the ignition and the heater pumping. For the first couple of minutes, I replayed our evening so far in my mind. And then it dawned on me that I was alone in Patch's Jeep. His private space.

If I were Patch, and I wanted to hide something highly secretive, I wouldn't hide it in my room, my school locker, or even my backpack, all of which could be confiscated or searched without warning. I'd hide it in my shiny black Jeep with the sophisticated alarm system.

I unbuckled my seat belt and rummaged through the stack of textbooks near my feet, feeling a mysterious smile creep to my mouth at the thought of uncovering one of Patch's secrets. I wasn't expecting to find anything in particular; I would have settled for the combination to his locker or his cell phone number. Toeing around old school assignments cluttering the floor mats, I found a faded pine-scented air freshener, an AC/DC *Highway to Hell* CD, pencil stubs, and a receipt from the 7-Eleven dated Wednesday at 10:18 p.m. Nothing especially surprising or revealing.

I popped open the glove compartment and sifted through the operating manual and other official documents. There was a gleam of chrome, and my fingertips brushed metal. I pulled out a steel flashlight and turned it on, but nothing happened. I unscrewed the bottom, thinking the flashlight felt a little light, and sure enough, there were no batteries. I wondered why Patch kept a nonworking flashlight stored in his glove compartment. It was the last thought I had before my eyes homed in on the rusty liquid that had dried at one end of the flashlight.

Blood.

Very carefully, I returned the flashlight to the glove compartment and shut it out of sight. I told myself there were lots of things that would leave blood on a flashlight. Like holding it with an injured hand, using it to push a dead animal to the side of the road . . . swinging it with force against a body repeatedly until it broke skin.

With my heart thundering, I jumped on the first conclusion that presented itself. Patch had lied. He'd attacked Marcie. He'd dropped me off Wednesday evening, traded his motorcycle for the Jeep, and gone out looking for her. Or maybe their paths had intersected by chance and he'd acted on impulse. Either way, Marcie was hurt, the police were involved, and Patch was guilty.

Rationally, I knew it was a quick draw and a big leap, but emotionally, the stakes were too high to step back and think it over. Patch had a frightening past and many, many secrets. If brutal and senseless violence was one of them, I wasn't safe riding around alone with him.

A flash of distant lightning brightened the horizon. Patch exited the restaurant and jogged across the parking lot holding a brown bag in one hand and two sodas in the other. He went around to the driver's side and ducked inside the Jeep. He lifted his ball cap and scrubbed rain out of his hair. Dark waves flipped up everywhere. He handed me the brown bag. "One turkey sandwich, hold the mayo and pickles, and something to wash it down."

"Did you attack Marcie Millar?" I asked quietly. "I want the truth—now."

Patch lowered his 7UP from his mouth. His eyes sliced into mine. "What?"

"The flashlight in your glove compartment. Explain it."

"You went through my glove compartment?" He didn't sound annoyed, but he didn't sound pleased, either.

"The flashlight has dried blood on it. The police came to my house earlier. They think I'm involved. Marcie was attacked Wednesday night, right after I told you how much I can't stand her."

Patch gave a curt laugh, minus the humor. "You think I used the flashlight to beat up Marcie."

He reached behind his seat and dragged out a large gun. I screamed.

He leaned over and sealed my mouth with his hand. "Paintball gun," he said. His tone had chilled.

I divided looks between the gun and Patch, feeling a lot of white showing around my eyes.

"I played paintball earlier this week," he said. "I thought we went over this."

"Th-that doesn't explain the blood on the flashlight."

"Not blood," he said, "paint. We were playing Capture the Flag."

My eyes shifted back to the glove compartment storing the flashlight. The flashlight was . . . the flag. A mix of relief, idiocy, and guilt at accusing Patch swam through me. "Oh," I said lamely. "I'm—sorry." But it seemed a little too late for sorry.

Patch stared straight ahead through the windshield, his breathing deep. I wondered if he was using the silence to let go of a little steam. I had just accused him of assault, after all. I felt terrible about it, but my mind was too rattled to come up with the right apology.

"From your description of Marcie, it sounds like she's probably racked up a few enemies," he said.

"I'm pretty sure Vee and I top the list," I said, trying to lighten the mood, but not entirely joking, either.

Patch pulled up to the farmhouse and killed the engine. His ball cap was low over his eyes, but now his mouth held the suggestion of a smile. His lips looked soft and smooth, and I was having a hard time averting my eyes. Most of all, I was grateful he seemed to have forgiven me.

"We're going to have to work on your pool game, Angel," Patch said.

"Speaking of pool." I cleared my throat. "I'd like to know when and how you're going to collect on that . . . thing I owe you."

"Not tonight." His eyes watched mine closely, judging my response. I was caught between an easing of my mind and disappointment. But mostly disappointment.

"I have something for you," Patch said. He reached under his seat and pulled out a white paper bag with red chili peppers printed across it. A to-go bag from the Borderline. He set it between us.

"What's this for?" I asked, peeking inside the bag, having absolutely no idea as to what might be inside.

"Open it."

I pulled a brown cardboard box out of the to-go bag and lifted the lid. Inside was a snow globe with a miniature Delphic Seaport Amusement Park captured inside. Brass wires were bent roughly into a circle for the Ferris wheel and twisting loops for the roller coaster; flat sheets of tarnished metal formed the Magic Carpet ride.

"It's beautiful," I said, a little astonished that Patch had thought of me, let alone gone to the trouble of buying me a present. "Thank you. I mean it. I love it."

He touched the curved glass. "There's the Archangel, before it was remodeled." Behind the Ferris wheel a thin wire ribboned to form the hills and valleys of the Archangel. An angel with broken wings stood at the highest point, bowing his head, gazing down without eyes. "What really happened the night we rode it together?" I asked.

"You don't want to know."

"If you tell me you'll have to kill me?" I half joked.

"We're not alone," Patch answered, looking through the windshield.

I glanced up and caught my mom standing in the open doorway. To my horror, she stepped out and walked toward the Jeep.

"Let me do all the talking," I said, stuffing the snow globe back in the box. "Don't say a word—not one word!"

Patch hopped out and came around for my door. We met my mom halfway up the driveway.

"I didn't know you were going out," she told me, smiling, but not in a relaxed way. It was a smile that said, We'll talk later.

"It was sort of last minute," I explained.

"I came home right after yoga," she said. The rest was implied. Lucky for me, not so lucky for you. I'd been counting on her going out for smoothies with her friends after class. Nine times out of ten, she did. She turned her attention to Patch. "It's nice to finally meet you. Apparently my daughter's a big fan."

I opened my mouth to give an extremely concise introduction

and send Patch on his way, but Mom beat me to it. "I'm Nora's mom. Blythe Grey."

"This is Patch," I said, racking my brain for something to say that would bring the pleasantries to an abrupt halt. But the only things I could think of were screaming Fire! or faking a seizure. Somehow, both seemed more humiliating than braving a conversation between Patch and my mom.

"Nora tells me you're a swimmer," Mom said.

I felt Patch shake with laughter beside me. "A swimmer?"

"Are you on the school swim team, or is it a city league?"

"More . . . recreational," said Patch, passing me a questioning glance.

"Well recreational is good too," Mom said. "Where do you swim? The rec center?"

"I'm more of an outdoor guy. Rivers and lakes."

"Isn't that cold?" asked Mom.

At my side, Patch jerked. I wondered what I'd missed. Nothing about the conversation seemed out of the ordinary. And I had to side with my mom on this one. Maine was not a warm, tropical place. Outdoor swimming was cold, even in the summertime. If Patch really was swimming outdoors, he was either crazy or he had a high pain threshold.

"All right!" I said, taking advantage of the lull. "Patch needs to get going." Go! I mouthed at him.

"That's a very nice Jeep," Mom said. "Did your parents buy it for you?"

"I got it myself."

"You must have quite a job."

"I bus tables at the Borderline."

Patch was saying as little as possible, keeping himself carefully shadowed in mystery. I wondered what his life was like when he wasn't around me. At the way back of my mind, I couldn't stop thinking about his frightening past. Up until now I'd fantasized about discovering his deep, dark secrets because I wanted to prove to myself and to Patch that I was capable of figuring him out. But now I wanted to know his secrets because they were a part of him. And despite the fact that I routinely tried to deny it, I felt something for him. The more time I spent with him, the more I knew the feelings weren't going away.

Mom frowned. "I hope work doesn't get in the way of studying. Personally, I don't believe high school students should work during the school year. You have enough on your plates already."

Patch smiled. "It hasn't been a problem."

"Mind if I ask your GPA?" Mom said. "Is that too rude?"

"Gee, it's getting late—," I began loudly, consulting the watch I didn't wear. I couldn't believe my mom was being so uncool about this. It was a bad sign. It could only mean her first impression of Patch was worse than I'd feared. This wasn't an introduction. It was an interview.

"Two-point-two," Patch said.

My mom stared at him.

"He's joking," I said quickly. I gave Patch a discreet push in the direction of the Jeep. "Patch has things to do. Places to go. Pool to play—" I clamped a hand over my mouth.

"Play?" my mom said, sounding confused.

"Nora's referring to Bo's Arcade," Patch explained. "But that's not where I'm headed. I've got a few errands to run."

"I've never been to Bo's," she said.

"It's not all that exciting," I said. "You're not missing anything."

"Wait," said Mom, sounding a lot like a red flag had just sprung up in her memory. "Is it out on the coast? Close to Delphic Seaport? Wasn't there a shootout at Bo's several years ago?"

"It's tamer than it used to be," Patch said. I narrowed my eyes at him. He'd beaten me to the punch. I'd planned on outright lying about Bo's having any history of violence.

"Would you like to come in for ice cream?" Mom asked, sounding flustered, caught between doing the polite thing and acting on the impulse to drag me inside and bolt the door. "We only have vanilla," she added to sour the deal. "It's a few weeks old."

Patch shook his head. "I've got to get going. Maybe next time. It was nice meeting you, Blythe."

I took the break in conversation as my cue and pulled my mom toward the front door, relieved that the conversation hadn't been as bad as it could have been. Suddenly Mom turned back.

"What did you and Nora do tonight?" she asked Patch.

Patch looked at me and raised his eyebrows ever so slightly.

"We grabbed dinner in Topsham," I answered quickly. "Sandwiches and sodas. Purely harmless night."

The trouble was, my feelings for Patch weren't harmless.

CHAPTER

19

I LEFT THE SNOW GLOBE IN ITS BOX AND TUCKED it inside my closet behind a stack of argyle sweaters I'd poached from my dad. When I'd opened the present in front of Patch, Delphic had looked shimmery and beautiful, light swirling rainbows from the wires. But alone in my bedroom, the amusement park looked haunted. A camp ideal for disembodied spirits. And I wasn't entirely sure there wasn't a hidden camera inside.

After changing into a stretchy camisole and floral pj pants, I called Vee.

"Well?" she said. "How'd it go? Obviously he didn't kill you, so that's a good start."

"We played pool."

"You hate pool."

"He gave me a few pointers. Now that I know what I'm doing, it's not so bad."

"I bet he could give you pointers in a few other areas of your life."

"Hmm." Normally, her comment might have incited at least a flush from me, but my mood was too serious. I was hard at work, thinking.

"I know I've said this before, but Patch doesn't instill a deep sense of comfort in me," Vee said. "I still have nightmares about the guy in the ski mask. In one of my nightmares, he ripped off his mask, and guess who was hiding under it? Patch. Personally, I think you should treat him like a loaded gun. Something about him isn't normal."

This was exactly what I wanted to talk about.

"What would cause someone to have a V-shaped scar on their back?" I asked her.

There was a moment of silence.

"Freak," Vee choked. "You saw him naked? Where did it happen? His Jeep? His house? Your bedroom?"

"I did not see him naked! It was sort of an accident."

"Uh-huh, I've heard that excuse before," said Vee.

"He had a huge, upside down V-shaped scar on his back. Isn't that a little weird?"

"Of course it's weird. But this is Patch we're talking about. He has a few screws loose. I'm going to take a wild guess and say . . . gang fight? Prison scars? Skid marks from a hit-and-run?"

One half of my brain was keeping track of my conversation with Vee, but the other, more subconscious half had strayed. My memory went back to the night Patch dared me to ride the Archangel. I recaptured the creepy and bizarre paintings on the side of the cars. I remembered the horned beasts ripping the wings off the angel. I remembered the black upside-down V where the angel's wings used to be.

I almost dropped the phone.

"S-sorry, what?" I asked Vee when I realized she'd carried the conversation further and was waiting for my response.

"What. Happened. Next?" she repeated, enunciating each word. "Earth to Nora. I need details. I'm dying here."

"He got in a fight and his shirt ripped. End of story. There's no what-happened-next."

Vee sucked in a breath. "This is what I'm talking about. The two of you are out together . . . and he gets in a fight? What's his problem? It's like he's more animal than human."

In my mind I switched back and forth between the painting of the angel's scars and Patch's scars. Both scars had healed to the color of black licorice, both ran from the shoulder blades to the kidneys, and both curved out as they traveled the length of the back. I told myself there was a good chance it was merely a very creepy coincidence that the paintings on the Archangel depicted Patch's scars perfectly. I told myself a lot of things could cause scars like Patch's. Gang fight, prison scars, skid marks—just like Vee said. Unfortunately, all the excuses felt like lies. Like the truth was staring me in the face, but I wasn't brave enough to look back.

"Was he an angel?" Vee asked.

I snapped to myself. "What?"

"Was he an angel, or did he live up to his bad-boy image? Because, honestly? I'm not buying this whole he-didn't-try-anything version of the story."

"Vee? I have to go." My voice was strewn with cobwebs.

"I see how it is. You're going to hang up before I get the details on the big shebang."

"Nothing happened on the date, and nothing happened after. My mom met us in the driveway."

"Shut up!"

"I don't think she likes Patch."

"You don't say!" Vee said. "Who'd have guessed?"

"I'll call you tomorrow, okay?"

"Sweet dreams, babe."

Fat chance, I thought.

After I got off the phone with Vee, I walked down the hall to my mom's makeshift home office and booted up our vintage IBM. The room was small, with a pitched roof, more of a gable than a room. One greasy window with faded orange curtains from the 1970s looked out at the side yard. I could stand up to my full height in about 30 percent of the room. In the other 70 percent, the top of my hair brushed the exposed beams of the rafters. A single bare bulb hung there.

Ten minutes later the computer secured a dial-up connection to the Internet, and I typed "angel wing scars" into the Google search bar. I hovered with my finger above the enter key, afraid that if I went through with it, I'd have to admit I was actually considering the possibility that Patch was—well, not . . . human.

I hit enter and mouse-clicked on the first link before I could talk myself out of it.

FALLEN ANGELS: THE FRIGHTENING TRUTH

At the creation of the Garden of Eden, heavenly angels were dispatched to Earth to watch over Adam and Eve. Soon, however, some angels set their sights on the world beyond the garden walls. They saw themselves as future rulers over the Earth's population, lusting after power, money, and even human women.

Together they tempted and convinced Eve to eat the forbidden fruit, opening the gates guarding

Eden. As punishment for this grave sin and for deserting their duties, God stripped the angels' wings and banished them to Earth forever.

I skimmed down a few paragraphs, my heart beating erratically.

Fallen angels are the same evil spirits (or demons) described in the Bible as taking possession of human bodies. Fallen angels roam the Earth looking for human bodies to harass and control. They tempt humans to do evil by communicating thoughts and images directly to their minds. If a fallen angel succeeds in turning a human toward evil, it can enter the human's body and influence his or her personality and actions.

However, the possession of a human body by a fallen angel can take place only during the Hebrew month of Cheshvan. Cheshvan, known as "the bitter month," is the only month without any Jewish holidays or fasts, making it an unholy month. Between new and full moons during Cheshvan, fallen angels invade human bodies in droves.

My stare lingered on the computer monitor a few minutes after I finished reading. I had no thoughts. None. Just a complexity of emotions tangling inside me. Cold, panicky amazement and fore-boding among them.

An involuntary shudder roused me to my senses. I remembered the few times I was certain Patch had breached normal communication methods and whispered directly to my mind, just like the article claimed fallen angels could. Comparing this information with Patch's scars, was it possible . . . could Patch be a fallen angel? Did he want to possess my body?

I browsed quickly through the rest of the article, slowing when I read something even more bizarre.

Fallen angels who have a sexual relationship with a human produce superhuman offspring called Nephilim. The Nephilim race is an evil and unnatural race and was never meant to inhabit Earth. Although many believe the Great Flood at the time of Noah was intended to cleanse the Earth of Nephilim, we have no way of knowing if this hybrid race died out and whether or not fallen angels have continued to reproduce with humans since that time. It seems logical that they would, which means the Nephilim race is likely on the Earth today.

I pushed back from the desk. I crammed everything I'd read into a mental folder and filed it away. And stamped SCARY on the outside of the folder. I didn't want to think about it right now. I'd sort through it later. Maybe.

My cell phone buzzed in my pocket and I jumped.

"Did we decide avocados are green or yellow?" Vee asked. "I've already filled all my green fruit slots today, but if you tell me avocados are yellow, I'm in business."

"Do you believe in superheroes?"

"After seeing Tobey Maguire in *Spider-Man*, yes. And then there's Christian Bale. Older, but killer hot. I'd let him rescue me from sword-wielding ninjas."

"I'm being serious."

"So am I."

"When was the last time you went to church?" I asked.

I heard her pop a gum bubble. "Sunday."

"Do you think the Bible is accurate? I mean, do you think it's real?"

"I think Pastor Calvin is hot. In a fortysomething way. That pretty much sums up my religious conviction."

After I hung up, I went to my room and slid under the covers. I threw on an extra blanket to ward off the sudden chill. Whether the room was cold, or the icy feeling originated inside me, I wasn't sure. Haunting words like "fallen angel," "human possession," and "Nephilim" danced me off to sleep.

CHAPTER 20

I TOSSED ALL NIGHT. THE WIND GUSTED THROUGH THE OPEN fields rimming the farmhouse, spraying debris against the windows. I woke several times, hearing shingles being pulled from the roof and tumbling over the edge. Every small noise from the rattle of the windowpanes to my own creaking bedsprings had me jumping out of sleep.

Around six I gave up, dragged myself out of bed, and padded down the hall for a hot shower. Next I cleaned my room—my closet was looking slim, and sure enough, I filled the hamper with three loads of laundry. I was climbing the stairs with a fresh load when a knock sounded at the front door. I opened it to find Elliot standing on the doorstep.

He wore jeans, a vintage plaid shirt rolled to the elbows, sunglasses, and a Red Sox cap. On the outside, he looked all-American. But I knew better, and a jolt of nervous adrenaline confirmed it.

"Nora Grey," Elliot said in a patronizing voice. He leaned in and grinned, and I caught the sour tang of alcohol on his breath. "You've been causing me a lot of trouble lately."

"What are you doing here?"

He peered behind me into the house. "What's it look like I'm doing? I want to talk. Don't I get to come in?"

"My mom's asleep. I don't want to wake her."

"I've never met your mom." Something about the way he said it made the hairs on the back of my neck stand tall.

"I'm sorry, do you need something?"

His smile was half sloppy, half sneering. "You don't like me, do you, Nora Grey?"

By way of answer, I folded my arms across my chest.

He staggered back a step with his hand pressed to his heart. "Ouch. I'm here, Nora, as a last-ditch effort to convince you that I'm an average guy and you can trust me. Don't let me down."

"Listen, Elliot, I have a few things I need to—"

He drilled his fist into the house, smacking his knuckles against the siding hard enough to shake loose chipped paint. "I'm not finished!" he slurred in a heated voice. Suddenly he tipped his head back and laughed quietly. He bent over and placed his bleeding hand between his knees and groaned. "Ten dollars says I'm going to regret that later."

Elliot's presence made my skin crawl. I remembered back several days, when I actually thought he was good-looking and charming. I wondered why I'd been such an idiot.

I was contemplating closing the door and locking it, when Elliot pulled off his sunglasses, revealing bloodshot eyes. He cleared his throat, his voice coming out straightforward. "I came here because I wanted to tell you Jules is under a lot of stress at school. Exams, student government, scholarship applications, yadda, yadda, yadda. He's not acting like himself. He needs to get away from it all for a few days. The four of us—Jules, me, you, Vee—should go camping for spring break. Leave tomorrow for Powder Horn and come back Tuesday afternoon. It'll give Jules a chance to decompress." Every word that came out of his mouth sounded eerily and carefully rehearsed.

"Sorry, I already have plans."

"Let me change your mind. I'll plan the whole trip. I'll get the tents, the food. I'll show you what a great guy I am. I'll show you a good time."

"I think you should leave."

Elliot leaned his hand on the doorjamb, bending toward me.

BECCA FITZPATRICK

"Wrong answer." For a fleeting moment, the glassy stupor in his eyes disappeared, something twisted and sinister eclipsing it. I involuntarily stepped back. I was almost positive Elliot had it in him to kill. I was almost positive Kjirsten's death was on his hands.

"Leave, or I'm calling a cab," I said.

Elliot flung the screen door open so hard it smacked back against the house. He grabbed the front of my bathrobe and yanked me outside. Then he shoved me back against the siding and pinned me there with his body. "You're coming camping whether you want to or not."

"Get off me!" I said, twisting away from him.

"Or what? What are you going to do?" He had me by the shoulders now, and he knocked me back against the house again, rattling my teeth.

"I'll call the police." I had no idea how I said it so bravely. My breathing was rapid and shallow, my hands clammy.

"Are you going to shout for them? They can't hear you. The only way I'm letting you go is if you swear to go camping."

"Nora?"

Elliot and I both turned toward the front door, where my mom's voice carried out. Elliot kept his hands on me a moment longer, then made a disgusted noise and shoved me away. Halfway down the porch steps, he looked over his shoulder. "This isn't over."

I hurried inside and locked the door. My eyes started to burn. I dragged my back down the length of the door and sat on the entry rug, fighting the urge to sob.

My mom appeared at the top of the stairs, cinching her robe at the waist. "Nora? What's wrong? Who was at the door?"

I blinked my eyes dry in a hurry. "A guy from school." I couldn't keep the waver out of my voice. "He—he—" I was already in enough trouble over my date with Patch. I knew my mom was planning to attend a wedding and reception tonight for the daughter of a friend from work, but if I told her Elliot had roughed me up, there was no way she'd go. And that was the last thing I wanted, because I needed to drive to Portland and investigate Elliot. Even a sliver of incriminating evidence might be enough to put him behind bars, and until that happened, I wouldn't feel safe. I sensed a certain violence escalating inside him, and I didn't want to see what would happen if it blew out of control. "He wanted my *Hamlet* notes," I said flatly. "Last week he cheated off my quiz, and apparently he's trying to make a habit of it."

"Oh, honey." She came down beside me, stroking my damp hair, which had chilled since my shower. "I can understand why you're upset. I can call his parents if you'd like."

I shook my head.

"Then I'll make breakfast," Mom said. "Go finish dressing. I'll have everything ready by the time you come down."

I was standing in front of my closet when my cell phone rang.

"Did you hear? The four of us are going c-a-m-p-i-n-g for

BECCA FITZPATRICK

spring break!" said Vee, sounding bizarrely cheerful.

"Vee," I said, my voice trembling, "Elliot's planning something. Something scary. The only reason he wants to go camping is so he can get us alone. We're not going."

"What do you mean we're not going? This is a joke, right? I mean, we finally get to do something exciting over spring break, and you're saying no? You know my mom will never let me go alone. I'll do anything. Seriously. I'll do your homework for a week. Come on, Nora. One little word. Say it. It starts with the letter Y. . . ."

The hand holding my cell quivered, and I brought up my other hand to steady it. "Elliot showed up at my house fifteen minutes ago, drunk. He—he physically threatened me."

She was quiet a moment. "What do you mean by 'physically threatened'?"

"He dragged me out the front door and shoved me against the house."

"But he was drunk, right?"

"Does it matter?" I snapped

"Well, he has a lot going on. I mean, he was wrongly accused of being messed up in some girl's suicide, and he was forced to switch schools. If he hurt you—and I'm not justifying what he did, by the way—maybe he just needs . . . counseling, you know?"

"If he hurt me?"

"He was wasted. Maybe—maybe he didn't know what he was doing. Tomorrow he's going to feel horrible."

I opened my mouth, shut it. I couldn't believe Vee was siding with Elliot. "I have to go," I said curtly. "I'll talk to you later."

"Can I be completely honest, babe? I know you're worried about this guy in the ski mask. Don't hate me, but I think the only reason you're trying so hard to pin it on Elliot is because you don't want it to be Patch. You're rationalizing everything, and it's freaking me out."

I was speechless. "Rationalizing? Patch didn't show up at my door this morning and slam me against my house."

"You know what? I shouldn't have brought it up. Let's just drop it, okay?"

"Fine," I said stiffly.

"So . . . what are you doing today?"

I poked my head out the door, listening for my mom. The sound of a whisk scraping the side of a bowl carried up from the kitchen. Part of me didn't see the point in sharing anything else with Vee, but another part of me felt resentful and confrontational. She wanted to know my plans? Fine by me. It wasn't my problem if she didn't like them. "I'm driving to Portland as soon as my mom leaves for a wedding at Old Orchard Beach." The wedding started at 4 p.m., and with the reception following, my mom wouldn't get home until 9 p.m. at the earliest. Which gave me enough time to spend the evening in Portland, and beat her home. "Actually, I was wondering if maybe I could borrow the Neon. I don't want my mom to see the miles I put on my car."

"Oh, boy. You're going to spy on Elliot, aren't you? You're going to snoop around Kinghorn."

"I'm going to do a little shopping and grab dinner," I said, sliding hangers down the rack in my closet. I pulled out a long-sleeved tissue tee, jeans, and a pink-and-white-striped beanie I reserved for bad-hair days and weekends.

"And would grabbing dinner include stopping by a certain diner located a few blocks from Kinghorn Prep? A diner where Kjirsten what's-her-name used to work?"

"That's not a bad idea," I said. "Maybe I will."

"And are you going to actually eat, or just interrogate the workers?"

"I might ask a few questions. Do I get the Neon or not?"

"Of course you do," she said. "What are best friends for? I'll even come with you on this doomed little tromp. But first you have to promise you'll go camping."

"Never mind. I'll take the bus."

"We'll talk about spring break later!" Vee called into the phone before I was able to disconnect.

I'd been to Portland on several occasions, but I didn't know the city well. I stepped off the bus armed with my cell, a map, and my own inner compass. The buildings were redbrick, tall and slender, blocking the setting sun, which blazed out from below a thick stretch of storm clouds, settling the streets under a canopy of shadow. The storefronts all had verandas and quaint signs extending over the doors. The streets were lit by black witch-hat lamps. After several blocks, the congested streets opened up to a wooded area, and I saw a sign for Kinghorn Prep. A cathedral, steeple, and clock tower peered above the treetops.

I stayed on the sidewalk and rounded the corner onto 32nd Street. The harbor was only a few blocks away, and I caught glimpses of boats passing behind the shops as they came in to dock. Halfway down 32nd Street, I saw a sign for Blind Joe's diner. I pulled my interview questions out and read them over one last time. The plan wasn't to look like I was holding an official interview. I hoped that if I casually broached the subject of Kjirsten with the employees, I could tease out something the handful of reporters before me had somehow missed. Hoping the questions were stored to memory, I underhanded the list into the nearest trash can.

The door chimed when I entered.

The floor was yellow and white tile, and the booths were uphol-stered in nautical blue. Pictures of the harbor hung on the walls. I sat in a booth close to the door and shrugged out of my coat.

A waitress in a stained white apron appeared beside me. "Name's Whitney," she told me in a sour voice. "Welcome to Blind Joe's. Special today is the tuna fish sandwich. Soup of the day's lobster chowder." Her pen was poised to take my order.

"Blind Joe's?" I frowned and tapped my chin. "Why does that name sound so familiar?"

BECCA FITZPATRICK

"Don't you read the paper? We were in the news for a week straight last month. Fifteen minutes and all that."

"Oh!" I said with sudden clarity. "Now I remember. There was a murder, right? Didn't the girl work here?"

"That would be Kjirsten Halverson." She clicked her pen impatiently. "Want me to bring out a bowl of that chowder to start?"

I didn't want lobster chowder. In fact, I wasn't remotely hungry. "That must have been hard. Were the two of you friends?"

"Hell, no. You going to order or what? I'll let you in on a little secret. I don't work, I don't get paid. I don't get paid, I don't make rent."

Suddenly I wished the waiter across the room were taking my order. He was short, bald back to his ears, and his body type mimicked the toothpicks in the dispenser at the end of the table. His eyes never reached higher than three feet off the ground. As pathetic as I would have felt after the fact, one friendly smile from me might have been enough to have him spilling Kjirsten's entire life story. "Sorry," I told Whitney. "I just can't stop thinking about the murder. Of course, it's probably old news to you. You must have had reporters in here all the time asking questions."

She gave me a pointed look. "Need a few more minutes to look over the menu?"

"Personally, I find reporters irritating."

She leaned in, bracing a hand on the tabletop. "I find customers who take their own sweet time irritating."

hush, hush

I blew out a silent sigh and flipped open the menu. "What do you recommend?"

"It's all good. Ask my boyfriend." She gave a tight smile. "He's the cook."

"Speaking of boyfriends . . . did Kjirsten have one?" Nice segue, I told myself.

"Spill," Whitney demanded. "You a cop? A lawyer? A reporter?"

"Just a concerned citizen." It sounded like a question.

"Yeah, right. Tell you what. Order a milkshake, fries, the Angus burger, a bowl of chowder, and give me a twenty-five-percent tip, and I'll tell you what I told everybody else."

I weighed my options: my allowance or answers. "Done."

"Kjirsten hooked up with that kid, Elliot Saunders. The one in the papers. He was in here all the time. Walked her back to her apartment at the end of her shift."

"Did you ever talk to Elliot?"

"Not me."

"Do you think Kjirsten committed suicide?"

"How should I know?"

"I read in the newspaper that a suicide note was found in Kjirsten's apartment, but that there was also evidence of a break-in."

"And?"

"You don't find that a little . . . odd?"

"If you're asking if I think Elliot could have put the note in her apartment, sure I do. Rich kid like that could get away with anything. Probably hired somebody to plant the note. That's how it works when you got money."

"I don't think Elliot has a lot of money." My impression had always been that Jules was the wealthy one. Vee never stopped raving about his house. "I think he went to Kinghorn Prep on scholarship."

"Scholarship?" she repeated on a snort. "What's in the water you been drinking? If Elliot don't got big-time money, how'd he buy Kjirsten her apartment? Tell me that."

I struggled to hold my surprise in check. "He bought her an apartment?"

"Kjirsten never shut up about it. About drove me insane."

"Why would he buy her an apartment?"

Whitney stared down at me, hands on hips. "Tell me you ain't really that dumb."

Oh. Privacy. Intimacy. Got it.

I said, "Do you know why Elliot transferred out of Kinghorn?"

"Didn't know he did."

I juggled her answers with the questions I still wanted to ask, trying to summon them up from memory. "Did he ever meet friends here? Anyone other than Kjirsten?"

"How'm I supposed to remember that?" She gave a hard eye roll. "I look like I got one of them photographic memories?"

"How about a really tall guy? Really tall. Long blond hair, good-looking, tailored clothes."

She ripped a ragged fingernail off with her front teeth and dropped it inside the pocket of her apron. "Yeah, I remember that guy. Hard not to. All moody and quiet. He came in once or twice. Wasn't that long ago. Maybe around the time Kjirsten died. I remember 'cause we were serving corned beef sandwiches for St. Patrick's Day and I couldn't get him to order one. Just glared at me like he would have reached across the table and slit my throat if I'd stuck around reading the daily specials any longer. But I think I remember something. It's not like I'm nosy, but I do got ears. Sometimes I can't help hearing things. Last time the tall guy and Elliot came in, they were hunched over a table, talking about a test."

"A test at school?"

"How should I know? From the sound of it, the tall guy failed a test, and Elliot was none too happy about it. He shoved his chair back and stormed out. Didn't even eat all his sandwich."

"Did they mention Kjirsten?"

"The tall guy came in first, asked if Kjirsten was working. I told him no, she wasn't, and he got on his cell phone. Ten minutes later, Elliot strolls in. Kjirsten always handled Elliot's table, but like I said, she wasn't working, so I got it. If they talked about Kjirsten, I didn't hear. But it looked to me like the tall guy didn't want Kjirsten around."

"Do you remember anything else?"

"Depends. You going to order dessert?"

"I guess I'll have a slice of pie."

"Pie? I give you five minutes of my valuable time, and all you order is pie? I look like I got nothing better to do than chitchat with you?"

I glanced around the diner. It was dead. Other than a man hunched over a paper at the counter, I was the only customer.

"Okay . . ." I scanned the menu.

"You're going to want a raspberry lemonade to wash that pie down." She scribbled it on her pad. "And after-dinner coffee." More scribbling. "I'll be looking forward to an additional twenty-percent tip with that." She pinned me with a smug smile, then tucked her pad into her apron and sashayed back to the kitchen.

CHAPTER

21

OUTSIDE, THE WEATHER HAD SHIFTED TO COLD AND drizzling. The lampposts burned an eerie, sallow color that did little against the thick fog brewing along the streets. I hurried out of Blind Joe's, grateful I'd looked at the weather forecast earlier and brought my umbrella. As I passed storefront windows, I saw crowds gathering in the bars.

I was a few blocks from the bus stop when the now familiar icy feeling kissed the back of my neck. I'd felt it the night I was sure someone looked in my bedroom window, at Delphic, and again right before Vee walked out of Victoria's Secret wearing my jacket. I bent down, pretended to tie my shoelace, and cast a surreptitious glance around. The sidewalks on both sides of the street were empty.

The crosswalk light changed, and I stepped off the curb. Moving faster, I tucked my handbag under my arm and hoped the bus was on time. I cut through an alley behind a bar, slipped past a huddle of smokers, and came out on the next street over. Jogging up a block, I veered down another alley and circled back around the block. Every few seconds I checked behind me.

I heard the rumble of the bus, and a moment later it rounded the corner, materializing out of the fog. It slowed against the curb and I climbed aboard, heading home. I was the only passenger.

Taking a seat several rows behind the driver, I slouched to keep out of sight. He jerked the lever to close the doors, and the bus roared down the street. I was on the verge of offering a sigh of relief when I received a text message from Vee.

WHERE U AT?

PORTLAND, I texted back. YOU?

ME 2. AT A PARTY WITH JULES AND ELLIOT. LET'S MEET UP.

WHY ARE YOU IN PORTLAND?!

I didn't wait for her answer; I dialed her directly. Talking was faster. And this was urgent.

"Well? What say you?" Vee asked. "Are you in the partying mood?"

hush, hush

"Does your mom know you're at a party in Portland with two guys?"

"You're starting to sound neurotic, babe."

"I can't believe you came to Portland with Elliot!" I had a sinking thought. "Does he know you're on the phone with me?"

"So he can come kill you? No, sorry. He and Jules ran to Kinghorn to pick up something, and I'm chilling solo. I could use a wingwoman. Hey!" Vee shouted into the background. "Hands off, okay? O-F-F. Nora? I'm not exactly in the greatest area. Time is of the essence."

"Where are you?"

"Hang on . . . okay, the building across the street says one-seven-two-seven. The street is Highsmith, I'm pretty sure."

"I'll be there as soon as I can. But I'm not staying. I'm going home, and you're coming with me. Stop the bus!" I called to the driver.

He applied the brakes, and I was thrown against the seat in front of me.

"Can you tell me which way to Highsmith?" I asked him once I'd made it to the top of the aisle.

He pointed out the windows paneling the right side of the bus. "West of here. You planning to go on foot?" He surveyed me up and down. "'Cause I should warn you, it's a rough neighborhood."

Great.

I had to walk only a few blocks before I knew the bus driver had been right to warn me. The scenery changed drastically. The quaint storefronts were replaced by buildings spray-painted with gang graffiti. The windows were dark, barred up with iron. The sidewalks were desolate paths stretching into the fog.

A slow, rattling noise drifted through the fog, and a woman pushing a cart of garbage bags wheeled into view. Her eyes were raisins, beady and dark, and they twitched their way over me in almost predatory evaluation.

"What we got here?" she said through a gape of missing teeth.

I drew a discreet step back and clutched my handbag against me.

"Looks like a coat, mittens, and a pretty wool hat," she said. "Always wanted me a pretty wool hat." She pronounced the word prit-ee.

"Hello," I said, clearing my throat and trying to sound friendly. "Can you please tell me how much farther to Highsmith Street?"

She cackled.

"A bus driver pointed me in this direction," I said with less confidence.

"He told you Highsmith is this way?" she said, sounding irritated. "I know the way to Highsmith, and this ain't it."

I waited, but she didn't elaborate. "Do you think you could give me directions?" I asked.

"I got directions." She tapped her head with a finger that

strongly resembled a twisted, knotted twig. "Keep everything up here, I do."

"Which way is Highsmith?" I encouraged.

"But I can't tell you for free," she said in a chiding tone. "That's gonna cost you. A girl has to make a living. Nobody ever tell you ain't nothing in life free?"

"I don't have any money." Not much, anyway. Only enough for a bus fare home.

"You got a nice warm coat."

I looked down at my quilted coat. A chilly wind ruffled my hair, and the thought of peeling my coat off sent a flush of goose bumps down my arms. "I just got this coat for Christmas."

"I'm freezing my derrière off out here," she snapped. "You want directions or not?"

I couldn't believe I was standing here. I couldn't believe I was bartering my coat with a homeless woman. Vee was so far in debt to me she might never get out.

I shucked off my coat and watched her zip into it.

My breath came out like smoke. I hugged myself and stamped my feet, conserving body heat. "Can you please tell me the way to Highsmith now?"

"You want the long way, or the short way?"

"Sh-short," I chattered.

"That's gonna cost you too. Short way's got an additional fee attached. Like I said, always wanted me a pretty wool hat."

I tugged the pink and white beanie off my head. "Highsmith?" I asked, trying to hold on to the friendly tone as I passed it over.

"See that alley?" she said, pointing behind me. I turned. The alley was a half block back. "You take it, you come out on Highsmith on the other side."

"That's it?" I said incredulously. "One block over?"

"Good news is, you got a short walk. Bad news is, ain't no walk feel short in this weather. 'Course, I'm nice and warm now I got me a coat and a pretty hat. Give me those mittens, and I'll walk you there myself."

I looked down at the mittens. At least my hands were warm. "I'll manage."

She shrugged and wheeled her cart to the next corner, where she took up a post against the bricks.

The alley was dark and cluttered with trash bins, water-stained cardboard boxes, and an unrecognizable hump that may have been a discarded water heater. Then again, it just as easily could have been a rug with a body rolled inside. A high chain-link fence spanned the alley halfway down. I could hardly climb a four-foot fence on a good day, let alone a ten-foot one. Brick buildings flanked me on both sides. All the windows were greased over and barred.

Stepping over crates and sacks of trash, I picked my way down the alley. Broken glass crunched beneath my shoes. A flash of white darted between my legs, stealing my breath. A cat. Just a cat, vanishing into the darkness ahead.

hush, hush

I reached for my pocket to text Vee, intending to tell her I was close and to watch for me, when I remembered I'd left my cell phone in my coat pocket. Nice going, I thought. *What are the chances the bag lady will give you back your phone? Precisely*—slim to none.

I decided it was worth a try, and as I turned around, a sleek black sedan sped past the opening to the alley. With a sudden glow of red, the brake lights lit up.

For reasons I couldn't explain beyond intuition, I drew into the shadows.

A car door opened and the crackle of gunfire broke out. Two shots. The car door slammed and the black sedan screeched away. I could hear my heart hammering in my chest, and it blended with the sound of running feet. I realized a moment later that they were my feet, and I was running to the mouth of the alley. I rounded the corner and came up short.

The bag lady's body was in a heap on the sidewalk.

I rushed over and fell on my knees beside her. "Are you okay?" I said frantically, rolling her over. Her mouth was agape, her raisin eyes hollow. Dark liquid flowered through the quilted coat I'd been wearing three minutes ago.

I felt the urge to jump back but forced myself to reach inside the coat pockets. I needed to call for help, but my cell phone wasn't there.

There was a phone booth on the corner across the street. I ran to it and dialed 911. While I waited for the operator to pick up, I glanced back at the bag lady's body, and that's when I felt cold adrenaline shoot through me. The body was gone.

With a shaky hand, I hung up. The sound of approaching footsteps tapped in my ears, but whether they were near or far, I couldn't tell.

Clip, clip, clip.

He's here, I thought. *The man in the ski mask.*

I shoved a few coins into the phone and gripped the receiver with both hands. I tried to remember Patch's cell phone number. Squeezing my eyes shut, I visualized the seven numbers he'd written in red ink on my hand the first day we met. Before I could second-guess my memory, I dialed the numbers.

"What's up?" Patch said.

I almost sobbed at the sound of his voice. I could hear the crack of billiard balls colliding on a pool table in the background, and knew he was at Bo's Arcade. He could be here in fifteen, maybe twenty minutes.

"It's me." I didn't dare push my voice above a whisper.

"Nora?"

"I'm in P-Portland. On the corner of Hempshire and Nantucket. Can you pick me up? It's urgent."

I was huddled in the bottom of the phone booth, counting silently to one hundred, trying to remain calm, when a black

Jeep Commander glided to the curb. Patch slid the door to the phone booth open and crouched in the entrance.

He peeled off his top layer—a long-sleeved black T-shirt—leaving him in a black undershirt. He fit the neckhole of the T-shirt over my head and a moment later had my arms pushed through the sleeves. The shirt dwarfed me, the sleeves hanging down well past my fingertips. It mingled the smells of smoke, saltwater, and mint soap. Something about it filled the hollow places inside me with reassurance.

"Let's get you in the car," Patch said. He pulled me up, and I wrapped my arms around his neck and buried my face into him.

"I think I'm going to be sick," I said. The world tilted, including Patch. "I need my iron pills."

"Shh," he said, holding me against him. "It's going to be all right. I'm here now."

I managed a little nod.

"Let's get out of here."

Another nod. "We need to get Vee," I said. "She's at a party one block over."

While Patch drove the Jeep around the corner, I listened to my chattering teeth echo around inside my head. I'd never been this frightened in my life. Seeing the dead homeless woman conjured up thoughts of my dad. My vision was tinged with red, and hard as I tried, I couldn't flush out the image of blood.

"Were you in the middle of a pool game?" I asked, remembering the sound of billiard balls colliding in the background during our brief phone conversation.

"I was winning a condo."

"A condo?"

"One of those swank ones on the lake. I would have hated the place. This is Highsmith. Do you have an address?"

"I can't remember it," I said, sitting up taller to get a better look out the windows. All of the buildings looked abandoned. There was no trace of a party. There was no trace of life, period.

"Do you have your cell?" I asked Patch.

He slid a Blackberry out of his pocket. "Battery's low. I don't know if it will make a call."

I texted Vee. WHERE ARE YOU?!

CHANGE OF PLANS, she texted back. GUESS J AND E COULDN'T FIND WHAT THEY WERE LOOKING 4. WE'RE GOING HOME.

The screen drained to black.

"It died," I told Patch. "Do you have the charger?"

"Not on me."

"Vee's going back to Coldwater. Do you think you could drop me off at her house?"

Minutes later we were on the coastal highway, driving right along a cliff just above the ocean. I'd been this way before, and when the sun was out, the water was slate blue with patches of dark green where the water reflected the evergreens. It was night, and the ocean was smooth black poison.

hush, hush

"Are you going to tell me what happened?" Patch asked.

The jury was still out on whether or not I should tell Patch anything. I could tell him how after the bag lady tricked me out of my coat, she was shot. I could tell him I thought the bullet was meant for me. Then I could try explaining how the bag lady's body had magically vanished into thin air.

I remembered the crazed look Detective Basso had directed at me when I told him someone had broken into my bedroom. I wasn't in the mood to get eyeballed and laughed at again. Not by Patch. Not right now.

"I got lost, and a bag lady cornered me," I said. "She talked me out of my coat...." I wiped my nose with the back of my hand and sniffled. "She got my beanie, too."

"What were you doing all the way out here?" asked Patch.

"Meeting Vee at a party."

We were halfway between Portland and Coldwater, on a stretch of lush and unpopulated highway, when steam spewed suddenly from the hood of the Jeep. Patch braked, easing the Jeep to the roadside.

"Hang on," he said, swinging out. Lifting the hood of the Jeep, he disappeared out of sight.

A minute later he dropped the hood back in place. Brushing his hands on his pants, he came around to my window, gesturing for me to lower it.

"Bad news," he said. "It's the engine."

I tried to look informed and intelligent, but I had a feeling my expression just looked blank.

Patch raised an eyebrow and said, "May it rest in peace."

"It won't move?"

"Not unless we push it."

Of all the cars, he had to win the lemon.

"Where's your cell?" Patch asked.

"I lost it."

He grinned. "Let me guess. In your coat pocket. The bag lady really cashed in, didn't she?"

He scouted the horizon. "Two choices. We can flag down a ride, or we can walk to the next exit and find a phone."

I stepped out, shutting the door with force behind me. I kicked the Jeep's right front tire. I knew I was using anger to mask my fear of what I'd been through today. As soon as I was all alone, I'd break down crying.

"I think there's a motel at the next exit. I'll go c-c-call a cab," I said, my teeth chattering harder. "Y-y-you wait here with the Jeep."

He cracked a slight smile, but it didn't look amused. "I'm not letting you out of my sight. You're looking a little deranged, Angel. We'll go together."

Crossing my arms, I stood up to him. In tennis shoes, my eyes came level with his shoulders. I was forced to tilt my neck back to meet his eyes. "I'm not going anywhere near a motel with you." Best to sound firm so I was less likely to change my mind.

hush, hush

"You think the two of us and a slummy motel make for a dangerous combination?"

Yes, actually.

Patch leaned back against the Jeep. "We can sit here and argue this." He squinted up at the riotous sky. "But this storm is about to catch its second wind."

As if Mother Nature wanted her say in the verdict, the sky opened and a thick concoction of rain and sleet hailed down.

I sent Patch my coldest look, then blew out an angry sigh.

As usual, he had a point.

CHAPTER 22

TWENTY MINUTES LATER PATCH AND I WASHED UP AT the entrance to a low-budget motel. I had not spoken one word to him as we'd jogged through the sleeting rain, and now I was not only soaked, but thoroughly . . . unnerved. The rain cascaded down, and I didn't think we would be returning to the Jeep anytime soon. Which left me, Patch, and a motel in the same equation for an undetermined amount of time.

The door chimed on our way in, and the desk clerk stood

abruptly, dusting Cheetos crumbs off his lap. "What'll it be?" he said, sucking his fingers clean of orange slime. "Just the two of you tonight?"

"We n-n-need to borrow your phone," I chattered, hoping he could make sense of my request.

"No can do. Lines are down. Blame the storm."

"What do y-you mean the l-lines are d-down? Do you have a cell?"

The clerk looked to Patch.

"She wants a nonsmoking room," Patch said.

I swiveled to face Patch. *Are you insane?* I mouthed.

The clerk tapped a few keys at his computer. "Looks like we've got . . . hang on . . . Bingo! A nonsmoking king."

"We'll take it," said Patch. He looked sideways at me, and the edges of his mouth tipped up. I narrowed my eyes.

Just then the lights overhead blinked out, plunging the lobby into darkness. We all stood silent for a moment before the clerk fumbled around and clicked on an industrial-size flashlight.

"I was a Boy Scout," he said. "Back in the day. 'Be prepared.'"

"Then you m-m-must have a cell phone?" I said.

"I did. Until I couldn't pay the bill anymore." He drew his shoulders up. "What can I say, my mom's cheap."

His mom? He had to be forty. Not that it was any of my business. I was far more concerned what my mom would do when she arrived home from the reception and found me gone.

"How do you want to pay?" the desk clerk asked.

"Cash," Patch said.

The desk clerk chuckled, bobbing his head up and down. "It's a popular form of payment here." He leaned close and spoke in confidential tones. "We get a lot of folks who don't want their extracurricular activities traced, if you know what I mean."

The logical half of my brain was telling me I couldn't actually be considering spending the night at a motel with Patch.

"This is crazy," I told Patch in an undertone.

"I'm crazy." He was on the brink of smiling again. "About you. How much for the flashlight?" he asked the clerk.

The clerk reached below the desk. "I've got something even better: survival-size candles," he said, placing two in front of us. Striking a match, he lit one. "They're on the house, no extra charge. Put one in the bathroom and one in the sleeping area and you'll never know the difference. I'll even throw in the matchbook. If nothing else, it'll make a good keepsake."

"Thanks," Patch said, taking my elbow and walking me down the hall.

At room 106, Patch bolted the door behind us. He set the candle on the nightstand, then used it to light the spare. Lifting his baseball cap, he shook the ends of his hair like a wet dog.

"You need a hot shower," he said. Taking a few steps backward, he ducked his head inside the bathroom. "Looks like bar soap and two towels."

I tilted my chin up a fraction. "You can't f-force me to stay here." I'd only agreed to come this far because I didn't want to stand out in the downpour, for one, and I had high hopes of finding a phone, for two.

"That sounded more like a question than a statement," said Patch.

"Then ans-s-swer it."

His rogue smile crept out. "It's hard to concentrate on answers with you looking like that."

I glanced down at Patch's black shirt, wet and clinging to my body. I brushed past him and shut the bathroom door between us.

Cranking the water to full hot, I peeled out of Patch's shirt and my clothes. One long black hair was plastered to the shower wall, and I trapped it in a square of toilet paper before flushing it. Then I stepped behind the shower curtain, watching my skin glow with heat.

Massaging soap into the muscles along my neck and down through my shoulders, I told myself I could handle sleeping in the same room as Patch. It wasn't the smartest or safest arrangement, but I'd personally see to it that nothing happened. Besides, what choice did I have . . . right?

The spontaneous reckless half of my brain laughed at me. I knew what it was thinking. Early on I'd felt drawn to Patch by a mysterious force field. Now I felt drawn to him by something entirely different. Something with a lot of heat involved. A connection tonight was inevitable. On a scale of one to ten, that terrified me about an eight. And excited me about a nine.

BECCA FITZPATRICK

I shut off the water, stepped out, and patted my skin dry. One glance at my soaked clothes was all I needed to know I had no desire to put them back on. Maybe there was a coin-operated dryer nearby . . . one that didn't require electricity. I sighed and pulled on my camisole and panties, which had survived the worst of the rain.

"Patch?" I whispered through the door.

"Done?"

"Blow out the candle."

"Done," he whispered back through the door. His laughter, too, sounded so soft it could have been whispered.

Snuffing out the bathroom candle, I stepped out, meeting total blackness. I could hear Patch breathing directly in front of me. I didn't want to think about what he was—or wasn't— wearing, and I shook my head to fragment the picture forming in my mind. "My clothes are soaked. I don't have anything to wear."

I heard the sound of wet fabric sliding like a squeegee over his skin. "Lucky me." His shirt landed in a wet heap at our feet.

"This is really awkward," I told him.

I could feel him smiling. He stood way, way too close.

"You should shower," I said. "Right now."

"I smell that bad?"

Actually, he smelled that good. The smoke was gone, the mint stronger.

Patch disappeared inside the bathroom. He relit the candle and left the door ajar, a sliver of light stretching across the floor and up one wall.

I slid my back down the wall until I was seated on the floor, then tipped my head against the wall. In all honesty, I couldn't stay here tonight. I had to get home. It was wrong to stay here alone with Patch, vow of prudence or not. I had to report the bag lady's body. Or did I? How was I supposed to report a vanished body? Talk about insane—which was the terrifying direction my thoughts were starting to go anyway.

Not wanting to dwell on the insanity idea, I concentrated on my original argument. I couldn't stay here knowing Vee was with Elliot, in danger, when I was safe.

After a moment's consideration I decided I needed to rephrase that thought. Safe was a relative term. As long as Patch was around, I wasn't in harm's way, but that didn't mean I thought he was going to act like my guardian angel, either.

Right away, I wished I could take back the guardian angel thought. Summoning up my powers of persuasion, I banished all thoughts of angels—guardian, fallen, or otherwise—from my head. I told myself I probably *was* going insane. For all I knew, I'd hallucinated seeing the bag lady die. And I'd hallucinated seeing Patch's scars.

The water stopped, and a moment later Patch strolled out wearing only his wet jeans hanging low on his waist. He left the bathroom candle lit and the door wide. Soft color glowed through the room.

One quick look and I could tell Patch clocked several hours a week running and lifting weights. A body that defined didn't come without sweat and work. Suddenly I felt a little self-conscious. Not to mention soft.

"Which side of the bed do you want?" he asked.

"Uh . . ."

A fox smile. "Nervous?"

"No," I said as confidently as possible under the circumstances. And the circumstances were that I was lying through my teeth.

"You're a bad liar," he said, still smiling. "The worst I've seen."

I put my hands on my hips and communicated a silent *Excuse me?*

"Come here," he said, pulling me to my feet. I felt my earlier promise of resistance melting away. Another ten seconds of standing this close to Patch and my defense would be blown to smithereens.

A mirror hung on the wall behind him, and over his shoulder I saw the upside-down V scars gleaming black on his skin.

My whole body went rigid. I tried to blink the scars away, but they were there for good.

Without thinking, I slid my hands up his chest and around to his back. A fingertip brushed his right scar.

Patch tensed under my touch. I froze, the tip of my finger quivering on his scar. It took me a moment to realize it wasn't actually my finger moving, but me. All of me.

I was sucked into a soft, dark chute and everything went black.

23

I WAS STANDING IN THE LOWER LEVEL OF BO'S ARCADE WITH my back to the wall, facing several games of pool. The windows were boarded, and I couldn't tell if it was day or night. Stevie Nicks was coming through the speakers; the song about the white-winged dove and being on the edge of seventeen. Nobody seemed surprised by my sudden appearance out of thin air.

And then I remembered I was wearing nothing but a cami and panties. I'm not all that vain, but standing in a crowd composed entirely of the opposite sex, my essentials barely covered, and nobody even looked at me? Something was . . . off.

I pinched myself. Perfectly alive, as far as I could tell.

Waving a hand to clear away the hazy cloud of cigar smoke, I spotted Patch across the room. He was sitting at a poker table, kicked back, holding a hand of cards close to his chest.

I padded barefoot across the room, crossing my arms over my chest, making sure to keep myself covered. "Can we talk?" I hissed in his ear. There was an unnerved quality to my voice. Understandable, since I had no idea how I'd come to find myself at Bo's. One moment I was at the motel, and the next I was here.

Patch pushed a short stack of poker chips into the pile at the center of the table.

"Like maybe now?" I said. "It's kind of urgent. . . ." I trailed off when the calendar on the wall caught my eye. It was eight months behind, showing August of last year. Right before I started sophomore year. Months before I met Patch. I told myself it was a mistake, that whoever was in charge of ripping off the old months had fallen behind, but at the same time I briefly and unwillingly considered the possibility that the calendar was right where it was supposed to be. And I was not.

I dragged a chair over from the next table and pulled up beside Patch. "He's holding a five of spades, a nine of spades, the ace of hearts . . ." I stopped when I realized that no one was paying attention. No, it wasn't that. No one could see me.

Footsteps lumbered down the stairs across the room, and the same cashier who'd threatened to throw me out the first time I'd come to the arcade appeared at the bottom of the stairwell.

"Someone upstairs wants a word with you," he told Patch.

Patch raised his eyebrows, transmitting a silent question.

"She wouldn't give her name," the cashier said apologetically. "I asked a couple of times. I told her you were in a private game, but she wouldn't leave. I can throw her out if you want."

"No. Send her down."

Patch played out his hand, gathered his chips, and pushed out of his chair. "I'm out." He walked to the pool table closest to the stairs, rested against it, and slid his hands inside his pockets.

I followed him across the room. I snapped my fingers in front of his face. I kicked his boots. I flat-out smacked his chest. He didn't flinch, didn't move.

Light footsteps sounded on the stairs, growing closer, and when Miss Greene stepped out of the darkened stairwell, I experienced a moment of confusion. Her blond hair was down to her waist and toothpick straight. She was wearing painted-on jeans and a pink tank top, and she was barefoot. Dressed this way, she looked even closer to my age. She was sucking on a lollipop.

Patch's face is always a mask, and at any given moment I have no idea what he's thinking. But as soon as he locked eyes on Miss Greene, I knew he was surprised. He recovered quickly, all emotion funneling away as his eyes turned guarded and wary. "Dabria?"

My heart hit a faster cadence. I tried to wrestle my thoughts together, but all I could think was, if I was really eight months in the past, how did Miss Greene and Patch know each other? She didn't have a job at school yet. And why was he calling her by her first name?

"How have you been?" Miss Greene—Dabria—asked with a coy smile, tossing the lollipop in the trash.

"What are you doing here?" Patch's eyes turned even more watchful, as if he didn't think "what you see is what you get" applied to Dabria.

"I sneaked out." Her smile twisted up on one side. "I had to see you again. I've been trying for a long time, but security—well, you know. It's not exactly lax. Your kind and my kind—we aren't supposed to mix. But you know that."

"Coming here was a bad idea."

"I know it's been a while, but I was hoping for a slightly more friendly reaction," she said, pushing her lips out in a pout.

Patch didn't answer.

"I haven't stopped thinking about you." Dabria dimmed her voice to a low, sexy pitch and took a step closer to Patch. "It wasn't easy getting down here. Lucianna is making excuses for why I'm absent. I'm risking her future as well as my own. Don't you want to at least hear what I have to say?"

"Talk." Patch's words didn't hold a shred of trust.

"I haven't given up on you. This whole time—" She broke off

and blinked back a sudden display of tears. When she spoke again, her voice was more composed but still held a wavering note. "I know how you can get your wings back."

She smiled at Patch, but he didn't return the smile.

"As soon as you get your wings back, you can come home," she said, speaking more confidently. "Everything will be like it was before. Nothing has changed. Not really."

"What's the catch?"

"There is no catch. You have to save a human life. Very judicious, considering the crime that banished you here in the first place."

"What rank will I be?"

All confidence scattered from Dabria's eyes, and I got the feeling he'd asked the one question she'd hoped to avoid. "I just told you how to get your wings back," she said, sounding a touch condescending. "I think I deserve a thank-you—"

"Answer the question." But his grim smile told me he already knew. Or had a very good guess. Whatever Dabria's answer was, he wasn't going to like it.

"Fine. You'll be a guardian, all right?"

Patch tipped his head back and laughed softly.

"What's wrong with being a guardian?" Dabria demanded. "Why isn't it good enough?"

"I have something better in the works."

"Listen to me, Patch. There's nothing better. You're kidding yourself. Any other fallen angel would jump at the chance to get their wings back and become a guardian. Why can't you?" Her voice was choked with bewilderment, irritation, rejection.

Patch pushed up from the pool table. "It was good seeing you again, Dabria. Have a nice trip back."

Without warning, she curled her fists into his shirt, yanked him close, and crushed a kiss to his mouth. Very slowly Patch's body turned toward her, his stance softening. His hands came up and skimmed her arms.

I swallowed hard, trying to ignore the stab of jealousy and confusion in my heart. Part of me wanted to turn away and cry, part of me wanted to march over and start shouting. Not that it would do any good. I was invisible. Obviously Miss Greene . . . Dabria . . . whoever she was . . . and Patch had a romantic past together. Were they still together now—in the future? Had she applied for a job at Coldwater High to be closer to Patch? Is that why she was so determined to scare me away from him?

"I should go," said Dabria, pulling free. "I've already stayed too long. I promised Lucianna I'd hurry." She lowered her head against his chest. "I miss you," she whispered. "Save one human life, and you'll have your wings again. Come back to me," she begged. "Come home." She broke away suddenly. "I have to go. None of the others can find out I've been down here. I love you."

As Dabria turned away, the anxiety vanished from her face. An expression of sly confidence replaced it. It was the face of someone who'd bluffed their way through a rough hand of cards.

Without warning, Patch caught her by the wrist.

"Now tell me why you're really here," he said.

I shivered at the dark undercurrent in Patch's tone. To an outsider, he looked perfectly calm. But to anyone who'd known him any length of time, it was obvious. He was giving Dabria a look that said she'd crossed a line and it was in her best interest to hop back across it—now.

Patch steered her toward the bar. He planted her on a bar stool and slid onto the one beside it. I took the one next to Patch, leaning in to hear him above the music.

"What do you mean, what am I here for?" Dabria stammered. "I told you—"

"You're lying."

Her mouth dropped. "I can't believe—you think—"

"Tell me the truth, right now," said Patch.

Dabria hesitated before answering. She gave him a fierce glare, then said, "Fine. I know what you're planning to do."

Patch laughed. It was a laugh that said, *I have a lot of plans. Which one are you referring to?*

"I know you've heard rumors about The Book of Enoch. I also know you think you can do the same thing, but you can't."

Patch folded his arms on the bar. "They sent you here to persuade me to choose a different course, didn't they?" A smile showed in his eyes. "If I'm a threat, the rumors must be true."

"No, they're not. They're rumors."

"If it happened once, it can happen again."

"It never happened. Did you even bother to read The Book of Enoch before you fell?" she challenged. "Do you know exactly what it says, word for holy word?"

"Maybe you could loan me your copy."

"That's blasphemous! You're forbidden to read it," she cried. "You betrayed every angel in heaven when you fell."

"How many of them know what I'm after?" he asked. "How big of a threat am I?"

She tossed her head side to side. "I can't tell you that. I've already told you more than I should have."

"Are they going to try to stop me?"

"The avenging angels will."

He looked at her with meaning. "Unless they think you talked me out of it."

"Don't look at me like that." She sounded like she was putting all her courage into sounding firm. "I won't lie to protect you. What you're trying to do is wrong. It's not natural."

"Dabria." Patch spoke her name as a soft threat. He might as well have had her by the arm, twisting it behind her back.

"I can't help you," she said with quiet conviction. "Not that way. Put it out of your mind. Become a guardian angel. Focus on that and forget The Book of Enoch."

Patch planted his elbows on the bar, radiating thought. After a moment he said, "Tell them we talked, and I showed interest in becoming a guardian."

"Interest?" she said, a bit incredulously.

"Interest," he repeated. "Tell them I asked for a name. If I'm going to save a life, I need to know who's at the top of your departing list. I know you're privy to that information as an angel of death."

"That information is sacred and private, and not predictable. The events in this world shift from moment to moment depending on human choices—"

"One name, Dabria."

"Promise me you'll forget about The Book of Enoch first. Give me your word."

"You'd trust my word?"

"No," she said, "I wouldn't."

Patch laughed coolly and, grabbing a toothpick from the dispenser, walked toward the stairs.

"Patch, wait—," she began. She hopped off the bar stool. "Patch, please wait!"

He looked over his shoulder.

"Nora Grey," she said, then immediately clamped her hands over her mouth.

There was a faint crack in Patch's expression—a frown of disbelief mixed with annoyance. Which made no sense since, if the calendar on the wall was correct, we hadn't met yet. My name shouldn't have sparked familiarity. "How is she going to die?" he asked.

"Someone wants to kill her."

"Who?"

"I don't know," she said, covering her ears and shaking her head. "There's so much noise and commotion down here. All the images blur together, they come too fast, I can't see clearly. I need to go home. I need peace and calm."

Patch tucked a strand of Dabria's hair behind her ear and looked at her persuasively. She gave a warm shudder at his touch, then nodded and shut her eyes. "I can't see . . . I don't see anything . . . it's useless."

"Who wants to kill Nora Grey?" Patch urged.

"Wait, I see her," said Dabria. Her voice turned anxious. "There's a shadow behind her. It's him. He's following her. She doesn't see him . . . but he's right there. Why doesn't she see him? Why isn't she running? I can't see his face, it's in shadow. . . ."

Dabria's eyes flew open. She sucked in a quick, sharp breath.

"Who?" Patch said.

Dabria curled her hands against her mouth. She was trembling as she raised her eyes to Patch's.

"You," she whispered.

My finger moved off Patch's scar and the connection broke. It took me a moment to reorient myself, so I wasn't ready for Patch, who wrestled me into the bed in an instant. He pinned my wrists above my head.

"You weren't supposed to do that." There was controlled anger in his face, dark and simmering. "What did you see?"

I got my knee up and clipped him in the ribs. "Get—off—me!"

He slid onto my hips, straddling them, eliminating the use of my legs. With my arms still stretched above my head, I couldn't do more than squirm under his weight.

"Get—off—me—or—I'll—scream!"

"You're already screaming. And it isn't going to cause a stir in this place. It's more of a whorehouse than a motel." He gave a hard smile that was all lethality around the edges. "Last chance, Nora. What did you see?"

I was fighting back tears. My whole body hummed with an emotion so foreign I couldn't even name it. "You make me sick!" I said. "Who are you? Who are you *really*?"

His mouth turned even more grim. "We're getting closer."

"You want to kill me!"

Patch's face gave away nothing, but his eyes grew cold.

"The Jeep didn't really die tonight, did it?" I said. "You lied. You brought me here so you could kill me. That's what Dabria said you want to do. Well, what are you waiting for?" I didn't have a clue where I was going with this, and I didn't care. I was spitting words in an attempt to keep my horror at bay. "You've been trying to kill me all along. Right from the start. Are you going to kill me now?" I stared at him, hard and unblinking, trying to keep tears from spilling as I remembered the fateful day he'd walked into my life.

"It's tempting."

I twisted beneath him. I tried to roll to my right, then to my left. I finally figured out I was wasting a lot of energy and stopped. Patch settled his eyes on me. They were blacker than I'd ever seen them.

"I bet you like this," I said.

"That would be a smart bet."

I felt my heart pounding clear down in my toes. "Just do it," I said in a challenging voice.

"Kill you?"

I nodded. "But first I want to know why. Of all the billions of people out there, why me?"

"Bad genes."

"That's it? That's the only explanation I get?"

"For now."

"What's that supposed to mean?" My voice rose again. "I get the rest of the story when you finally break down and kill me?"

"I don't have to break down to kill you. If I'd wanted you dead five minutes ago, you'd have died five minutes ago."

I swallowed at the less-than-cheerful thought.

He brushed his thumb over my birthmark. His touch was deceptively soft, which made it all the more painful to endure.

"What about Dabria?" I asked, still breathing hard. "She's the same thing you are, isn't she? You're both—angels." My voice cracked on the word.

Patch rotated slightly off my hips, but kept his hands at my wrists. "If I ease up, are you going to hear me out?"

If he eased up, I was going to bolt for the door. "What do you care if I run? You'll just drag me back in here."

"Yeah, but that would cause a scene."

"Is Dabria your girlfriend?" I could feel each ragged rise and fall of my chest. I wasn't sure I wanted to hear his answer. Not that it mattered. Now that I knew Patch wanted to kill me, it was ridiculous that I even cared.

"Was. It was a long time ago, before I fell to the dark side." He gave a hard smile, attempting humor. "It was also a mistake." He rocked back on his heels, slowly releasing me, testing to see if I'd fight back. I lay on the mattress, breathing hard, my elbows propping me up. Three counts went by, and I hurled myself at him with all the force I had.

I shoved against his chest, but other than swaying back slightly, he didn't move. I scrambled out from under him and took my fists to him. I hammered his chest until the bottoms of my fists began to throb.

"Done?" he asked.

"No!" I drove my elbow down into his thigh. "What's the matter with you? Don't you feel anything?"

I rose to my feet, found my balance on the mattress, and kicked him as hard as I could in the stomach.

"You've got one more minute," he said. "Get your anger out of your system. Then I take over."

I didn't know what he meant by "take over," and I didn't want to find out. I made a leaping run off the bed, with the door in sight. Patch snagged me midair and backed me against the wall. His legs were flush with mine, front to front down the length of our thighs.

"I want the truth," I said, struggling not to cry. "Did you come to school to kill me? Was that your aim right from the start?"

A muscle in Patch's jaw jumped. "Yes."

I swiped a tear that dared escape. "Are you gloating inside? That's what this is about, isn't it? Getting me to trust you so you could blow it up in my face!" I knew I was being irrationally irate. I should have been terrified and frantic. I should have been doing everything in my power to escape. The most irrational part of all was that I still didn't want to believe he would kill me, and no matter how hard I tried, I couldn't smother that illogical speck of trust.

"I get that you're angry—," said Patch.

"I am ripped apart!" I shouted.

His hands slid up my neck, searing hot. Pressing his thumbs gently into my throat, he tipped my head back. I felt his lips come against mine so hard he stopped whatever name I'd been about to call him from coming out. His hands dropped to my shoulders, skimmed down my arms, and came to rest at the small of my back. Little shivers of panic and pleasure shot through me. He tried to pull me against him, and I bit him on the lip.

He licked his lip with the tip of his tongue. "Did you just bite me?"

"Is everything a joke to you?" I asked.

He dabbed his tongue to his lip again. "Not everything."

"Like what?"

"You."

The whole night felt unbalanced. It was hard to have a show-down with someone as indifferent as Patch. No, not indifferent. Perfectly controlled. Down to the last cell in his body.

I heard a voice in my mind. *Relax. Trust me.*

"Omigosh," I said with a burst of clarity. "You're doing it again, aren't you? Messing with my mind." I remembered the article I'd pulled up when I Googled fallen angels. "You can put more than words in my head, can't you? You can put images—very real images—there."

He didn't deny it.

"The Archangel," I said, finally understanding. "You tried to kill me that night, didn't you? But something went wrong. Then you made me think my cell phone was dead, so I couldn't call Vee. Did you plan to kill me on the ride home? I want to know how you're making me see what you want!"

His face was carefully expressionless. "I put the words and images there, but it's up to you if you believe them. It's a riddle. The images overlap reality, and you have to figure out which is real."

"Is this a special angel power?"

He shook his head. "Fallen angel power. Any other kind of angel wouldn't invade your privacy, even though they can."

Because other angels were good. And Patch was not.

Patch braced his hands against the wall behind me, one on either side of my head. "I put a thought in Coach's mind to redo the seating chart because I needed to get close to you. I made you think you fell off the Archangel because I wanted to kill you, but I couldn't go through with it. I almost did, but I stopped. I settled for scaring you instead. Then I made you think your cell was dead because I wanted to give you a ride home. When I came inside your house, I picked up a knife. I was going to kill you then." His voice softened. "You changed my mind."

I sucked in a deep breath. "I don't understand you. When I told you my dad was murdered, you sounded genuinely sorry. When you met my mom, you were nice."

"Nice," Patch repeated. "Let's keep that between you and me."

My head spun faster, and I could feel my pulse beating in my temples. I'd felt this heart-pounding panic before. I needed my iron pills. Either that, or Patch was making me think I did.

I tilted my chin up and narrowed my eyes. "Get out of my mind. Right now!"

"I'm not in your mind, Nora."

I bent forward, bracing my hands on my knees, sucking air. "Yes, you are. I feel you. So this is how you're going to do it? Suffocate me?"

Soft popping sounds echoed in my ears, and a blurry black framed my vision. I tried to fill my lungs, but it was like the air had disappeared. The world tilted, and Patch slipped sideways in my vision. I flattened my hand to the wall to steady my balance. The deeper I tried to inhale, the tighter my throat constricted.

Patch moved toward me, but I flung my hand out. "Get away!"

He leaned a shoulder on the wall and faced me, his mouth set with concern.

"Get—away—from—me," I gasped.

He didn't.

"I—can't—breathe!" I choked, clawing at the wall with one hand, clutching my throat with the other.

Suddenly Patch scooped me up and carried me to the chair across the room. "Put your head between your knees," he said, guiding my head down.

I had my head down, breathing rapidly, trying to force air inside my lungs. Very slowly I felt the oxygen creep back into my body.

"Better?" Patch asked after a minute.

I nodded, once.

"Do you have iron pills with you?"

I shook my head.

"Keep your head down and take long, deep breaths."

I followed his instructions, feeling a clamp loosen around my chest. "Thank you," I said quietly.

"Still don't trust my motives?"

"If you want me to trust you, let me touch your scars again."

Patch studied me silently for a long moment. "That's not a good idea."

"Why not?"

"I can't control what you see."

"That's kind of the point."

He waited a few counts before answering. His voice was low, emotions untraceable. "You know I'm hiding things." There was a question attached to it.

I knew Patch lived a life of closed doors and harbored secrets. I wasn't presumptuous enough to think even half of them revolved around me. Patch lived a different life outside the one he shared with me. More than once I'd speculated what his other life might be like. I always got the feeling that the less I knew about it, the better.

My lip wobbled. "Give me a reason to trust you."

Patch sat on the corner of the bed, the mattress sinking under his weight. He bent forward, resting his forearms on his knees. His scars were in full view, the candlelight dancing eerie shadows across their surface. The muscles in his back heightened, then relaxed. "Go ahead," he said quietly. "Keep in mind that people change, but the past doesn't."

Suddenly I wasn't so sure I wanted this. On almost every level, Patch terrified me. But deep down, I didn't think he was going to kill me. If that was what he wanted, he would have done it already. I glanced at his gruesome scars. Trusting Patch felt a lot more comfortable than slipping into his past again and having no idea what I might find.

But if I backed out now, Patch would know I was terrified of him. He was opening one of the closed doors just for me and only because I'd asked for it. I couldn't make a request this heavy, then change my mind.

"I won't get trapped in there forever, will I?" I asked.

Patch gave a short laugh. "No."

Summoning my courage, I sat on the bed beside him. For the second time tonight, my finger brushed the peaked ridge of his scar. A hazy gray crowded my vision, working from the edges in. The lights went out.

CHAPTER 24

I WAS ON MY BACK, MY CAMI SPONGING UP MOISTURE beneath me, blades of grass poking the bare skin on my arms. The moon overhead was nothing more than a sliver, a grin tipped on its side. Other than the rumble of distant thunder, all was quiet.

I blinked several times in succession, helping my eyes hurry and adapt to the scant light. When I rolled my head sideways, a symmetrical arrangement of curved twigs poking up from the grass solidified in my vision. Very slowly I pulled myself up. I couldn't tear my eyes away from the two black orbs staring at me from just above the curved twigs. My mind worked to place the familiar image. And then, with a horrific flash of recognition, I knew. I was lying next to a human skeleton.

I crawled backward until I came up against an iron fence. I pushed through the muddled moment and recaptured my last memory. I'd touched Patch's scars. Wherever I was, it was somewhere inside his memory.

A voice, male and vaguely familiar, carried through the darkness, singing a low tune. Turning toward it, I saw a labyrinth of headstones stretching like dominoes into the mist. Patch was crouched on top of one. He wore only Levi's and a navy T-shirt, even though the night wasn't warm.

"Moonlighting with the dead?" called the familiar voice. It was rough, rich, and Irish. Rixon. He slouched against a headstone opposite Patch, watching him. He stroked his thumb across his bottom lip. "Let me guess. You've got it in your mind to possess the dead? I don't know," he said, wagging his head. "Maggots squirming in your eyeholes . . . and your other orifices, might be carrying things a bit too far."

"This is why I keep you around, Rixon. Always seeing things from the bright side."

"Cheshvan starts tonight," Rixon said. "What are you doing arsing around in a graveyard?"

"Thinking."

"Thinking?"

"A process by which I use my brain to make a rational decision."

The corners of Rixon's mouth pulled down. "I'm starting to worry about you. Come on. Time to go. Chauncey Langeais and Barnabas await. The moon turns at midnight. I confess I've got my eye on a betty in town." He gave a catlike purr. "I know you like them red, but I like 'em fair, and once I get into a body, I intend to take care of unfinished business with a blonde who was making eyes at me earlier."

When Patch didn't move, Rixon said, "Are you daft? We've got to go. Chauncey's oath of fealty. Not ringing a bell? How about this. You're a fallen angel. You can't feel a thing. Until tonight, that is. The next two weeks are Chauncey's gift to you. Given unwillingly, mind you," he added on a conspirator's grin.

Patch gave Rixon a sidelong glance. "What do you know about *The Book of Enoch*?"

"About as much as any fallen angel: slim to none."

"I was told there's a story in *The Book of Enoch*. About a fallen angel who becomes human."

Rixon doubled over with laughter. "You lost your mind, mate?" He welded the outer edges of his palms together, making an open book with his hands. "*The Book of Enoch* is a bedtime story. And a good one, by the looks of it. Sent you straight to dreamland."

"I want a human body."

"You'd best be happy with two weeks and a Nephil's body. Half-human is better than nothing. Chauncey can't undo what's been done. He swore an oath, and he has to live up to it. Just like last year. And the year before that—"

"Two weeks isn't enough. I want to be human. Permanently." Patch's eyes cut into Rixon's, daring him to laugh again.

Rixon raked his hands through his hair. "*The Book of Enoch* is a fairy tale. We're fallen angels, not humans. We never were human, and we never will be. End of story. Now, quit arsing around and help me figure out which is the way to Portland." He craned his neck back and observed the inky sky.

Patch swung down off the headstone. "I'm going to become human."

"Sure, mate, sure you can."

"*The Book of Enoch* says I have to kill my Nephil vassal. I have to kill Chauncey."

"No, you don't," Rixon said with a note of impatience. "You've got to possess him. A process by which you take his body and use it as your own. Not to put a damper on things, but you can't kill Chauncey. Nephilim can't die. And have you thought of this? If you could kill him, you couldn't possess him."

"If I kill him, I'll become human and I won't need to possess him."

Rixon squeezed the inner corners of his eyes as if he knew his argument was falling on deaf ears and it was giving him a headache.

BECCA FITZPATRICK

"If we could kill Nephilim, we would have found a way by now. I'm sorry to tell you, lad, but if I don't get into the arms of that blond betty soon, my brains will bake. And a few other parts of my—"

"Two choices," said Patch.

"Eh?"

"Save a human life and become a guardian angel, or kill your Nephil vassal and become human. Take your pick."

"Is this more Book of Enoch rubbish?"

"Dabria paid me a visit."

Rixon's eyes widened, and he snorted a laugh. "Your psychotic ex? What's she doing down here? Did she fall? Lost her wings, did she?"

"She came down to tell me I can get my wings back if I save a human life."

Rixon's eyes got wider. "If you trust her, I say go for it. Nothing wrong with being a guardian. Spending your days keeping mortals out of danger . . . could be fun, depending on the mortal you're assigned."

"But if you had a choice?" Patch asked.

"Aye, well, my answer depends on one very important distinction. Am I roaring drunk . . . or have I completely lost my mind?" When Patch didn't laugh, Rixon said soberly, "There's no choice. And here's why. I don't believe in The Book of Enoch. If I were you, I'd aim for guardianship. I'm half considering the deal myself. Too bad I don't know any humans on the brink of death."

There was a moment's silence, then Patch seemed to shake off his thoughts. He said, "How much money can we make before midnight?"

"Playing cards or boxing?"

"Cards."

Rixon's eyes sparkled. "What do we have here? A pretty boy? Come here and let me give you a proper clatter." He hooked Patch around the neck, pinning him in the crook of his elbow, but Patch got him around the waist and dragged Rixon to the grass, where they took turns throwing clobbering punches.

"All right, all right!" Rixon bellowed, throwing his hands up in surrender. "Just 'cause I can't feel a bloody lip doesn't mean I want to spend the rest of the night walking around with one." He winked. "Won't increase my chances with the ladies."

"And a black eye will?"

Rixon lifted his fingers to his eyes, probing. "You didn't!" he said, swinging a fist at Patch.

I pulled my finger away from Patch's scars. The skin on the back of my neck prickled, and my heart pumped much too fast. Patch looked at me, a shadow of uncertainty in his eyes.

I was forced to accept that maybe now wasn't the time to rely on the logical half of my brain. Maybe this was one of those times when I needed to step out of bounds. Stop playing by the rules. Accept the impossible.

"Then you're definitely not human," I said. "You really are a fallen angel. A bad guy."

That squeezed a smile out of Patch. "You think I'm a bad guy?"

"You possess other people's . . . bodies."

He accepted the statement with a nod.

"Do you want to possess my body?"

"I want to do a lot of things to your body, but that's not one of them."

"What's wrong with the body you have?"

"My body is a lot like glass. Real, but outward, reflecting the world around me. You see and hear me, and I see and hear you. When you touch me, you feel it. I don't experience you in the same way. I can't feel you. I experience everything through a sheet of glass, and the only way I can cut through that sheet is by possessing a human body."

"Or part-human."

Patch's mouth tightened at the corners. "When you touched my scars, you saw Chauncey?" he guessed.

"I heard you talking to Rixon. He said you possess Chauncey's body for two weeks every year during Cheshvan. He said Chauncey isn't human either. He's Nephilim." The word rolled off my tongue in a whisper.

"Chauncey is a cross between a fallen angel and a human. He's immortal like an angel but has all the mortal senses. A fallen angel who wants to feel human sensations can do it in a Nephil's body."

"If you can't feel, why did you kiss me?"

Patch traced a finger along my collarbone, then headed south, stopping at my heart. I felt it pounding through my skin. "Because I feel it here, in my heart," he said quietly. "I haven't lost the ability to feel emotion." He watched me closely. "Let me put it this way. Our emotional connection isn't lacking."

Don't panic, I thought. But already my breathing was faster, shallower. "You mean you can feel happy or sad or—"

"Desire." A barely-there smile.

Keep moving forward, I told myself. Don't give your own emotions time to catch up. Deal with them later, after you have answers. "Why did you fall?"

Patch's eyes held mine for a couple of counts. "Lust."

I swallowed. "Money lust?"

Patch stroked his jaw. He only did that when he wanted to conceal what he was thinking, the giveaway to his thoughts being his mouth. He was fighting a smile. "And other kinds. I thought if I fell, I'd become human. The angels who'd tempted Eve had been banished to Earth, and there were rumors that they'd lost their wings and become human. When they left heaven, it wasn't this big ceremony we were all invited to. It was private. I didn't know their wings were ripped out, or that they were cursed to roam Earth with a hunger to possess human bodies. Back then, nobody had even heard of fallen angels. So it made sense in my mind, that if I fell, I'd lose my wings and become human. At the time, I was crazy about a human girl, and it seemed worth the risk."

"Dabria said you can get your wings back by saving a human life. She said you'll be a guardian angel. You don't want that?" I was confused why he was so set against it.

"It's not for me. I want to be human. I want it more than I've ever wanted anything."

"What about Dabria? If the two of you aren't together anymore, why is she still here? I thought she was a regular angel. Does she want to be human too?"

Patch went deathly still, all the muscles up his arm going rigid. "Dabria's still on Earth?"

"She got a job at school. She's the new school psychologist, Miss Greene. I've met with her a couple times." My stomach gave a hard twist. "After what I saw in your memory, I thought she took the job to be closer to you."

"What exactly did she tell you when you met with her?"

"To stay away from you. She hinted at your dark and dangerous past." I paused. "Something about this is off, isn't it?" I asked, feeling an ominous prickle make its way down my spine.

"I need to take you home. Then I'm going to the high school to look through her files and see if I can find something useful. I'll feel better when I know what she's planning." Patch stripped the bed bare. "Wrap yourself in these," he said, handing me the bundle of dry sheets.

My mind was working hard to make sense of the fragments of information. Suddenly my mouth went a little dry and sticky. "She still has feelings for you. Maybe she wants me out of the picture."

Our eyes locked. "It crossed my mind," Patch said.

An icy, disturbing thought had been banging around inside my head the past few minutes, trying to get my attention. It practically shouted at me now, telling me Dabria could be the guy in the ski mask. All along I thought the person I hit with the Neon was male, just like Vee thought her attacker was male. At this point, I wouldn't put it past Dabria to deceive us both.

After a quick trip to the bathroom, Patch emerged wearing his wet tee. "I'll go get the Jeep," he said. "I'll pull around to the back exit in twenty. Stay in the motel until then."

AFTER PATCH LEFT, I PUT THE CHAIN ON THE DOOR. I dragged the chair across the room and rammed it under the door handle. I checked to make sure the window locks were in place. I didn't know if locks would work against Dabria—I didn't even know if she *was* after me—but I figured it was better to play it safe. After pacing around the room for a few minutes, I tried the phone on the nightstand. Still no dial tone.

My mom was going to kill me.

I'd sneaked behind her back and gone to Portland. And how was I supposed to explain the whole "I checked into a motel with Patch" situation? I'd be lucky if she didn't ground me through the end of the year. No. I'd be lucky if she didn't quit her job and apply to substitute teach until she found a full-time job locally. We'd have to sell the farmhouse, and I'd lose the only connection to my dad I had left.

Approximately fifteen minutes later I peered through the peephole. Nothing but blackness. I unbarred the door, and just as I was about to tug it open, lights flickered on behind me. I whirled around, half expecting to see Dabria. The room was still and empty, but the electricity was back.

The door opened with a loud click and I stepped into the hall. The carpet was bloodred, worn bald down the center of the hallway, and stained with unidentifiable dark marks. The walls were painted neutral, but the paint job was sloppy and chipping.

Above me, a neon green sign spelled the way to the exit. I followed the arrow down the hall and around the corner. The Jeep rolled to a stop on the other side of the back door, and I dashed out and hopped in on the passenger side.

No lights were on when Patch pulled up to the farmhouse. I experienced a guilty squeeze in my stomach and wondered if my mom was driving around, looking for me. The rain had died, and fog pressed against the siding and hung on the shrubs like Christmas tinsel. The trees dotting the driveway were permanently twisted and

BECCA FITZPATRICK

misshapen from constant northern winds. All houses look uninviting with the lights off after dark, but the farmhouse with its small slits for windows, bowed roof, caved-in porch, and wild brambles looked haunted.

"I'm going to walk through," Patch said, swinging out.

"Do you think Dabria's inside?"

He shook his head. "But it doesn't hurt to check."

I waited in the Jeep, and a few minutes later Patch walked out the front door. "All clear," he told me. "I'll drive to the high school and come back here as soon as I sweep her office. Maybe she left something useful behind." He didn't sound like he was counting on it.

I unbuckled my seat belt and ordered my legs to carry me quickly up the walk. As I turned the doorknob, I heard Patch back down the driveway. The porch boards creaked under my feet and I suddenly felt very alone.

Keeping the lights off, I crept through the house room by room, starting with the first floor, then working my way upstairs. Patch had already cleared the house, but I didn't think an extra pair of eyes would hurt. After I was sure no one was hiding under the furniture, behind the shower curtains, or in the closets, I tugged on Levi's and a black V-neck sweater. I found the emergency cell phone my mom kept in a first-aid kit under the bathroom sink and dialed her cell.

She picked up on the first ring. "Hello? Nora? Is that you? Where are you? I've been worried sick!"

I drew a deep breath, praying the right words would come to me and help me talk my way out of this.

"Here's the deal—," I began in my most sincere and apologetic voice.

"Cascade Road flooded and they closed it. I had to turn back and get a room in Milliken Mills—that's where I am now. I tried calling home, but apparently the lines are down. I tried your cell, but you didn't pick up."

"Wait. You've been in Milliken Mills this whole time?"

"Where did you think I was?"

I gave an inaudible sigh of relief and lowered myself onto the edge of the bathtub. "I didn't know," I said. "I couldn't get ahold of you, either."

"What number are you calling from?" Mom asked. "I don't recognize this number."

"The emergency cell."

"Where's your phone?"

"I lost it."

"What! Where?"

I came to the rocky conclusion that a lie of omission was the only way to go. I didn't want to alarm her. I also didn't want to be grounded for an interminable length of time. "It's more like I misplaced it. I'm sure it will pop up somewhere." On a dead woman's body.

"I'll call you as soon as they open the roads," she said.

Next I called Vee's cell. After five rings I was sent to voice mail.

"Where are you?" I said. "Call me back at this number ASAP." I snapped the phone shut and tucked it into my pocket, trying to convince myself Vee was fine. But I knew it was a lie. The invisible thread tying us together had been warning me for hours now that she was in danger. If anything, the feeling was heightening with each passing minute.

In the kitchen I saw my bottle of iron pills on the counter, and I immediately went for them, popping the cap and swallowing two with a glass of chocolate milk. I stood in place a moment, letting the iron work into my system, feeling my breathing deepen and slow. I was walking the milk carton back to the fridge when I saw her standing in the doorway between the kitchen and laundry room.

A cold, wet substance pooled at my feet, and I realized I'd dropped the milk. "Dabria?" I said.

She tilted her head to one side, showing mild surprise. "You know my name?" She paused. "Ah, Patch."

I backed up to the sink, putting more distance between us. Dabria didn't look anything like she did at school as Miss Greene. Tonight her hair was tangled, not smooth, and her lips were brighter, a certain hunger reflected there. Her eyes were sharper, a smudge of black ringing them.

"What do you want?" I asked.

She laughed, and it sounded like ice cubes tinkling in a glass. "I want Patch."

hush, hush

"Patch isn't here."

She nodded. "I know. I waited down the street for him to leave before I came in. But that's not what I meant when I said I want Patch."

The blood pounding through my legs circled back to my heart with a dizzying effect. I put one hand on the counter to steady myself. "I know you were spying on me during the counseling sessions."

"Is that all you know about me?" she asked, her eyes searching mine.

I remembered the night I was sure someone had looked in my bedroom window. "You've been spying on me here, too," I said.

"This is the first time I've been to your house." She dragged her finger along the edge of the kitchen island and perched herself on a stool. "Nice place."

"Let me refresh your memory," I said, hoping I sounded brave. "You looked in my bedroom window while I was sleeping."

Her smile curved high. "No, but I did follow you shopping. I attacked your friend and planted little hints in her mind, making her think Patch hurt her. It wasn't a far stretch. He's not exactly harmless to begin with. It was in my best interest to make you as frightened of him as possible."

"So I'd stay away from him."

"But you didn't. You're still standing in our way."

"In your way of what?"

"Come on, Nora. If you know who I am, then you know how this works. I want him to get his wings back. He doesn't belong on Earth. He belongs with me. He made a mistake, and I'm going to correct it." There was absolutely no compromise in her voice. She got off the stool and walked around the island toward me.

I backed along the edge of the outer counter, keeping space between us. Racking my brain, I tried to think of a way to distract her. Or escape. I'd lived in the house sixteen years. I knew the floor plan. I knew every secret crevice and the best hiding places. I commanded my brain to come up with a plan: something spur-of-the-moment and brilliant. My back met with the sideboard.

"As long as you're around, Patch won't return with me," Dabria said.

"I think you're overestimating his feelings for me." It seemed like a good idea to downplay our relationship. Dabria's possessiveness appeared to be the main force driving her to act.

An incredulous smile dawned on her face. "You think he has those feelings for you? All this time you thought—" She broke off, laughing. "He's not staying because he loves you. He wants to kill you."

I shook my head. "He's not going to kill me."

Dabria's smile hardened at the edges. "If that's what you believe, you're just another girl he's seduced to get what he wants. He has a talent for it," she added shrewdly. "He seduced your name right out of me, after all. One soft touch from Patch was all it took. I fell under his spell and told him death was coming for you."

I knew what she was talking about. I'd witnessed the exact moment she was referring to inside Patch's memory.

"And now he's doing the same thing to you," she said. "Betrayal hurts, doesn't it?"

I shook my head slowly. "No—"

"He's planning to use you as a sacrifice!" she erupted. "See that mark?" She thrust her finger at my wrist. "It means you're a female descendant of a Nephil. And not just any Nephil, but Chauncey Langeais, Patch's vassal."

I glanced at my scar, and for one heart-stopping moment, I actually believed her. But I knew better than to trust her.

"There's a sacred book, *The Book of Enoch*," she said. "In it, a fallen angel kills his Nephil vassal by sacrificing one of the Nephil's female descendants. You don't think Patch wants to kill you? What's the one thing he wants most? Once he sacrifices you, he'll be human. He'll have everything he wants. And he won't come home with me."

She unsheathed a large knife from the wood block on the counter. "And that's why I have to get rid of you. It appears that one way or another, my premonitions were right. Death is coming for you."

"Patch is coming back," I said, my insides sickening. "Don't you want to talk this over with him?"

"I'll make it quick," she continued. "I'm an angel of death. I carry souls to the afterlife. As soon as I finish, I'll carry your soul through the veil. You have nothing to be afraid of."

BECCA FITZPATRICK

I wanted to scream out, but my voice was trapped at the back of my throat. I edged around the sideboard, putting the kitchen table between us. "If you're an angel, where are your wings?"

"No more questions." Her voice had grown impatient, and she began closing the distance between us in earnest.

"How long has it been since you left heaven?" I asked, stalling. "You've been down here for several months, right? Don't you think the other angels have noticed you're missing?"

"Not another step," she snapped, raising the knife, scattering light off the blade.

"You're going to a lot of trouble for Patch," I said, my voice not nearly as devoid of panic as I wanted. "I'm surprised you don't resent him for using you when it suits his purpose. I'm surprised you want him to get his wings back at all. After what he did to you, aren't you happy he's banished here?"

"He left me for a worthless human girl!" she spat, her eyes a fiery blue.

"He didn't leave you. Not really. He fell—"

"He fell because he wanted to be human, like her! He had me— he had me!" She gave a scoffing laugh, but it didn't mask the anger or sorrow. "At first I was hurt and angry, and I did everything in my power to forget about him. Then, when the archangels figured out he was seriously attempting to become human, they sent me down here to change his mind. I told myself I wasn't going to fall for him all over again, but what good did it do?"

"Dabria . . . ," I began softly.

"He didn't even care that the girl was made from the dust of the earth! You—all of you—are selfish and slovenly! Your bodies are wild and undisciplined. One moment you're at the peak of joy, the next you're on the brink of despair. It's deplorable! No angel will aspire to it!" She flung her arm in a wild arc across her face, wiping away tears. "Look at me! I can barely control myself! I've been down here too long, submerged in human filth!"

I turned and ran from the kitchen, knocking over a chair and leaving it behind me in Dabria's path. I raced down the hall, knowing I was trapping myself. The house had two exits: the front door, which Dabria could reach before me by cutting through the living room, and the back door off the dining room, which she blocked.

I was shoved hard from behind, and I pitched forward. I skidded down the hall, coming to a stop on my stomach. I rolled over. Dabria hovered a few feet above me—in the air—her skin and hair ablaze in blinding white, the knife pointed down at me.

I didn't think. I kicked my leg up with all my strength. I arched into the kick, bracing with my nonkicking leg, and aimed for her lower arm. The knife was knocked out of her hand. As I got my feet under me, Dabria pointed at the lamp on a small entryway table, and with a sharp fling of her finger, sent it flying at me. I rolled away, feeling shards of glass slide under me as the lamp shattered on the floor.

BECCA FITZPATRICK

"Move!" Dabria commanded, and the entry bench slid to barricade the front door, blocking my exit.

Scrambling forward, I took the stairs two at a time, using the banister to propel me faster. I heard Dabria laugh behind me, and the next instant the banister broke free, crashing to the hall below. I threw my weight back to keep from falling over the unguarded edge. Catching my balance, I raced up the final stairs. At the top I flung myself into my mom's bedroom and slammed the French doors shut.

Racing to one of the windows flanking the fireplace, I looked down two stories to the ground. There were three bushes in a rock bed directly below, all their foliage gone since autumn. I didn't know if I'd survive a jump.

"Open!" Dabria commanded from the other side of the French doors. A crack split up the wood as the door strained against the lock. I was out of time.

I ran to the fireplace and ducked under the mantel. I had just pulled my feet up, bracing them against the inside of the flue, when the doors swung open, slamming back against the wall. I heard Dabria stride to the window.

"Nora!" she called in her delicate, chilling voice. "I know you're close! I sense you. You can't run and you can't hide—I'll burn this house down room by room if that's what it takes to find you! And then I'll burn my way through the fields behind. I'm not leaving you alive!"

A glow of bright gold light sizzled to life outside the fireplace, along with the roaring *whoosh* of fire igniting. The flames sent shadows dancing in the pit below. I heard the snap and crackle of fire eating up fuel—most likely the furniture or wood floors.

I stayed cramped in the flue. My heart throbbed, sweat leaking from my skin. I drew several breaths, exhaling slowly to manage the burn in my tightly contracted leg muscles. Patch had said he was going to the school. How long until he came back?

Not knowing if Dabria was still in the room, but fearing that if I didn't leave now, the fire would trap me in, I lowered one leg into the pit, then the other. I came out from under the mantel. Dabria was nowhere in sight, but the flames were licking up the walls, smoke choking all air from the room.

I hurried down the hall, not daring to go downstairs, thinking Dabria would expect me to try to escape through one of the doors. In my bedroom I opened the window. The tree outside was close enough and sturdy enough to climb. Maybe I could lose Dabria in the fog behind the house. The nearest neighbors were just under a mile away, and running hard, I could be there in seven minutes. I was about to swing my leg out the window when a creak sounded down the hall.

Quietly closing myself inside the closet, I dialed 911.

"There's someone in my house trying to kill me," I whispered to the operator. I had just given my address when the door to my room eased open. I held perfectly still.

BECCA FITZPATRICK

Through the slats in the closet door, I watched a shadowy figure enter the room. The lighting was low, my angle was off, and I couldn't see a single distinguishing detail. The figure parted the window blinds, peering out. It fingered the socks and underwear in my open drawer. It picked up the silver comb on my bureau, studied it, then returned it. When the figure turned in the direction of the closet, I knew I was in trouble.

Sliding my hand over the floor, I felt for anything I could use in my defense. My elbow bumped a stack of shoe boxes, toppling them. I mouthed a curse. The footsteps trod closer.

The closet doors opened, and I hurled a shoe out. I grabbed another and threw it.

Patch swore in an undertone, yanked a third shoe out of my hands, and hurled it behind him. Wrestling me out of the closet, he got me on my feet. Before I could register relief at discovering him and not Dabria in front of me, he pulled me against him and wrapped his arms around me.

"Are you okay?" he murmured in my ear.

"Dabria's here," I said, my eyes brimming with tears. My knees trembled, and Patch's hold was the only thing keeping me up. "She's burning down the house."

Patch handed me a set of keys and curled my fingers around them. "My Jeep's parked on the street. Get in, lock the doors, drive to Delphic, and wait for me." He tipped my chin up to face him. He brushed a kiss across my lips and sent a flash of heat through me.

"What are you going to do?" I asked.

"Take care of Dabria."

"How?"

He slid me a look that said, Do you really want details?

The sound of sirens wailed in the distance.

Patch looked to the window. "You called the police?"

"I thought you were Dabria."

He was already on his way out the door. "I'll go after Dabria. Drive the Jeep to Delphic and wait for me."

"What about the fire?"

"The police will handle it."

I tightened my grip on the keys. The decision-making part of my brain was split, running in opposite directions. I wanted to get out of the house and away from Dabria, and meet up with Patch later, but there was one nagging thought I couldn't shake free. Dabria had said Patch needed to sacrifice me to become human.

She hadn't said it lightly, or to get under my skin. Or even to harden me against him. Her words had come out cold and serious. Serious enough that she tried to kill me to stop Patch from getting to me first.

I found the Jeep parked on the street, just like Patch had said. I put the keys in the ignition and floored the Jeep down Hawthorne. Figuring it was pointless to try Vee's cell again, I dialed her home phone instead.

"Hi, Mrs. Sky," I said, trying to sound like nothing was out of the ordinary. "Is Vee there?"

"Hi, Nora! She left a few hours ago. Something about a party in Portland. I thought she was with you."

"Um, we got separated," I lied. "Did she say where she was going after the party?"

"She was thinking about seeing a movie. And she isn't answering her cell, so I assume she has it turned off for a show. Is everything okay?"

I didn't want to frighten her, but at the same time, I wasn't about to say everything was okay. Not one bit of it felt okay to me. The last time I'd heard from Vee, she was with Elliot. And now she wasn't answering her cell.

"I don't think so," I said. "I'm going to drive around and look for her. I'll start at the movie theater. Will you search the promenade?"

CHAPTER

26

I T WAS THE SUNDAY NIGHT BEFORE THE START OF SPRING
break, and the movie theater was packed. I got in the ticket
line, continually looking around for signs that I'd been followed. Nothing alarming so far, and the press of bodies offered
good cover. I told myself Patch would take care of Dabria and that
I had nothing to worry about, but it didn't hurt to be vigilant.

Of course, deep inside, I knew Dabria wasn't my biggest worry.
Sooner or later Patch was going to figure out I wasn't at Delphic.

Based on past experience, I didn't have any illusions about being able to hide long-term from him. He would find me. And then I'd be forced to confront him with the question I was dreading. More specifically, I dreaded his answer. Because there was a shadow of doubt at the back of my mind, whispering that Dabria had been telling the truth about what it would take for Patch to get a human body.

I stepped up to the ticket window. The nine-thirty movies were just starting.

"One for The Sacrifice," I said without thinking. Immediately I found the title eerily ironic. Not wanting to reflect further on it, I fished in my pockets and pushed a wad of small bills and coins under the window, praying it was enough.

"Jeez," the teller said, staring at the coins spilling under the window. I recognized her from school. She was a senior, and I was pretty sure her name was Kaylie or Kylie. "Thanks a lot," she said. "It's not like there's a line or anything."

Everyone behind me muttered a collective expletive.

"I cleaned out my piggy bank," I said, attempting sarcasm.

"No kidding. Is it all here?" she asked, expelling a drawn-out sigh as she pushed the coins into groups of quarters, dimes, nickels, and pennies.

"Sure."

"Whatever. I don't get paid enough for this." She swept the money into the cash drawer and slid my ticket under the window. "There are these things called credit cards. . . ."

hush, hush

I grabbed the ticket. "Did you happen to see Vee Sky come in tonight?"

"Bee who?"

"Vee Sky. She's a sophomore. She was with Elliot Saunders."

Kaylie or Kylie's eyes bugged out. "Does it look like a slow night? Does it look like I've just been sitting here, memorizing every face that walks past?"

"Never mind," I breathed, heading for the doors leading inside.

Coldwater's movie theater has two screens, behind doors on either side of a concession counter. As soon as the ticket guy ripped my ticket in half, I tugged on the door to theater number two and ducked inside to darkness. The movie had started.

The theater was almost full, except for a few isolated seats. I walked down the aisle, looking for Vee. At the bottom of the aisle I turned and walked across the front of the theater. It was hard to distinguish faces in the darkness, but I was pretty sure Vee wasn't here.

I exited the theater and walked over to the show next door. It wasn't as crowded. I did another walk-through, but again, I didn't see Vee. Taking a seat near the back, I tried to settle my mind.

This whole night felt like a dark fairy tale I'd strayed into and couldn't find my way back out of. A fairy tale with fallen angels, human hybrids, and sacrificial killings. I rubbed my thumb over my birthmark. I especially didn't want to think about the possibility that I was descended from one of the Nephilim.

I pulled out the emergency cell phone and checked for missed calls. None.

I was tucking the phone in my pocket when a carton of popcorn materialized beside me.

"Hungry?" asked a voice from just over my shoulder. The voice was quiet and not especially happy. I tried to keep my breathing calm. "Stand up and walk out of the theater," Patch said. "I'll be right behind you."

I didn't move.

"Walk out," he repeated. "We need to talk."

"About how you need to sacrifice me to get a human body?" I asked, my tone light, my insides feeling leaden.

"That might be cute if you thought it was true."

"I do think it's true!" Sort of. But the same thought kept returning—if Patch wanted to kill me, why hadn't he already?

"Shh!" said the guy next to me.

Patch said, "Walk out, or I'll carry you out."

I flipped around. "Excuse me?"

"Shh!" the guy beside me hissed again.

"Blame him," I told the guy, pointing at Patch.

The guy craned his neck back. "Listen," he said, facing me again. "If you don't quiet down, I'll get security."

"Fine, go get security. Tell them to take him away," I said, again signaling Patch. "Tell them he wants to kill me."

"*I* want to kill you," hissed the guy's girlfriend, leaning around him to address me.

hush, hush

"Who wants to kill you?" the guy asked. He was still looking over his shoulder, but his expression was puzzled.

"There's nobody *there*," the girlfriend told me.

"You're making them think they can't see you, aren't you?" I said to Patch, awed by his power even as I despised his use of it.

Patch smiled, but it was pinched at the corners.

"Oh, jeez!" said the girlfriend, throwing her hands in the air. She rolled her eyes furiously at her boyfriend and said, "Do something!"

"I need you to stop talking," the guy told me. He gestured at the screen. "Watch the show. Here—have my soda."

I swung into the aisle. I felt Patch move behind me, unsettlingly close, not quite touching. He stayed that way until we were out of the theater.

On the other side of the door, Patch hooked my arm and guided me across the foyer to the ladies' room.

"What is it with you and girls' bathrooms?" I said.

He steered me through the door, locked it, and leaned back against it. His eyes were all over me. And they showed every sign of wanting to rattle me to death.

I was backed up against the counter, my palms digging into the edge. "You're mad because I didn't go to Delphic." I raised one shaky shoulder. "Why Delphic, Patch? It's Sunday night. Delphic will be closing soon. Any special reason you wanted me to drive to a dark, soon-to-be deserted amusement park?"

He walked toward me until he was standing close enough that I could see his black eyes beneath his ball cap.

"Dabria told me you have to sacrifice me to get a human body," I said.

Patch was quiet a moment. "And you think I'd go through with it?"

I swallowed. "Then it's true?"

Our eyes locked. "It has to be an intentional sacrifice. Simply killing you won't do it."

"Are you the only person who can do this to me?"

"No, but I'm probably the only person who knows the end result, and the only person who would attempt it. It's the reason I came to school. I had to get close to you. I needed you. It's the reason I walked into your life."

"Dabria told me you fell for a girl." I hated myself for experiencing irrational pangs of jealousy. This wasn't supposed to be about me. This was supposed to be an interrogation. "What happened?"

I desperately wanted Patch to give away some clue to his thoughts, but his eyes were a cool black, emotions tucked out of sight. "She grew old and died."

"That must have been hard for you," I snapped.

He waited a few counts before answering. His tone was so low, I shivered. "You want me to come clean, I will. I'll tell you everything. Who I am and what I've done. Every last detail. I'll dig it all up, but you have to ask. You have to want it. You can see who I was, or you can see who I am now. I'm not good," he said, piercing me with eyes that absorbed all light but reflected none, "but I was worse."

I ignored the roll in my stomach and said, "Tell me."

"The first time I saw her, I was still an angel. It was an instant, possessive lust. It drove me crazy. I didn't know anything about her, except that I would do whatever it took to get close to her. I watched her for a while, and then I got it in my head that if I went down to Earth and possessed a human body, I would be cast out of heaven and become human. The thing is, I didn't know about Cheshvan. I came down on a night in August, but I couldn't possess the body. On my way back to heaven, a host of avenging angels stopped me and ripped out my wings. They tossed me out of the sky. Right away I knew something was wrong. When I looked at humans, all I could feel was an insatiable craving to be inside their bodies. All my powers were stripped, and I was this weak, pathetic thing. I wasn't human. I was fallen. I'd realized I'd given it all up, just like that. All this time I've hated myself for it. I thought I'd given it up for nothing." His eyes focused singularly on me, leaving me feeling transparent. "But if I hadn't fallen, I wouldn't have met you."

My conflicting emotions weighed so heavily inside my chest, I thought they might suffocate me. Biting back tears, I forged ahead. "Dabria said my birthmark means I'm related to Chauncey. Is that true?"

"Do you want me to answer that?"

I didn't know what I wanted. My whole world felt like a joke,

BECCA FITZPATRICK

and I was the last one to get the punch line. I wasn't Nora Grey, average girl. I was the descendant of someone who wasn't even human. And my heart was smashing itself to pieces over another nonhuman. A dark angel. "Which side of my family?" I said at last.

"Your dad's."

"Where's Chauncey now?" Even though we were related, I liked the idea of him being far away. Very far away. Far enough that the link between us might not feel as real.

His boots were flush with the toes of my tennis shoes. "I'm not going to kill you, Nora. I don't kill people who are important to me. And you top the list."

My heart did a nervous flip. My hands were pressed against his stomach, which was so hard even his skin didn't give. I was keeping a pointless safeguard between us, since not even a towering electrical fence would make me feel secure from him.

"You're impinging on my private space," I said, inching backward.

Patch gave a barely there smile. "Impinging? This isn't the SAT, Nora."

I tucked a few stray hairs behind my ears and took one sizable step sideways, skirting the sink. "You're crowding me. I need— room." What I needed were boundaries. I needed willpower. I needed to be caged up, since yet again I was proving I couldn't be trusted in Patch's presence. I should have been bolting for the door, and yet . . . I wasn't. I tried convincing myself I was staying because I needed answers, but that was only part of it. It was the other part I didn't want to think about. The emotional part. The part that was pointless fighting.

"Are you keeping anything else from me?" I wanted to know.

"I'm keeping a lot of things from you."

My insides took a steep dive. "Like?"

"Like the way I feel about being locked up in here with you." Patch braced one hand against the mirror behind me, his weight tipping toward me. "You have no idea what you do to me."

I shook my head. "I don't think so. This isn't a good idea. This isn't right."

"There's all kinds of right," he murmured. "On the spectrum, we're still in the safe zone."

I was pretty sure the self-preserving half of my brain was screaming, *Run for your life!* Unfortunately, blood roared in my ears, and I wasn't hearing straight. Obviously I wasn't thinking straight either.

"Definitely right. Usually right," Patch continued. "Mostly right. Maybe right."

"Maybe not right now." I sucked in some air. Out of the corner of my eye I noticed a fire alarm drilled into the wall. It was ten, maybe fifteen feet away. If I was fast, I could cross the room and pull it before Patch stopped me. Security would come running. I'd be safe. And that's what I wanted . . . wasn't it?

"Not a good idea," Patch said with a soft shake of his head.

BECCA FITZPATRICK

I bolted for the fire alarm anyway. My fingers closed on the lever and I pulled down to sound the alarm. Only, the lever didn't budge. As hard as I tried, I couldn't get it to move. And then I recognized Patch's familiar presence in my head, and I knew it was a mind game.

I swiveled around to face him. "Get out of my head." I stormed back and shoved hard against his chest. Patch took a step back, steadying himself.

"What was that for?" he asked.

"For this whole night." For making me crazy about him when I knew it was wrong. He was the worst kind of wrong. He was so wrong it felt right, and that made me feel completely out of control.

I might have been tempted to hit him square in the jaw had he not taken me by the shoulders and pinned me against the wall. There was hardly any space left between us, just a thin boundary of air, but Patch managed to eliminate it.

"Let's be honest, Nora. You've got it bad for me." His eyes held a lot of depth. "And I've got it bad for you." He leaned into me and put his mouth on mine. A lot of him was on me, actually. We touched base at several strategic locations down our bodies, and it took all my willpower to break away.

I pulled back. "I'm not finished. What happened to Dabria?"

"All taken care of."

"What exactly does that mean?"

"She wasn't going to keep her wings after plotting to kill you. The moment she tried to get back into heaven, the avenging angels would have stripped them. She had it coming sooner or later. I just sped things up."

"So you just—tore them off?"

"They were deteriorating; the feathers were broken and thin. If she stayed on Earth much longer, it was a signal to every other fallen angel who saw her that she'd fallen. If I didn't do it, one of them would have."

I dodged another one of his advances. "Is she going to make another unwanted appearance in my life?"

"Hard to say."

Lightning quick, Patch caught hold of the hem of my sweater. He reeled me into him. His knuckles brushed the skin of my navel. Heat and ice shot through me simultaneously. "You could take her, Angel," he said. "I've seen both of you in action, and my bet's on you. You don't need me for that."

"What do I need you for?"

He laughed. Not abruptly, but with a certain low desire. His eyes had lost their edge and were focused wholly on me. His smile was all fox . . . but softer. Something just behind my navel danced, then coiled lower.

"Door's locked," he said. "And we have unfinished business."

My body seemed to have swept aside the logical part of my brain. Smothered it, in fact. I slid my hands up his chest and looped my arms around his neck. Patch lifted me at the hips, and I wrapped my legs around his waist. My pulse pounded, but I didn't mind one little bit. I crushed my mouth to his, soaking up the ecstasy of his mouth on mine, his hands on me, feeling on the verge of bursting out of my skin—

The cell phone in my pocket rang to life. I pulled away from Patch, breathing heavily, and the phone rang a second time.

"Voice mail," Patch said.

Deep in the recesses of my consciousness, I knew answering my phone was important. I couldn't remember why; kissing Patch had made every last harbored worry evaporate. I untangled myself from him, turning away so he wouldn't see how worked up ten seconds of kissing him had made me. Internally I was screaming with joy.

"Hello?" I answered, resisting the urge to wipe my mouth for smeared lip gloss.

"Babe!" Vee said. We had a bad connection, the crackle of static cutting across her voice. "Where are you?"

"Where are you? Are you still with Elliot and Jules?" I flattened a hand against my free ear to hear better.

"I'm at school. We broke in," she said in a voice that was naughty to perfection. "We want to play hide-and-seek but don't have enough people for two teams. So . . . do you know of a fourth person who could come play with us?"

An incoherent voice mumbled in the background.

"Elliot wants me to tell you that if you don't come be his partner—hang on—what?" Vee said into the background.

Elliot's voice came on. "Nora? Come play with us. Otherwise, there's a tree in the common area with Vee's name on it."

Pure ice flowed through me.

"Hello?" I said hoarsely. "Elliot? Vee? Are you there?"

But the connection was dead.

CHAPTER 27

"WHO WAS THAT?" PATCH ASKED.

My whole body was ringing. It took me a moment to answer. "Vee broke into the high school with Elliot and Jules. They want me to meet them. I think Elliot's going to hurt Vee if I don't go." I looked up at Patch. "I think he's going to hurt her if I do."

He folded his arms, frowning. "Elliot?"

"Last week at the library I found an article that said he was questioned in a murder investigation at his old school, Kinghorn Prep. He walked into the computer lab and saw me reading it. Ever since that night, I've gotten a bad vibe from him. A really bad vibe. I think he even broke into my bedroom to steal the article back."

"Anything else I should know?"

"The girl who was murdered was Elliot's girlfriend. She was hanged from a tree. Just now on the phone he said, 'If you don't come, there's a tree in the common area with Vee's name on it.'"

"I've seen Elliot. He seems cocky and a little aggressive, but he doesn't strike me as a killer." He dipped into my front pocket and extracted the Jeep's keys. "I'll drive over and check things out. I won't be long."

"I think we should call the police."

He shook his head. "You'll send Vee to juvie for destruction of property and B and E. One more thing. Jules. Who is this guy?"

"Elliot's friend. He was at the arcade the night we saw you."

His frown deepened. "If there was another guy, I would remember."

He opened the door and I followed him out. A janitor wearing black slacks and a work-issue maroon shirt was sweeping bits of popcorn in the lobby. He did a double take at the sight of Patch exiting the ladies' room. I recognized him from school. Brandt Christensen. We had English together. Last semester I'd helped him write a paper.

"Elliot is expecting me, not you," I told Patch. "If I don't show up, who knows what will happen to Vee? That's a risk I'm not going to take."

"If I let you come, you'll listen to my instructions and follow them carefully?"

"Yes."

"If I tell you to jump?"

"I'll jump."

"If I tell you to stay in the car?"

"I'll stay in the car." It was mostly true.

Out in the parking lot of the theater, Patch aimed his key fob at the Jeep, and the headlights blinked. Suddenly he came to a halt and swore under his breath.

"What's wrong?" I said.

"Tires."

I dropped my gaze and sure enough, both tires on the driver's side were flat. "I can't believe it!" I said. "I drove over two nails?"

Patch crouched by the front tire, running his hand around the circumference. "Screwdriver. This was an intentional attack."

For a moment I thought maybe this was another mind trick. Maybe Patch had his reasons for not wanting me to go to the high school. His feelings about Vee were no secret, after all. But something was missing. I couldn't feel Patch anywhere inside my head. If he was altering my thoughts, he'd found a new way to accomplish it, because as far as I could tell, what I was seeing was real.

"Who would do that?"

He rose to his full height. "The list is long."

"Are you trying to tell me you have a lot of enemies?"

"I've upset a few people. A lot of folks place bets they can't win. Then they blame me for walking off with their car, or more."

Patch walked one space over to a coupe, opened the driver's side door, and took a seat behind the steering wheel. Reaching under it, his hand disappeared.

"What are you doing?" I asked, standing in the open doorway. It was a waste of breath since I was well aware of what he was doing.

"Looking for the spare key." Patch's hand reappeared, holding two blue wires. With some skill, he removed the ends of the wires and tapped them together. The engine turned over, and Patch looked out at me. "Seat belt."

"I'm not stealing a car."

He shrugged. "We need it now. They don't."

"It's *stealing*. It's wrong."

Patch didn't look the least bit troubled. In fact, he looked a little too relaxed in the driver's seat. *This isn't the first time he's done this*, I thought.

"First rule of auto theft," he said on a smile. "Try not to hang around the crime scene longer than necessary."

"Hang on one minute," I said, holding up a finger.

I jogged back to the theater. On my way inside, the glass doors reflected the parking lot behind me, and I saw Patch swing out of the coupe.

BECCA FITZPATRICK

"Hi, Brandt," I said to the boy still flicking popcorn into a long-handled dustpan.

Brandt looked up at me, but his attention was quickly drawn over my shoulder. I heard the theater doors open and sensed Patch move behind me. His approach wasn't all that different from a cloud eclipsing the sun, subtly darkening the landscape, hinting of a storm.

"How's it going?" Brandt said uncertainly.

"I'm having car trouble," I said, biting my lip and trying on a sympathetic face. "I know I'm putting you in an awkward position, but since I helped you with that Shakespeare paper last semester . . ."

"You want to borrow my car."

"Actually . . . yes."

"It's a piece of junk. It's no Jeep Commander." He looked right at Patch like he was apologizing.

"Does it run?" I asked.

"If by run you mean do the wheels roll, yeah, it runs. But it's not for loan."

Patch opened his wallet and handed over what looked like three crisp hundred-dollar bills. Reining in my surprise, I decided the best thing to do was play along.

"I changed my mind," Brandt said, eyes wide, pocketing the money. He fished in his pockets and underhanded Patch a pair of keys.

"What's the make and color?" Patch asked, catching the keys.

hush, hush

"Hard to tell. Part Volkswagen, part Chevette. It used to be blue. That was before it corroded to orange. You'll fill the tank up before you return it?" Brandt said, sounding like he had his fingers crossed behind his back, pressing his luck.

Patch peeled out another twenty. "Just in case we forget," he said, stuffing it into the front pocket of Brandt's uniform.

Outside, I told Patch, "I could have talked him into giving me his keys. I just needed a little more time. And by the way, why do you bus tables at the Borderline if you're loaded?"

"I'm not. I won the money off a pool game a couple nights back." He pushed Brandt's key in the lock and opened the passenger-side door for me. "The bank is officially closed."

Patch drove across town on dark, quiet streets. It didn't take long to arrive at the high school. He rolled Brandt's car to a stop on the east side of the building and killed the engine. The campus was wooded, the branches twisted and bleak and holding up nothing but a damp fog. Behind them loomed Coldwater High.

The original part of the building had been constructed in the late nineteenth century, and after sunset it looked very much like a cathedral. Gray and foreboding. Very dark. Very abandoned.

"I just got a really bad feeling," I said, eyeing the school's black voids for windows.

"Stay in the car and keep out of sight," Patch told me, passing over the keys. "If anybody comes out of the building, take off." He got out. He was wearing a fitted black crewneck tee, dark Levi's, and boots. With his black hair and dusky skin, it was hard to distinguish him from the background. He crossed the street and, in a matter of moments, blended completely into the night.

CHAPTER

28

FIVE MINUTES CAME AND WENT. TEN MINUTES stretched to twenty. I struggled to ignore the hair-raising feeling that I was under surveillance. I peered into the shadows ringing the school.

What was taking Patch so long? I shuffled through a few theories, feeling more uneasy by the moment. What if Patch couldn't find Vee? What would happen when Patch found Elliot? I didn't think Elliot could overpower Patch, but there was always a chance—if Elliot had the element of surprise.

The phone in my pocket rang, and I jumped out of my skin.

"I see you," Elliot said when I answered. "Sitting out there in the car."

"Where are you?"

"Watching you from a second-story window. We're playing inside."

"I don't want to play."

He ended the call.

With my heart in my throat, I got out of the car. I looked up at the dark windows of the school. I didn't think Elliot knew Patch was inside. His voice came across impatient, not angry or irritated. My only hope was that Patch had a plan and would make sure nothing happened to me or Vee. The moon was clouded over, and under a shadow of fear I walked up to the east door.

I stepped into semidarkness. My eyes took several seconds to make something of the shaft of streetlight falling through the window encased in the top half of the door. The floor tiles reflected a waxy gleam. Lockers were lined up on either side of the hallway like sleeping robotic soldiers. Instead of a peaceful, quiet feeling, the halls radiated hidden menace.

The outside lights illuminated the first several feet into the hallway, but after that, I could see nothing. Just inside the door was a panel of light switches, and I flipped them on. Nothing happened.

Since the power was working outside, I knew the electricity inside had been shut off by hand. I wondered if this was part of Elliot's plan. I couldn't see him, and I couldn't see Vee. I also couldn't see Patch. I was going to have to feel my way through each room in the school, playing a slow game of elimination until I found him. Together we would find Vee.

Using the wall as my guide, I crept forward. On any given weekday, I passed down this stretch of hall several times, but in the darkness it suddenly seemed foreign. And longer. Much longer.

At the first intersection I mentally assessed my surroundings. Turning left would lead to the band and orchestra rooms and the cafeteria. Turning right would lead to administrative offices, as well as a double staircase. I continued straight, heading deeper into the school, toward the classrooms.

My foot caught on something, and before I could react, I went sprawling to the floor. Hazy gray light filtered through a skylight directly overhead as the moon broke between clouds, illuminating the features of the body I'd tripped on. Jules was on his back, his expression fixed in a blank stare. His long blond hair was tangled over his face, his hands slack at his sides.

I pushed back on my knees and covered my mouth, panting air. My legs trembled with adrenaline. Very slowly, I rested my palm on Jules's chest. He wasn't breathing. He was dead.

I jumped to my feet and choked on a scream. I wanted to call out for Patch, but that would give my location away to Elliot—if he didn't already know it. I realized with a start that he could be standing feet away, watching me as his twisted game unfolded.

The overhead light faded, and I made a frantic survey of the hall. More endless hallway stretched ahead. The library was up a short flight of stairs to my left. Classrooms started on the right. On a split moment's decision, I chose the library, groping through the blackening halls to get away from Jules's body. My nose dripped, and I realized I was crying soundlessly. Why was Jules dead? Who killed him? If Jules was dead, was Vee also?

The library doors were unlocked, and I fumbled my way inside. Past the bookshelves, at the far end of the library, were three small study rooms. They were soundproof; if Elliot wanted to isolate Vee, the rooms were an ideal place to put her.

I was just about to start toward them when a masculine groan carried through the library. I came to a halt.

The lights out in the hall powered to life, illuminating the darkness of the library. Elliot's body lay a few feet away, his mouth parted, his skin ashen. His eyes rolled my way, and he reached an arm out to me.

A piercing scream escaped me. Whirling around, I ran for the library doors, shoving and kicking chairs out of my way. Run! I ordered myself. Get to an exit!

I staggered out the door, and that's when the lights in the hall died, plunging everything once again to black.

"Patch!" I tried to scream. But my voice caught, and I choked on his name.

Jules was dead. Elliot was almost dead. Who had killed them? Who was left? I tried to make sense of what was happening, but all reason had left me.

A shove to my back threw me off balance. Another shove sent me flying sideways. My head smashed against a locker, stunning me.

A narrow beam of light swept across my vision, and a pair of dark eyes behind a ski mask swirled into focus. The light came from a miner's headlamp secured over the mask.

I pushed up and tried to run. One of his arms shot out, cutting off my escape. He brought up his other arm, trapping me against the locker.

"Did you think I was dead?" I could hear the gloating, icy smile in his voice. "I couldn't pass up one last chance to play with you. Humor me. Who did you think the bad guy was? Elliot? Or did it cross your mind that your best friend could do this? I'm getting warm, aren't I? That's the thing about fear. It brings out the worst in us."

"It's you." My voice rattled.

Jules ripped off the headlamp and ski mask. "In the flesh."

"How did you do it?" I asked, my voice still trembling. "I saw you. You weren't breathing. You were dead."

"You're giving me too much credit. It was all you, Nora. If your mind wasn't so weak, I couldn't have done a thing. Am I making you feel bad? Is it discouraging to know that out of all the minds I've invaded, yours tops the list as easiest? And most fun."

I licked my lips. My mouth tasted a strange combination of dry and sticky. I could smell the fear on my breath. "Where's Vee?"

He slapped my cheek. "Don't change the subject. You really should learn to control your fear. Fear undermines logic and opens up all sorts of opportunities for people like me."

This was a side of Jules I'd never seen. He'd always been so quiet, so sullen, radiating a complete lack of interest in everyone around him. He stayed in the background, drawing little attention, little suspicion. Very clever of him, I thought.

He grabbed my arm and jerked me after him.

I clawed at him and twisted away, and he drove his fist into my stomach. I stumbled backward, gasping for air that did not come. My shoulder dragged down a locker until I sat crumpled on the floor. A ribbon of air slipped down my throat, and I choked on it.

Jules touched the tracks my nails had carved in his forearm. "That's going to cost you."

"Why did you bring me here? What do you want?" I couldn't keep the hysteria from my voice.

He yanked me up by my arm and dragged me farther down the hall. Kicking a door open, he thrust me inside and I went down, my palms colliding with the hard floor. The door slammed behind me. The only light came from the headlamp, which Jules held.

The air held the familiar odors of chalk dust and stale chemicals. Posters of the human body and cross-sections of human cells decorated the walls. A long black granite counter with a sink stood at the front of the room. It faced rows of matching granite lab tables. We were inside Coach McConaughy's biology room.

A flash of metal caught my eye. A scalpel lay on the floor, tucked against the wastebasket. It must have been overlooked by both Coach and the janitor. I slid it into the waistband of my jeans just as Jules hauled me to my feet.

"I had to cut the electricity," he said, setting the headlamp on the nearest table. "You can't play hide-and-seek in the light."

Scraping two chairs across the floor, he positioned them facing each other. "Have a seat." It didn't sound like an invitation.

My eyes darted to the panel of windows spanning the far wall. I wondered if I could crank one open and escape before Jules caught me. Amid a thousand other self-preserving thoughts, I told myself not to appear frightened. Somewhere in the back of my mind I remembered that advice from a self-defense class I'd taken with Mom after my dad died. Make eye contact . . . look confident . . . use common sense . . . all easier said than done.

Jules pushed down on my shoulders, forcing me into a chair. The cold metal seeped through my jeans.

"Give me your cell phone," he ordered, hand held out for it.

"I left it in the car."

He breathed a laugh. "Do you really want to play games with me? I've got your best friend locked somewhere in the building. If you play games with me, she's going to feel left out. I'll have to think up an extra-special game to make it up to her."

I dug out the phone and passed it over.

With superhuman strength, he bent it in half. "Now it's just the two of us." He sank into the chair facing mine and stretched his legs out luxuriously. One arm dangled off the seat back. "Let's talk, Nora."

I bolted from the chair. Jules hooked me around the waist before I'd made it four steps and shoved me back into the chair.

"I used to own horses," he said. "A long time ago in France, I had a stable of beautiful horses. The Spanish horses were my favorite. They were caught wild and brought directly to me. Within weeks I had them subdued. But there was always the rare horse that refused to be broken. Do you know what I did with a horse that refused to be broken?"

I shuddered for an answer.

"Cooperate, and you have nothing to fear," he said.

I didn't for one moment believe him. The gleam in his eyes wasn't sincere.

"I saw Elliot in the library," I was surprised by the waver in my voice. I didn't like or trust Elliot, but he didn't deserve to die slowly and in pain. "Did you hurt him?"

He scooted closer, as if to share a secret. "If you're going to commit a crime, never leave evidence. Elliot's been an integral part of everything. He knows too much."

"Is that why I'm here? Because of the article I found about Kjirsten Halverson?"

huṣh, huṣh   359

Jules smiled. "Elliot failed to mention that you know about Kjirsten."

"Did Elliot kill her . . . or did you?" I asked on a cold snap of inspiration.

"I had to test Elliot's loyalty. I took away what was most important. Elliot was at Kinghorn on scholarship, and nobody let him forget it. Until me. I was his benefactor. In the end, it came down to choosing me or Kjirsten. More succinctly, choosing money or love. Apparently there's no pleasure in being a pauper among princes. I bought him off, and that's when I knew I could rely on him when it came time to dealing with you."

"Why me?"

"You haven't figured it out yet?" The light highlighted the ruthlessness in his face and created the illusion that his eyes had turned the color of molten silver. "I've been toying with you. Dangling you by a string. Using you as a proxy, because the person I really want to harm can't be harmed. Do you know who that person is?"

All the knots in my body seemed to come undone. My eyes moved out of focus. Jules's face was like an Impressionist painting—blurred around the edges, lacking detail. Blood drained from my head, and I felt myself start to slip off the chair. I'd felt this way enough times before to know I needed iron. Soon.

He slapped my cheek again. "Focus. Who am I talking about?"

"I don't know." I couldn't push my voice above a whisper.

"Do you know why he can't be hurt? Because he doesn't have

a human body. His body lacks physical sensation. If I locked him up and tortured him, it wouldn't do any good. He can't feel. Not an ounce of pain. Surely you've got a guess by now? You've been spending a lot of time with this person. Why so silent, Nora? Can't figure it out?"

A trickle of sweat crept down my back.

"Every year at the start of the Hebrew month of Cheshvan, he takes control of my body. Two whole weeks. That's how long I forfeit control. No freedom, no choice. I don't get the luxury of escaping during those two weeks, loaning my body out, then coming back when it's all over. Then I might be able to convince myself it wasn't really happening. No. I'm still in there, a prisoner inside my own body, living every moment of it," he said in a grinding tone. "Do you know what that feels like? Do you?" he shouted.

I kept my mouth shut, knowing that to talk would be dangerous. Jules laughed, a rush of air through his teeth. It sounded more sinister than anything I'd ever heard.

He said, "I swore an oath allowing him to take possession of my body during Cheshvan. I was sixteen years old." He shrugged, but it was a rigid movement. "He tricked me into the oath by torturing me. After, he told me I wasn't human. Can you believe it? Not human. He told me my mother, a human, slept with a fallen angel." He grinned odiously, sweat sprinkling his forehead. "Did I mention I inherited a few traits from my father? Just like him, I'm a deceiver. I make you see lies. I make you hear voices."

Just like this. Can you hear me, Nora? Are you frightened yet?

He tapped my forehead. "What's going on in there, Nora? Awfully quiet."

Jules was Chauncey. He was Nephilim. I remembered my birthmark, and what Dabria had told me. Jules and I shared the same blood. In my veins was the blood of a monster. I shut my eyes, and a tear slid out.

"Remember the night we first met? I jumped in front of the car you were driving. It was dark and there was fog. You were already on edge, which made it that much easier to deceive you. I enjoyed scaring you. That first night gave me a taste for it."

"I would have noticed it was you," I whispered. "There aren't many people as tall as you."

"You're not listening. I can make you see whatever I want. Do you really think I'd overlook a detail as condemning as my height? You saw what I wanted you to see. You saw a nondescript man in a black ski mask."

I sat there, feeling a tiny crack in my terror. I wasn't crazy. Jules was behind all of it. He was the crazy one. He could create mind games because his father was a fallen angel and he'd inherited the power. "You didn't really ransack my bedroom," I said. " You just made me think you did. That's why it was still in order when the police arrived."

He applauded slowly and deliberately. "Do you want to know the best part? You could have blocked me out. I couldn't have touched your mind without your permission. I reached in, and you never resisted. You were weak. You were easy."

It all made sense, and instead of feeling a brief moment of relief, I realized how susceptible I was. I was stripped wide open. There was nothing stopping Jules from sucking me into his mind games, unless I learned to block him out.

"Imagine yourself in my place," said Jules. "Your body violated year after year. Imagine a hatred so hard, nothing but revenge will cure it. Imagine expending large sums of energy and resources to keep a close eye on the object of your revenge, waiting patiently for the moment when fate presented you an opportunity not just to get even, but to tip the scales in your favor." His eyes locked on mine. "You're that opportunity. If I hurt you, I hurt Patch."

"You're overestimating my value to Patch," I said, cold sweat breaking out along my hairline.

"I've been keeping a close eye on Patch for centuries. Last summer he made his first trip to your house, though you didn't notice. He followed you shopping a few times. Every now and then, he made a special trip out of his way to find you. Then he enrolled at your school. I couldn't help but ask myself, what was so special about you? I made an effort to find out. I've been watching you for a while now."

Nothing short of dread gripped me. Right then, I knew it was never my dad's presence I'd felt, following me like a phantom guardian. It was Jules. I felt the same ice-cold, unearthly presence now, only amplified a hundred times.

"I didn't want to draw Patch's suspicion and backed off," he continued. "That's when Elliot stepped forward, and it didn't take him long to tell me what I'd already guessed. Patch is in love with you."

It all clicked into place. Jules hadn't been sick the night he disappeared into the men's room at Delphic. And he hadn't been sick the night we went to the Borderline. All along it was the simple fact that he had to remain invisible to Patch. The moment Patch saw him, it would all be over. Patch would know Jules—Chauncey— was up to something. Elliot was Jules's eyes and ears, feeding information back to him.

"The plan was to kill you on the camping trip, but Elliot failed to convince you to come," Jules said. "Earlier today, I followed you out of Blind Joe's and shot you. Imagine my surprise when I found I'd killed a bag lady dressed in your coat. But it all worked out." His tone relaxed. "Here we are."

I shifted in my seat, and the scalpel slid deeper into my jeans. If I wasn't careful, it would slip out of reach. If Jules forced me to stand, it might slide all the way down my pant leg. And that would be the end of that.

"Let me guess what you're thinking," said Jules, rising to his feet and sauntering to the front of the room. "You're starting to wish you'd never met Patch. You wish he'd never fallen in love with you.

Go on. Laugh at the position he's put you in. Laugh at your own bad choice."

Hearing Jules talk about Patch's love filled me with irrational hope.

I fumbled the scalpel out of my jeans and jumped from my seat. "Don't come near me! I'll stab you. I swear I will!"

Jules made a guttural sound and flung his arm across the counter at the front of the room. Glass beakers shattered against the chalkboard, papers fluttering down. He strode toward me. In a panic, I brought the scalpel up as hard as I could. It met his palm, slicing through skin.

Jules hissed and drew back.

Not waiting, I plunged the scalpel down into his thigh.

Jules gaped at the metal protruding from his leg. He jerked it out using both hands, his face contorting in pain. He opened his hands, and the scalpel fell with a clatter.

He took a faltering step toward me.

I shrieked and dodged away, but my hip clipped the edge of a table; I lost my footing and tumbled down. The scalpel lay several feet away.

Jules flipped me on my stomach and straddled me from behind. He pressed my face into the floor, crushing my nose and muffling my screams.

"Valiant attempt," he grunted. "But that won't kill me. I'm Nephilim. I'm immortal."

I grabbed for the scalpel, digging my toes into the floor to stretch those last, vital inches. My fingers fumbled over it. I was so close, and then Jules was dragging me back.

I brought my heel up hard between his legs; he groaned and went limp off to one side. I scrambled to my feet, but Jules rolled to the door, kneeling between me and it.

His hair hung in his eyes. Beads of sweat trickled down his face. His mouth was lopsided, one half curled up in pain.

Every muscle in my body was coiled, ready to spring into action.

"Good luck trying to escape," he said with a cynical smile that seemed to require a lot of effort. "You'll see what I mean." Then he sank to the ground.

CHAPTER

I HAD NO IDEA WHERE VEE WAS. THE OBVIOUS THOUGHT came to me to think like Jules—where would I hold Vee hostage if I were him?

He wants to make it hard to escape and hard to be found, I reasoned.

I brought up a mental blueprint of the building, narrowing my attention to the upper levels. Chances were, Vee was on the third floor, the highest in the school—except for a small fourth floor, which was more of an attic than anything else. A narrow staircase accessible only from the third floor led up to it. There were two bungalow-style classrooms at the top: AP Spanish and the eZine lab.

Vee was in the eZine lab. Just like that, I knew it.

Moving as quickly as I could through the darkness, I felt my way up two flights of stairs. After some trial and error, I found the narrow staircase leading to the eZine lab. At the top, I pushed on the door.

"Vee?" I called softly.

She let out a small moan.

"It's me," I said, taking each step with care as I maneuvered up an aisle of desks, not wanting to knock over a chair and alert Jules to my location. "Are you hurt? We need to get out of here." I found her huddled at the front of the room, hugging her knees to her chest.

"Jules hit me over the head," she said, her voice rising. "I think I passed out. Now I can't see. I can't see anything!"

"Listen to me. Jules cut the electricity and the shades are drawn. It's just the darkness. Hold my hand. We have to get downstairs right now."

"I think he damaged something. My head is throbbing. I really think I'm blind!"

"You're not blind," I whispered, giving her a small shake. "I can't see either. We have to feel our way downstairs. We're going to leave through the exit by the athletics office."

"He's got chains on all the doors."

A moment of rigid silence dropped between us. I remembered Jules wishing me luck escaping, and now I knew why. A perceptible chill rippled from my heart through the rest of my body. "Not the door I came in," I said at last. "The far east door is unlocked."

"It must be the only one. I was with him when he chained the others. He said that way nobody would be tempted to go outside while we played hide-and-seek. He said outside was out-of-bounds."

"If the east door is the only one left unlocked, he'll try to block it. He'll wait for us to come to him. But we're not going to. We're going out a window," I said, devising a plan off the top of my head. "On the opposite end of the building—this end. Do you have your cell?"

"Jules took it."

"When we get outside, we have to split up. If Jules chases us, he'll have to choose one of us to follow. The other will get help." I already knew who he'd choose. Jules had no use for Vee, except to lure me here tonight. "Run as hard as you can and get to a phone. Call the police. Tell them Elliot is in the library."

"Alive?" Vee asked, her voice trembling.

"I don't know."

We stood huddled together, and I felt her pull her shirt up and wipe her eyes. "This is all my fault."

"This is Jules's fault."

"I'm scared."

"We're going to be fine," I said, attempting to sound optimistic. "I stabbed Jules in the leg with a scalpel. He's bleeding heavily. Maybe he'll give up chasing us and go get medical attention."

A sob escaped Vee. We both knew I was lying. Jules's desire for revenge outweighed his wound. It outweighed everything.

Vee and I crept down the stairs, keeping tight to the walls, until we were back on the main floor.

"This way," I whispered in her ear, holding her hand as we speed-walked down the hall, heading farther west.

We hadn't walked very far when a guttural sound, not quite laughter, rolled out of the tunnel of darkness ahead.

"Well, well, what do we have here?" Jules said. There was no face attached to his voice.

"Run," I told Vee, squeezing her hand. "He wants me. Call the police. Run!"

Vee dropped my hand and ran. Her footsteps faded depressingly fast. I wondered briefly if Patch was still in the building, but it was more of a side thought. Most of my concentration went into not passing out. Because once again, I found myself all alone with Jules.

"It will take the police at least twenty minutes to respond," Jules told me, the tap of his shoes drawing closer. "I don't need twenty minutes."

I turned and ran. Jules broke into a run behind me.

Fumbling my hands over the walls, I turned right at the first intersection and raced down a perpendicular hall. Forced to rely on the walls to guide me, my hands slapped over the sharp edges of lockers and doorjambs, nicking my skin. I made another right, running as fast as I could for the double doors of the gymnasium.

The only thought pounding through my head was that if I could get to my gym locker in time, I could lock myself inside it. The girls' locker room was wall-to-wall and floor-to-ceiling with oversize lockers. It would take Jules time to break into each one individually. If I was lucky, the police would arrive before he found me.

I flung myself into the gym and ran for the attached girls' locker room. As soon as I pushed on the door handle, I felt a spike of cold terror. The door was locked. I rattled the handle again, but it didn't give. Spinning around, I searched frantically for another exit, but I was trapped in the gym. I fell back against the door, squeezed my eyes shut to stave off fainting, and listened to my breath hitch up.

When I reopened my eyes, Jules was walking into the haze of moonlight trickling through the skylights. He'd knotted his shirt around his thigh; a stain of blood seeped through the fabric. He was left in a white undershirt and chinos. A gun was tucked into the waistband of his pants.

"Please let me go," I whispered.

"Vee told me something interesting about you. You're afraid of heights." He lifted his gaze to the rafters high above the gym. A smile split his face.

hush, hush

The stagnant air was sodden with the smells of sweat and wood varnish. The heat had been turned off for spring break and the temperature was icy. Shadows stretched back and forth across the polished floor as the moonlight broke through the clouds. Jules stood with his back to the bleachers, and I saw Patch move behind him.

"Did you attack Marcie Millar?" I asked Jules, ordering myself not to react and give Patch away.

"Elliot told me there's bad blood between the two of you. I didn't like the idea of someone else having the pleasure of tormenting my girl."

"And my bedroom window? Did you spy on me while I was sleeping?"

"Nothing personal."

Jules stiffened. He stepped forward suddenly and jerked on my wrist, spinning me around in front of him. I felt what I feared was the gun press into the nape of my neck. "Take off your hat," Jules ordered Patch. "I want to see the expression on your face when I kill her. You're helpless to save her. As helpless as I was to do anything about the oath I swore to you."

Patch took a couple of steps closer. He moved easily, but I sensed his tightly reined caution. The gun probed deeper, and I winced.

"Take another step and this will be her last breath," Jules warned.

Patch glanced at the distance between us, calculating how quickly he could cover it. Jules saw it too.

"Don't try it," he said.

"You're not going to shoot her, Chauncey."

"No?" Jules squeezed the trigger. The gun clicked, and I opened my mouth to scream, but all that came out was a tremulous sob.

"Revolver," Jules explained. "The other five chambers are loaded."

Ready to use those boxing moves you're always bragging about? Patch said to my mind.

My pulse was all over the place, my legs barely holding me up. "W-what?" I stammered.

Without warning, a rush of power coursed into me. The foreign force expanded to fill me. My body was completely vulnerable to Patch, all my strength and freedom forfeited as he took possession of me.

Before I had time to realize just how much this loss of control terrified me, a crushing pain spiked through my hand, and I realized Patch was using my fist to punch Jules. The gun was knocked loose; it skidded across the gym floor out of reach.

Patch commanded my hands to slam Jules backward against the bleachers. Jules tripped, falling into them.

The next thing I knew, my hands were closing on Jules's throat, flinging his head back against the bleachers with a loud crack! I held him there, pressing my fingers into his neck. His eyes widened, then bulged. He was trying to speak, moving his lips unintelligibly, but Patch didn't let up.

I won't be able to stay inside you much longer, Patch spoke to my thoughts. *It's not Cheshvan and I'm not allowed. As soon as I'm cast out, run. Do you understand? Run as fast as you can. Chauncey will be too weak and stunned to get inside your head. Run and don't stop.*

A high humming sound whined through me, and I felt my body peeling away from Patch's.

The vessels in Jules's neck jumped out and his head drooped to one side. *Come on*, I heard Patch urge him. *Pass out . . . pass out . . .*

But it was too late. Patch vanished from inside me. He was gone so suddenly, I was left dizzy.

My hands were in my control again, and they sprang away from Jules's neck on impulse. He gasped for air and blinked up at me. Patch was on the floor a few feet away, unmoving.

I remembered what Patch had said and sprinted across the gym. I flung myself against the door, expecting to sail into the hall. Instead it was like hitting a wall. I shoved the push bar, knowing the door was unlocked. Five minutes ago I'd come through it. I hurled all my weight against the door. It didn't open.

I turned around, the adrenaline letdown causing my knees to shake. "Get out of my mind!" I screamed at Jules.

Pulling himself up to sit on the lowest rise of the bleachers, Jules massaged his throat. "No," he said.

I tried the door again. I got my foot up and kicked the push bar.

I smacked my palms against the door's slit of a window. "Help! Can anyone hear me? Help!"

Looking over my shoulder, I found Jules limping toward me, his injured leg buckling under each step. I squeezed my eyes shut, trying to focus my mind. The door would open as soon as I found his voice and swept it out. I searched every corner of my mind but couldn't find him. He was somewhere deep, hiding from me. I opened my eyes. Jules was much closer. I was going to have to find another way out.

Drilled into the wall above the bleachers was an iron ladder. It reached to the grid of rafters at the top of the gym. At the far end of the rafters, on the opposite wall, almost directly above where I stood, was an air shaft. If I could get to it, I could climb in and find another way down.

I broke into a dead sprint past Jules and up the bleachers. My shoes slapped the wood, echoing through the empty space, making it impossible to hear whether Jules was following me. I got my footing on the first ladder rung and hoisted myself up. I climbed one rung, then another. Out of the corner of my eye, I saw the drinking fountain far below. It was small, which meant I was high. Very high.

Don't look down, I ordered myself. Concentrate on what's above. I tentatively climbed one more rung. The ladder rattled, not properly welded to the wall.

Jules's laughter carried up to me, and my concentration slipped.

Images of falling flashed in my mind. Logically, I knew he was planting them. Then my brain tilted, and I couldn't remember which way was up or down. I couldn't decipher which thoughts were mine and which belonged to Jules.

My fear was so thick it blurred my vision. I didn't know where on the ladder I stood. Were my feet centered? Was I close to slipping? Clenching the rung with both hands, I pressed my forehead against my knuckles. *Breathe*, I told myself. *Breathe!*

And then I heard it.

The slow, agonizing sound of metal creaking. I closed my eyes to suppress a dizzy spell.

The metal brackets securing the top of the ladder to the wall popped free. The metallic groan changed to a high-pitched whine as the next set of brackets down tore from the wall. I watched with a scream trapped in my throat as the entire top half of the ladder broke free. Locking my arms and legs around the ladder, I braced myself for the backward fall. The ladder wavered a moment in air, patiently succumbing to gravity.

And then it all happened quickly. The rafters and skylights faded away into a dizzying blur. I flew down until, suddenly, the ladder slammed to a stop. It bounced up and down, perpendicular to the wall, thirty feet above ground. The impact jerked my legs loose, my hands my only attachment to the ladder.

"Help!" I screamed, my legs bicycling through air.

The ladder lurched, dropping several more feet. One of my

shoes slid down my foot, caught on my toe, then dropped. Far too long later, it hit the gym floor.

I bit down on my tongue as the pain in my arms deepened. They were tearing out of their sockets.

And then, through the fear and panic, I heard Patch's voice. *Block him out. Keep climbing. The ladder's intact.*

"I can't," I sobbed. "I'll fall!"

Block him out. Close your eyes. Listen to my voice.

Swallowing, I forced my eyes shut. I clung to Patch's voice and felt a sturdy surface take shape beneath me. My feet were no longer hanging in air. I felt one of the ladder rungs digging into the balls of my feet. Focusing with resolve on Patch's voice, I waited until the world crept back into place. Patch was right. I was on the ladder. It was upright, secured to the wall. I regained a measure of determination and continued climbing.

At the top I eased myself precariously onto the closest rafter. I got my arms around it, then swung my right leg up and over. I was facing the wall, with my back to the air shaft, but there was nothing I could do now. Very carefully, I rose up on my knees. Using all my concentration, I starting inching backward across the expanse of the gym.

But it was too late.

Jules had climbed quickly, and was now less than fifteen feet away from me. He climbed onto the rafter. Hand over hand, he dragged himself toward me. A dark slash on the inside of his wrist

hush, hush

caught my eye. It intersected his veins at a ninety-degree angle and was nearly black in color. To anyone else, it might have looked like a scar. To me, it meant so much more. The family connection was obvious. We shared the same blood, and it showed in our identical marks.

We were both straddling the rafter, sitting face-to-face, ten feet apart.

"Any last words?" Jules said.

I looked down, even though it made me dizzy. Patch was far below on the gym floor, still as death. Right then, I wanted to go back in time and relive every moment with him. One more secret smile, one more shared laugh. One more electric kiss. Finding him was like finding someone I didn't know I was searching for. He'd come into my life too late, and now was leaving too soon. I remembered him telling me he'd give up everything for me. He already had. He'd given up a human body of his own so I could live.

I wobbled accidentally, and instinctively dropped lower to balance myself.

Jules's laughter carried like a cold whisper. "It makes no difference to me whether I shoot you or you fall to your death."

"It does make a difference," I said, my voice small but confident. "You and I share the same blood." I lifted my hand precariously, showing him my birthmark. "I'm your descendant. If I sacrifice my blood, Patch will become human and you'll die. It's written in The Book of Enoch."

BECCA FITZPATRICK

Jules's eyes were devoid of light. They were trained on me, absorbing every word I spoke. I could tell by his expression that he was weighing my words. A flush rose in his face, and I knew he believed me. "You—," he sputtered.

He slid toward me with frantic speed, simultaneously reaching into his waistband to draw the gun.

Tears stung my eyes. With no time for second thoughts, I threw myself off the rafter.

A DOOR OPENED AND CLOSED. I WAITED TO HEAR footsteps approach, but the only sound came from the ticking of a clock: a rhythmic, steady pounding through the silence.

The sound began to fade, winding down. I wondered if I would hear it stop completely. I suddenly feared that moment, unsure of what came after.

A much more vibrant sound eclipsed the clock. It was a

reassuring, ethereal sound, a melodic dance on air. Wings, I thought. Coming to take me away.

I held my breath, waiting, waiting, waiting. And then the clock began to go in reverse. Instead of slowing, the beat became more certain. A spiral-like liquid formed inside me, coiling deeper and deeper. I felt myself pulled into the current. I was sliding down through myself, into a dark, warm place.

My eyes flickered open to familiar oak paneling on the sloped ceiling above me. My bedroom. A sense of reassurance flooded over me, and then I remembered where I'd been. In the gym with Jules.

A shiver slid over my skin.

"Patch?" I said, my voice hoarse from disuse. I tried to sit up, then gave a muffled cry. Something was wrong with my body. Every muscle, bone, cell was sore. I felt like one giant bruise.

There was movement near the doorway. Patch leaned against the doorjamb. His mouthed was pressed tight and lacked its usual twinge of humor. His eyes held more depth than I'd ever seen before. They were sharpened by a protective edge.

"That was a good fight back in the gym," he said. "But I think you could benefit from a few more boxing lessons."

On a wave, everything came back to me. Tears rolled up from deep inside me. "What happened? Where is Jules? How did I get here?" My voice cracked with panic. "I threw myself off the rafter."

"That took a lot of courage." Patch's voice turned husky, and he stepped all the way inside my bedroom. He closed the door behind him, and I knew it was his way of trying to lock out all the bad. He was putting a divide between me and everything that had happened.

He walked over and sat on the bed beside me. "What else do you remember?"

I tried to piece my memories together, working backward. I remembered the beating wings I'd heard shortly after I flung myself off the rafter. Without any doubt, I knew I'd died. I knew an angel had come to carry my soul away.

"I'm dead, aren't I?" I said quietly, reeling with fright. "Am I a ghost?"

"When you jumped, the sacrifice killed Jules. Technically, when you came back, he should have too. But since he didn't have a soul, he had nothing to revive his body."

"I came back?" I said, hoping I wasn't filling myself with false hope.

"I didn't accept your sacrifice. I turned it down."

I felt a small Oh form at my mouth, but it never quite made it past my lips. "Are you saying you gave up getting a human body for me?"

He lifted my bandaged hand. Underneath all the gauze, my knuckles throbbed from punching Jules. Patch kissed each finger, taking his time, keeping his eyes glued to mine. "What good is a body if I can't have you?"

Heavier teardrops rolled down my cheeks, and Patch pulled me

BECCA FITZPATRICK

to him, tucking my head against his chest. Very slowly the panic edged away, and I knew it was all over. I was going to be all right.

Suddenly I pulled away. If Patch had turned down the sacrifice, then—

"You saved my life. Turn around," I ordered solemnly.

Patch gave a sly smile and indulged my request. I rucked his T-shirt up to his shoulders. His back was smooth, defined muscle. The scars were gone.

"You can't see my wings," he said. "They're made of spiritual matter."

"You're a guardian angel now." I was still too much in awe to wrap my mind around it, but at the same time I felt amazement, curiosity . . . happiness.

"I'm your guardian angel," he said.

"I get my very own guardian angel? What, exactly, is your job description?"

"Guard your body." His smile tipped higher. "I take my job seriously, which means I'm going to need to get acquainted with the subject matter on a personal level."

My stomach went all fluttery. "Does this mean you can feel now?"

Patch watched me in silence for a moment. "No, but it does mean I'm not blacklisted."

Downstairs, I heard the quiet rumble of the garage door gliding open.

"My mom!" I gasped. I found the clock on the nightstand. It was just after two in the morning. "They must have opened the bridge. How does this whole guardian angel business work? Am I the only person who can see you? I mean, are you invisible to everyone else?"

Patch stared at me like he hoped I wasn't serious.

"You're not invisible?" I squeaked. "You have to get out of here!" I made a movement to push Patch off the bed but was cut short by a searing jab in my ribs. "She'll kill me if she finds you in here. Can you climb trees? Tell me you can climb a tree!"

Patch grinned. "I can fly."

Oh. Right. Well, okay.

"The police and fire department were here earlier," Patch said. "The master bedroom will need to be gutted, but they stopped the fire from spreading. The police will be back. They're going to have a few questions. If I had to guess, they already tried reaching you on the cell you called 911 on."

"Jules took it."

He nodded. "I figured. I don't care what you tell the police, but I'd appreciate it if you left me out of it." He slid my bedroom window open. "Last thing. Vee got to the police in time. Paramedics saved Elliot. He's in the hospital, but he'll be all right."

Down the hall, at the bottom of the stairs, I heard the house door shut. My mom was inside.

"Nora?" she called. She tossed her purse and keys on the entry table. Her high heels clicked across the wood floors, almost at a running pace. "Nora! There's police tape on the front door! What is going on?"

I looked to the window. Patch was gone, but a single black feather was pressed to the outer pane, held in place by last night's rain. Or angel magic.

Downstairs, my mom flicked on the hall light, a faint ray of it stretching all the way under the crack at the bottom of my door. I held my breath and counted seconds, assuming I had about two more before—

She shrieked. "Nora! What happened to the banister!"

Good thing she hadn't seen her bedroom yet.

The sky was a perfect, rinsed blue. The sun was just starting to fan out across the horizon. It was Monday, a brand-new day, the horrors of the past twenty-four hours far behind. I had five hours of sleep under my belt, and other than the all-over body pain that came from being sucked into death, then spat back out, I felt remarkably refreshed. I didn't want to hang a black cloud over the moment by reminding myself that the police were expected to arrive any minute to take my statement on the night's events. I still hadn't made up my mind what I was going to tell them.

I padded to the bathroom in my nightshirt—mentally blocking the question of how I'd changed into it, since I'd presumably been wearing clothes when Patch brought me home—and sped through my morning routine. I splashed cold water on my face, scrubbed my teeth, and tamed my hair back into a rubber band. In my bedroom, I pulled on a clean shirt, clean jeans.

I called Vee.

"How are you doing?" I asked.

"Good. How are you?"

"Good."

Silence.

"Okay," Vee said in a rush, "I am still totally freaked out. You?"

"Totally."

"Patch called me in the middle of the night. He said Jules roughed you up pretty bad, but that you were okay."

"Really? Patch called you?"

"He called from the Jeep. He said you were asleep in the backseat and he was driving you home. He said he just happened to be driving past the high school when he heard a scream. He said he found you in the gym, but that you'd fainted from pain. The next thing he knew, he looked up and saw Jules jump off the rafter. He said Jules must have snapped, a side effect from all the burdensome guilt he felt over terrorizing you."

I didn't realize I was holding my breath until I let go of it. Obviously, Patch had manipulated a few details.

"You know I'm not buying it," Vee continued. "You know I think Patch killed Jules."

BECCA FITZPATRICK

In Vee's position, I'd probably think similarly. I said, "What do the police think?"

"Turn on the TV. There's live coverage right now, Channel Five. They're saying Jules broke into the school and jumped. They're ruling it a tragic teen suicide. They're asking people with information to call the hotline listed at the bottom of the screen."

"What did you tell the police when you first called it in?"

"I was scared. I didn't want to get busted for B and E. So I called in anonymously from a pay phone."

"Well," I said at last, "if the police are ruling it a suicide, I guess that's what happened. After all, this is modern-day America. We have the benefit of forensics."

"You're keeping something from me," said Vee. "What really happened after I left?"

This is where it got sticky. Vee was my best friend, and we lived by the motto No Secrets. But some things are just impossible to explain. The fact that Patch was a fallen-turned-guardian angel topped the list. Directly below it was the fact that I'd jumped off a rafter and died, but was still alive today.

"I remember Jules cornering me in the gym," I said. "He told me all the pain and fear he was going to inflict. After that, the details get hazy."

"Is it too late to apologize?" Vee said, sounding more sincere than she had in our whole friendship. "You were right about Jules and Elliot."

hush, hush

"Apology accepted."

"We should go to the mall," she said. "I feel this overwhelming need to buy shoes. Lots of them. What we need is some good old-fashioned shoe-shopping therapy."

The doorbell rang, and I glanced at the clock. "I have to give the police my statement about what happened last night, but I'll call you after that."

"Last night?" Vee's tone shot up with panic. "They know you were at the school? You didn't give them my name, did you?"

"Actually, something happened earlier in the night." Something named Dabria. "I'll call you soon," I said, hanging up before I had to lie my way through another explanation.

Limping down the hall, I'd made it as far as the top of the stairs when I saw who my mom had invited inside.

Detectives Basso and Holstijic.

She led them into the living room, and although Detective Holstijic collapsed onto the sofa, Detective Basso remained standing. He had his back to me, but a step creaked halfway through my descent, and he turned around.

"Nora Grey," he said in his tough cop voice. "We meet again."

My mom blinked. "You've met before?"

"Your daughter has an exciting life. Seems like we're here every week."

My mom aimed a questioning glance at me and I shrugged, clueless, as if to guess, *Cop humor?*

BECCA FITZPATRICK

"Why don't you have a seat, Nora, and tell us what happened," Detective Holstijic said.

I lowered myself into one of the plush armchairs opposite the sofa. "Just before nine last night I was in the kitchen drinking a glass of chocolate milk when Miss Greene, my school psychologist, appeared."

"She just walked into your house?" Detective Basso asked.

"She told me I had something she wanted, and that's when I ran upstairs and locked myself in the master bedroom."

"Back up," said Detective Basso. "What was this thing she wanted?"

"She didn't say. But she did mention she's not a real psychologist. She said she was using the job to spy on students." I divided a glance among everyone. "She's crazy, right?"

The detectives shared a look.

"I'll run her name, see what I can find," Detective Holstijic said, pulling himself back to his feet.

"Let me get this straight," Detective Basso said to me, "She accused you of stealing something that belonged to her, but she never said what?"

Another sticky question. "She was hysterical. I only understood half of what she was saying. I ran and locked myself inside the master bedroom, but she broke down the door. I was hiding inside the flue of the fireplace, and she said she'd burn the house down room by room to find me. Then she started a fire. Right there in the middle of the room."

hush, hush

"How did she start the fire?" my mom asked.

"I couldn't see. I was in the flue."

"This is crazy," Detective Basso said, shaking his head. "I've never seen anything like this."

"Is she going to come back?" my mom asked the detectives, coming over to stand behind me and placing her hands protectively on my shoulders. "Is Nora safe?"

"Might want to see about getting a security system installed." Detective Basso opened his wallet and held out a card to Mom. "I vouch for these guys. Tell them I sent you, and they'll give you a discount."

A few hours after the detectives left, the doorbell rang again.

"That must be the alarm system company," Mom said, meeting me in the hall. "I called, and they said they'd send a guy out today. I can't stand the thought of sleeping here without some kind of protection until they find Miss Greene and lock her away. Didn't the school even bother to check her references?" She opened the door, and Patch stood on the porch. He wore faded Levi's and a snug white T-shirt, and he held a toolbox in his left hand.

"Good afternoon, Mrs. Grey."

"Patch." I couldn't quite nail my mom's tone. Surprise mixed with discomfiture. "Are you here to see Nora?"

Patch smiled. "I'm here to spec your house for a new alarm system."

"I thought you had a different job," said Mom. "I thought you bussed tables at the Borderline."

"I got a new job." Patch locked eyes with me, and I warmed in a lot of places. In fact, I was dangerously close to feverish. "Outside?" he asked me.

I followed him out to his motorcycle.

"We still have a lot to talk about," I said.

"Talk?" He shook his head, his eyes full of desire. *Kiss*, he whispered to my thoughts.

It wasn't a question, but a warning. He grinned when I didn't protest, and lowered his mouth toward mine. The first touch was just that—a touch. A teasing, tempting softness. I licked my lips and Patch's grin deepened.

"More?" he asked.

I curled my hands into his hair, pulling him closer. "More."

ACKNOWLEDGMENTS

Thanks to Caleb Warnock and my fellow writers at Writing in Depth; I couldn't have asked for truer friends to make this journey. A shout-out to Laura Andersen, Ginger Churchill, and Patty Esden, who never let me quit and who were honest (even when I didn't want it). Special thanks to Eric James Stone for tying the ribbon on the package.

I owe Katie Jeppson, Ali Eisenach, Kylie Wright, Megan and Josh Walsh, Lindsey Leavitt, and Riley and Jace Fitzpatrick thanks, too, for everything from babysitting, to information on surgical procedures, to communal brainstorming, to undeserved patience.

It has been sheer fun working with Emily Meehan, my savvy editor, and my many friends at Simon and Schuster BFYR who've cheered me on and worked behind the scenes to make this all happen—Justin Chanda, Anne Zafian, Courtney Bongiolatti, Dorothy Gribbin, Chava Wolin, Lucy Ruth Cummins, Lucille Rettino, Elke Villa, Chrissy Noh, Julia Maguire, and Anna McKean. Thank you!

I'm especially thankful that Catherine Drayton came into my life at just the right time. Thanks for helping me make it this far. I'll never forget the phone call when I learned my book had been sold. . . .

Thanks to James Porto for a cover that blew away my expectations. I owe my copy editor, Valerie Shea, a big thank-you as well.

Most of all, thanks to my mom. For everything. XOXO.

Need some more?

Get a sneak peek at the sequel!

crescendo

P ATCH WAS STANDING BEHIND ME, HIS HANDS on my hips, his body relaxed. He stood two inches over six feet tall and had a lean, athletic build that even loose-fit jeans and a T-shirt couldn't conceal. The color of his hair gave midnight a run for its money, with eyes to match. His smile was sexy and warned of trouble, but I'd made up my mind that not all trouble was bad.

Overhead, fireworks lit up the night sky, raining streams of color into the Atlantic. The crowd oohed and aahed. It was late June, and Maine was jumping into summer with both feet, celebrating the beginning of two months of sun, sand, and tourists with deep pockets. I was celebrating two months of sun, sand, and plenty of exclusive time with Patch. I'd enrolled in one summer school course—chemistry—and had every intention of letting Patch monopolize the rest of my free time.

The fire department was setting off the fireworks on a dock that couldn't have been more than two hundred yards down the beach from where we stood, and I felt the boom of each one vibrate in the sand under my feet. Waves crashed into the beach just down the hill, and carnival music tinkled at top volume. The smell of cotton candy, popcorn, and sizzling meat hung thick in the air, and my stomach reminded me I hadn't eaten since lunch.

"I'm going to grab a cheeseburger," I told Patch. "Want anything?"

"Nothing on the menu."

I smiled. "Why, Patch, are you flirting with me?"

He kissed the crown of my head. "Not yet. I'll grab your cheeseburger. Enjoy the last of the fireworks."

I snagged one of his belt loops to stop him. "Thanks, but I'm ordering. I can't take the guilt."

He raised his eyebrows in inquiry.

"When was the last time the girl at the hamburger stand let you pay for food?"

"It's been a while."

"It's been *never*. Stay here. If she sees you, I'll spend the rest of the night with a guilty conscience."

Patch opened his wallet and pulled out a twenty. "Leave her a nice tip."

It was my turn to raise my eyebrows. "Trying to redeem yourself for all those times you took free food?"

"Last time I paid, she chased me down and shoved the money in my pocket. I'm trying to avoid another groping."

It sounded made up, but knowing Patch, it was probably true.

I hunted down the end of a long line that wrapped around the hamburger stand, finding it near the entrance to the indoor carousel. Judging by the size of the line, I estimated a fifteen-minute wait just to place my order. One hamburger stand on the entire beach. It felt un-American.

After a few minutes of restless waiting, I was taking what must have been my tenth bored look around when I spotted Marcie Millar standing two spots back. Marcie and I had gone to school together since kindergarten, and in the eleven years since, I'd seen more of her than I cared to remember. Because of her, the whole school had seen more of my underwear than necessary. In junior high, Marcie's usual MO was stealing my bra from my gym locker and pinning it to the bulletin board outside the main offices, but occasionally she got creative and used it as a centerpiece in the cafeteria—both my A cups filled with vanilla pudding and topped with maraschino cherries. Classy, I know. Marcie's skirts were two sizes too small and five inches too short. Her hair was strawberry blond, and she had the shape of a Popsicle stick—turn her sideways and she practically disappeared. If there was a scoreboard keeping track of wins and losses between us, I was pretty sure Marcie had double my score.

"Hey," I said, unintentionally catching her eye and not seeing any way around a bare-minimum greeting.

"Hey," she returned in what scraped by as a civil tone.

Seeing Marcie at Delphic Beach tonight was like playing What's Wrong with This Picture? Marcie's dad owned the Toyota dealership in Coldwater, her family lived in an upscale hillside neighborhood, and the Millars took pride in being the only citizens of Coldwater welcomed into the prestigious Harraseeket Yacht Club. At this very minute, Marcie's parents were probably in Freeport, racing sailboats and ordering salmon.

By contrast, Delphic was a slum beach. The thought of a yacht club was laughable. The sole restaurant came in the form of a whitewashed hamburger stand with your choice of ketchup or mustard. On a good day, fries were offered in the mix. The entertainment slanted toward loud arcades and bumper cars, and after dark, the parking lot was known to sell more drugs than a pharmacy.

Not the kind of atmosphere Mr. and Mrs. Millar would have their daughter polluting herself in.

"Could we move any slower, people?" Marcie called up the line. "Some of us are starving to death back here."

"There's only one person working the counter," I told her.

"So? They should hire more people. Supply and demand."

Given her GPA, Marcie was the last person who should be spouting economics.

Ten minutes later, I'd made progress, and stood close enough to the hamburger stand to read the word MUSTARD scribbled in black Magic Marker on the communal yellow squirt bottle. Behind me, Marcie did the whole shifting-weight-between-hips-and-sighing thing.

"Starving with a capital S," she complained.

The guy in line ahead of me paid and carried off his food.

"A cheeseburger and a Coke," I told the girl working the stand.

While she stood over the grill making my order, I turned back to Marcie. "So. Who are you here with?" I didn't particularly care who she'd come with, especially since we didn't share any of the same friends, but my sense of courtesy got the better of me. Besides, Marcie hadn't done anything overtly rude to me in weeks. And we'd stood in relative peace the past fifteen minutes. Maybe it was the beginning of a truce. Bygones and all that.

She yawned, as if talking to me was more boring than waiting in line and staring at the backs of people's heads. "No offense, but I'm not in a chatty mood. I've been in line for what feels like five hours, waiting on an incompetent girl who obviously can't cook two hamburgers at once."

The girl behind the counter had her head ducked low, concentrating on peeling premade hamburger patties from the wax paper, but I knew she'd heard. She probably hated her job. She probably secretly spat on the hamburger patties when she turned her back. I wouldn't be surprised if at the end of her shift, she went out to her car and wept.

"Doesn't your dad mind that you're hanging out at Delphic Beach?" I asked Marcie, narrowing my eyes ever so slightly. "Might tarnish the estimable Millar family reputation. Especially now that your dad's been accepted into the Harraseeket Yacht Club."

Marcie's expression cooled. "I'm surprised your dad doesn't mind you're here. Oh, wait. That's right. He's dead."

My initial reaction was shock. My second was indignation at her cruelty. A knot of anger swelled in my throat.

"What?" she argued with a one-shoulder shrug. "He's dead. It's a fact. Do you want me to lie about the facts?"

"What did I ever do to you?"

"You were born."

Her complete lack of sensitivity yanked me inside out—so much so that I didn't even have a comeback. I snatched my cheeseburger and Coke off the counter, leaving the twenty in its place. I wanted badly to hurry back to Patch, but this was between me and Marcie. If I showed up now, one look at my face would tell Patch something was wrong. I didn't need to drag him into the middle. Taking a moment alone to collect myself, I found a bench within sight of the hamburger stand and sat down as gracefully as I could, not wanting to give Marcie the power to ruin my night.

The only thing that could make this moment worse was knowing she was watching, satisfied she'd stuffed me into a little black hole of self-pity. I took a bite of cheeseburger, but it left a bad taste in my mouth. All I could think of was dead meat. Dead cows. My own dead father.

I threw the cheeseburger into the trash and kept walking, feeling tears slip down the back of my throat.

Hugging my arms tightly at the elbows, I hurried toward the shack of bathrooms at the edge of the parking lot, hoping to make it behind a stall door before the tears started falling. There was a steady line trickling out of the women's room, but I edged my way through the doorway and positioned myself in front of one of the grime-coated mirrors. Even under the low-watt bulb, I could tell my eyes were red and glassy. I wet a paper towel and pressed it to my eyes. What was Marcie's problem? What had I ever done to her that was cruel enough to deserve this?

Drawing a few stabilizing breaths, I squared my shoulders and constructed a brick wall in my mind, placing Marcie on the far side of it. What did I care what she said? I didn't even like her. Her opinion meant nothing. She was rude and self-centered and attacked below the belt. She didn't know me, and she definitely didn't know my dad. Crying over a single word that fell from her mouth was a waste.

Get over it, I told myself.

I waited until the red rimming my eyes faded before leaving

the restroom. I roamed the crowd, looking for Patch, and found him at one of the ball toss games, his back to me. Rixon was at his side, probably wagering money on Patch's inability to knock over a single weighted bowling pin. Rixon was a fallen angel who had a long history with Patch, and their ties ran deep to the point of brotherhood. Patch didn't let many people into his life, and trusted even fewer, but if there was one person who knew all his secrets, it was Rixon.

Up until two months ago, Patch had also been a fallen angel. Then he saved my life, earned his wings back, and became my guardian angel. He was supposed to play for the good guys now, but I secretly sensed that his connection to Rixon, and the world of fallen angels, meant more to him. And even though I didn't want to admit it, I sensed that he regretted the archangels' decision to make him my guardian. After all, it wasn't what he wanted.

He wanted to become human.

My cell phone rang, jarring me from my thoughts. It was my best friend Vee's ringtone, but I let voice mail take her call. With a squeeze of guilt, I vaguely noted it was the second call of hers I'd avoided today. I justified my guilt with the thought that I'd see her first thing tomorrow. Patch, on the other hand, I wouldn't see again until tomorrow evening. I planned to enjoy every minute I had with him.

I watched him pitch the ball at a table neatly lined with six bowling pins, my stomach giving a little flutter when his T-shirt crept up in the back, revealing a stripe of skin. I knew from experience that every inch of him was hard, defined muscle. His back was smooth and perfect too, the scars from when he'd fallen once again replaced with wings—wings I, and every other human, couldn't see.

"Five dollars says you can't do it again," I said, coming up behind him.

Patch looked back and grinned. "I don't want your money, Angel."

"Hey now, kids, let's keep this discussion PG-rated," Rixon said.

"All three remaining pins," I challenged Patch.

"What kind of prize are we talking about?" he asked.

"Bloody hell," Rixon said. "Can't this wait until you're alone?"

Patch gave me a secret smile, then shifted his weight back, cradling the ball into his chest. He dropped his right shoulder, brought his arm around, and sent the ball flying forward as hard as he could. There was a loud crack! and the remaining three pins scattered off the table.

"Aye, now you're in trouble, lass," Rixon shouted at me over the commotion caused by a pocket of onlookers, who were clapping and whistling for Patch.

Patch leaned back against the booth and arched his eyebrows at me. The gesture said it all: Pay up.

"You got lucky," I said.

"I'm about to get lucky."

"Choose a prize," the old man running the booth barked at Patch, bending to pick up the fallen pins.

"The purple bear," Patch said, and accepted a hideous-looking teddy bear with matted purple fur. He held it out to me.

"For me?" I said, pressing a hand to my heart.

"You like the rejects. At the grocery store, you always take the dented cans. I've been paying attention." He hooked his finger in the waistband of my jeans and pulled me close. "Let's get out of here."

"What did you have in mind?" But I was all warm and fluttery inside, because I knew exactly what he had in mind.

"Your place."

I shook my head. "Not going to happen. My mom's home. We could go to your place," I hinted.

We'd been together two months, and I still didn't know where Patch lived. And not for lack of trying. Two weeks into a relationship seemed long enough to be invited over, especially since Patch lived alone. Two months felt like overkill. I was trying to be patient, but my curiosity kept getting in the way. I knew nothing about the private, intimate details of Patch's life, like the color of paint on his walls. If his can opener was electric or manual. The brand of soap he showered with. If his sheets were cotton or silk.

"Let me guess," I said. "You live in a secret compound buried in the underbelly of the city."

"Angel."

"Are there dishes in the sink? Dirty underwear on the floor? It's a lot more private than my place."

"True, but the answer's still no."

"Has Rixon seen your place?"

"Rixon is need-to-know."

"I'm not need-to-know?"

His mouth twitched. "There's a dark side to need-to-know."

"If you showed me, you'd have to kill me?" I guessed.

He wrapped his arms around me and kissed my forehead. "Close enough. What time's curfew?"

"Ten. Summer school starts tomorrow." That, and my mom had practically taken a part-time job finding opportunities to drop the knife between me and Patch. If I'd been out with Vee, I could say with absolute certainty that my curfew would have stretched to ten thirty. I couldn't blame my mom for not trusting Patch—there was a point in my life when I'd felt similarly—but it would have been extremely convenient if every now and then she relaxed her vigilance.

Like, say, tonight. Besides, nothing was going to happen. Not with my guardian angel standing inches away.

ABOUT THE AUTHOR

BECCA FITZPATRICK's Hush, Hush Saga, including Hush, Hush; Crescendo; and Silence, all debuted as New York Times bestsellers. She graduated college with a degree in health, which she promptly abandoned for storytelling. When not writing, she's most likely running, prowling sale racks for shoes, or watching crime dramas on TV. She lives in Colorado with her family. Find out more at beccafitzpatrick.com.

Love is lost but never forgotten . . .

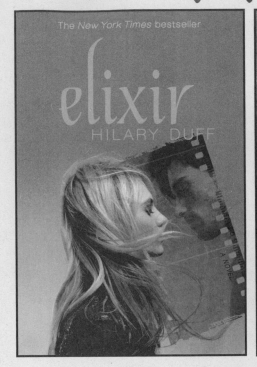

Don't miss the *elixir* series
by New York Times bestselling author

HILARY DUFF

EBOOK EDITIONS ALSO AVAILABLE